THE
CRUELEST
CUT

BOOKS BY GENE RONTAL

THE
CRUELEST
CUT

A Detective Ben Dailey, M.D. Mystery

GENE RONTAL

CAMEL
PRESS
Kenmore, WA

CAMEL
PRESS

A Camel Press book published by Epicenter Press

Epicenter Press
6524 NE 181st St.
Suite 2
Kenmore, WA 98028

For more information go to:
www.Camelpress.com
www.Coffeetownpress.com
www.Epicenterpress.com
www.generontalbooks.com

This is a work of fiction. Names, characters, places, brands, media, and incidents are either the product of the author's imagination or are used fictiously.

Design by Scott Book and Melissa Vail Coffman

The Cruelest Cut
Copyright © 2021 by Gene Rontal

Previously published by Sterling House

ISBN: 978-1-60381-266-5 (Trade Paper)
ISBN: 978-1-60381-267-2 (eBook)

Printed in the United States of America

To Ellen

Life is short and the art long.

—*Hippocrates*

CHAPTER 1

"**A**RE YOU SURE YOU TWO WANT TO SEE THIS?"
I stood motionless next to the murder victim, the ordeal of uttering anything trapping me somewhere between fear and curiosity. Allan Davis, the Wayne County Medical Examiner, glared impatiently for an answer, his eyes shifting from me to the powerfully built black man next to the autopsy table. After a moment of indecision, we both nodded silently.

Davis drew the shroud downward from the victim's head. At first, I couldn't quite understand what I was looking at, just amorphous, bloody tissue. Then I looked at the head: there wasn't any hair. It took me a moment to realize why. He had been scalped.

I felt sick and mesmerized at the same time.

"Gentlemen, what you are seeing is a modern-day version of a skinning," Davis intoned.

As he spoke, I studied the uncovered face and saw that skin had been removed in neat, linear strips, leaving thin white zebra stripes of cadaveric skin. Against the dark facial musculature, it produced a hideous red and white mask, like some horrific preternatural monster.

"Whoever did this was meticulous," I said, trying to intellectualize the dreadful calamity in front of me.

"That, Dr. Dailey, is because this is most likely a ritual murder, and those usually involve some type of design that only the killer understands," Davis said without wavering. He pulled the sheet down further. As on the face, ribbons of skin had been removed from the exposed chest and abdominal musculature.

I glanced at Lieutenant George Sennett, standing next to me, and saw that he had backed away from the body. The muscles of his jaw were clenching and unclenching. "Is this the way they brought him in?" he asked.

The M.E. barely nodded as he reached silently under the edge of the table and withdrew a small oscillating saw to start opening the skull.

"What are those, Dr. Davis?" Sennett asked, pointing at several clear glass jars on the shelf behind Davis.

Davis put down the blade, picked up one of the jars, and showed it to both of us. "They contain the heart, lungs, and kidneys. We're required to section the major organs. Everything else is gross, un-sectioned material only, unless there is some reason for further analysis."

As he put the jar back, I looked at the victim's face again, then his hands. "He has no nails," I said almost to myself.

Davis looked pleasantly surprised. "Obviously, doctor, your days in the anatomy lab weren't wasted. You are correct, each one was pulled out. And that's not all. This victim died of asphyxiation."

Davis turned and pulled out another jar from the storage shelf. It held two ovoid objects floating in formaldehyde.

"Don't tell me . . ." Sennett gasped.

Davis nodded solemnly. "Yes, his testicles. We found them in his throat. I assume that's what choked him to death."

My chest got hot and my mouth was suddenly parched. Sennett turned away. I heard him breathing slowly and deeply.

"Dr. Davis," Sennett interjected weakly, trying to swallow and clear his throat at the same time. "The only death I've ever seen like this was that young girl who was mutilated and killed several years ago." His words came out slowly, as if the memory had irritated a festering ulcer.

"True, but that crime was solved," Davis replied. "Besides, from the needle marks on his arm this looks more like a drug killing to me."

Sennett nodded. "Considering the circumstances, it's a possibility. There was a note with the body. It read, *The wage of sin is death.*"

"Any idea of the significance?" Davis asked, placing the glass specimen bottle back on the shelf.

Sennett looked back at the body and then ran a handkerchief over his sweating face. "We have a few ideas we're working on." Sennett's voice dropped, and he turned to leave, mumbling to Davis that he had seen enough. We walked away from the table, allowing the M.E. to spend the rest of his day muddling through the dead man's tissues.

Sennett looked down at the floor as we walked past Davis's office, then into the hallway. "Well, that was . . ." Sennett began before he ran down the hall and into the men's bathroom. The sound of his eructation echoed down the corridor.

Chapter 2

I WAITED FOR SENNETT ON THE SIDEWALK outside of the building and looked absently from the Medical Examiner's office southward to the downtown Detroit skyline. As I did, I thought about an architect friend of mine who once told me he despised the Wayne County Morgue, because it represented an architectural metaphor for Detroit. He maintained that this tasteless and prosaic building, housing the worst of the city's misery, was purposefully placed so that its windows could overlook the Renaissance Center, the city's dying attempt at resurrection. I used to think that his theory was a bunch of artistic psychobabble. After what I just saw, I wasn't so sure he was wrong.

I looked back at the entrance again and this time saw Sennett walking slowly from the door. He stopped for a moment and took a deep breath. Outside, in the bright sunlight and inhaling the fresh air, he seemed revived. But not totally. I think if I had mentioned a double cheeseburger and fries, it would have sent him praying once again to the porcelain gods. "Okay, Lieutenant, now you can explain to me why you dragged me down here to witness this."

Sennett stood at the front steps and pulled out his sunglasses. "I'm sorry about dumping you into this mess, Ben. When there's a murder, I make it a point of going to the autopsy. I hate it, but it gives me a chance to see the murder, get into the killer's head. Davis didn't tell me it was going to be that bad. I think he enjoys the shock value," he replied, putting on his dark Ray-Bans.

"All you said was that there was a murder and you wanted my advice. I'm a doctor, not a policeman. What advice could I possibly give you?"

"I didn't want to tell you over the phone. It's about Jordan."

At the mention of Jordan Dalkind, I felt myself come to attention. "What about her?" I watched as Sennett flipped his coat over his opposite shoulder, exposing a 9-millimeter SIG Sauer poking over his hip.

"This guy on the table was named Hamoud Ishaki."

"Who's he?"

"Didn't you see the paper this morning, Ben?" he asked.

"No. I try not to obscure my opinions with the facts." As a matter of record, I usually only read the sports page of the local rag.

"It made the front page." He opened the car door and reached for the paper on the front seat.

I scanned it quickly. The headline read "Arab Community Claims Bias in Federal Charges." I read further. They cited Jordan by name as the lead prosecutor. Hamoud Ishaki's name was mentioned as one of the named suspects.

"That's great," I said. "There are 500,000 people in the Detroit area of Middle Eastern descent. Now one of them is killed, and my girlfriend is right in the middle of it. Why do the newspapers want to pick on her?"

He explained that Jordan was the lead prosecutor in a drug case involving several Lebanese-American suspects. The claim from her detractors focused on charges of prosecutorial misconduct. I wasn't completely surprised at the accusations. Jordan was conscientiously silent about her work, but after reading the article, I recalled a conversation I had with her a few months ago. "She said she was working on a matter that involved the Arab community and worried that, because she was Jewish, there could be some ramifications if there was an indictment. I tried to press her to find out more, but she changed the subject. Now it was front page news.

"So what's the big deal? If they're guilty, they'll get what they deserve," I said anxiously. "Jordan is doing her job."

"In a perfect world that's right, but not when a man named Bill Yaldo is involved." As Sennett spoke, he started walking again, taking slow measured steps.

"Who?"

"He is one of the richest Arab-Americans in Detroit. The word at the station is that he has property, a few businesses, and lots of cash."

"Why would he be involved?"

"For one thing, Ishaki was his grandson."

Sennett described the murder victim as someone bound for trouble from the start—a broken family, in and out of juvenile homes, and a couple of brushes with the law. His latest problem involved drugs.

"Hamoud Ishaki was important to the Feds," Sennett continued. "They had evidence that he was transporting pseudoephedrine hydrochloride across the border into Canada."

"That's a cold medicine. The over-the-counter stuff," I murmured.

"Right. Broken down it can be made into amphetamines. Once they get to that point, it's sold as a narcotic. Crystal is the street name. There's millions in it. The drug money is used for Arab terrorist activities. It's a big business."

By the time I had made the simple assumption that he should be arrested, we were at the front of Sennett's sedan. "So why is my fiancée getting all this attention?" I asked.

Sennett described how, based on the FBI information, Jordan was getting ready to go to a Federal grand jury to get a sealed indictment on some of the most prominent Arab businessmen in the city. Those close to the case assumed that someone leaked the information to the paper.

"How does a leak like that happen?" As I spoke, I was momentarily distracted by a man at the corner in a heavy overcoat, greasy brown cotton pants, and dirty white tennis shoes, clutching a paper cup and yelling at some imaginary combatant. He was making his way toward us.

"There is some suspicion that Yaldo might have been part of the scheme to discredit Jordan. He has friends in high and low places—judges, an Arab congressman from his district, a U.S. Senator, and probably some informant inside the Federal building, just to name a few. The ethnic profiling claim is just a dodge to divert attention from the crime."

When I asked what they could do to Jordan, he told me that was the reason he wanted me at the autopsy. He said I needed to know what kind of people we were dealing with. He finished by claiming that when they wanted to get someone, they wouldn't quit.

"What do you mean 'get someone?'" I asked, feeling more and more anxious.

Sennett explained that the Feds were getting ready to make a plea bargain with Ishaki and get him to testify against his co-conspirators. They assumed someone found out that he was going to rat on them and ordered a contract murder intended to send a message to the others involved: Don't drop out of line.

"Ben, I wanted you to know that a death threat was called in to Jordan's personal office."

At the words my whole body stiffened. I looked at him closely. His face was an impenetrable mask behind his mirrored sunglasses.

"It's not that unusual. Threats get called in all the time. The Feds have a policy of recording all non-recognized incoming calls," Sennett continued.

"What was the call about?" I asked cautiously.

"This one was different. The voice was garbled, but it was clearly directed at Jordan, and it said '*Wheresoever ye be, death will overtake you.*'"

"What's that from?" I asked.

"I sent it to Washington to see what it meant. They think it might be from the Koran. We traced the call. It came from an outside phone booth at a gas station in the city. No prints, no identification of the caller. For all we know it could have been a crank call. Other than assuming it came from the Arab community and that it's related to Jordan's case, there isn't much more we can do at this point," he continued.

I asked him if Jordan knew about my being here. He said she did, but wasn't happy about it. I thought about the dead Ishaki kid and the fuss in the paper. Now, I was really alarmed. "What are you doing to protect her?" I asked shakily.

"You know Jordan. Her first words were that she didn't want protection. She figures she can take care of herself."

"What do you mean take care of herself?" I asked angrily. "There are laws against threatening a Federal prosecutor."

As I finished speaking, our man on the street saw us and made a beeline for the car. He was holding the cup in the air and yelling something about Vietnam and the war. I thought that his madness fit this morning perfectly. Sennett walked over to him, took a dollar out of his pocket and stuck it in his cup. A half toothless smile came across the man's face, and he shuffled away. Sennett strode back toward his car.

"See, Ben, just like that bum, the law and the truth can be very different things. Panhandling is illegal, but the truth is, I feel sorry for the guy."

I thought about the newspaper story. If the dead kid's grandfather was as powerful as he was made out to be, why make an overt threat against Jordan? It would just make him more of a target for the Feds. It made no sense.

But then, who could make sense of anything as gruesome as the murder victim we had just seen? I asked him how I could help. His reply was that right now there was nothing anyone could do but wait and see. I didn't think he meant to, but his words left me feeling as helpless and frightened and anxious as I had been in a long time. That fear sealed my resolve. I would protect Jordan with my life.

Sennett started up the car and put it in gear. I called to him through the open window. "Hey, Lieutenant, you be careful."

"Right back at you," he growled.

CHAPTER 3

WITH A THREAT TO JORDAN and nothing solid to go on, I felt vulnerable and anxious. The situation wasn't made any better when I tried calling and couldn't reach her. Even her secretary didn't know where she was. This just wasn't like Jordan to be out of contact. I was about to phone Sennett when my nurse, Katie Andrews, called and told me there was an emergency at the office. Someone from the board of trustees at the hospital had called and insisted that I see a patient immediately. At first, I was going to tell them I had a problem, and couldn't be there, but I decided that panicking wouldn't solve anything. When I finally reached Sennett, he said the same thing. The only thing left to do was to head back to the clinic and take care of the emergency.

Walking in through the back door, I entered my private office and stood for a moment, gazing absentmindedly around the room. It wasn't that much to look at—just a blonde wood desk, a computer, and a few pictures. Behind the desk on the wall was my medical diploma from Ann Arbor and my framed membership plaques from several prestigious societies.

They all pronounced me a laryngologist, a doctor who specializes in diseases of the voice box. At one time I was thought of as one of the country's experts in the treatment of voice disorders, but being spuriously cast off of a hospital staff will quickly plunder a reputation. And like the long trailer on a movie, bad news sometimes lasts longer than the film. Now, back in practice after so many forgotten years, I understood how fleeting personal recognition is.

My gaze fell onto a small glass shelf below the diplomas. In the middle was a small Michigan football, signed by my coach, signifying my four years of gutting it out on the hamburger squad. Next to it was a photograph of me with a long-legged woman in red stretch pants on a snow-covered ridge in the

Rockies, with the peaks of the Maroon Bells rising behind her. It was Jordan holding her Völkl skis in one hand and a red helmet in the other, long hair cascading over her black Arc'teryx jacket and a bright smile illuminating her face. I was part of the landscape, staring at her with admiration. Then I thought about my conversation with Sennett.

I was about to pick the phone up and call Jordan when Katie walked in to inform me that the woman who was sent over was pacing the waiting room, asking when I was going to see her. I had no choice now, so I told her to bring the patient in and then keep trying Jordan's phone.

Katie handed me the chart, and I quickly scanned her entry information. Frances Gallagher was in her mid-fifties and lived on one of the fanciest streets in the suburbs. Walking into the examining room, she was exactly what I had expected: an elegantly dressed woman in a gray suit and peach colored silk blouse, both open to the third button, so that a hint of her surgically implanted breasts would be evident to all. She had an almost too-smooth face, a string of pearls at her neck, and a very large diamond on her hand. I introduced myself.

"I'm so glad to meet you," she said breathlessly. "I'm a friend of Brad Dixon. You must know him from the board of trustees. When I told him I had a problem, he said you were a *special* person, and I simply *must* come to see you. He said you were the *best* there was when it comes to voice work. I do hope this won't take too long, because I have an appointment downtown in about an hour."

There it was. In ten seconds she had given me her bona fides: rich, important, demands special care.

But there was something else that I noticed about her. When she spoke, she had a peculiar double tone to her voice, something called diplophonia. Most voice specialists can detect it a mile away. It's a warning sign of significant vocal cord disease.

"Well, the best guy is the one who fixes you up," I said with a smile. "Now tell me about your problem."

"I think I've got sinus trouble or a touch of allergies. My voice has been hoarse for about three months."

I asked her the usual questions regarding her hoarseness. When it came to tobacco, she said she had been smoking filtered cigarettes since she was fifteen, then added that doctors always blamed everything on smoking. I had heard that one many times before, always from hardcore smokers.

When I finished taking her history, I examined her head and neck. Everything seemed fine, except her voice. Then I took a laryngeal mirror, heated it to prevent it from fogging, and placed it in her mouth. I adjusted my headlight and shone the light against the mirror to see the reflection of her vocal cords. It took me a few seconds of looking to confirm what I expected: her left vocal cord was covered with a whitish lesion. Probably cancer.

I removed the mirror and placed it on the examining table next to me.

She had already pulled out her compact and was adjusting her lipstick. "Mrs. Gallagher, there is a problem with your vocal cord."

"What is it, a little laryngitis? I'm sure antibiotics will do fine. They always have in the past."

"Have you seen your regular doctor about this?"

"Several times. I'm sure you know Rudy Chambers. He's chief of staff at Community." She looked at her diamond-studded Cartier watch impatiently.

Yeah, I knew Rudolph J. Chambers. He was a society sycophant who earned his living making $400 house calls on rich people. "Your left vocal cord has a lesion on it."

"What kind of lesion?"

"It looks like it may be a small tumor."

"Is it cancer?" she asked.

When I replied that it might be, she stared at me for a moment, trying to digest what I had said. "Oh, my Lord. This can't possibly be true. It's just laryngitis."

"We'll need to get a biopsy. Then I'll be able to give you an exact answer."

Her turned-up nose turned up a little higher. "Absolutely not! I'm calling a friend of mine. He knows someone at the Mayo Clinic. This can't possibly be true."

With that she stood, picked up her black leather Louis Vuitton handbag, and walked out of the room, leaving me to fend for myself among the discarded proletariats. I speculated she left thinking Mr. Dixon was wrong. I wasn't the greatest doctor after all.

I guess at one point in my career I might have been bothered by her outburst, but not anymore. Some people want to kill the messenger, and I wasn't quite ready for that. So I shrugged the confrontation off as useless energy and walked back to the nurse's station to dictate my notes. Halfway down the hallway, Katie came running up to me. "Jordan just called," she said with a touch of agitation. "She's at the emergency room at St. Vincent's and sounded upset, something about having contractions."

Suddenly, Mrs. Gallagher's fit of pique seemed inconsequential. This was my child they were talking about.

CHAPTER 4

As I RACED TO THE ER it suddenly occurred to me that my slow motion relationship with Jordan Dalkind was now in fast forward. It was during what I refer to as the dark days of my life that we had met two years ago. I had been forced off the staff at St. Vincent's Hospital in Detroit for a death I didn't cause. What ensued could only be described as the spiraling collapse of a line of dominoes. Divorce from a barren marriage and a loss of self-esteem had left me nearly broke and emotionally bankrupt. I have to admit there were times when I thought my life wasn't worth saving.

I was living like a vagabond on my old sailboat on Lake St. Clair, barely making ends meet by performing medical insurance evaluations. It was Christmas and things were slow, so the insurance agent, thinking he was being kind, asked me to simply gather some medical information on the death of a female client. It wasn't so simple. The deceased was the victim of a deranged man who shot her.

Coincidentally, Jordan had just moved to Detroit as the Assistant Federal Prosecutor for the Eastern District of Michigan, and this was her first murder case. Oddly, the woman's death became intertwined with my own dismissal from the hospital. As I slowly pieced together the puzzle, I solved the crime and resurrected my good name.

My status of having slipped from grace never seemed to bother her. In fact, we had fallen in love, and now she was carrying our child. Miraculously, I now had everything I had ever wanted back within my grasp. I promised myself that I would never let anything screw up my life again.

Entering through the large sliding doors of St. Vincent's emergency center, my anxiety became more manageable when I saw Jordan standing by the counter in the waiting room. She was wearing a tight-fitting shirt with low-riding pants that made her eight-month pregnant bump contrast oddly with her exquisite body. It was a look that excited me as much as the first time I had met her.

She told me everything was alright. The doctor said it was uterine cramps. Right. Uterine cramps to obstetricians, cardiac stimulators to doctors who are about to become fathers.

"Trying to see if I can stand the pressure?" I asked.

"No," she replied sweetly, "I was just checking your response time in case I needed to make a fast trip to the hospital." She smiled reassuringly back at me. It was an engaging smile accompanied by a sense of calm and composure. Only her eyes spoke of her intensity.

"How'd I do?" I asked. My shirt was clinging to me with the perspiration of someone who had just gone three rounds with a heavy bag.

"Not bad. The doctor said first deliveries average sixteen hours, so you had plenty of time."

My voice changed to serious as we walked outside. "You heard about the autopsy, didn't you?" I asked.

"Yes, and I'm aggravated that I wasn't there."

"I think George was looking out for your wellbeing. And so am I. These threats are nothing to fluff off and neither is the anxiety it brings."

She glared at me. "I can take care of myself, doctor. I don't need someone running interference for me." Then she smiled. "But I understand."

I was about to get into my car when my cell phone rang. It was Sennett. "We might have a lead," he said.

"What is it?" I asked.

"There's a gang leader on the West Side." Sennett didn't wait for my reply. "He's known as the Reverend Ikeda Walker, a.k.a. Icky Walker. He runs the D-Hood. That's a gang on the West Side. He calls himself the Reverend, because he always quotes the Bible. I spoke with some of the boys at the Hate Crime Unit. They think that note in the Ishaki murder might be his style. Do you know where Jordan is? With everything that's gone on, I think she should be there."

I handed the phone to Jordan, and after a brief conversation, she gave it back to me. Her eyes had turned flinty and the business tone had returned to her voice. "We'll meet Sennett downtown."

At the reception desk at Detroit Police Headquarters we were greeted by a balding, red-faced sergeant who looked a little like the jelly donut sitting on the counter in front of him. Sennett was standing beside him.

"ID," the sergeant grumbled, looking annoyed that we had interrupted his repast.

Jordan showed her Federal Prosecutor's ID. He grunted and then reached his hand out for mine. I thrust my fingers into my back pants pocket and pulled out my Special Deputy badge, which read, *Benjamin Dailey, M.D., Police Surgeon*. To make my title official, they paid me a few bucks every year to perform some perfunctory functions, like exams on some of the department bigwigs. I had to admit, I liked pulling that badge out of my pocket.

The sergeant raised his eyebrows so high they almost touched his combover. "Man," he said, staring at my bright gold shield, "in all the years I've been checking people in at this station, I've never seen one of these."

"Yeah, well, trust me, the doc here earned this one," Sennett said.

The sound of the sergeant dropping my shield on the counter startled me for a moment. He had slapped it down in front of him and was punching some numbers into the computer. From the side I could see my image come up on the screen.

He picked up the badge again and rubbed the edges carefully, as if to assure himself that it wasn't a plastic fake. Then he looked up at me. "You're a doctor, huh?" he asked, as he put the shield back in my wallet.

"Most of the time that's what I do." He handed the leather case back to me across the counter.

"Well, make sure you keep it in the case. It's sharp. You could cut yourself. The department wouldn't want its police surgeon hurting his hands. You never know when you may need them." He laughed loudly at his joke.

For our part we all smiled politely and started walking past his counter toward the elevator. As we did, we heard him muttering. "Police surgeon, now ain't that a first."

Jordan and I made our way up to the second floor and waited for another half hour in the metal chairs outside of Sennett's office, while he took care of some phone calls. Every now and then I would peek down the hallway and watch the stream of felons parading past us, headed to the lock-up. Some of them did the perp-walk, and some stared defiantly at anyone who would look. One thing Detroit wasn't short of was hardcore scumbags.

Ten minutes later an officer poked his head around the corner and into Sennett's office. "They've got Icky Walker in the I-room, Lieutenant." Sennett straightened himself up and started walking toward the hallway.

We followed him down a brightly lit passageway of glazed cement blocks that reminded me of the trek to the principle's office—a walk I made many times as a kid. At the end of the hall was a steel plated door and a cramped interview room. Inside sat Icky Walker, at least two hundred and seventy pounds of fearsome indignation with muttonchops, gold jewelry, and a short-clipped Afro. He looked like Mr. T, except for his bracelets. They were police-issue.

Jordan and I watched through a one-way mirror as Sennett interrogated the prisoner. The lieutenant was good, but Walker wouldn't bend. His hard-ass responses were made in a high-pitched voice that made him seem almost juvenile. The sound of him speaking gave me an involuntary shiver. Big men with little voices can be very dangerous.

The lieutenant must have recognized this too, because he was doggedly persistent in his interrogation. Regardless, every question he asked was stonewalled by Icky Walker. After an exasperating hour of questioning, Sennett approached Walker from behind and spoke softly. I could hear something about grabbing his ankles at Jackson Prison.

That's when Walker's demeanor changed. Sennett asked him again if he had ever met Ishaki. The prisoner shifted in his seat for a moment and then miraculously remembered someone with a name like Ishaki having been mentioned, calling him by his nickname, Harry. He spoke about a party store, called the Acey Deucy, on Sturdevant and Dexter. That was all he knew.

Sennett must have believed him, because when he was finished, he motioned for the guard to get him out of the room. Walker rose and shambled to the door. As he reached the entrance, he looked back at Sennett and pointed his finger at the Lieutenant. "*Vengeance is mine; I will repay saith the Lord.*" After he spoke, his face softened and he smiled, then walked out, laughing down the hallway.

When he left, Jordan and I came in from the other room. Jordan wasted no time getting to the point. "C'mon Lieutenant, let's find the Acey Deucy Party Store and talk to some people."

"Jordan, don't you think you've had enough for one day?" I asked.

This time she just shrugged. Sennett looked at her for a moment, waiting for her to answer, then offered his opinion. "I think we should, but I've got a feeling it's going to be a dead end."

"Why?" Jordan asked.

"Don't get me wrong. Icky Walker is bad," Sennett said. "But after grilling him, I don't think he knows much."

"What are you going to do?" I asked.

He stopped for a moment and ruminated on the question, then he spoke. "We have no choice. I'm going to the neighborhood around the Acey-Deucy and following the lead."

"What about me?" Jordan asked.

"No offense, but I'm not too good at delivering babies."

Jordan gave him a look that didn't exactly bridge the gender gap. "This is partly my problem, Lieutenant. Don't forget I'm the one being threatened."

Sennett frowned. He was past kidding around. "C'mon, Jordan. Don't you think this is taking it a little too far?"

Before she could speak, I answered for her. "Jordan isn't going. I am."

"On what basis?" Sennett asked. There was a tone of relief in his voice.

"On the basis that it involves a threat to Jordan and our child, and if I don't go, you'll have to deal with her. Besides, I'm legit." I fingered the deputy card in my pocket and pulled it out to show Sennett.

"You really like this police stuff, don't you?" Sennett asked.

"As long as I come back alive."

Sennett looked over at Jordan. She held up her hands in mock surrender. "Just make sure you keep Ben out of trouble," she said with an I've-been-through-this-before resignation in her voice.

The Lieutenant looked at me for a moment, then tapped the piece inside his coat and smiled. "Just stay behind me and try not to be too white. This is just going to be a little conversation with some people, nothing violent."

I looked over at Jordan. She was quiet, maybe disappointed. I understood her feelings. When I was exiled from the hospital for five years, there wasn't a day that I didn't yearn to be in my profession and part of the game.

CHAPTER 5

I MET SENNETT AT HIS OFFICE around three-thirty, and we took an unmarked car out of the garage. I think the lieutenant liked going into the heart of the gang-infested neighborhoods unannounced. He once told me that walking into a joint he knew was ruled by thugs and showing his badge gave him a real sense of satisfaction, the kind that said *you don't control this turf, the law does*.

Nonetheless, badge or not, he still didn't take any chances, even if it was just to interview people. He checked his Sig before we left and made sure there was a cruiser in the district. George Sennett was a tough sonofabitch, no doubt. But he was also careful.

We drove down Dexter Avenue, south of the Davison Expressway. In the 1950s, this area of Detroit was a bustling commercial district, full of markets and stores and people. In the 1960s, it was the heart of the riots that devastated the city. Now it was a no-man's land of dilapidated buildings, with the windows of unairconditioned apartments flung open in response to the afternoon sun.

He turned the car down Sturdevant, a couple of blocks from Dexter Avenue. In the distance I could see a barber pole and the edge of a blue neon party store sign.

The hot, shimmering streets were mostly empty in the late afternoon; just an old couple wheeling a small pull-cart with groceries, two middle aged men sitting at the corner under the awning of a corner store, taking a pull from the bottles inside their brown bags, and three young toughs in lowrider jeans, hips strutting down the street, as if they were keeping time to some unheard music.

"Are we going to the Acey Deucy first?" I asked.

"We'll try it, but on a nice day like this in the city you never know whether these places are open or not. If we can't find out anything at the party store, we'll visit Jackson's Barbershop at the end of the street. If you want to know anything in a neighborhood like this, it's the first place you go."

Sennett parked in the middle of the block, under the shade of an old maple tree. As we got out of the car, he handed me a large envelope and asked me to bring it along. Then he took off his jacket, slung it over his shoulder, and mopped his brow. It was so hot, his shirt was already soaked.

We walked to a yellow building on the corner. Over the entrance the sign read Acey Deucy, and under it in bold red script were the words "Checks Cashed." The front door was locked with a closed sign behind the glass door. Sennett gave me an I-told-you-so look and motioned me down the street toward a red and white barber pole sticking out from the plate glass window of a store.

Jackson's Barbershop was sandwiched between The First Church of the Blessed Word, a storefront church, and the Acey Deucy on the corner. As we walked there, Sennett told me that he and Levi "Lefty" Jackson went to the same high school. He played football and Lefty was the starting pitcher on the state championship baseball team. Ever since they had remained best friends.

When we entered, the air was refreshingly cool and smelled of pomade and after shave lotion. There was no one there except for a lean black man sitting in the barber chair reading the newspaper. He had a bald head, smooth, light brown, freckled skin, and gray-green eyes that lit up with surprise. "Lieutenant! Man, how you be?"

"I'm doing fine, Lefty, just fine."

"Well, you don't look so fine. You're sweatin' so much, I thought you came from a laundromat." He started laughing at his joke, so hard it brought tears to his eyes.

"Hot weather and bad air conditioning. It's a problem."

Lefty glanced over at me. "Say, Lieutenant, what are you and that distinguished looking white man doing down at my shop?"

"This is Dr. Benjamin Dailey. He's helping me on a case."

"A doctor investigating crime, huh? Sounds kind of fishy to me. You know, back the day, I knew a colored boy from Jackson, Mississippi, named Frank Barnes. Good kid. Man, could he hit! He left the league after two years and went back to college. Went on to become a famous heart surgeon. Made a lot more money than any of us."

I was going to ask him if Frank Barnes ever investigated murders, when Sennett interjected. "Lefty, an Arab boy got killed a couple of days ago," he said quietly. "We think he might have had some dealings at the Acey Deucy. You know a kid named Hamoud Ishaki?" His face turned serious.

"Well, let's see . . . . I knew some Arab-looking kid that used to hang out there named Harry. I cut his hair once in a while. He was a strange kid. Big talker. You know the kind, 'I can hit anyone's fastball, inside, outside, down low, up high.' Lotta talk, you know what I mean?"

"Show him the photos, Doc," Sennett said. I pulled a copy of a photograph of Hamoud Ishaki out of the manila envelope I was carrying.

Lefty nodded. "That's him all right."

"There's some talk that Icky Walker might have been involved," Sennett continued.

I looked out the window onto the street while Lefty explained that he didn't think Walker would bother with a kid like Ishaki. Not good enough to kill. In this neighborhood it didn't get much more worthless than that.

"Did this boy, Harry, look like trouble?" Sennett asked.

"Nah, he didn't look that tough to me. Just a lot of talk."

I looked over at Sennett. "Another dead end," I said dejectedly.

"Maybe yes, maybe no," Lefty said. "Abdul, from the store, told me something interesting while I was cutting his hair. An Arab guy was in the Acey Deucy a few days ago, asking a bunch of questions about Harry. Everyone clams up."

"Any idea who he was?"

"He'd been down at the store once before, but no one paid any attention. He asked Abdul to call him if Harry ever came down there. Abdul's a nice guy. He likes baseball."

"Do you know the man's name?"

"Sure, the guy gave Abdul a card. He described the man to me, then wrote his name down. Abdul knows I can get information out of anyone, certainly better than he can. Abdul was suspicious of him, but he's suspicious of everyone. Anyway, the man never came in."

Lefty reached into the drawer under the ultraviolet box that held his utensils and handed Sennett the name and number. It said Ahmad Masri and listed a phone number in Dearborn. Sennett pocketed the slip of paper. "Thanks, Lefty. When we gonna play again?"

"When you learn how to get out of a sand trap?" Lefty laughed. The overhead light reflected off his gold front tooth, so that he looked as if he had a small light bulb in his mouth.

"Next week at Palmer. I've got to get my money back."

We didn't say much else. I shook hands with the ex-quarterback turned barber and walked out, wondering about the connection between Ahmad Masri and the late Hamoud Ishaki. On the way back to the station, Sennett told me he had to make a statement to the press on the murder. He didn't sound enthusiastic.

As soon as I was back in my car, I called Jordan and arranged to meet her at Gus's Diner for dinner. Gus Katsopopoulos had a place in Greektown next to the gambling casino. The diner had been there long before gambling came, and Gus hoped it would be there long after.

I found Jordan standing outside the restaurant. The sun was still out at seven o'clock, and the warm June breeze coming off the river felt soothing. It was a feeling Midwesterners spent all winter yearning for and all summer enjoying.

A short and burly man with hairy arms, bushy eyebrows, and a perpetual five o'clock shadow waved to us as we walked in. Gus Katsopopoulos came over and gave Jordan a big hug. He had intelligent, dark eyes and an infectious grin with wide-spaced white teeth that contrasted brightly against his dark face. I looked at him holding Jordan and thought of a koala bear hugging a curvaceous tree limb.

"Hey Doc, how come you got such a good-looking woman?"

"Luck of the draw, Gus."

"Yeah, well you musta had a good hand." Gus knew how we met, and I think it always tickled him to have been there at the start.

Jordan sat down at the window table and picked up a menu. Before she even opened it, Gus yelled over to the cook behind the broad Formica counter, "Hey, Joey, bring the doc and his wife two gyros and a Greek."

"*Soon-to-be-wife* and make that three gyros and a large Greek, Gus," Jordan interjected. "I'm eating for two."

"Or maybe three . . .," I explained to no one in particular and then looked around as if someone else had spoken.

"I love men," Jordan retorted, a look of utter disgust covering her face. "They should try carrying around thirty or forty extra pounds for nine months. You fall in love with every bathroom you see, your back aches, and your feet feel like two lead weights."

"That's why God, in his infinite wisdom, gave women a uterus," I said, thinking I was being funny.

"Yeah, and that's why the devil, in *his* infinite wisdom, gave Lorena Bobbit a knife."

That's when Gus really cracked up. "Doc, don't mess with this woman. I think you're out of your league."

"No question." I looked around at the empty diner. "Say, where is everyone tonight?" I asked, anxious to get my foot out of my mouth.

"Ask the city council. They're the ones that wanted the casino. They said it would be wall to wall people." Gus should have studied sociology, because he had a pretty good take on the city. He explained how the casinos did nothing but keep the poor people poorer and increased the racial disparity of the city.

Listening to Gus, I looked at the casino across the street. Through the large plate glass windows, I saw faceless people pushing the buttons on the slot machines in a sort of rhythmic chaos, and wondered if they could somehow harness that energy for something useful.

Jordan unfolded her napkin and paused momentarily, deciding whether to put it on her lap or over her distended middle. Then she asked, "What happened with Sennett?"

"Not much. Just spent some time talking with one of the best left-handed high school quarterbacks to ever play the game."

"Oh, yeah? And what did he say?"

"The word on the street is that Icky Walker didn't kill Ishaki, but he did mention someone else that might be involved. Sennett's got the name written down. Other than that, there was nothing solid to go on."

By this time Gus was back at the table. Jordan studied him for a moment. "Gus, you're a smart guy. Let me ask you a question."

"Shoot."

"Suppose the police are watching a guy they think has committed a crime. If you were the criminal, would you ever threaten someone just to bait the police, knowing they were watching?"

Gus thought a moment. "Come to think of it, I saw it happen once in the old country. Two guys had a long-standing argument over the price of fish at the market. The police knew about it, but never thought either one would do anything. Then the one guy pulls a knife and threatens the owner with the police looking."

"Over fish?"

"That's what it looked like. Turns out the owner of the market was trying to make it with the other guy's girlfriend. The one guy was losing face over the girl. The price of the fish was just an excuse."

"See, Ben, the whole story sounds fishy to me," she deadpanned.

We all started to laugh. Then Gus went back to his kitchen, Jordan focused on her gyro, and I thought about Hamoud Ishaki lying on the table, and then about his grandfather. It was hard to believe that Bill Yaldo was the kind of person who would threaten Jordan in the face of the publicity he had created. He seemed too smart.

CHAPTER 6

THE NIGHT WAS COOL and the warm breeze coming off the lake gave the water an almost sensual feeling as it washed back and forth over my naked body. Each time it did I felt myself get harder, as if some unseen, unknown erotic force was pulling at me.

Then I realized it was a hand that had inserted itself between my legs. Soft and gentle. But where was it coming from? Slowly a head appeared out of the water. It had the face of Julie McFarland. How did she get here?

She smiled and rose up out of the water, her firm breasts rubbing against my chest. She brought one of them up to my mouth and ran the nipple up and down my lips.

I could feel myself getting hotter, in spite of the water. I watched as her wet body rose above me, presenting a perfect view of the carefully waxed hair between her legs. I was transfixed as the lips on her cleft beckoned my erection toward the dark inside of her. Then, out of nowhere, I thought to myself, where was Jordan? What was I doing with Julie? I struggled to consciousness, my eyes suddenly opening. My heart was beating wildly. I was sweating and disoriented. Now I felt guilty.

Julie McFarland was a nurse in the operating room. She had a nasty reputation, and a few days ago she had come on to me during a chance meeting when I was leaving the hospital. I had ignored her and thought it was over. Obviously not. I was calmer now, but still excited. Why was I thinking about Julie? It didn't take me long to realize that Jordan's pregnancy and the associated lack of sex were the cause.

As I looked over at Jordan sleeping peacefully on the pillow next to me, I yearned to say something to her. I had made a few advances lately, but she hadn't seemed interested. Like last night. I rubbed her back for a few minutes. That was usually our sign. Instead, she turned on her side and went to sleep. I didn't want to press the issue. Not expressing my feelings is one of my worst faults. I wondered how long it would take my blue balls to change my ways.

I struggled out of bed and made it to the bathroom. It usually takes about twenty minutes of standing in front of the mirror, splashing water on my face and shaving, before I can function. I call it my organizational time. This morning I was slower than usual in getting organized. By the time I had finished, my recent ardor was only a memory.

I got dressed and went downstairs. Our dog, Buck, was waiting for me in the kitchen, panting with excitement. He was a yellow Lab, and if I do say so myself, one of the smartest dogs ever. We walked outside, and I watched as he wheeled around the grass on the front lawn. It was all part of our early summer ritual. I found a stick and threw it to him. He bounded to the twig and rushed to bring it back, dropping it at my feet. I smiled at him like a proud parent.

Brett Zielinski drove by in his car and threw the paper on the driveway. He stopped for a moment, and we chatted. He was a star pitcher on his high school team and was going to college on a scholarship. Nice boy. I thought to myself that, if I had a son, I'd like him to be like Brett.

I waved at him as he drove away and then took a few minutes to yank out a couple of unsuspecting green weeds that had invaded my garden. When I was done, I whistled for Buck, waited a few moments for him to come, and walked back in the house.

Inside, I set the paper on the kitchen table and glanced at the front page. The headline screamed out at me. "Prominent Arab Leader Found Shot to Death." I read on:

>Bill Yaldo, President of the Arab Council for Equality (ACE), was found dead in his car in an abandoned field near Michigan Avenue. He was shot through the head. A spokesman for ACE blamed subversive agents from Zionist organizations and vowed to help find the murderer.
>
>Yaldo was the grandfather of Hamoud Ishaki, a young Arab, who was also recently murdered. Yaldo had been critical of the federal prosecutor's office's tactics regarding certain allegations against members of the Arab American community. Most of his condemnation had been directed toward Assistant Federal Prosecutor Jordan Dalkind, claiming that the prosecutor was using innuendo and misleading facts in her investigation.
>
>Ms. Dalkind is the fiancée of Dr. Benjamin Dailey. Dailey, recognized in his own right as a surgeon, is perhaps best known

for his dramatic uncovering of a string of murders at St. Vincent's Hospital. When asked if Dr. Dailey had any connection in the investigation, the prosecutor's office had no comment.

After reading the article, I guessed Yaldo wasn't as smart as I had thought. And neither was I. Hamoud Ishaki, Bill Yaldo and now Jordan and me all in the same article.

I wondered if I should stay 'til Jordan read the article, then glanced at my watch and realized I was running late. Discussing the news would have to wait until I was home for dinner.

Six minutes into the twenty-five minute drive to the hospital, I called Sennett and found him at his office. It was seven-thirty in the morning.

"I suppose you're calling about that stuff in the paper, huh?" he growled.

"Yeah, it was on my mind."

"Well, don't believe everything you read. Those rags try to stir up something any time they can."

Remembering the columns written about me and the heinous malpractice I was accused of committing, I could only agree. I was a convicted man before I ever stepped into the courtroom. "So, what is the *real* truth?"

Sennett sighed deeply. "The real truth is we found this guy Yaldo with a single shot in the head. I would have almost thought it was a suicide, except there was no gun and no note."

I turned off the Lodge Expressway as Sennett explained that he had cleared Walker of any involvement and was working on Lefty's tip. I asked him if Yaldo's death had anything to do with the threat against Jordan. He said to forget about it.

"Why?"

"Yaldo's associates don't have the same political clout. The chance of something happening to Jordan is considerably less."

"Any other good news?"

"Yeah. There were traces of amphetamines on the floor of Yaldo's car. It would appear to confirm the Feds' suspicions."

"And for this, Jordan's life is threatened."

Sennett said I had to sit tight and wait. I wondered if he would be as calm if he were in my shoes. "There's one other thing, Ben." The tone of his voice turned somber. "I got a note."

"From who?"

"The killer."

"What did it say?"

"It was a recognition letter, to show the magnitude of his greatness."

I pulled to the shoulder of the road just to catch my breath. The thought that the killer was looking for kudos for such a horrific crime made me sick. "Was there a signature?"

"Yeah, it was signed 'Friend of the Devil.' We ran a search on the font. It came from Microsoft Word. We'll never find who sent it; there are millions of copies," he said dejectedly. "I know you're worried about Jordan, but I'm not convinced there is connection."

I wanted to say thanks, but somehow that word didn't seem appropriate, so I grunted a goodbye and hung up. This whole affair was giving my crankiness new meaning.

By the time I finished my call with Sennett, I was at St. Vincent's. As soon as I hit the entrance, my growling stomach decided I should stop for a bagel and a cup of coffee in the doctors' dining room. Before my five-year exile from the hospital, I used to enjoy going there for the banter, but when my case went public, I quickly became *una persona non grata*.

Sure, after I had uncovered the series of murders I was welcomed back like a conquering hero. So-called friends who shunned me now greeted me as a revered colleague. Who were they kidding? I could have had a chip on my shoulder, but what good would that have done? Besides, if it hadn't happened, I might have never met Jordan, and that was worth any pain I might have suffered.

I sat down at a polished round table by the window and was soon joined by two anesthesiologists I worked with, Carl Fairchild and Larry Schneider, along with another doctor I didn't recognize. Schneider introduced Mark Shackley, a young orthopedic surgeon who had recently joined the staff. He then began what sounded like an ongoing argument with Fairchild about the management of a patient on the floor that had almost died of pulmonary complications from an anesthetic.

The discussion lasted for about five minutes. It was a little embarrassing listening to two grown men having a full-blown argument over what seemed like a minor medical issue. Fairchild—tall, athletically built, with an almost too-perfect Aryan face and a pedigree of Eastern schools behind him—seemed to be winning until Schneider quoted some obscure medical journal. The latter was the Mutt to Fairchild's Jeff, a medium-sized man with short reddish hair graying at the temples, brush-cut in a style that made him look hip in an effeminate way. When he saw that he had verbally pinned the other doctor, a smile of victory spread across his face.

These academic arguments with Fairchild were becoming legendary at St. Vincent's, and I wanted no part of them. "I'm sure there are two sides to every argument," I said, trying to defuse the situation.

"Well, I guess that says it all, doesn't it?" Larry said sarcastically.

"Not with you, Larry. You always need the last word. So, I'm bringing the case up to the Morbidity and Mortality Conference next week," Fairchild replied in a serious tone.

"And I will get the last word," Larry replied. Fairchild seemed unfazed by the threat. Instead they both got up from the table and strode down the hallway arguing, this time about Mozart. Shackley followed a few steps behind them, shaking his head.

After they left, I sat down in a leather chair for a few minutes and read about the Tigers in *The Free Press*. When I was done, I picked up my coffee from the table and started down the hallway. I wondered about those two guys and how far they would take their arguments. Schneider was too opinionated, Fairchild was an academic snob. Every difference of opinion seemed like life and death to them. Then I thought about Hamoud Ishaki and Bill Yaldo, and suddenly life and death became more real to me.

CHAPTER 7

Aᴛᴛᴇʀ ᴛʜᴇ ᴅᴇᴀᴛʜ ᴏꜰ Bɪʟʟ Yᴀʟᴅᴏ things seemed to cool down, except for the weather. The beautiful days of late June turned into a blistering early July dry spell. No rain in two weeks. Feast or famine; there was never any in-between when it came to weather in the Midwest.

I would have thought that the absence of any direct threats would have made Jordan feel better. Instead, she seemed to absorb the heat like dry sand, her chin dragging on the floor. On Thursday we were supposed to go the art museum for a fundraiser with George, but I could tell her heart wasn't in it, which was surprising, since she had minored in art history in college and wouldn't have missed the Van Gogh show for anything.

"What happened?" I asked, as she walked into the foyer of our townhouse. She turned her back to me to close the door. I could tell she was upset, so I touched her on the shoulders, as if trying to help her out of the coat she wasn't wearing, trying to show her I could be attentive and sympathetic.

"The pressure got to be too much. Ferguson suspended me from the case."

I heard the news with mixed emotions. I wanted to believe that the government is an ecumenical place where only the truth survives, but I'd learned otherwise. In a bureaucracy, rules and job security are everything. Jordan's boss, Jim Ferguson, was a bureaucratic sycophant. Anything that made him look bad and interfered with his career path immediately became someone else's problem. It angered me because I knew how much Jordan cared about her job, and because Ferguson was making her his Judas goat. But part of me was relieved—at this juncture of her pregnancy, she didn't need this kind of aggravation.

I looked at my watch. I wasn't about to let her get depressed. "Aren't we supposed to go to the museum?"

"I'm not much in the mood."

"Come on. It'll be good for you. We're meeting George down there. Besides, it's Van Gogh. I can study his ears, and you can tell me all about his painting."

It didn't take much convincing. Often Jordan could drop her irritations like bad habits, but she wouldn't forget them. I pitied Ferguson in the long run.

She changed quickly. As I had found out, pregnancy obviated choices when it came to clothes. Still, when she came down the stairs, I drank her in with my eyes. She was wearing a blouson shirt tied at the hip over black capri pants.

Even in her pregnancy, she was gorgeous, and I confess to stripping her in my mind's eye, watching her descend the staircase, and feeling myself grow unruly. God knows, over the past couple of months, her pregnancy and sex seemed like distant cousins. I wanted to say something, but after the other night, I didn't want to press the issue.

When she came to the bottom of the stairs, I stopped her for a moment and looked into her shimmering, light green eyes, the most beautiful eyes I had ever seen. I almost felt guilty at my selfish lust. Then I put my arms around her and felt her full breasts against my chest. She must have sensed my ardor, because she didn't resist. As she pressed closer, I automatically slid my hands over her firm buttocks.

She pulled backward for a moment, her eyes half-closed, yet quizzical. "I love you, Ben. Just not now. I'm sorry, I'm just not there right now," she said.

I stepped away for a moment. She must have seen the hurt in my eyes.

"I understand, believe me, I do," she continued. "It's not you. I have so much on my mind, with the wedding, the baby, and now this problem at work. It's sometimes too much." I could see how upset she was and cursed myself over my own selfishness.

The ride to the Institute of Art, one of Detroit's remaining jewels, was pretty quiet. It wasn't until we were on the Lodge Freeway that I started talking. "Are you quiet because of Ferguson?"

"No, just trying to sort my thoughts out after a long day," she said with a smile. "I couldn't care less about Ferguson. He's simply a bureaucrat. I'm more worried about the fallout from this, the publicity, what it will do to us. You saw your name in the paper, didn't you?"

I nodded. "Forget about the publicity. It's there whether I like it or not. What about the wedding?"

"You know how much I've looked forward to the day and to having a baby. The most exciting things in my life are happening all at once. I want to enjoy everything and not miss out."

"You will, trust me," I said, "but maybe it's time to pack it in for a while. Let's get married, have the kid. Leave this thing with Ferguson behind us. Right now, you don't need this kind of aggravation."

"I agree. Still, I want to see this thing through."

We were on Woodward, passing the replica of Rodin's *The Thinker* that guarded the front steps of the art museum. A large spotlight searched the sky. I pulled my Grand Wagoneer up to the valet. It looked a little *sans-culotte* next to the Mercedes and Jaguars that encircled the entrance, but that's part of the reason I had bought a Jeep.

Suddenly, as I pulled the key out of the ignition, Jordan turned to me, touching my hand. "I don't leave anything unfinished, Ben, and I won't be intimidated. I don't care about the threats. You know I would never abuse the power of my office."

"Of course not. It's cowards like Ferguson who abuse your office's dignity."

Jordan paused, pondered my sudden wisdom, smiled winsomely at me, and then squeezed my hand. "I'm glad you understand," she said, kissing me on the cheek. I nodded with the knowledge that understanding and satisfaction can be distant cousins.

We left the car and waded through a throng of people toward the exhibit, smiling familiarly at a bunch of people whose names we couldn't remember. After searching the crowd for a few moments, I finally saw George standing next to the bar. I took Jordan's hand and guided her over to him. "It took me two seconds to figure out where you would be, Lieutenant."

"Drink is the curse of the working class," he said, giving me an innocent, George Jefferson smile. It seemed so incongruous from a man so physically imposing.

As we walked past Diego Rivera's magnificent murals, I told George that I was surprised to see him at an art exhibit. He said he was there at the request of his chief, as kind of a police representative. Besides, he said, he wanted to show his softer side.

Jordan heard our talking and interrupted us. "You guys can banter all you want, but I'm going to look at the show."

We followed her as she walked into the gallery and began looking at the series of paintings from Van Gogh's residence in Arles. As the paintings drew her into their creator's private world, I could see her beautiful eyes brighten. We were standing in front of the famous self-portrait of the artist in a yellow straw hat.

"You see his work with oil?" she commented. "The way he layers it, the unusual colors that up close seem strange, but far away seem so vibrant? He was a genius."

"I couldn't agree more," said a voice from behind us.

We turned around to see Carl Fairchild standing next to a tawdry-looking woman with tousled blonde hair splayed in skillful disarray, a short, tight, black skirt, six-inch spike heels, and a black lace tank top that left nothing to the imagination. It was Julie McFarland, and her see-it-all appearance didn't surprise me.

After my encounter with her at the hospital, she would have been at the bottom of my list of people I wanted to see. I introduced Jordan and Sennett, and we chatted for a few minutes. They were a study in contrasts, Madonna vs. Slut, fulfilled happiness vs. loneliness looking for a mate. Thankfully, it seemed that Julie couldn't care less that I was there. It appeared that she had found what she wanted.

On the other hand, Fairchild was absolutely charming. "Do you like the Impressionists?" Jordan asked him.

As I looked at some of the other pictures, I could hear Carl giving his critique of the show by comparing Van Gogh to the Renaissance sculptures. Seems as though medicine wasn't the only thing upon which he had an opinion.

I anticipated that Jordan might be sorry she asked the question, so I tried to rescue her. "Jordan, one thing you must learn about Dr. Fairchild," I said. "He has his opinions."

"I'm not sure he's wrong," she said in Carl's defense. "It's a tough call. The Italian sculptors found beauty in portraying the human form, while Van Gogh portrayed his troubled soul."

"My point exactly," Fairchild continued. "The sculptors created life. Van Gogh created turbulence. Take the David sculpture. The perfection of the human form, even down to the nails on his feet. And the gaze, the anticipation, the inner vision that left him with no doubt he could slay Goliath."

"Well, I can certainly see you understand the art that you like," Jordan said, ever the diplomat. "Perhaps one day we should compare notes on our favorite paintings."

Fairchild looked away suddenly. "Yes, well, maybe sometime." Then he turned to Sennett. "What did you say your name was?"

"George Sennett."

Fairchild gazed at him for a moment, then snapped his fingers. "I thought I recognized you. Aren't you that detective I saw on the news last night discussing the murder of that young Arab boy?"

Sennett nodded silently. He looked uncomfortable at the attention.

"Terrible business," Fairchild said.

As Fairchild spoke, I was becoming more and more uneasy. I knew the last thing Sennett wanted to talk about was business.

"Yeah, it is," Sennett replied, trying not to linger on the subject.

Fairchild looked away from the lieutenant and over at the paintings. Then he turned back. "Well, at least he didn't have to worry about trying to find perfection in an imperfect world like Van Gogh. It's almost a curse, don't you think?"

Sennett didn't reply. Just then a friend of Fairchild's came up, and soon he was off like a wandering minstrel, mingling elsewhere in the crowd and spewing his education to anyone who would listen. For her part, Julie McFarland had her arm wrapped inside of his, her hip tightly pressed against his upper thigh. She had the hook in this one, and there was no way he was getting off.

"The man has an attitude, doesn't he?" Sennett asked.

"That's just Carl," I said. "He's an aristocratic snob, still living his Ivy League education. If he couldn't say something obtuse, it wouldn't be him. He's harmless as long as he stays out of the operating room and sticks to crossword puzzles." Jordan stared after him as he walked down the gallery.

"Art snobs. I know the type," she said. "Funny, though, everything matches except that woman he is with. She looks like... what was it you once called some woman you saw, George?"

Sennett smiled. "Like she could suck the chrome off a bumper hitch." Then he turned to me. "You know her?"

I said she was a scrub nurse that I worked with occasionally at St. Vincent's. I added that she wasn't my type, but then wished I hadn't protested so much. If Jordan had any qualms about Julie, my statement must have been sufficient, because she immediately turned her attention to the buffet table.

"Hungry?" I asked.

"I thought you'd never get around to the problem at hand," she said, smiling.

We made our way to the buffet table, which was stacked with Middle Eastern food—babaghanouge, humus, tabouli, lamb chops, and pita bread. Between us we had had three of everything. When we were finished, we checked out the rest of the exhibit. It was spectacular; the work in Arles, the collaboration with Gaugin, and the deterioration of a relationship that might have sent Van Gogh into the depression that ultimately ended his life. I wondered if Van Gogh was secretly gay.

As we walked down the gallery, our chance meeting with Fairchild and Julie crossed my mind. Not that it was strange to see him there, but, if I had to bet on a doctor from the hospital that would have been at an art exhibit, it would have been Larry Schneider. Then I admonished myself for my prejudice.

At the end of the exhibit we said goodbye to Sennett and left the art institute around nine o'clock, just in time to avoid the Mercedes crush. On the way home I realized I was a lot more tired than I thought. It wasn't until I got to the front door and heard Buck yapping that I became more alert. If I hadn't, I might have missed the note taped to the front door.

I picked up the piece of paper. It looked as if it had been typed on a computer. I started reading and a chill came over me.

> *I appreciated the news conference yesterday. I was also pleased to find the name of the famous Dr. Benjamin Dailey in the newspaper. As a man who has solved crimes, you must be impressed with my genius.*
>
> *Yes, I killed him. And it was glorious. Eliminating the*

non-believer and ridding the world of such alien trash. I am
God's messenger.

I thought you would like to know how I did it. He was
strapped to a table. I told him he was guilty of sins and that he
must die for his imperfection. But as a lesson, I instructed him
that he would first have his ability to procreate eliminated. With
that I removed his testicles.

As you can imagine he was not too happy, so I had to keep
him quiet. That is why they were found in his throat. I must say
it gave me great sexual stimulation.

Now that I know you are involved, I plan to keep you in the
loop. I trust you are happy for me.

Friend of the Devil

P.S.—I saw your girlfriend's picture in the paper. She's a fox.

Jordan, who had been looking over my shoulder, asked quietly, "What do
you make of this, Ben?"

I was angry and puzzled. The press had drawn me into this for no reason.
Other than my relationship with Jordan, what could I possibly do for this killer? I looked at her face. It was pale in the light of the front porch. Lines skirted
her eyes and the corners of her mouth. Fear had a way of doing that. "The killer
knows where we live, and he wants us to know that. I'm going to call Sennett."

Jordan opened the door to let Buck out and then turned to me. "See, I told
you the publicity was bad. This is exactly what I was worried about."

I did my best to settle Jordan down, then I called Sennett. He was at our
house a little after midnight. He spent some time studying the letter and then
made a phone call. Outwardly, he tried not to seem overly concerned, but at the
same time he told us that as a precaution he would have a couple of his boys,
as he put it, "look after our house." He said he would call me in the office in
the morning. Neither of us fell asleep until we saw the unmarked car in front
of the house.

Things always seem better in the daytime. The following morning was no
exception. The unmarked car was still in front of our house and the street appeared peaceful in the morning sunshine. I reached the office convinced that
things were under control. Ten minutes later I didn't have time to think about
Hamoud Ishaki, murder, or threatening notes. That's because I got the first of
two phone calls regarding Frances Gallagher, the socialite with the throat tumor. One was from a throat specialist I knew in Boston, and the other was
from a doctor I had never heard of before from the Mayo Clinic. I patiently explained what I had found on my examination, but I detected a certain amount
of haughtiness from both doctors. Frances Gallagher had big-time money, the

kind of dough that gets people's attention quickly. They both listened to my diagnosis before lecturing me on their treatment protocols. Then I was dismissed.

It was about two o'clock when Sennett called me back. "I thought you would want to know that we might be close to solving the murder."

"That's a positive statement," I said with relief. "Jordan doesn't need this kind of trouble right now."

There was a pause at the other end, as if Sennett was preparing to say something important. "We arrested that guy Masri today. We found some incriminating evidence that links him to the Ishaki murder. In addition, he also happens to be Bill Yaldo's best friend. Kind of a murderer's ménage à trois."

That's what I loved about George Sennett, the ability to make the horrible sound even more dreadful. "Do you think he was responsible for the note on my front door?"

"Maybe. Or it could be just a crank note from someone who saw the article in the paper."

"Some crank note. It scared the crap out of us."

"I know," Sennett said. "But I'm confident enough about this collar that I've pulled the boys off your detail."

I guessed if Sennett was confident, why shouldn't I feel the same?

CHAPTER 8

AFTER SENNETT TOLD US OF THE ARREST, we both decided that we weren't going to let these threats rule our lives, which was part of the reason why we walked into the northern suburb of Birmingham. The other reason was Jordan's thirty-sixth birthday.

Birmingham is the metropolitan area's answer to the squalor and hopelessness of Detroit. The town covers about ten square blocks and is nestled between a busy boulevard and some of the nicest housing and best restaurants Detroit has to offer.

We ate at a small Italian bistro, spending most of the time talking about wedding plans and the baby. It seemed peaceful, and I felt more at ease than I had in several weeks. It was around twilight when we started walking back to our home, about four blocks from the downtown area.

I say our home, but it was actually Jordan's. When we had decided to live together, she had a place, and I didn't. Now we had an arrangement. She paid the mortgage, and I paid for everything else. Not that I hadn't offered to pay for everything, but Jordan wasn't that way. Independence was very important to her and had been all her life.

As we neared the house, I noticed a red Toyota Camry parked in front, a light on inside the car and a man behind the wheel with a woman in the passenger seat. It made me wish that Sennett's men hadn't left.

I was tempted to confront the driver, but Jordan was tired, and I didn't feel like getting into an altercation. We had gotten as far as the front walk when I heard a car door open. I turned around quickly and saw a tall man walking toward us, carrying something under his arm. In the darkening twilight, I couldn't make out his face. With the note on our door, the threats against

Jordan, and a natural fear born of experience, I kept my fists clinched. I had been through this before.

Jordan walked quickly to the front door and opened it. As soon as she was inside, she flicked on the porch light, put Buck on a leash next to her, and reached into her shoulder purse. Instinctively, I knew she had her hand on her Walther PPK.

Buck started barking as I started toward the tall man. I was about ten feet away when I recognized the stranger. It was Mark Shackley, the young surgeon I had met in the doctors' dining room. Next to him was a woman in her early thirties, tall and thin, with jet-black hair. She had nice legs that were squeezed into jeans that seemed a little too tight. I figured her to be in her late twenties.

Shackley came up the sidewalk and stopped a few feet from the front porch. "I'm so sorry to disturb you at this hour, Dr. Dailey, but there was no answer at your home and we really wanted to speak with you." He turned slightly to the woman next to him. "This is my wife, Karin." I said hello, then took his hand and shook it, relieved that there was nothing to be alarmed about.

I turned to Jordan and nodded. Her hand came out of the purse.

"It must be pretty important. I don't usually see anyone at this hour coming up to my front steps. And call me Ben, I like it better. Come on in."

Shackley looked sheepish as he and his wife walked past me into the foyer. I introduced them to Jordan and within a few moments Buck was licking Mark on the face. "You're a pretty big guy. You play basketball?" I asked.

By the time we had reached the living room, he had explained that he had grown up in Indiana and everyone in Indiana played basketball. The problem was that he was too slow and didn't have a great shot. He figured he'd do better with his brains. Smart kid.

We walked into the living room and sat down on the couch. Shackley's wife grasped her knees and looked uncomfortable. I noticed her glancing at a sunset photo of a campsite on Big Trout Lake in the Algonquin. Jordan had taken it on one of our trips into Canada.

Jordan walked in as they were looking at the picture. "It's a nice shot, isn't it?" Jordan asked. It seemed to break the ice.

"Mark and I like camping a lot. We've been to Yellowstone," Karin said. "It was great." I detected a slight accent to her voice, but I couldn't quite place it.

They were easy to talk with and within a few minutes we found out that they had been married for just over a year and that Karin was an OBGYN physician who had just joined a practice at St. Vincent's. Still it was strange for them to come to the house unannounced, so I asked them how long they had been waiting for us.

They looked at each other, seemingly unsure of what to say. Then Karin spoke up. "We came early and waited. We didn't want to miss you. We're terribly sorry to drop in on you this way."

Jordan must have sensed their discomfort, because she suddenly asked if they wanted some coffee. When they said they would, she invited them into the kitchen. It didn't take long for her to set four cups on the glass table in the corner, and we sat down.

I put some cream in my mug and then turned to Mark. "Okay, what was so important for the two of you to come out late at night? I can't imagine it's about medicine."

Mark leaned forward, as if to get my attention better. "We've got a serious problem in the family," he said, hesitating slightly. "And, well, I had heard from some of the guys at the hospital that you had some experience in this type of situation, that you were the best."

I ignored the compliment. "What kind of situation?" I asked guardedly.

"It's kind of in the crime business."

I eyed him for a second, trying to detect a deceit that wasn't there. "I'm a doctor, so don't expect too much."

Mark nodded, as if he understood what I meant. "It's Karin's father. He's got himself into some trouble."

"What kind of trouble?"

"Mark, let me tell." Karin stiffened in her chair. She had a beautiful face, smooth skin, dark curly hair, and full, red lips. Her voice was firm, but I could see her hands were trembling slightly as she held the coffee cup in front of her. "There was a killing, actually two murders. It was in the paper. An Arab boy was tortured to death. Then a man named Bill Yaldo was killed. A suspect was arrested."

I looked over at Jordan with surprise, then turned back to Karin. "What does that have to do with you?"

"My maiden name is Masri. The man who was arrested is my father, Ahmad."

"What happened?" I asked, trying to sound detached from a murder I already knew about.

"The police arrested him. They said they suspected him of being involved in the dead man's murder. They said something about probable cause and a search warrant. Nothing like this has ever happened to us." I looked over at Mark. His head was down now and the toe of one of his big shoes was tracing the grouted lines of the floor tile.

"Do you have an attorney?" Jordan asked.

"My father doesn't want one because he claims he's innocent. The judge appointed a public defender, some young guy just out of law school."

I disregarded the critique. "Tell me, what's your father-in-law like, Mark?" I asked.

Mark described his father-in-law as ardently devoted to Arab causes, "a my-way-or-the-highway" type of person. After spending his life growing up in a Presbyterian family, playing ball at the YMCA, and attending Notre Dame, he said he felt like they were on different planets. There was a definite rancor in his voice.

"Is he a fundamentalist or a militant?" Jordan asked.

"Neither." Karin interjected. "He's never made a political statement since he's been here."

"He is accused of a heinous crime. Could he have done it?" I asked.

Karin's face blanched. "I know my father is not without faults. He was involved in the civil war in Lebanon, and I'm sure he did things of which he is not proud. Things he felt he had to do to protect our lives and our families."

"Why did he leave?" I asked.

"My mother died from a car bomb. He worshipped her, and her death changed him forever. That's when he moved to America."

I asked her if her father had ever been involved in any conflicts since he had been in America. She denied it, saying the only conflicts she knew he was involved with had to do with social causes, like finding jobs for immigrants. She said he was tired of fighting, but even in this country there was always some kind of ethnic discord. "When you're an Arab in a country of Christians," she said, "people stereotype you before they know you."

"Did your father know Yaldo?" Jordan asked.

Karin explained that the two men were friends in Lebanon, but then lost track of one another. Her father came to America first and brought her to Chicago, where they lived for several years. When Yaldo came to America, he called her father and begged him to come to Detroit. He even helped him start his restaurant in Dearborn, The Oasis. She mentioned that when Hamoud Ishaki was born, the family asked Masri to be the godfather.

Jordan wondered if Karin's father would have had any reason to be angry with Mr. Yaldo. She said that she always thought there was some kind of old score that had never been settled between the two men. She suspected it was over her mother. "But my father would never settle a difference by killing someone."

When Karin stopped speaking, I decided to cut to the chase. "Okay, exactly what can I do for you?" I interjected.

Before they could answer, I heard Buck growling at something at the back door. It wasn't like him, so I excused myself and walked down the hallway. The dog was barking and this time his teeth were showing. His response alarmed me.

I turned on the light outside and picked up the flashlight from the closet next to the door. I put Buck on a leash and opened the door slowly, shining my flashlight from side to side. There was no one there, but he was still growling, so I went into the small courtyard that constituted our backyard. Buck pulled me to the back gate. It led into the alley behind the house, and it was open. I knew I had closed it.

Now I was alarmed. I looked over the gate and down the alley. Suddenly, a trash can overturned and clattered on the asphalt. Buck strained at the leash, barking. I shone the flashlight in the direction of the sound and thought I saw a figure in the darkness, but it was late, and I couldn't be sure. When I looked again there was no one there, and I wasn't about to go chasing a shadow at this hour. By the time I had surveyed the alley a second time, Buck had quieted down. I locked the gate and brought him back to the house, dead-bolted the back door, and took the leash off the dog. He curled up on the mat in the back hall. His excitement was over, but maybe mine was just beginning, I thought.

I walked back into the kitchen. Jordan looked up at me and asked if everything was okay, and I told her the gate had swung open in the wind. Then I mentioned how smart our dog was. Everyone nodded with the patronizing smile of people who knew how obsessed dog owners were. When I sat back down, I resumed the conversation.

Mark took over. "We're both young doctors. We don't need this kind of publicity. We've started new practices, and this thing could wreck us. To move now would be economic suicide." He then explained that he and his wife wanted to hire me to investigate the accusations against his father-in-law. My immediate response was to suggest that they get a lawyer.

"We need something outside of the normal legal channels," Mark stammered. "We want to know if he really is guilty."

I wanted to tell them that, in police work, there was often a large gap between being innocent and being convicted, but I didn't have the heart. I wanted to tell them I wasn't a detective, I was just a doctor, but I couldn't. Instead I suggested what I always did to a patient with a serious disease—don't give up hope.

"We won't. That's why we came tonight," Karin said.

I got up from the table, walked over to the window, and stared out into the darkness for a few moments. When I was done ruminating, I came back and sat at the table. "Let me see if I can find something to help you with. I'll tell you this, if he's clearly guilty, I'm not interested."

"Fair enough," Mark said, as he handed me a brown file folder. "This folder has some family pictures, including some photos of Hamoud, a little history of my father-in-law, and some addresses of people who know him."

"I'll look this stuff over when I get a chance," I said. The conversation seemed over, and I got up from my chair, but Shackley was hesitant to let the matter drop.

"Dr. Dailey, I hate to ask this, but we need to know how much you charge. I know you're a doctor and all, but nothing is for free. Karin and I are just getting started. We can pay you, but not all at once."

"Mark, I don't want anything. If something good comes of all this, that would be payment enough."

"Like a contingency fee, without the contingency."

I laughed. "Yeah, kind of like that."

"Thank you," he said, shaking my hand. Karin also grabbed my hand but didn't say anything.

As they walked out, I thought about what he had said. *The guys said you were the best.* I wondered what he meant. I had always thought I'd be the best doctor, but that wasn't what he was referring to. Then I remembered what Sennett had once told me. Once you stared death in the face, you would never be looked at the same. Maybe he was right.

I stood in the foyer with Jordan as they walked back to their car. "Everything all right with the dog?" she asked. I told her what I found, and she didn't seem alarmed, so I didn't press the issue further. Then she looked at me for a moment. "Ben, I'm wondering if you will ever be able to . . ."

"Don't say it, Jordan. I'm thinking the same thing, and the answer is I don't know how to get rid of being a detective."

CHAPTER 9

I WAS BACK IN THE OFFICE the next morning at eight o'clock. It took until eight-thirty for Mrs. Gallagher's newest doctor to call me. His name was Thornton Calliston Rodgers III from The Center for Cancer Care in New York. I had met him a few times, but I doubted he remembered. He was the original jug full of water with a cork rammed home.

We spoke for a few minutes, during which time he told me that Mrs. Gallagher had flown in the previous day to see him. He lectured me on his findings and then declared that this was most likely a benign lesion. After which he proceeded to tell me his treatment plan, followed by a summary of his statistics.

I think "hello" and "goodbye" were the two words I managed to insert into the conversation. I wanted to help this poor woman, but there were some people that you just can't get through to. By the time I hung up, I was giving thanks to the gods of medicine that Mrs. Gallagher had sought her care elsewhere.

It was just after I had seen my last patient of the day when I called Sennett to tell him about Mark and Karin. He listened for a moment and then asked if we could meet at Jordan's office later that afternoon. He wanted to tell me something about the case, and said he felt safer talking in the office of a Federal attorney. George Sennett always did things by the book.

Jordan's office was on Fort Street, a couple of blocks from the Detroit River. They should have called the McNamara Building an armed fortress and not a building. It had started out as a drab, governmental knock-off of Bauhaus architecture, but, since the Oklahoma City bombing, it seemed more imposing than ever.

The cold facade was enhanced by an austere entranceway guarded by metal detectors and federal officers. This included a mandatory pat down before you could get to the prosecutor's office. I don't think it bothered me as much as it did Sennett. One of the policemen who was guarding the entrance knew him and, when he saw Sennett, muttered something about a ball game and how the lieutenant's home run was really a foul. Sennett shrugged his shoulders, but I had a feeling it cost someone some dough.

It must have been stuck in their craw for a while, because they practically had him undressed by the time he made it past the lobby. One of the guards mentioned something to the officer behind the metal detector about a full body cavity search, loud enough for Sennett to hear. When Sennett stepped back a pace, they winked at each other and let him by.

We took the elevator to Jordan's office on the eleventh floor. No one was in, so we slipped inside and sat down on the leather chairs in front of her desk. Sennett took off his jacket while I looked around.

Flowers in a vase, French lace runner on the credenza behind her, the smell of perfume. It was a feminine office, no question. But there was also a hard side—a certificate for marksmanship and a citation from the U.S. Attorney General for her work on a case in Miami. There used to be a photograph of her fiancé, Matt. That and the remembrance of his death in a drug bust were packed away somewhere, but I knew the memory still ran deep. She had told me the story of their relationship in a matter-of-fact way. After that she didn't say much, and I never pursued it.

There were two photos at the corner of the credenza. One of us together in Aspen and the other a picture of her in a SWAT outfit. I had gone to the range with her a couple of times. Seeing her put five straight shots in the target's head, I had a feeling she wouldn't hesitate on the real thing.

Sennett studied the picture closer. "I never realized Jordan was into the military thing," he mused.

"That was back when she worked for the DA's office in Miami. She was engaged to an FBI agent at the time."

Sennett raised his eyebrows. "Really. What happened?"

"Jordan doesn't like talking about it. Apparently, she asked him to let her go on a stakeout of a building near the pier. It was a late-night deal and the drug gang they were watching had an alarm around the building. One of the agents tripped the wire and all hell broke out. Matt, her fiancé, saw Jordan was trapped and ran to protect her. He died taking a bullet meant for her," I said sadly.

Sennett's eyes narrowed, and the sadness that only a police officer could have spread over his face. He was just about to say something when Jordan walked into the room.

"Just checking the place out or coming for a longer stay?" she asked.

I looked up. "No, I figured I'd move my office into the Federal building," I said. "Maybe I'd get paid quicker by Medicare."

"Possibly, but by the time you signed all the forms, I think you'd be begging to be back in your office." A smile crossed her lips, and I laughed.

She went behind her desk and sat down. She looked good as a lawyer, sitting tall in her light brown suit, a cameo necklace just above the collar of her blouse, and reading glasses perched inquisitively on the end of her nose. She turned from me and looked at Sennett for an answer.

"I wanted Ben to tell me about his meeting with Masri's daughter in front of you so that there would be no conflict about who said what," Sennett stated clearly.

"You're sure it's not privileged?" I asked.

"Not unless you signed a contract. That's one of the reasons I wanted to meet with you in Jordan's office. This is a Federal case and I don't want any misunderstanding." Jordan nodded. By-the-book Sennett.

I told him about our meeting with Mark and Karin Shackley. Then I asked him about the suspect. "Everything points to Ahmad Masri," he said.

"What do you mean?"

"It turns out he may have had an ax to grind with Yaldo."

"Over what?"

"Something in the old country. Who knows?" Sennett went on to tell us they were holding Masri on probable cause. The confidence of yesterday was gone from his voice. It was clear that he was worried about his case. As he spoke, I looked out the window toward the Detroit River. A freighter was relentlessly churning its way to Lake Erie. The day seemed so peaceful, too peaceful to be talking about violent death.

Jordan slowly removed her glasses and looked over at Sennett. "Lieutenant, tell me about the other murder, the one that was similar to the Ishaki boy."

Sennett looked around the room for a moment, visibly upset, and then down at his brawny arms, bulging out of his blue, short-sleeved shirt. Sennett had a hard time talking about his feelings. He rhythmically squeezed his fists, rippling the muscles in his forearm.

"About fifteen years ago we had a murder-torture victim, a young girl named Stacey Issacson. She had been molested. A broomstick . . ."

Sennett picked up a pencil from Jordan's desk, as if he were looking at the murder weapon. "She had her neck cut open and her jugular vein removed. It was wrapped around her wrist like a bracelet," he continued. "It was terrible. Her father was a doctor who did abortions in the inner city. The body was left hanging from a light pole near his clinic. We figured it was some kind of hate thing by a pro-lifer or some white supremacist group. We had ten guys working on the case, day and night."

Jordan interjected. "Aside from the obvious relationship of the victim to the doctor, what made you believe it was related to his abortion work?"

"There was a note left beside the body. Just the usual revenge-type doggerel. The thing that led us to believe it might be the work of a white supremacist was the swastika that was drawn on the bottom of the note."

"I remember reading something about it in the Miami papers. The murder was solved, wasn't it?" Jordan asked.

"Yeah, we found the perpetrator floating in the Detroit River."

"Why did you think he was the killer?" Jordan asked.

"He had a record. His name was James Carrington. In his wallet was the name of the victim. We tracked down his apartment and found newspaper articles and personal items that led us to believe he was the killer."

He described the perp as an ex-Marine Corps medic, who had helped in the autopsy room at Bethesda Naval Hospital. In addition, he had been photographed, protesting at the abortion clinic. When Jordan asked if there could be a connection, Sennett emphatically replied that this murder appeared to be a separate incident. "Masri is my man, I'm sure."

As he spoke, I thought about the young girl's murder. A horrific crime that was solved. Or was it? If Sennett wasn't so sure they had found the killer, I wouldn't have been inclined to agree.

Jordan's voice brought me back to the conversation. "And you have this man, Masri, in custody?" she asked.

Sennett nodded. "We've got him on some circumstantial evidence right now. Like I said, there was some type of conflict between him and Bill Yaldo. In a few days we should have enough facts to wrap it up. Do you see any problems?"

"Depends on the judge," Jordan said firmly. Her voice, stone cold and precisely accurate, made me glad I wasn't Ahmad Masri.

"That's what my captain said," Sennett replied. "Right now, I'm just going to follow the rules and see where it takes us."

"And why has it taken you to my office?" Jordan asked with the slightest of smiles.

"This may have some Federal implications, including hate crime statutes," Sennett said gravely. "That's a job for your department. But you've seen what can happen. If we don't have our case airtight, we're not going anywhere, especially in this community."

"I agree."

Sennett explained that his biggest problem was getting anything out of a close-mouthed Arab community. Since I had become friendly with the Shackleys, he wanted to know if I would cooperate with him in sharing information.

"Isn't that a violation of some kind of ethical standard?" I asked.

"This isn't the Hippocratic Oath, and there's no doctor-patient confidentiality. I'm not asking for medical information. This is murder, and anything that might be of advantage to us within the law is fair game."

"I guess it's up to Ben," she said. "There are no legal issues."

No legal issues, only moral ones. Isn't that how it always is?

"These people sound like survivors. Not unlike our relatives from the camps." Jordan tapped her pen on the edge of her desk, then put the end in her mouth, chewing thoughtfully.

"Yeah, religious and economic survivors," Sennett replied.

"There is something about religion that brings out the worst and the best in people," Jordan said.

"And sometimes religion is used as an excuse for something else," I interjected, "but isn't saying that a big assumption? I have a number of Middle Eastern patients. They seem to be honest, hardworking people, anxious to be American citizens."

"Exactly," Sennett said. "That's why I'd like both of you to sift through the information, just to get another set of eyes on the process." As he spoke, he looked over at the credenza as if he would find some answer in Jordan's SWAT team picture.

"Anything in particular?" I asked.

"I'm not sure. Free-floating hunches are not my style."

"It's not hunches, Lieutenant, it's instinct," I replied. "Maybe you need to listen to your inner thoughts." I thought again about the dead girl whose murder was solved.

"What do you mean?"

"You don't have a lot of faith in hunches. You deal in facts. I see the same thing in medicine. The young kids that come out of medical school call it 'evidence-based medicine'—a series of tests that always lead you to the answer."

"You sound skeptical."

"I like to think outside of the box once in a while, like the similar murder a few years ago. Check it out. See if there is something else that's similar."

Sennett's hands were spread out in front of him now. The tension was gone. "Maybe I'll go to the crime lab tomorrow. Do you two want to come along?"

"I guess it wouldn't hurt. I'm already involved," I said, without a lot of enthusiasm.

Jordan nodded her head reluctantly. "Just remember that involvement can be dangerous," she cautioned me.

With my history, I knew why. I was about to say something smart. Then I thought of Jordan's former fiancé, Matt, and Hamoud Ishaki, his balls in his throat. I looked around Jordan's office. Lace runner, flowers, a beautiful view down the river. The only thing missing was an emesis basin.

CHAPTER 10

T HE NEXT DAY WE MET SENNETT at the Detroit Police Department crime lab, which was housed a couple of blocks from headquarters in a converted elementary school. It looked like a pretty ordinary building from the outside and stayed ordinary until we passed through the double steel vault door. There we introduced ourselves to Jerome Michaels, ex-special forces and now assigned to guard detail at the lab.

Jerome stood up from his desk. He was a wiry five-ten with bulging veins sticking out like latticework on his arms and hands. I suspected that under his tight, dark blue Detroit Police uniform shirt was a six-pack that could stop a battering ram. It was obvious to me that whatever was in this building required more than run-of-the-mill security.

"Running in the Marine Corps marathon again with combat boots and a forty-pound pack, Jerome?" Sennett asked.

Jerome nodded nonchalantly, then looked down at his visitor list. "She's in the ballistic room," he said in a deep baritone voice, pointing us to proceed down the hallway. Jerome was the kind of man who had too many things on his mind to bother with small talk.

The "she" he was referring to was Florence Clevenger, Chief Investigator at the Detroit Police Crime Lab. We found her behind a glass enclosure with earmuffs on and a Smith and Wesson in her hand. She was a black woman with a closely-clipped natural, a high forehead, small, almond-shaped eyes, and sensuous red lips that made her intelligent face look sexy. When she saw us, she pointed to her covered ears and motioned us to back out of the room.

We watched from the hall as she expertly squeezed off four bullets into an enclosed shooting case and then retrieved them. I looked at her more closely.

She had a boyish, athletic body with slim hips and long legs. From the way she handled the S&W, I suspected that she was the kind of woman who opened her own doors.

When she finished, she walked over to Sennett and smiled. It was an engaging, hard-to-not-like-you smile, incongruous for a woman who spent her life solving vicious crimes. It was also the smile of someone with more than just a passing acquaintance with the lieutenant. Sennett seemed a little uncomfortable.

"Hey, Bubba, you've come back to get educated!" she said taking off her ear protectors and walking out of the room.

"Don't get too excited, Flo. It's a visit, not a semester," Sennett replied. He proceeded to introduce Jordan and me. She greeted us, then took the bullets from the gun and put them under a microscope. "New stuff, Flo?" Sennett asked.

"We found a gun in the dumpster near a club where a rapper was killed." She had two bullets under the scope. "That's it," she said, "the rifling is identical. This is the murder weapon. Now all you guys have to do is find the perp."

She put the bullets in an evidence box, shut off her microscope, and motioned for us to sit in the chairs in her lab. "Now what's this business regarding the Issacson murder all about? I thought it was a done deal," Flo said with a frown.

Sennett explained the similarities between the murders of Hamoud Ishaki and the Issacson girl and asked for another look at the evidence.

"No problem, George." She punched the keys on the Dell 5500 in front of her, and soon paper was spitting out of the printer like mulch from a woodchipper. Sennett went to the machine and picked up the papers, which were summary sheets of the Issacson murder. Ghastly information. It was hard to look through the pages; a young woman that had been assaulted, tortured, and mutilated, while alive.

We examined the other papers, including a copy of the note at the murder scene. My eyes shifted quickly across the smudged piece of paper to a red and black swastika at the bottom. I thought about my grandfather's family, incinerated in the Holocaust. It made me sick. "What was the significance of that note?" I asked.

"The quote was from the Bible, but beyond that it's anyone's guess."

We looked at the pictures. As we did, I glanced up and looked around the room filled with filing cabinets, glass beakers, and Bunsen burners. If I wasn't with the police, it could have been a college chemistry lab.

Sennett passed me the coroner's report. I noted that the pathologist was Allan Davis. Somehow, I couldn't get away from him. It was disturbing.

"How sure are you that the man you found was the killer?" My innocent question must have seemed like a challenge, because Flo scrutinized me for a moment. I think the word "sure" meant a lot to her. Her professional credibility was at stake and *sure* had to be positive beyond a reasonable doubt.

"We were ninety-nine percent convinced. You're a doctor, right?" Her voice was strong, and her question was direct. There was no nonsense in the Clevenger household. I nodded. "What do you tell your patients? Are you always one hundred percent right?"

"Not usually."

"So, you use the weight of the evidence to make a diagnosis. Most of the time you're right. Sometimes the system fails. It's that way in forensics. There's always a slim chance that we could be wrong."

I nodded at her logic. "How about in this case?"

Clevenger went on to describe how they had found the victim's driver's license on his person and pieces of the murdered girl's clothing decorating his apartment. "In addition," Clevenger continued, "there was a diary with a complete confession. It was a total package."

Sitting near her desk, I picked up two remaining bullets that were on her blotter. "It's too bad you didn't have the gun, or something like that."

"Show the doc that other note, Flo," Sennett probed. Flo nodded and handed me a single sheet of paper, which I read to myself.

> *I almost botched the job, and it was all my fault. I should have known her old man would have had security. He ran an abortion clinic. It was all there for me to see. I just didn't see it.*
>
> *When the security guys spotted the girl in my car, I had no choice. I had to get rid of her in a hurry. I must admit it took away a lot of the excitement from her death. I wanted it slow and satisfying. I wanted to explain to her how her life was useless, how her mother was a whore, and how imperfect she was.*
>
> *Instead, it was what I refer to as untidy. I had to pull away quickly from the side street. She was fighting and screaming so loud I had to stop the car and beat her into submission.*
>
> *She was still breathing when I was done, so I pulled into an abandoned field, put her in the backseat, and undressed her. When I was finished with her, I was satisfied with the exception that she never heard my lecture. I will be more careful. There will be no more mistakes.*

I passed the note to Jordan. "I don't get it," I said.

"The dead girl's father ran an abortion clinic in Ypsilanti. In retrospect, Carrington was a perfect suspect. We had implicated him on some other trouble we'd had with an abortion clinic in Flint. But it was the nonviolent type of action; you know demonstrations, picketing. We didn't put it together until we found him in the Detroit River." Sennett seemed irritated as he spoke. I suspected it was because the guy was already dead. I'm sure he would have liked to spend some time with him in the interrogation room.

"What about DNA testing?" I asked.

"That was fifteen years ago. Our lab wasn't set up to perform the test as a routine at that time. Besides, everything was so clear-cut, we didn't feel we needed it."

"Okay, Flo," Sennett continued, "we know Carrington killed Stacy Issacson. He had some medical knowledge. Now you've got another murder that was no ordinary crime of passion. The doc is suggesting there's a connection."

"There are some similarities," Flo said thoughtfully. "The killer is someone who studied his victim closely before the crime. He appeared to be meticulous."

"But you don't think there is a connection between this killing and any other murder?" I asked again.

Flo appeared unfazed by my persistence. "No. We've combed the data banks. Since the Issacson murder fifteen years ago, there haven't been any other cases that weren't solved. All of our information from computers, DNA, and fingerprints is negative. And we found James Carrington. This looks like a new killer on the loose, and he is very, very dangerous."

"Is there any doubt about Carrington?" Jordan asked.

"Perfect evidence and a motive. It was a complete forensic package."

"How would you profile this new killer?" Jordan asked.

Clevenger described how most killers like this one are seeking some kind of attention. "That's why they usually include a letter of some kind," she said. "While they may or may not have a sexual proclivity for the same sex, they definitely have sexual perversions and deficiencies that they are trying to fulfill. Inadequacies are common. The act of killing produces sexual power. They usually start early in life killing animals and then work their way up to humans." When Jordan asked her if Ishaki's murder might be a terrorist or a political statement, Flo thought it wasn't.

Jordan found a seat next to a glass cabinet filled with NIH pamphlets and several textbooks on DNA testing. She pulled out one of the books and studied the cover for a few seconds. Then she turned back to Flo. "Do you believe Masri perpetrated this crime?" Jordan asked. Flo nodded.

I was back to rubbing the bullets in my hand. This whole business was making me nervous. "How sure are you of this?"

"The only thing that dissuades me is the absence of hard evidence, the DNA."

"What about the fact that he has a family?" I asked.

"Is his wife alive?" Flo asked.

"She was killed in Lebanon from a car bomb," I replied.

"That was most likely the trigger," she said triumphantly. "He probably cracked after that. And the murder coincides with the time he's been here. Killers like this want to make a statement about something. Prove a point, no matter how obscure, no matter how displaced their rage. It's as if they wanted to get even with someone."

"For instance?" I asked, placing the bullets back on her desk.

"Look at Jack the Ripper," Flo replied. "He claimed he was ridding society of prostitutes, but he was probably trying to rid himself of his own demons. He kept writing letters, taunting the police in London, just like this note is taunting us."

"Do you think the person who killed Hamoud Ishaki had the same motive?" Jordan asked.

"Maybe," Flo responded, "But whatever the motivation, I suspect that whoever did this killing is actually playing some kind of intricate game known only to him. We just don't understand it."

Clevenger went on to explain that almost all of these types of killings are overt and perverted public demonstrations that reflect upon a childhood of abuse, an abusive relationship between parents, or a sudden act of violence that changed their lives. In each case notoriety plays an important role. "Take the Green River Killer, Gary Leon Ridgeway, in Washington state, or the BTK killer in Kansas," she said. "They killed and mutilated dozens of people, all the while taunting the police with notes and misleading clues."

"I read about them in the paper," Jordan added.

"That's exactly what the killer would want you to say," Flo replied. "The need for public attention is one of the main things that drives them to kill. They crave the recognition of their own self-proclaimed greatness."

Sennett, who all this time had been quietly studying the papers on the Issacson murder, shook his head. "All these killers eventually make some kind of mistake. In Ridgeway's situation, he left a paint fragment at a crime site, paint from the plant where he worked. When one of his victims escaped a murder attempt, she went to the police. They had a list of employees at the plant, and she identified him through a picture." He paused a moment and smiled. "How I love good, old-fashioned police work."

"That may be true, but right now we don't even know if we are dealing with a serial killer," Flo replied.

"What about the testicles in Ishaki's throat?" I interjected.

"Probably a diversion from the evidence, an attempt to distract us from the style of murder. It would seem on the surface that Hamoud Ishaki was the victim of a type of murder sometimes carried out by terrorists and other subversive groups in the Middle East," Flo explained. "The Taliban tortured their victims by skinning them alive."

"Great. Just another thing to inflame the community," Sennett said.

"That's a problem. The public wants a killer found. The evidence seems to fit. The police are anxious to get this out of their hair." I looked around Flo's office again. Test tubes, large, leather-bound books, computers, the kind of materials that produced tests even the most skeptical sleuth couldn't argue against. "Okay, what do you need to prove Masri is the murderer?" I asked.

"We have to get a DNA sample that we can compare to a hair found on Hamoud Ishaki's shirt," Flo said. "The hair's DNA was different than the victim's DNA. Let me show you the DNA findings."

Her voice seemed clinically detached and emotionless as she pulled out two files and showed how the chromatographic lines matched between blood found on a victim and that of a killer. She spoke about the genes of a possible killer the way I spoke about incisions and sutures. Then she produced a hair found on Hamoud Ishaki's shirt and one of the victim's. The two hairs didn't match.

"If the lieutenant gets me a hair from the guy they have in jail, I'll test it. A match makes the case."

"That shouldn't be hard," Sennett replied. "Let's go now and see if he can oblige."

Flo seemed a little disappointed when Sennett rose along with us to leave. She told us to come back anytime. When it came to Sennett, I sensed she meant it.

I stepped into the sunshine outside of the lab and took a deep breath. I had learned enough for one morning. A stiff breeze blowing from the south filled my lungs. I told Sennett that I would call him later.

Jordan and I walked to the car and got inside. Once the engine started and the windows were down, I told Jordan to call her boss and tell him she was going to be tied up for the rest of the afternoon stalking a dangerous animal.

We both needed a relief from the horrid killings, especially Jordan with her pregnancy. I wanted her to take her mind off of the investigation. She was a sports addict. That's why I decided we should spend the rest of the day at Comerica Park watching the Tigers play baseball. Of the many reasons to come down to the city, the Red Wings, Lions, and Tigers were three of the best.

Detroiters take their sports seriously. They're proud, hardworking, blue-collar people who are tired of watching the reputation of their city decline with every drop in the census. That's why they cling to their sports teams for a respect not bestowed by the media. When Detroit teams win, they win. And lately the Tigers were winners.

It actually turned out to be a pretty good game. The Tigers decided to make a contest of it. It got down to the bottom of the ninth. The Detroit first baseman hit a walk-off home run and the fans erupted. You have to be patient with the Tigers, otherwise you'd go insane.

I was walking out of the stadium when my cell phone rang. It was Sennett.

"Ben, I got some news on the DNA of that hair sample."

"Don't leave me hanging, Lieutenant."

"It didn't match."

"Another good plan gone awry?" I asked.

"So far we're still on a fishing expedition."

"From the sound of your voice it appears that you need better bait."

"Yeah, well, I need more than jokes to keep this guy Masri in the slammer. If I don't get something soon, he's out of here."

"Maybe he's innocent."

"Maybe, but there's too much coincidence here. His godchild looked like a gangster-in-training, and he hated Bill Yaldo. I know a bad player when I see one."

"Sounds like the same story I used to hear about the Tigers."

CHAPTER 11

I HAD AGREED TO MEET MARK SHACKLEY and his wife the next afternoon to visit her father. They were waiting for me when I arrived outside the Wayne County Jail near Beaubien and Fort streets. What I didn't expect were the TV cameras.

As I walked up to the couple, Mark had a pained expression on his face, as if to say *I have no idea what to do now*. A reporter came up to me when she saw that I was talking with Mark. She looked like she was in her late twenties, an eager beaver ready for a story.

"Say, aren't you Ben Dailey, the surgeon?" she asked, thrusting a microphone with her station's call sign on it into my face.

I nodded.

"Are you working on this case for Mr. Masri?" This time she pressed her face a little closer to me so her cameras would get all of us in the picture. I backed away.

"I have no comment. I'm a doctor and a friend of the Shackleys."

"Do you think Mr. Masri was responsible for this heinous crime?"

"No comment." I walked away with Mark and Karin into the jail.

Mark looked at me with dismay. "I'm sorry. I wish I could have warned you."

"It's all right. No harm was done. We'll go out the back way after we see Karin's father."

"Are we ready?" Mark asked.

"I wish I knew. I don't know what to expect with this meeting." As soon as I said it, I regretted showing my lack of certainty. I glanced at Karin. If it bothered her, she didn't show it.

"There is one thing," she said. "Before we go in, Ben, be prepared for my father. He's from the old school. He doesn't like American ways. Everything with him is tough. He prides himself on his inner strength. He'll want to see just how tough you can be."

"Does he like America?"

"He loves it here, especially the freedom. But he thinks Americans are all soft."

"Why does he live here?"

"Because after the war, there was no place for him," Karin said with a sigh. "Everything was politics, and his side lost. With it went his job. He had relatives here in the States. They begged him to come."

"Tell me about your mother," I said. A change came over her face. A few new lines around her eyes, a slight downturn of her lower lip.

She described her mother as a wonderful woman, intelligent and funny. "She was in a building, looking for my father, when the car bomb went off," she said, "and he was never the same after that. His life was wrapped in guilt."

"That's understandable."

"The whole weight of his life has made him difficult to deal with. Still, he is my father and my only family other than Mark."

"Well," I said, "don't worry about me. I'm tough too. Let's go and see him."

We crossed Beaubien Street and entered the county jail. Six officers sat at the front desk with blue uniform shirts stretched tight over their protruding bellies. I thought about Jerome Michaels at the crime lab and wondered if the cadre of policemen at the jail was a case of quantity over quality.

The sergeant at the information desk pointed us to the lock-up. It was on the third floor. We were packed into an elevator with three officers, who were laughing about something. I could see Mark reach down and grab hold of Karin's hand. She looked up and smiled.

When we got off, we were escorted into a room with a thick metal door, a worn, yellow tiled floor, and a single metal table with several chairs around it. It was similar to the one I had seen Ikeda Walker in, only cleaner. I looked down at the floor where brownish stains were ingrained in the tile. I knew old blood when I saw it, I just didn't know who it belonged to. On the opposite wall was a single window.

We waited in silence for about five minutes, as both Shackleys fidgeted in their chairs. I saw Mark nervously doodling something on a pad of paper.

Suddenly, the silence was broken when a door opened and through it walked a guard, followed by a man in an orange jumpsuit labeled "WCJ," Wayne County Jail. It was the feeder jail to Jackson Prison, a repository of the scummiest criminals in the state. I recognized the prisoner from the pictures on Sennett's desk. Even so, he was more striking in person. His hair was a curly salt and pepper that extended down to his trimmed beard and mustache. His lip curled upward and his thick, slanted brows gave his face an imperious, almost cruel look. He walked toward the table with a slight limp and stopped at the metal chair, holding his body proudly erect. As he sat down, he looked over at his daughter. There was no smile, only a piercing gaze.

"So, you brought me two Americans. What is this about?"

"Papa, I've brought them to help you." Karin's voice had changed from the doctor in charge to a child talking to her father. She blinked several times, and her body seemed to become smaller in the chair.

"Who is this other man?" he asked, looking at me.

"This is Dr. Benjamin Dailey. He is a doctor at the hospital who was wrongly accused of something similar to your situation. He understands what is happening."

Masri turned and looked at me.

"So, you are a doctor. Do you practice at the same hospital as my daughter?"

"Yes, I do."

"I would assume that is what you know best, right?" Masri said.

"That's correct."

"So, if you were going to help me, this would be on a part-time basis, is that right?"

"I suppose so." His cross-examination was irritating. Shouldn't he be grateful that the three of us cared?

He looked at me sternly. "What nationality are you?"

I knew what that meant. "Hebrew," I replied.

"I see. And you as a Jew are going to help an Arab, such as I?"

"We're all human beings, and each one of us at one time or another needs a helping hand."

"Ah, a diplomat and a doctor. Impressive. Tell me, Dr. Dailey, what is it that you could do for me?"

"I'm not sure, right now," I answered, suddenly feeling much less confident than I had only moments earlier. "Your daughter has asked me to help, and I am trying to gather as much information as possible."

"But you are not a policeman or a detective, is that right?"

"No, I . . ."

"You see, Karin, you have brought me an amateur, a dabbler in matters that should not concern him. I don't need this man." I could feel my face redden as he spoke.

"Papa! You are talking to a respected man, a doctor."

"I have seen your people, your doctors. They told me I would never walk again. Back then it was only my will. And now it is my will again. I will not waste my time with your Jewish philosopher. Guard!"

With that he got up and walked to the door. The officer was there to escort him out.

"Mr. Masri," I pleaded, "I came here to help you, on behalf of your daughter and her husband. They believe in your innocence. Please keep that in mind when you think about this meeting later in your cell."

He didn't even turn to say goodbye to his daughter.

Tears welled up in Karin's eyes as she watched her father leading the way to his cell. When he left, she turned back to me. "Whatever my father is, he is not a killer. I know it. He is not an evil man. He's so angry at everything, but there is love inside that man, I know."

"Sometimes love is hard to find," I said. "Besides, he is right on one thing. I am a fulltime doctor, not a detective."

I think Karin realized that there was no future in trying to deal with her father directly, because she suggested that I visit a waiter-friend of his at the Oasis Restaurant. I didn't think it would get me very far, but I didn't want them to feel like I was giving up already, so I agreed.

Mark Shackley helped his wife out of the chair and down to the elevator.

We stood outside of the jail for a moment. I looked at our reflection in the large windows. Here we were, three highly educated, well-meaning professionals, but stupid at the same time. To think we could heal a man who hates because of a broken heart would be pure vanity. The best we could do would be to see that justice was served.

When I thought back about my own struggle to free myself from the corruption that had exiled me from my profession, I realized just how precious justice was. If I could give this to these people, I could live with that. I looked at Karin for a moment. "What's the name of your father's friend?" I asked.

IT WAS LATE AFTERNOON WHEN I LEFT the jail and made my way to the one refuge that had kept me sane all these years. The Pipeline, a small jazz club near the waterfront in Detroit's warehouse district.

The place wasn't much to look at from the outside, a simple sign and a pair of wrought iron lamps announcing the entrance. On the inside it was the premier jazz club in a city known for its music. And I was the filler man, playing piano on Thursday nights between sets.

The light was dim in the club when I entered, except for the filtered afternoon sun coming in the front window and illuminating the stage like one of those old Blue Note album covers. I half-expected to see Bogart coming out from the side of the stage, cigarette in hand, trying to shrug off the night before.

There were only a couple of customers at the bar, both of whom were engaged in a vigorous discussion of politics with Charlie, the bartender and resident politician, philosopher, and consummate sports analyst.

Sid Blanton, who owned the joint, was sitting on the edge of the stage cleaning his sax. When he saw me, he smiled. "Damn, Doc," he said, with a growling Louis Armstrong tone to his voice, the result of a near-death experience from a tumor I removed from his voice box. "I've been waiting all day for you. My hands have been itchin' for my sax. You ready to play?" Sid was about five-eight, with a smooth, balding head that glistened in the light. He wore an open yellow shirt, dark green pants, and deep red shoes. The effect was pure cool. And that's the way he played.

"You know I'm not always the most punctual," I said, sitting down next to him.

He said he couldn't agree more, claiming that the ten minutes he'd had to wait for me to perform his tracheotomy and save his life were the longest ten minutes of his life. We laughed at the gallows humor with the nervous chuckle of two people who survived a near-death experience and knew how close life and death were. Charlie brought over a couple of Labatts, and we chatted for a while. After about ten minutes, I finally got the nerve up to tell him my problem—I needed a band for the wedding. To my relief, it took him ten seconds of thought until he said he could find an eight-piece band for Jordan. One-half of my wedding problems were solved.

When we finished our drinks, we went up to the stage and played for about half an hour, knocking around some Art Blakely stuff. About halfway through Blakely's version of *Lester Left Town*, Jordan walked in. Even though I hadn't told her where I was going, she knew my haunts. I gave her a wink as she sat down at a corner table near the stage. She smiled back, a sweet smile, the one that held my heart.

I gave the piece we were playing a little extra improvisation, just for her. While I tried to replace Cedar Walton on the piano, I wound up being Ben Dailey, which was good enough that we got a long round of applause from the three people in the club. If there was one thing Sid and I had learned after our years of playing together, it was that it pays to stack the crowd.

I got up from the piano, walked over to Charlie to get another Labatt and a bottle of Perrier, and then sat down at a table near the door with Jordan. I was relieved she hadn't been there for my conversation with Sid.

Jordan seemed happy. Sid came over and sat with us. "That was a good lick, Sid," Jordan exclaimed, smiling.

"Give it up to the doc. He was on."

"You think he could be big time, Sid?" she asked.

"You never know. In the music business, luck is a big part of success."

I glanced over at Sid and swirled the beer around in my glass. "Luck and who you know. One thing is for sure, just because someone doesn't have a big name, doesn't mean he can't be someone big."

"For instance . . .?" Jordan asked.

Sid started to talk about some of the guys he knew thirty years ago who had made it, when Charlie called him over to the bar.

Jordan watched until Sid was out of earshot. "Ben, I've got more bad news regarding your Mr. Masri. In addition to the argument he had with Bill Yaldo, several people came forward, indicating that they had witnessed an altercation between him and Hamoud Ishaki. He accused Ishaki of defaming his wife's family, the memory of his father, and the teachings of Islam. The witnesses said that, according to Masri, if Ishaki was guilty, he would be skinned alive and his soul would be left to the devil."

I wondered to myself how much more incriminating news I could take. "The last part really is a nice touch. Was there anything about the other murder?" I asked.

Jordan explained that the police had questioned Masri about whether he had ever heard of James Carrington. Apparently, at one time Carrington drove a truck for a food service company that stopped at Masri's restaurant. Then she laid the big one on me. "The judge has released Masri on bail."

I was startled. "I didn't think that was possible with that kind of crime."

"It shouldn't be, but the judge was Roger Pilkington. He's an inner city liberal. The people love him. They call him the freeman's judge. That's why he is always re-elected."

"Which people?" I asked. "The people who are victims or the perpetrators?"

According to Jordan, Pilkington's legal decisions focused on two issues—any underdog whose plight would play well in the newspapers or anyone who had enough money to pay him off. "In this case, it was bail money."

"Who paid his tab?"

"As far as we know, it was his bail bondsman."

"Pretty good credit to get that kind of money."

"Or he knew someone," Jordan replied stiffly.

My head was swimming, and I was sick of spending my time with Jordan talking about death and murder. I wanted to change the subject. "I got Sid to line up a band for our wedding."

At the mention of the wedding, her demeanor changed, and her eyes brightened. "That's great. I can't wait to go over the music with him. What about the caterer?"

I knew I should have kept my mouth shut. "I've had a little trouble with that, but I think I have it under control."

"What do you mean you think?" Jordan asked with a certain amount of alarm.

"There was a scheduling conflict with the original caterer. His chef was scheduled at two places. He said he couldn't do ours."

"What are we going to do? It's getting late to get a caterer."

"I called Gus and . . ."

Jordan's face twisted itself into a pout. "Gus? Ben, you can't. I love him, but he can't cater our wedding. What is he going to serve, the Mr. K special?"

"He told me he's able to do it. He said he would make something special. Something we would be proud of."

"Like what?"

"He spat out a bunch of Greek names. I couldn't remember them all."

"Ben!"

"Jordan, Gus is our friend. I couldn't say no."

Tears started at the corner of Jordan's eyes. "This is special, Ben. I'm only going to get married once. It means so much."

I winced. Was I that much of a thoughtless oaf? Then I thought about the man she once loved, the guy who died heroically. Had she ever said that to him? *Never mind*, I told myself, *that was then, this is now.* "Trust me, Jordan. Gus will do a great job. I know it."

There was no reply, so I looked down at the table and cursed myself for doing this to Jordan. If I had been a cartoon, I would have started whistling.

Chapter 12

The next morning, I went down to the public library to read about the murder of Stacy Issacson. Somewhere in the stacks there had to be a clue. The library was right across the street from the Detroit Institute of Arts. It was one of the few imposing cultural landmarks still present in a city ravaged by unemployment, white flight to the suburbs, and rampant crime. When I looked at the manicured lawn, the white marble steps, and the striking magnitude of the building, it gave me hope that someone still cared.

I left my car parked on the street. I didn't have any change, so I took an on-duty Detroit Police tag that Sennett had given me and hung it on the mirror. Nothing like knowing someone.

I walked inside and was shown to a computer. It took a few questions and a prolonged stint at the machine before I made it to the stacks. Once there, I found a series of articles on the Stacy Issacson murder. There were pictures of the girl and her father and the site where she was found. Much of the gruesome detail was left out.

I went back to the computer for more information, and that's when I found an article detailing the murder in the magazine section of *The New York Times*. This time very little was left untouched. Most of it dealt with the capture of the killer, James Carrington. It was a story of diligent police work and luck.

I went through the article carefully, taking notes, including the names of friends, the car Stacy drove, and even her father's history. He had graduated from Penn, took a residency at Hopkins in OB, and then had a stint as a professor at Ann Arbor. That's where Sennett probably came into contact with the case—he had been on the force in Ann Arbor before he came to Detroit.

There was an article about Issacson's clinic in Ypsilanti, taking care of indigent women with unwanted pregnancies. I noticed a small blurb about his activity in Jewish Zionist organizations. Perhaps there was more to the murder of his daughter than abortion, like a hate crime or something like that. Regardless, as Flo said, the evidence made Carrington appear like a sure bet for the murder.

Once I got the vital information down, I studied the murder. Stacey had been sexually assaulted, but no semen was ever found on the body. The only tangible clue from the killer was the note left at the murder scene.

When I finished, I went back over the things I knew about Hamoud Ishaki. He was older than Stacy Issacson, and he was male. Other than that, the murder was similar to the other killings. Even the notes were similar. If the evidence hadn't been so complete against Carrington, I would have said the murders had been done by the same person.

After two hours of staring at microfilm, my eyes were burning from concentration, and my mind was staggering from a tour through the sordid details of a heinous crime. I needed to get away from murder and torture.

I walked out of the library and into the midday sunshine. I thought about Stacey's father. How would I have felt? What kind of anger must he be harboring, even now? It was unimaginable. I thought about the child Jordan was carrying. Would I kill someone to protect that infant? The question didn't need an answer.

THE REST OF THE DAY WAS A DRAG. I saw a few patients, but it was hard to focus on their needs. Doctors are like any other service providers; the patient expects their undivided attention, even if their personal lives are a shamble, their psyches distraught, their souls in turmoil.

I finished seeing patients at around five and stayed an extra hour trying to make sense of all the papers on my desk. It seemed as though in the twenty-plus years I had been practicing, the paperwork had grown exponentially. Most of it was compliance forms for federal regulations. Without them, life could be so sweet. Yet without them, my practice would be restricted to the likes of the aristocratic Mrs. Gallagher. That realization bent my head to the desk and set my pen dancing.

At about six I looked at my watch and reached for my car keys. Karin Shackley had arranged for me to go down to The Oasis and meet her father's friend, who was a waiter there. Fortunately, Jordan had a night meeting and knew I'd be late.

I made my way to the Southfield Expressway and headed south. It was dodge 'em driving all the way. For some reason, Detroiters view this twenty-mile stretch of highway as their own personal autobahn. No dallying in the passing lanes and forget the speed limit. You had to be on your toes. By the time I got to Michigan Avenue, I was ready to go home.

I drove through downtown Dearborn at around seven-thirty. It was a town that once housed one of the most overt segregationists in American history, Orville Hubbard. Redlining and racial profiling were the order of the day. The joke was that the slogan on all Dearborn police cars, "Keep Dearborn Clean," really meant "Keep Dearborn White."

Hubbard died in 1978. By then his city had changed, but not in the way he had hoped. Its streets of white vinyl–sided houses were now occupied, not by the African Americans he had hoped to keep out, but by Arab-Americans. It had become one of the largest Arab neighborhoods outside of the Middle East. And, ironically, just like Orville Hubbard, its occupants guarded their heritage fiercely, especially in east Dearborn where the most Arabs in the Detroit area were located. Here, Arabic was spoken at almost every establishment, and it wasn't unusual to see women with hijabs and men sporting thawb and sandals.

As I drove east on Michigan Avenue, I could see the leftover sun in my rearview mirror. Clusters of kids at the corner park were still in full frenzy. I stopped for a red light at the intersection of Michigan and Oak for a moment and watched a ball game on a local playground between kids no older than ten or eleven. It reminded me of forty years earlier, playing behind the grade school in a pickup game. Only now it was soccer instead of baseball.

A car horn shook me out of my reverie. I looked ahead and then focused on a red neon sign that was intermittently flashing *The Oasis*.

I pulled up to the one-story white building that featured a picture of a horse rearing, its forefeet slashing the air, an Arab sheik on its back. I looked for a parking space amongst the posse of Cadillacs and Continentals that ringed the side street. Finally, a valet came out and took my car. I was feeling all right until I got out and gave him the keys. Then I began to wonder what I was doing there, but by this time it was too late.

I walked inside, not sure of what to expect. I glanced around, though it took a few moments for my eyes to adjust to the subdued lighting. I saw men seated near a small stage, most dressed in dark suits, a couple with open-collar shirts. Multicolored lights surrounded the dance floor, and a small bandstand awaited the night's action. I looked to the side. Next to the entrance were two bouncers, who looked like the two timekeeping stone giants, Gog and Magog, on the clock tower at the Henry Ford Museum. Cross them and I was sure they would hammer out their form of justice.

I told them I was there to see Frank Moladi. They pointed me to the maitre d', who showed me to a table close to the stage. Obviously, I was on the A-list.

Walking to the table, I half-expected to see Masri. It almost seemed strange that he wasn't there. I looked around again at the twenty white-clothed tables circling the dance floor. I was the only non-Arab in the place.

The maitre d' motioned to the waiter to come to the table. "What would you like, sir?" He spoke with a thick accent. English clearly wasn't the primary language of The Oasis.

"I'm looking for a waiter named Moladi." In the background I could see the members of the band beginning to set up.

"Have a seat at the table. I will have him bring you a drink."

Another waiter arrived with a bottle and placed it on the table with a carafe of water. He was tall and thin, with a large Semitic nose and a widow's peak with black hair plastered on his head, held permanently in place by a thick coat of gel. I watched as he poured a small amount of white liquid into a glass, then filled the rest with water.

"I'm not sure that drinking is what I'm after. Mr. Masri's daughter asked me to come by and speak with Frank Moladi. Is that you?"

"I am. I understood that you would be coming here." His voice was deep and reassuring, and I instantly felt at ease.

"I need some information about Ahmad Masri. I'm trying to help him and his family against the accusations that have been made against him."

"Please, it is our custom to greet strangers by offering them a drink. This is Touma Arak. It contains *arak*, our native liquor. I assure you, you will enjoy it."

I'm not much for drinking, but I had the feeling that not accepting would have been a major faux pas, so I took a sip. The milky-white fluid had a delicious flavor. "It tastes like licorice."

"Exactly, my friend. The Greeks call it ouzo. You have never been here before?"

"First time."

"Are you staying for the show?"

"I hadn't intended to. I really came here to speak with you about Mr. Masri. You know him well?"

"About as well as any man."

"His daughter, Karin, told me you would be able to give me some useful information about him. She wants me to help her father, but so far, I haven't been much help."

Moladi stared at me for a moment, then his eyes darted around the room. He had a long neck and a razor-cut, trimmed beard that ran into the cleft in his chin. His eyes were obscured by shaded, thin-rimmed black wire glasses. When he spoke, his lips curled into a half-smile, as if he were playing a prank. The mention of Masri's name took the smile away.

"Please, before we speak, stay for the show. I will order for you. I assure you that you will enjoy it." I was going to object, but it was too late. He walked across the empty stage to another waiter and spoke for several seconds in Arabic. When he returned, he seemed more relaxed.

He sat down next to me and refilled my glass from the bottle of arak. As he did, he spoke of Masri's wife, Sherita, and the anger that Masri carried from her death. He intimated that there was nothing his friend wouldn't do in the "old country."

"What about his family?" I asked.

"His family is his daughter. He dominated her. She was going to be a success no matter what."

I was eating, drinking, and talking. Moladi had now taken a seat next to me. I thought it was a little strange, but no one seemed to object. He poured me another drink, and we talked.

I sipped the drink and stared at him for a moment. "He was supposed to have a fight with Bill Yaldo in which he threatened him."

"It never happened. It is just some of Ahmad's enemies trying to make trouble for him."

"What enemies?"

"Oh, just people jealous of his success."

By now the band had started up: a clarinet, a guitar, tambourines, and the light roll of a snare drum. The *arak* was beginning to dull my alertness. "Did Masri work with you in Beirut?"

"He was part of the team."

"What team?"

"We were working on new biochemical formulations for generic drugs."

"Ah, no DAW's in Beirut." I could feel my voice slurring and hear myself laughing at my own words.

I looked out on the stage. In the center of the dance floor, a beautiful, dark-haired woman in a thin veiled skirt stepped forward. I could see her taut belly undulating behind the gauzy material. She had a veil in each hand that she swirled over her head as she moved bare-footed from one table to another. My eyes began to blur with the motion. The band began a rhythmic song in the background, as the woman heightened her gyrating dance on the wooden floor. I heard clapping from the audience and foreign words floated in my ears.

The music became louder. Slowly and deliberately, she came closer to my seat. She swirled in front of me, scarves of red and blue flashing in front of my eyes like a kaleidoscope. It was dizzying, almost hypnotic as her hips undulated from side to side and her pelvis thrust out in front of her.

There was more clapping and shouting in the background. I could barely hear it now. All I could see was the girl pulsating in front of me. I wanted to say something, but the words never came out. The scene before me felt like a dream, and I needed to sleep.

CHAPTER 13

I BEGAN TO WAKE UP WITH JORDAN AT MY SIDE. At least it seemed like Jordan. She was whispering into my ear and stroking me gently. I felt her slide down alongside of me, kissing my chest and stomach. I vaguely remembered my dream with Julie McFarland. But this seemed real. As much as I wanted to say something, I couldn't find the words. The woman next to me persisted.

I felt her hands move deeper into my groin and her lips surrounded me. The movement was exciting, stimulating, but something felt wrong. I struggled to sit upright, my eyes trying to focus on her rising and falling head.

Her hands surrounded me more tightly and the throbbing became more intense as her mouth closed over my now full erection. I saw her hair in the light, black and glistening. An alarm went off in my head as I realized this wasn't Jordan's hair. I pulled back suddenly.

As I did, I shook my head to clear my eyes and looked over at the dark-haired girl lying naked next to me. Light was streaming in through the window. My clothes were on the floor. Then I remembered the dancing girl from last night.

I looked at the phone next to the bed. A matchbook reading *Dearborn's Finest* stared at me. A motel and a naked woman. What had I done?

I swung my feet over the bed, bending over to collect my clothes. My head was aching, and I was dizzy. I bent over and struggled to get my clothes on. Once I did, I looked over at the girl.

Without her makeup, she looked ordinary. Her eyes were vacant with that clock-watching look that said she needed to move on to her next job. The large rounded breasts that stood so firm last night sagged against her side. Her nipples were flat against their brown areolae. I looked at her abdomen and caught a glimpse of the hair between her legs.

When she saw that, she smiled at me and crooked her finger, as if to lure me back. Then she whispered something in Arabic that I didn't understand. I could see the missing teeth at the back of her mouth, a mouth that was just a few minutes ago urging me on. I smiled back weakly, then all but ran for the door.

I opened it and caught my breath in the early morning air. My groin was aching from near ejaculation. I longed to finish the job with Jordan, but at the same time I was ashamed. The word trust popped into my mind. I felt as if I had violated a bond that I thought was ironclad. How had I succumbed so quickly? Was I drugged or was it just the alcohol?

These thoughts raged through my mind as I stared over a railing at Michigan Avenue. I was on the second floor of a small motel. Over the balcony I saw cars crawling back and forth along the six-lane highway. I knew someone would look up at me and assume I was one of those rent-by-the-hour customers. I had wondered the same thing every time I had passed by a cheap motel filled with pickup trucks and Cadillacs.

A few doors down stood a swarthy man dressed in a gray gabardine suit, stationed at the hallway by the stairs. From the bulge in his jacket, I figured he was carrying. "Where are we?" I asked weakly.

"The Casbah Motel just off Michigan Avenue. Mr. Masri asked me to extend his apologies and to escort you to your car."

Masri. I should have known. He probably taped the whole thing, whatever that thing was. I was insane with guilt. What had I done?

When we reached the car, the man handed me my keys. I didn't want to look at his face, only get in the car. As I opened the door, I glanced furtively around, afraid that someone might recognize me. Who was I kidding? I was the only Anglo down here.

I got behind the wheel and started the engine. As soon as I had moved onto Michigan Avenue, a feeling of relief inundated my head. At least I was moving out of this neighborhood. Some detective I was. False pride is a damning emotion.

I picked up my cell phone. My first call was to Jordan.

"Where have you been?" she asked, angrily. "Do you think I might have been worried about you? I was going to call George."

"Look, Jordan, I don't blame you. I'm sorry I didn't come home last night. I was out at Ahmad Masri's place. I had a little too much to drink, so they put me up in a motel. Compliments of the management."

"What were you doing, checking out the belly dancers in Dearborn?"

She didn't know how close to the truth she was.

"They served something called *arak*. I must have had too much and passed out. I guess they didn't want to have a friend of Masri's daughter get in trouble." A partial truth at this point was better than nothing.

"You should know better, Ben. *Arak* is one of the strongest drinks you can get." I knew she trusted me. I couldn't find a place to stow my guilt.

"For a man who drinks as little as I do, anything stronger than beer is out of my league."

"How do you feel now?" I could sense she was almost laughing at my incompetence.

"Like someone stuck an M-80 in my head," I muttered, "but at least I found out that Ahmad Masri was a complex man capable of many things, the least of which is mayhem of one sort or another."

"Any good qualities?"

"The only good thing anyone tells me about him is his daughter, Karin. She was his prize. From what they say, she is as good as her press clippings."

"Pretty nice legacy for a male-dominated society, wouldn't you say?"

"Yeah, especially when you see her father's friends."

"By the way, George Sennett called last night."

"I'll give him a call. Listen, I have to run to the hospital." I was anxious to get off the phone and glad that Jordan hadn't pressed me any further about my assignation last night. My only solace was that I didn't remember.

I dialed George. He answered, but sounded irritated. "You don't sound so good, Lieutenant."

"Neither do you, Ben."

"I have an excuse." I told him about my night at The Oasis but left out a few important parts, especially the dancer and the Casbah Motel, since, at this point, I wasn't sure what had happened. Before I unloaded something as personal as that, I wanted to think it over.

That's when he told me there had been a new kidnapping. An eighteen-year-old boy was missing. It made me sick. "What do you do in a case like that?"

"Check on leads, look for evidence, and get publicity. We try to get as much in the papers as possible. Someone might recognize him. If we don't get any results, I'll call you. By the way, how's your investigation on Masri going?"

"I haven't learned a lot. Why?" I asked.

"He was supposed to check in this morning," Sennett barked. "We haven't heard from him yet. We've got a warrant to search his house."

"It's still early, George."

"Yeah, maybe you're right. Thanks for the advice."

I hung up and looked at my watch. I had to get to the office. As I drove off, a feeling of malaise enveloped me, and it wasn't my hangover. Kidnapping, Masri missing. In medicine, coincidence was rare—most things that happened were connected to each other. I wondered whether the same was true with the law.

I FELT LIKE SHIT WHEN I REACHED THE HOSPITAL. Then I looked at myself in the rearview mirror and saw that I had hangover written all over my face. Maybe I just wasn't cut out for the noir gumshoe racket.

I parked in the doctor's lot and walked through the back entrance to the operating room and into the surgeon's lounge. My chances of not running into anyone I knew were slim, but that was the only place with a shower. Unfortunately, when I reached the lounge, it was filled with the usual suspects, mostly anesthesiologists waiting for surgeons. In the corner were the dynamic duo, Larry Schneider and Carl Fairchild. Schneider was humming a tune and working on *The New York Times* crossword puzzle. He glanced up for a moment.

"Dailey, you look like shit," he said, curling his nose as if I'd been scraped off his shoe.

"Looks can be deceiving. I feel worse than that."

"Sick?"

I decided that Schneider was not on my need-to-know list, so I just said I thought I had a flu bug. I was about to say something else when he held up his crossword puzzle and asked to anyone who would listen, "A six-letter word for a woods play."

"Let me see it," Fairchild responded, suddenly interested in the conversation. Reluctantly, Larry handed him the newspaper, and Carl carefully folded the edges until they lined up perfectly. Then he studied it for a moment. "Birdie." He made it sound like it was obvious to anyone with a brain.

"How did you know that?" Larry looked at him, both astonished and annoyed that Fairchild had one-upped him.

"Not everything in a crossword puzzle is as it seems. There's always a theme. You just have to recognize it. It's an art form."

"What kind of art?" Schneider asked.

"These games are symbolic art. Patterns of words. It's a perfection of pattern and design." Fairchild was on the lecture circuit again.

"Excuse me, but I beg to differ," Larry said. "A puzzle is predesigned to be solved, so it has to perfect. In art there is always a search for perfection that isn't always attained." Here we go again. Couldn't they have a conversation without a debate?

"Well, tell me this, Larry," Fairchild responded. "Is medicine an art or a science?" I could sense the argument starting again.

"I'm not sure I know what you're getting at, Carl."

"Medicine is a science. A perfect science. Sure, we haven't perfected everything yet. That is merely the science we don't know. But, if you say it is an art, then you imply a human factor that supposes there is a mystical reasoning in the profession."

At that moment one of the nurses poked her head in the room.

"The patient is in the room, Dr. Fairchild."

Carl looked down at his watch, almost as if he was preaching to the wrong crowd. He shrugged his round shoulders and moved his head, like a boxer avoiding a punch. I was surprised at the ripple of his arm muscles as he moved to get out of the chair. When he finally stood up, he turned to Schneider. "By the way, Larry, I see that the airway case we talked about is being discussed at this week's Morbidity and Mortality Conference."

"Can't admit when you're on the wrong side of an argument?" Schneider said, calmly.

"Quite the contrary," Fairchild replied. "I think it falls into the science we don't know. I think the discussion will be quite enlightening." Then he turned to me. "I was hoping you would be there, Ben." When summoned, you rarely had a choice in avoiding the M and M conference.

Schneider looked over defiantly at Fairchild. Suddenly, a sneering black frown crossed his face. It was the same look of disdain I had seen before. "Why is he doing this?" he asked, getting up from his chair and moving toward the door.

"Relax, Larry. It's education, nothing else," I said calmly. His facial tension eased.

"Maybe," he replied, indecisively. I had the distinct impression that Larry felt persecuted.

At that point Carl walked to the door. As he looked back, he said, "It's happy gas time, gentlemen." Schneider followed him into the hallway leading to the operating rooms, and they continued to chatter about medicine.

As they walked out of the room, I felt perplexed. I couldn't figure either of them out—Fairchild trying to skewer Schneider, and then clasping him on the back as if nothing had happened. Then there was Schneider, with a temper so raw he would flare up at the least provocation. He would be a difficult colleague for anyone.

I got up, poked my head through the door to the operating room, and coerced one of the techs to get me a razor from a surgical prep kit. I took it into the washroom and lathered up. Once I had finished shaving, I showered and put on a pair of surgical scrubs. I looked in the mirror. Not perfect, but acceptable.

CHAPTER 14

I ARRIVED AT THE OFFICE just before my morning hours started to find the waiting room was already full. I didn't have to time think about the night before, so I buried myself in my work. It lasted until about noon, when Katie came up to me.

"Dr. Dailey, a man dropped this off for you this morning just after the office opened."

I looked at the manila envelope. "Did he say who he was?"

"No, but he was in a hurry. He spoke with an accent."

"Thanks, Katie."

I sat down at my desk and gazed at the envelope, not knowing what to expect, and opened it slowly. Inside were some pictures and a VHS cassette. I stared at them for a moment. My stomach started to knot. There were three color Polaroids and an eight and half by eleven blowup of me naked in bed with the dancer from last night. I was at full attention and the girl looked like she was in the throes of ecstasy. It looked like what I imagined they sell in one of those triple x magazines at an adult bookstore.

I picked up the envelope and felt something inside. I opened the flap and pulled out a note. It said:

> *I have no use for you. You have no need for me. I despise your people. Stay away from my daughter and stay away from me before you get hurt.*
>
> *Masri*

I felt sick to my stomach. It was a setup. Probably the whole staff of The

Oasis was in on it. All of them were protecting Masri. Karin was naïve and so was I. A loyalty started in the battlefield of Beirut was not going to be extinguished just because the locale had shifted to America.

I looked at the nautical clock on my desk, a gift from Jordan. It was just after nine. I picked up the pictures and put them in the envelope. Another pang of guilt knifed through me.

My gaze dropped down on the desk, and I surveyed the patient schedule for the day. It was full. Whatever my personal problems, I had patients waiting, and they didn't care whether I was guilty of an indiscretion or not. So I put the package in a drawer in my desk and went back to seeing patients.

It was a struggle. Katie must have noticed my distraction, because she asked if I was all right. When I told her I had a long night, she looked at the schedule and canceled the last three patients. I was grateful she had the wisdom to do something I couldn't. Twenty minutes later I was downtown and walking in the warm afternoon sunshine. As I walked, I tried to dissect what had happened. Maybe they found someone who looked like me and they took those pictures? Then I ran the photos through my mind again. There was no question that was me. Drugs and drink and a bedroom scene. It was pretty tawdry.

I went over to Gus's for a sandwich and ate it at one of his outdoor tables, while I stared across at the river and wished I were on my boat. The wind was blowing from the west. With the following current and my sloop on a broad reach, I could be in Port Clinton in seven hours. Any place away from here.

Gus sat down beside me with a look of concern. "What's the matter, Doc? You look lost."

"No, just thinking. Listen, you're sure about this wedding thing, right? I don't want to put you on the spot."

"Relax, Doc, I got no problem. I'm going to get my cousin, Nick, to help. We're going to get some grills. You'll love it."

Wonderful, I thought, Gus and his cousins. I was about to ask Gus what he planned on grilling—hoping for lobster, but anticipating hot dogs—when he was called inside.

I sat there for a few minutes more and then I walked back to my car parked in the deck across the street. Once inside I turned around and reached for some paper on the back seat. That's when I noticed it, a single black Nike baseball shoe sitting next to my briefcase. Inside the shoe was a note typed on computer paper:

> *I know you like baseball, so do I. The game has made me very*
> *happy. I know you are happy for me too. Aren't you proud?*
>
>   *Friend of the Devil*

I looked at the shoe for a moment and then re-read the note. It was on the same paper that had been used for the note that was on my door. Masri was out and the notes reappeared. What the shoe meant was unclear, but I felt it was no coincidence that it coincided with the new disappearance.

I picked up my cell phone and called Sennett. He wasn't there, so I left a message with Sergeant Knudsen to have the lieutenant meet me at Poppleton Park that afternoon.

GEORGE SENNETT WAS WAITING FOR ME at the small park near our town house. He was sitting on a bench, watching a group of kids playing ball on the sandlot. One of them, a gangly youngster of about twelve, was throwing some heat, and a smaller boy was ducking out of the way. Each time the ball went wild, the batter had to retrieve it from the backstop. I sat down next to him. On the next pitch, the smaller boy nailed a high hard one over the fence.

"Nothing like baseball on a sunny afternoon, huh, Doc? Makes you feel young again."

"Maybe," I said distractedly. "Somebody else must feel the same way, because they left this present for me on my back seat."

A deep scowl came across his face. "I thought we had gotten rid of this when we arrested Masri. Now he's out and it's started again." He stopped for a moment and looked at the shoe. "I guess it fits. The boy we're looking for is a star baseball player. He played for Clawson High."

A shiver of fear went through me. "What's his name?" I asked apprehensively.

"Brett Zielinski. Why? You know someone on the team?" Sennett asked.

"Brett delivers the newspaper to my house. I wondered why I hadn't seen him for the past couple of days. I guess I know what the baseball shoe means," I said fearfully, half-expecting Sennett to tell me they had found the boy. I was genuinely afraid. "What are you going to do?"

"I went public today on TV. There was a press conference. I made a little speech begging the public to help, and then we showed pictures of the missing kid."

By this time, the boys who had been playing ball had picked up their things and were walking off the field. One of them cracked a joke and they all started laughing. I wondered if they knew Brett Zielinski.

"Any leads?"

"I get the usual crank calls and the I'm-sure-I-saw-him sightings. Then the parents call me every hour. It's very upsetting," Sennett replied.

"What about Masri?" I asked.

"Not a word. Disappeared. And get this—after we let him go, Flo found some blood on the clothes in Masri's house that matches Hamoud Ishaki's blood. There's no way that Masri son of a bitch is innocent."

"Great," I replied, scraping the sand under the bench with my shoe. "So much for the legal system."

Sennett turned to me on the bench. "I'll need to take the shoe and the note down to forensics. I doubt that Flo will find any prints, but you never know. We're playing in a league with someone bad." The two boys passed by us. Sennett smiled and gave them the thumbs up sign. They both laughed.

"It's like you told me once, trouble follows me like white on rice."

"Are you still going to help that doctor at the hospital?"

I shook my head. "I may be dumb, but I'm not stupid. I don't need any more of that. What I do need to do is tell Masri's daughter. I have to go over there today. That should be fun."

"A lot more fun than trying to find the murderer of some kid who's been mutilated and tortured to death."

"Yeah," I replied dolefully.

"Well, at least there's one thing that should make you feel better."

"What's that?"

Sennett went on to explain that, with Ishaki and Yaldo dead, the FBI was changing the focus of the investigation to a hate crime. Furthermore, now that Jordan was off the case, there didn't appear that there was much of motive for anyone to involve her.

"I guess that make sense, but how do you explain the Zielinski kid? He delivered my newspaper. That's more than just a coincidence. And where does that leave your investigation of Masri?"

"Trust me, I'm convinced Masri is involved. You can rest assured that I'll get him." As he said it, he picked up a small twig from the ground and snapped it in half with his fingers. "But there's more to it than just that."

He made it clear that, while Brett Zielinski hadn't been found yet, he assumed that the boy was dead. And since the young man wasn't part of the Arab community, there had to be some other pattern to the crime. I probably should have followed the ignorance is bliss theory, but instead I asked him why.

"It's my guess that the original threat message wasn't directed at Jordan," he muttered.

"Then who is he sending it to?" I asked, half-expecting the answer I didn't want to hear.

"I wasn't sure until you showed me this latest message, but now I'm convinced. After the initial call to Jordan's office, look who has been getting the messages: you and me. That's who I think they were really meant for. Masri and whoever else is perpetrating these crimes are purposely taunting you and me."

"I don't want to take any chances with Jordan on the basis of a hunch."

"Neither do I. We're still going to keep a watch out until we find out more."

When I asked him if he had any other ideas, he shrugged his broad shoulders dejectedly in a show of ignorance and got up to leave. As he did, I put my hand on his forearm and asked him to stay for a moment. Then I explained what had happened at The Oasis. After I finished the story, his face brightened and he chuckled, as if to say that, compared to what he had seen so far, it was no big deal. He said we'd make a call on the waiter and see what he had to say. This time when he finished, we both stood up.

I sighed. Sennett's dark mood and the events that were swirling around this case were beginning to depress me. As we both reached our cars, I turned to face him. "George, how did we get ourselves into this mess?"

"Like I told you once, Doc, once you're part of the people, your life ain't never gonna be the same." Now I knew what he meant.

MY MEETING WITH THE SHACKLEYS went exactly as I thought—lousy. It wasn't easy to have TV crews hanging around your house. Now I had to tell them I couldn't help them. I hated giving up on a patient. This felt just as bad.

I explained that the police had a motive for her father to kill Bill Yaldo. I also told her about my meeting with Frank Moladi, but left out the exact details.

She seemed ashamed but not surprised. Apparently lacing *arak* with opium is an old trick. I had wondered if I had been drugged, but I couldn't blame her that it happened. Now that I knew, it was hard for me to accept I was that naive.

When I explained that I could no longer help her, she seemed to understand. Suddenly, I felt relief. As I got up to leave, she grabbed my sleeve and thanked me. I knew the doctor in me couldn't let the patient die, but I wasn't ready to tell Karin Shackley that.

She walked me to the door, and I shook her hand. Going back to my car, I felt as I had felt many times before, overcome by the feeling of having failed, of not having cured the patient, of having to tell the family how sorry I was. You're only as good as your skill and your luck, and sometimes that's just not enough. It's an awful feeling all doctors have to face, and it never gets easier.

I got back into my car and backed down the driveway. As I drove toward the expressway, I felt a huge load had been lifted off my shoulders, as if everything was done with, and, because I had been wronged, I was free to back out of the whole situation. Then I thought about The Oasis Club and the naked woman in bed. I was pissed at myself for not being smarter and at Masri for slitting the throat of my better angel with a curved knife. I wanted to believe I was done, but the little demon in my head who always tortured me in the name of virtue whispered glibly that I would keep at this case, that I hadn't been tortured enough.

CHAPTER 15

IT WASN'T UNTIL I LOOKED AT MY APPOINTMENT LIST the next morning that I realized that the Anesthesia Department's Morbidity and Mortality conference was scheduled for noon. It was a forum for the anesthesiologists and surgeons to discuss mishaps and learn from their mistakes. Theoretically, it should be an excellent program, a form of self-examination. In reality, it sometimes took the form of a witch-hunt, depending on who had the complication.

In the case of Carl Fairchild and Larry Schneider, they each had their own agenda. To Fairchild this was an academic debate, a platform of reaffirmation of his Ivy League education. In Schneider's case, it was just the opposite. He lived for the day he could take an academic snob like Fairchild and make him eat crow.

Today the conference lasted for over an hour as the two men debated the management of their airway case. It was the general consensus that it ended in a draw, a fact that probably irritated both men.

Fairchild shrugged his shoulders after it was over. Larry, on the other hand, still appeared to bear the anger of an inconclusive decision. The look he gave Fairchild as they stepped down from the podium was something out of a psych ward.

I'm sure they were going to have more words, but I couldn't stay for that. My pager went off calling me for my scheduled surgery. The case was booked for an hour to remove a small nodule from the vocal cord of a local disc jockey. The actual procedure took fifteen minutes. The remaining time was spent setting the room up and listening to the nurses chatter about the recent murder and the new report of a missing teenager. Everyone seemed to have an opinion. The conversation was giving me a headache.

I didn't have long to think more about it, because the phone began ringing at the end of the operation. The circulating nurse picked it up and answered quietly. She listened for a moment and then turned to me. "It's Katie. She said Jordan called and wanted to meet you this afternoon at her office. She said it was important, but it wasn't about her."

I got dressed as quickly as possible and made it down to the McNamara Building in record time, considering road construction and the insane back-up of traffic caused by three or four Detroit police officers, stopping drivers who weren't wearing their seatbelts. I guessed that the city figured this was as good a way to stimulate the economy as anything they had tried before.

I parked my car in the visitor's deck and high-tailed it up to her office. Jordan was pacing the room as I entered. For one of the few times I had known her, her desk appeared messy with several folders spread out and a couple of photographs lying to the side. She appeared relieved when I walked in unannounced. "Thanks for coming so quickly. I had to show you this stuff."

"What stuff is that?"

"Don't think I'm crazy, but I noticed something this morning after you left."

Like I said, the little man in my head wasn't going to let me out of this case, no way, no how. "What's that?" I asked.

She pulled out the newspaper picture of the missing boy, Brett Zielinski, from the folder. Next to it she placed a photograph of another boy. "What do you notice about these two pictures?"

I studied them carefully. The boys had the same widow's peak, the same arched eyebrows, and the same prominent jaw with a midline cleft. There was a definite resemblance. The only difference was their hair color.

"They look like they could be brothers."

"Exactly what I thought."

"Where did you get them?"

"I was going through a folder that Karin Shackley gave you."

"I recognize that photo now," I said, suddenly intrigued. "That's Hamoud Ishaki."

Jordan nodded. "Correct. He was fourteen when this snapshot was taken."

"What are you saying?"

"I saw the photos together by chance. It struck me as strange. Could they be related?"

"Impossible," I said, snorting derisively.

"Maybe you're right, but what if it wasn't impossible? How could you prove it?" Jordan asked.

"We'd have to find the parents and interview them."

"And what do you say to them? Excuse me, are you the biological parents of this boy?" Her lawyer's cynicism cut to the chase and put me on the defensive.

"I guess we could test their parents' DNA for paternity," I muttered, giving in a little. I looked at the photos again. The resemblance between the boys was remarkable.

"You know, that's the trouble with scientists. They rely too heavily on laboratory tests. I don't need a lab test to tell me they look alike."

Low-tech investigation. The use of the mind. "It's just a photograph, Jordan. What if we are wrong? You said it yourself. We could never make a case from what we have. We need a fact. It may be far more complicated than comparing photographs."

Jordan looked pensive for a moment. "We have to assume that there is a connection between the disappearance of the Zielinski boy and the death of Hamoud Ishaki."

"That's a big leap of faith, since we're not completely sure that there is a connection."

I was about to say something else when my cell phone rang. It was Sennett. They had found Brett Zielinski. He was propped up, seated on home plate at American Legion Field in Royal Oak with his right arm amputated and resting in his lap. His baseball glove was still on his hand. Sennett said something else. This time there was an audiotape at his office.

I was heartsick. Brett Zielinski, a hardworking, star athlete, a good kid. Why would anyone want to kill him? Then I remembered the baseball shoe on the back seat of my car. Jordan was right—it wouldn't take a leap of faith now.

CHAPTER 16

IT'S HARD TO LOOK AT ANYONE WHO'S BEEN MURDERED, especially someone I knew, a teenager who hadn't yet realized life's fruits, life's joys. It was especially hard to see him lying out on the slab in Allan Davis's morgue, but it wasn't as bad as the first time. It angered me that I was getting used to this. It felt like I was taking on Davis's profession.

After Sennett had called, I told Jordan I would be at the morgue and not to worry if I was late. The drive was short, and I was already in the autopsy room when Davis and Sennett walked in. I had planned to tell the lieutenant I was through with the Masri case, but Jordan's revelation had hooked me. I wasn't quite ready to quit yet.

"Now look at this. The killer neatly cut off the arm, as if he had used an electric saw," Davis said, shuffling through his specimens.

The lieutenant seemed more in charge of his emotions than he did the last time we were down here. "What do you make of it?" Sennett asked almost pleadingly.

"This torture killing is similar to that of the other boy," Davis said.

"You think this is a serial killer then?" I asked.

"If two makes a series, then it is," Sennett responded. "Then there was the audiotape that was sent to me. Listen to it."

He withdrew the pocket recorder from his pocket and pressed the play button. The voice had the monotone of a person disguising his identity:

"I thought you would like to know what I know about Brett Zielinski. You might find it interesting.

Death is the reason for life. Without the thrill of torture there could be no meaning, no excitement, no reason for enduring the fools around me. Killing is all I need. My palms began to sweat as I listened.

I saw him up close playing baseball. He was a tall, good looking kid, with a mop of sandy brown hair, long gangly arms, and an infectious grin. The uniform on his back read Colburn's Department Store, and it was dirty, the result of a slide into second to break up a double play, a diving catch in left field, and a game-winning single. I know that because I watched him play before I killed him.

I waited by his car. I was wearing a minister's suit. Nice touch, don't you think? I told him I was a friend of his Uncle Jim. He seemed to like that I was. I told him I took a video of his diving catch. He wanted to see it, so he came over to my van. When he was inside, I locked the doors. He struggled to get out, but I clubbed him into submission. It was a little messy. But I had my way with him. Aren't you happy for me?

"There was something else," Davis said.

"What?" Sennett asked, almost afraid to answer.

"There was a picture and a note." His voice dropped to a nearly inaudible register as he handed the packet to Sennett.

He opened it, staring at the photo. I could see his eyes narrowing and the veins in his neck stand out above his collared shirt. He looked at it for another moment, then silently handed it to me. I wish he hadn't. It was a photograph of a baseball with a zero drawn on it and a smiley face in the center. The note read:

"A no-hitter. Pretty funny, don't you think?"
                                              Yours truly,
                                         Friend of the Devil

"The same name," I said, trying to divert my anger.

"He's taunting us with his sickness," Sennett growled. "I want that bastard, and I want him now."

"He's getting what he wants, George. These killers all want attention. Someone to recognize their genius. Isn't that what Flo said?" I asked.

I could almost feel the heat of Sennett's anger. When I looked at him, I could see the strain of the two murders showing on his face and in his bearing. I tried not to think about my emotions, and instead focused back on the case. Whoever was doing this knew about anatomy. Maybe Masri was studying his daughter's medical books. But how would he know a young kid like Brett Zielinski?

My thought was interrupted as Davis picked up a paper from his desk and handed it to Sennett. "There was some hair that the crime boys picked up on the body," he said. "If the DNA matches Masri, he's our killer. The DNA doesn't lie."

"Maybe yes, maybe no." Sennett started to sound defensive. I don't think he liked being pinned to conclusions that he only wished were right.

I looked back at the table with the young boy on it. What difference did it make now? The killer had extracted what he wanted, no matter who he was. At least Brett Zielinski wasn't suffering any more.

I was about to say something when Davis's assistant walked in. "Lieutenant, there are a bunch of reporters and television cameras outside. I think you should speak with them."

Sennett's face took on the look of frustration and anger once again. "That's the last thing I want. How the hell can I speak with them? I haven't even called the parents." He remained pensive for a moment, then turned to Davis. "Nothing about this note or the baseball photo to anyone, including the press. I want to let this settle down before we do any more damage to anyone."

Davis turned to Sennett and gave him that crazy, half-cocked grin that only he was capable of. "Not a word from me." Then he paused for moment. "What if the killer knew his victims. Wouldn't that be the cruelest cut of all?" he chortled, impressed at his double entendre. When we didn't respond, he turned silently back to his papers, with the annoyed look of a comic whose audience wasn't smart enough to understand.

I assumed that Davis's gallows humor was his insulation from the gruesomeness of his job, but I still found it annoying. I could only think of Brett Zielinski's family and the pain they must be going through. It was at times like this that I was glad this was Sennett's fulltime job and not mine. Then I looked at the people in the room and the grotesque picture in Sennett's hand and realized there was no escape for me either.

I WAS WITH JORDAN IN HER OFFICE the next morning when the call came through. It was Sennett. "Flo just called me with the hair sample taken off the dead boy. It matches with Masri. Are you satisfied now? This bastard killed him. And now we have a motive."

"Huh?"

"I spoke with the parents. Brett went to a school with a high percentage of Arab kids. Apparently, he got into a fight with one of them. He kicked the crap out of the other boy."

"So? Kids get into fights all the time."

"This isn't like the old days, where you duke it out and that's that," Sennett said grimly. "There's so much ethnic bashing and violence on television and the movies, and no one is satisfied with just a fight. Masri had a reputation. Maybe someone told him about the fight and asked for help."

I thought Sennett was stretching it by linking Masri to a boyhood fight. Still, I could understand his frustration. He had people searching the entire city, and not a peep had been heard.

"Would you ask Flo if she minds if Jordan and I come by and ask her a few questions?" I questioned.

"That's a leading question, Doc. Usually when you ask questions, there's trouble following right behind."

"Jordan had a hunch. I wanted to ask Flo about it," I said, trying to sound casual.

"Did I ever tell you I hate hunches?" he replied.

"Yeah, I've heard you say that before."

"What have you got?" Sennett asked.

"I'm just trying to prove that science and technology triumph over ignorance and superstition."

Sennett spoke with Flo and we made arrangements to meet her in a half hour. Jordan and I left her office on Fort Street and drove up to Jefferson, past *The Fist* a gift from Sports Illustrated to the city. It was called *The Fist* because that was exactly what it was, a larger-than-life metal sculpture of Joe Louis' clenched hand; a symbol to anyone who drove by that this was Detroit, a place that deserved respect. For a city that had survived the riots, it seemed like a strange gesture.

It didn't take long to drive to the crime lab. We made our way to Flo's office. When she saw Jordan and me together, she smiled. "Another visit to the crime lab. This is becoming a regular thing."

We sat down and Jordan explained her theory that Ishaki and the Zielinski boy might be related. "You're our last chance. Do you have any DNA samples from the Zielinski kid?" Jordan asked.

Flo thought about it for a moment and then went to her files. She pulled out the results of the DNA testing on the two victims and studied them for what seemed like countless minutes, writing and counting. When she was done, she put her pen down, shook her head, and then looked up at us.

"Unbelievable, simply unbelievable."

"What?"

"If this was a paternity case, these two specimens would be a dead-on match."

"How can that be? There is absolutely no relationship between the families. They're from different ends of the planet, ethnically, racially, culturally."

Flo shrugged her shoulders. "My job is to tell you what I see, not explain how it happened."

"Is there any chance that you could be wrong?" I asked.

I think she might have taken my question as an affront, because she sighed like a weary professor, tired of instructing her pupils. "We use fragment lengths of the DNA. The shorter the fragment lengths, the greater the chance of error. These are long fragments. These two men have a 99% chance of having the same parent."

I was mystified, and so, it seemed, was everyone else in the room. Flo picked up the phone on her desk and dialed Sennett. It took her a couple of minutes to describe Jordan's observation regarding the photographs and then the DNA tests. When she was done, she handed the phone to me.

"So somehow these two vics are genetically related," he said, his voice was hard, businesslike. "Ahmad Masri. I'll find that bastard, if takes the rest of my career."

"How? There hasn't been a sighting of him for days. Where are you going to start?" I asked.

"I know," he replied, his voice suddenly sounding deflated

"Remember what you've always told me, George. Police work is putting one brick on top of another."

"All right, I remember. Now what?" he replied, sounding as if he were at his wits' end.

"The only ones that can answer that are the Zielinskis."

"Then let's talk with them," he said.

I gave the phone back to Flo, and she spoke to Sennett for another minute. While she did, I explained to Jordan what Sennett had said. She didn't seem enthralled with the notion of going over to the Zielinski's home. "Don't forget, this was your idea," she said with an irritated tone to her voice.

MARY ANNE AND JOHN ZIELINSKI LIVED IN CLAWSON, one of a number of middle-class neighborhoods that surrounded Birmingham. Most of the people that lived there worked for the Big Three. The Zielinskis lived in a modest home, left over from a subdivision built in the late '60s. I had read their story in the newspaper. Both parents worked, they went to church on Sundays, and they had two children, who were high achievers. Especially Brett.

He was a straight A student in high school, the starting quarterback on the state champion high school football team, and a lock to be taken in the professional baseball draft next year. By all accounts he was an All-American kid, liked by everyone that met him, including me. It made his murder that much more upsetting.

As we walked up the steps to the home, I wondered how we were going to question Brett's paternity. I was glad Jordan was with me. Something told me it would be easier for a woman to ask that kind of question, although a male doctor, even a head and neck surgeon like me, lent credibility to evidence like the DNA results I was about to present.

We rang the bell, and John Zielinski opened the door. He was a large man with close-cropped brown hair, big shoulders, and a no-nonsense look to his face. It was the look of a man who was used to working hard and earning what he made. But there was bewilderment in his eyes, too, behind his proud sense of self. I looked at him and tried to put myself in his place. How would I feel? The murder of a son was a betrayal, an overwhelming injustice, an insult to a man that had always done the right thing.

Sennett introduced Jordan as a Federal prosecutor and me as the police surgeon assigned to the case. Mr. Zielinski invited us into the house. It was a three-bedroom ranch built on a slab. There was a living room to the left. On the right was a dining room with an antique wooden table and wooden chairs with blue needlepoint seat covers. Behind the table was a matching hutch with a dozen or so ceramic plates lining the shelves. Through the dining room I could see the clean white kitchen and a comfortable family room overlooking a neatly manicured backyard.

Mr. Zielinski asked us to sit at the dining room table. As we did, a woman in her late forties entered from the kitchen. She was plump, medium height with blonde hair, honest blue eyes, and the beginning of a full face that would someday grace a loving grandmother. John Zielinski introduced us to his wife, Mary Anne.

Before anyone started speaking, Sennett stepped forward and expressed our condolences, and then Jordan began talking. "Mrs. Zielinski, you may wonder why a Federal prosecutor is present. I am here because Hamoud Ishaki, the first young man who was murdered, was the subject of a Federal investigation. As you know, there may be a connection."

"I don't see any connection other than I know that he was also murdered and tortured," John Zielinski replied quizzically.

Jordan explained that she had come into possession of a photograph of Ishaki at about the same age as their son, Brett. She laid the two pictures on the table in front of the parents.

The Zielinskis stared at them. "What are you trying to show us?" Mrs. Zielinski asked.

"These two boys have an amazing resemblance," Jordan stated, while pointing to the two faces in front of her.

"I'm sorry, Ms. Dalkind, but this makes no sense. There are thousands of people that look alike. What does this prove?" Mr. Zielinski asked, his face reddening.

"This is where it gets hard, sir," Sennett interjected. "On a hunch, we ran DNA testing on samples from your son and tissue from the dead boy, Hamoud Ishaki. They were . . . identical."

"Excuse me, but what does that mean?" I could see Mr. Zielinski was getting more anxious. A hint of accusation colored his voice.

"It means that within a reliability of 99%, your son and Hamoud Ishaki have the same father," I said, trying to lend some professional authority to the statement.

There was a stunned silence in the room. John Zielinski looked over at his wife, a menacing scowl darkening his face. Far less than anger, his face bore the aspect of vindication.

He said nothing, and his silence spoke loudly.

As we waited for a reply, my eyes shifted to the hutch, and I studied the colorful plates, each one issued for a new year. Finally, when he didn't respond, I continued. "Mr. Zielinski, we want to test your DNA," I said, trying to deflect the anger from Jordan.

"I know what the truth is, and I'm not afraid to find out your results," Mr. Zielinski grumbled.

Mrs. Zielinski, however, lost the look of the matronly grandmother. Her face had taken on a hardness that startled me.   "I don't see what . . ." she began.

"Stop it," Zielinski ordered. She blanched and looked at him, stunned but silent.

I glanced at Sennett, then proceeded to remove the vials, alcohol pad, and a tourniquet from my pocket that I had taken from my office. "Sir, I need to draw some blood from your arm to check your DNA and compare it to samples from both boys." Strangely, Mr. Zielinski said nothing as I stood up and walked over to him. When I asked him to sit down in the chair, he didn't flinch. I took out a couple of cotton swabs and asked him to open his mouth, I then inserted the swabs and rubbed the lining from the inside of his cheek. When I finished, I put the swabs in a sterile vial. During the procedure, he didn't flinch. It was almost as if he was relishing the chance to vindicate himself. After I put the swabs away, he remained silent. His wife didn't speak either.

Sennett asked them if they wanted to tell us anything else, but they shook their heads silently, almost in unison. I guessed that Sennett could have invoked some kind of police rule to get them to say more. Instead, he thanked them and told them we were working on the case as hard we could. The Zielinskis' impassive faces told us that wasn't enough.

CHAPTER 17

It was Thursday night, and I was at my regular gig, playing the intermission sets at The Pipeline. It was also my chance to cool down and try to digest what was happening to me. I had just finished playing Ellington's version of "Satin Doll". I got a nice hand from the audience and then walked over to the bar, picked up a Labatt from Charlie, and found a corner table that was empty. As I took a long pull from the bottle, I thought to myself that one thing was certain: I was in this investigation for the long haul. The direct communication to me from the killer and Jordan's insistence that I help in the investigation had made that choice clear.

But when Sennett asked me to arrange a meeting with Karin Shackley at the hospital, I wasn't sure I wanted to be part of it. For one thing, I was no longer working for them.

Sennett and I had met with Karin in the doctors' lounge that day. Recalling the meeting, I think she may have been intimidated by the glowering hulk of the lieutenant and his gruff demeanor, but in spite of that, she was open and offered to help in any way she could. In the end she didn't have much to say that wasn't already known about her father.

However, rehashing the conversation in my mind, I recalled that she did tell us one interesting thing. Hamoud Ishaki's mother had an arranged marriage at age thirteen. Her husband was an intolerant sort of a person, and, when she developed some back problems and couldn't do work around the house, he became abusive. The abuse became serious when the child was born and didn't look anything like the father or the mother. He accused the mother of having an affair and walked out on her. Two months later the mother committed suicide. Bill Yaldo raised his grandson, but Karin claimed that Yaldo never cared for the boy.

In the semi-darkness of the club, I started thinking about Hamoud Ishaki's torture and death. I imagined him fighting for his life as somebody came at him with a knife, ready to cut off his family jewels. I wondered what I would have done. I looked at my watch. It was after ten, and I had to get home. I was tired and confused, but I stayed at the table for a few more minutes as Sid started into his last set. I was about to leave when the door opened, and George Sennett walked in. He looked exhausted.

"Looking for some music or looking for me?"

"I need to speak with you," he barked with a tone of frustration. "I checked all your spots, and this was the last one."

"It's the mark of a good detective, finding his man."

He didn't laugh. Instead he sat down and ordered two more Labatt Blues from Charlie. We drank straight from the bottle, sitting there for a few minutes in silence, just listening to Sid play. The trio was right in the middle of the Brubeck's version of "These Foolish Things". Sid was improvising slow and quiet, almost as if he knew I wanted to talk. There was a clinking of glasses and the usual barroom chatter. I asked George why he wanted to see me.

"Flo looked at all of the autopsy specimens again for DNA. She put all of the results on the table. We looked at all of them together. I think she wanted to educate me. You know, make it easier, keep talking to me."

"What happened?"

"We put the specimens side by side and studied the chromatographs. It was clear that Mr. Zielinski is not the boy's father."

"How would Hamoud Ishaki and Brett Zielinski have the same father? It makes no sense," I said as much to myself as to Sennett.

Sennett rolled the bottle back and forth in his palms, as if he were rubbing Aladdin's lamp. Finally, he looked up. "There's something else, Ben. Since this is a murder investigation and we had the specimen, I compared the DNA test on Ahmad Masri. He was not related to either Hamoud Ishaki or Brett Zielinski."

"So Masri's not the father and neither is John Zielinski." I thought about the murder of Stacey Issacson. "This guy, Carrington, who killed Stacey Issacson . . . did you do a DNA profile on him?"

This time Sennett was quick to respond. "We were developing a data bank at the time on all murderers. We went back and looked at his DNA. He wasn't related either."

"Any other ideas?" I asked, full of ideas of my own.

"We're working on it," Sennett said tiredly. "I should know later this afternoon. Unless we can find the father, we can't prove anything."

In the background, Bennie Perkins was going through his alto sax solo, so sweet and yet so melancholy. "From what I read, the FBI hasn't come up with a DNA bank of the entire population yet," I said. "So ,what are you going to do, check every male in the area for a DNA match?" Sennett shook his head disconsolately.

Bennie and Sid moved into the duet portion, moving up and down the scale in a rhythmic improvisation. "I've been doing some thinking, George. Hamoud Ishaki had his nails removed. Every one of them."

Sennett's eyes flashed in the light from the table candle. "It's an interesting fact, but so what? Unless we can find them somewhere else it makes no difference."

I looked out on the dance floor. There were four couples out there now. Two of them were older men with women in their twenties. They were dancing close, close enough to upset their wives. Old men with young women. I wondered if they said that about me and Jordan.

"Maybe yes, maybe no. Let's put ourselves in Hamoud Ishaki's shoes. This killer is a sadist. He doesn't stop at anything."

Sennett was eyes were fixed on me. "Your point?"

"Allan Davis tells me that Ishaki had his testicles cut off," I pointed out.

"I'm sick enough. Do I have to hear that again?"

"Think about it. Someone is taking a knife to your manhood, what are you going to do?"

"Fight like hell."

"Right. You'd bring your hands down to where he had the knife. You'd claw at him. Fight like hell."

"What are you getting at?"

"The underside of your nails would be filled with his skin, right?"

"The killer removed them. Davis didn't report anything."

"Maybe. Davis reported everything on the autopsy except the testicles."

"What do you mean?"

"I mean he pulled the victim's balls out of the mouth and put them in a jar. I saw them. They weren't part of Davis's organ sections. Even for him it was a bit too much."

"So you think Davis didn't examine them well?"

"I'm sure he did, but maybe there's a remnant of something there." I felt as if I was grasping at very small straws, but what else did I have to go on?

"OK," Sennett grumbled. "Let's roust our friendly doctor out of the sack and get him down to the morgue."

"He's probably still at home reading the latest issue of *Golf Digest*."

Sennett stood up looking determined, like a prize fighter that's been sick of getting hammered. "Fuck that shit. I'll get his ass down to the morgue right now."

My third visit to the morgue was no charm. If I thought Davis was pissed the last time they had called him down, this time I knew he would be livid when he heard the request came from me. That's why I asked Sennett to call him. After all, Davis was an employee of the county. What could he say?

"Lieutenant," Davis said, sourly, "I hope Dr. Dailey hasn't brought you down here on a field trip. I'm on call, but I'm not a slave to stupid ideas."

"Stupid to you, but to gumshoes like me, it's just work." Davis looked a little scornful. "Okay," Sennett said, "suppose I tell you this is police business, so forget your bullshit." Davis looked taken back by the force of Sennett's words.

"What do you need?"

"I need to see the specimen in the jars of Hamoud Ishaki."

"Which one?"

"I want to see his testicles."

Davis looked shocked. "What for?"

"We need to see them, Allan," I said. "It's important." I was firm but friendly.

Davis fished around on a shelf until he found the jars with Ishaki's name on them. He pushed aside a couple of bottles until he brought down one containing two walnut-sized round objects. I was feeling sick all over again.

I think Davis, though, actually enjoyed our revulsion, examining the glands as if they were plums on a fruit stand. "Normal in appearance. Nothing that would remotely appear unusual."

He was about to put them back in the jar when I looked at the formaldehyde. I picked up the container and stared at it closely. At the bottom was a thin, red piece of what looked like tissue sitting at the bottom.

"Allan, what is that small red thing on the bottom of the jar?"

"Probably just debris."

"Could it be something else?"

"Like what?" he asked confrontationally.

"I'm not the pathologist, Allan."

Davis stared at the bottom of the jar again with a look of uncertainty. He removed the black top and reached in with a long metal forceps to retrieve the object. When he did, he held it up to the light.

"It looks like a piece of rubber or plastic," he said, the defiance out of his voice.

"Plastic? From where?" Sennett blurted.

"How the hell should I know?" Davis responded angrily.

"Can we look at it under the microscope?" I asked.

I think he would have refused if we hadn't had a history together. Then again, the lieutenant was in no mood for petulant displays of ego, so Davis relented. "I'll do it. It'll just take a couple of minutes."

Sennett and I walked out of the lab and into the hallway to wait.

"You actually think Davis is going to come up with something?" Sennett asked.

"We'll know soon." I nodded toward the doorway just as Davis walked through it toward us.

"It looks a piece of a surgical glove, Ben," he said with a puzzled expression. "Whatever that means."

"Is there anything on it?"

"Just blood."

"The victim's or someone else's?" Sennett asked.

"You guys never quit, do you?" Davis asked, back to his crotchety self.

"It's the job, Allan. It makes you that way," Sennett said matter-of-factly.

Never quit, I thought, confused and excited at the discovery. That's what doctors do. Davis should have learned that in medical school.

UNLIKE DAVIS, FLO CLEVENGER DIDN'T SEEM TO MIND being called in the middle of the night, especially when Sennett told her we might have a break in the case. We met her at the Detroit Police lab just before midnight and explained what we had found. She ran the chromatographs in thirty minutes. "You guys have hit the jackpot," Flo said with a tone of excitement.

"How do you mean?" Sennett asked.

"I mean that from a paternity standpoint, the blood on the piece of glove that you brought me matches perfectly with the DNA from the other specimens."

"You mean the swabs were that of the boys' father?" Sennett asked.

"Unless I'm mistaken, that's what it is," Flo replied.

"So ,it is possible that the person who murdered Hamoud Ishaki might have been his father," I said, now more confused than educated.

"Correct, Ben." Flo nodded solemnly as she spoke.

"And maybe Masri is not involved," I added.

"All we know is that Masri was not the father and his DNA is not in that jar," Sennett said stiffly. "But I've been a cop for twenty-five years. He's involved. I know guilty when I see it."

"Yeah. Don't forget the blood of the dead kid on his clothes," Flo interjected.

"But is it possible that all of these DNA tests are coming back with the same person? Could it be that these were planted findings?" I asked.

"Maybe on Masri, but the tissues from Carrington and the two dead boys are theirs. But let's table that for a moment. For one thing, they couldn't fake the paternity tests," Flo said.

I excused myself, telling Sennett and Flo that I wanted to call Jordan. I stepped outside in the hallway and telephoned her. All I got was a busy signal.

As I walked back to Flo's office, I noticed a line of photographs on the wall. I looked closer and saw that there were pictures of men and women in dress uniforms. Under each were the name and the title of lab director. I stared at a one taken back in the late forties. It was the face of an elderly white man with a thin, pinched nose, high forehead, and tired, deep-set eyes. I wondered how many crimes he could have solved with all this new technology and how many criminals had gotten away.

Then I thought about the DNA findings we had just found. What had we proven? The murderer and the father were one and the same. Fine. But who? Then I thought about Stacey Issacson and James Carrington. These murders were too much like Stacey's to be a coincidence.

I walked back into the Flo's office. Sennett was on his cell phone. I waited until he put the phone back in his pocket. "George," I said flatly, "we need to check out the remains of Stacey Issacson and see if her DNA matches."

"You won't quit on that theory, will you?" he asked, with resignation in his voice. I shook my head. "Well, it will have to wait for now. That was Homicide. They found a coat, shoes, and personal effects in a dumpster in Dearborn, near The Oasis. There was blood on them."

"Any idea as to the owner?"

"Yeah, the clothes belonged to Bill Yaldo. There was blood on the coat that belonged to Yaldo."

"Any ideas?" I asked.

"Like I said, I know guilty when I see it. And I don't need any fancy DNA testing," Sennett replied, an edge back in his voice. "This has to be Masri. Who else? He is a sick, dangerous, and very smart killer. Don't ever forget that, Doc."

"I won't," I replied. "I just want to find out more about the Issacson murder."

"You really believe there's a relationship to the Issacson murder," Flo said with some surprise in her voice.

"I'm not that smart," I answered. "All I know is the killer was related to Hamoud Ishaki and Brett Zielinski, and he wasn't Masri."

Sennett looked disconcerted. "I've got to sort this thing out. Right now, I've got a lot on my plate." He started toward the door and we followed him out, through the hallway and into the parking lot.

It was a dark, moonless night. When I had arrived at our cars, I looked up at the eight-foot chain link fence with razor wire on the top and felt a little more secure behind the fence than outside. I opened my car and got in and sat for a moment. After looking at the specimen and getting the DNA results, I felt confused and unprotected. Whoever was committing these crimes was smart, probably a lot smarter than me. Now, looking outside the fence, the thought occurred to me that maybe I should wait for Jerome to come back in the morning.

That thought didn't last long as I saw the automatic gate go up and watched as Flo and Sennett drove off. I was bushed, but I was also angry. I should have been home, enjoying the weather instead of following leads on a murder and examining a dead man's testicles. I wished Karin Shackley had never contacted me. I wished I wasn't in the detective business.

Then I thought of George Sennett, a man so driven to find a vicious killer that he practically forgot to eat and sleep. George was my friend and he needed my help. Just what that help was I hadn't figured out, but somehow, I knew I had to. I brought the Wagoneer to the gate, which opened slowly. I eased out onto the dark street.

CHAPTER 18

I TURNED LEFT AND SWITCHED ON MY bright lights. As I did, I thought to myself that I had been down this path before—ensnared by events into an investigation I didn't want. It bothered me. Not so much for myself, but for Jordan. I needed her help, but the two most important events in her life were about to happen, and I didn't want anything to spoil them. Besides, anxiety and pregnancy weren't a good mix.

Not that Jordan ever complained. When it came to things like this, she was a rock. I was beginning to think it was my anxiety, not hers. As I drove away from the police lab, I felt a little guilty. Who was I to be that paternalistic? After all, didn't she get herself into this case all on her own? Maybe I didn't want an answer.

I felt a little on edge as I drove down the narrow street. It was dark, and once I got away from the brightly lit parking lot, the illumination was barely adequate. I looked both ways before continuing. There wasn't any traffic at this hour and before I knew it Sennett and Flo had disappeared in the distance. Nevertheless, I proceeded slowly toward Woodward Avenue. When I reached the intersection, I noticed a single pair of headlights behind me. I turned onto the main thoroughfare.

The headlights followed. I kept looking at them as I drove down toward Six Mile Road. It wasn't long before I noticed that the vehicle started to gain on my car.

I slowed for the yellow light ahead at the Woodward intersection but thought better of it. The car behind me was getting closer, so, instead, I accelerated through the intersection and made a hard left. I thought my move had lost him, but I wasn't fast enough. I looked again at my side mirror and saw that the vehicle had made the light.

My hands gripped the steering wheel tighter. I was scared now. This wasn't just an idle coincidence—I was being followed. As the vehicle got closer, I could see that what I thought was a car was really a van. I slowed again so I could see if I could recognize anything about the van or who was driving it.

I glanced quickly at the side of the vehicle. There was some Arabic writing on the side and a name I couldn't make out. Then I pulled up slightly and looked again at the driver. In the light from the halogen streetlamps, it looked for all the world like Moladi.

I didn't have time to decide who it was, because the driver suddenly swerved his van into my lane. I yanked the wheel to the right and accelerated again, just missing a parked car. I saw the red light ahead. Suddenly there was a bright flash from the van and a thud against my briefcase.

A bullet. It took a moment to realize I was being shot at. Then came the fear as a flush came over me and my heart began racing. I felt my hands grip the wheel tighter.

I had to go through the red light. Out of the corner of my eye I saw a car coming down the side street. I looked at my speedometer. It read almost seventy, and the van was closing. There was a risk, but I had to take it. I could see the headlights of the approaching car and heard the wailing of its horn. All I could think about was Jordan. We both squeaked through the intersection just as a car crossed behind us.

As soon as we were through, I slammed on the brakes and saw smoke from the tires in my rearview mirror. The van kept going, but suddenly I saw him touch his brakes. I waited until the last minute, then swung my car across the median and into the southbound lanes. At that time of night there was no traffic.

His van turned toward me in my rearview mirror. If I couldn't shake this guy, I knew I was in trouble. I looked back in the mirror again and saw the lights of the van behind me, as the driver made the turnaround. The lights edged closer.

It was happening again. I could see my car careening wildly down a twisting, mountain road in Colorado, chased by a desperate killer intent on ending my life. There was the sound again, shots ringing out and the shattering of glass. Staying alive, using my head. It was all that had kept me alive back then. Now, amazingly, my terror polished my mind, enabling crisis-mode decisions and cool, razor-sharp responses again. I meant to survive.

A traffic light up ahead changed from green to yellow. I jammed my foot against the accelerator, looking from side to side to see if traffic was coming across the intersection. I had gone beyond the point of return. The speedometer read 75 mph as I roared past the low-slung strip buildings that lined Woodward. Lights flashed up ahead, a multi-colored blur. As I sped past, I saw the patrol car.

The police were after me immediately, sirens wailing and lights flashing. I pulled over and stopped in front of a twenty-four hour McDonald's. The van flew past. I tried to make out the license plate tag, but it was too dark and, now that I was safe, I was shaking too hard to see clearly. All I could do was sit with my arms outstretched and the heels of my hands against the steering wheel, waiting for my chance to explain what had happened to the cops.

Two officers, one big guy and a smaller woman, slowly walked out of their blue Crown Vic. I could see them proceeding cautiously toward the back of the Wagoneer. This was no average traffic stop. They each took a side of my car, their hands on their holsters. Officer Big tapped harshly on the driver's side window with his nightstick. I rolled down the window and offered my driver's license and police badge with a trembling hand. I had never been happier to see two police officers in my life.

I did the get-out-of-your-car thing and walked a straight line. When they determined that I wasn't drunk and saw my police badge, they eased off. I was going to tell them the whole story, then I thought better of it. Instead I pled the only *mea culpa* a doctor can have; I was on my way to an emergency at the hospital.

They seemed to buy my story but gave me a ticket anyway. So much for professional courtesy. As they pulled away, I sat for a moment, trying to understand what had just happened to me. I looked up at the mirror and for a moment saw my father's visage. The same cheekbones, the same eyes studying my face for an answer. I had a momentary urge to call him, tell him about the dilemma I was in, ask for his advice. I almost thought of doing it, but at eighty-five it wasn't fair to put that burden on him. So, I started the car up and headed north to the house.

IT WAS THREE IN THE MORNING when I finally came home. I was carrying the exhaustion of a near-death experience and a case that was dragging me into the vortex of a dangerous whirlpool. Usually I park the car in the garage, but it was late, so I left it on the street. I opened the door and walked into the house quietly. The only light that was on was from a small lamp in the study. As I walked in, Buck came padding into the hallway, wagging his tail.

I patted his head and then peeked into the room. Jordan was asleep on the sofa, a crocheted Afghan covering her. A pang of remorse filled me, both from the strain I was putting on Jordan and the effect it might have on our unborn child. I felt helpless.

I was about to go upstairs, when Jordan awoke. "What time is it?" she asked, rubbing the sleep out of her eyes.

Buck was rubbing his head on my legs, so I started scratching him behind the ears. "A little after three in the morning. I'm sorry you waited up for me."

"Do you want to tell me where you've been?" There was a hint of accusation in her voice.

"I tried to call you, but all I got was a busy signal," I said a little defensively.

"I was home all night, waiting for you."

I looked over at the phone on the desk. It was off the hook. "Are you worried I was somewhere I shouldn't have been?"

By this time Jordan had awoken fully and was sitting with her legs crossed in front of her, the blanket on her lap. She was wearing a thin black t-shirt over her white cotton underwear. Her hair was down and in the soft lamplight, her face looked like she could have been in a Vermeer painting. "Maybe I am," she said. "This isn't the first time you've been out late at night. Is there something I'm doing? I know I haven't been the most affectionate lately." I could see her eyes glistening, she was close to breaking down.

I went over to the couch, sat next to her, and wrapped my arms around her shoulders. She didn't push me away this time, but she also didn't seem ready to forgive me for my absence just yet. I thought about my evening at The Oasis and now my near-miss at the hands of a drive-by shooter. Then there was the issue of sex, or lack thereof. Did she think I was staying out late just to avoid the issue? Or maybe she thought I was having an affair. I had to level with her.

I decided to move to the large upholstered chair next to couch so I could compose myself. After a couple of moments, I started telling her about the episode at The Oasis, explaining everything, including the drink that Moladi slipped me and the videotape.

"Where is the tape now?" she asked, the lawyer back in her voice.

"I have a copy. I suspect the original is with Moladi."

She didn't say anything, so I went on to tell her about this evening's events at the police lab, finishing with the chase, the van, and the errant bullet fired into my briefcase. I could see, as I continued, that her face was beginning to soften, and the hard look had gone out of her eyes. It was replaced by a look of sorrow.

"Why didn't you tell me?" she said with a tone of disappointment.

I shifted a little in my chair. "I didn't want to upset you and the baby. Besides, having a picture of your husband in bed with another woman is not conducive to conjugal bliss."

"Ben, when I lost Matt on that wharf in Miami, I vowed I would never let that happen again. I need to know what's happening. I'm not a child."

I felt bad. That's exactly how I was treating her. "I was going to, I just wanted to wait until I understood where this investigation was going. So much has happened." I explained the finding on the glove fragment and the DNA tests. Her reaction wasn't what I had anticipated.

"You've been in a shell just like you were before I met you. There is more to your behavior than just the case, isn't there?" she asked softly.

I was embarrassed at my weaknesses. I decided to confess. "I've been feeling well, you know, a little left behind. I needed you more than you'll ever know."

By this time she had left the couch and had squeezed herself next to me on the chair. She wrapped her arms around my neck and pulled my face close to hers. I felt the warmth of her lips.

"You might have been wrong not to tell me what was going on, but I let you down too. I was selfish, just too wrapped up in my own problems." By this time she had unbuckled my belt and her hand was slipping down inside of my pants. "I'll never let that happen again."

My hands felt for her panties, and I slipped them off. As I did, I slid my hand between her legs and felt her liquid softness. Then I suddenly stopped. "Are you sure this is okay?" I whispered hoarsely.

She grinned at me, putting her forefinger to her lip. "Shut up, Dailey." With that we both eased off the chair and onto the floor. As I entered her, I knew with certainty that this was not a dream.

I WALKED OUT OF THE HOUSE at seven the next morning, tired from everything that had happened last night, but without the anxiety I had felt for the past few weeks. That feeling lasted until I got to my car on the street. That's when I saw one of those flyers that people stick in your windshield wiper advertising cheap loan rates or a free pizza. I frowned at the annoyance and then looked at the other cars on the street. None of them had one. Now my senses were alerted. I lifted up the wiper, almost afraid to read what it said. I should have been. When I opened it up, it read:

I had fun last night. I hope you did too.
Friend of the Devil

I folded the paper and then opened the door to my car. When I got behind the wheel, I sat there wondering what to do. I felt angry, scared, and helpless, and all I could think of doing was to vent my frustration on Sennett.

When I called, he wasn't there, so I left a message and drove to my office. About halfway there, I stopped at a deli, bought my coffee and carbohydrate— a giant artery-clogging cinnamon pinwheel—and sat down on a stool in front of the counter. I opened up the paper. As if the note wasn't enough, there was Ahmad Masri's dour face all over the front page. The headline read, "Arab businessman suspected in second torture and murder." The article outlined his release on bail, some details of his past, and, of course, mentioned his daughter. A nationwide manhunt had begun. By the time I was finished, I was feeling sick to my stomach, and it wasn't entirely the pinwheel's fault.

I arrived at the office early, went in through the back door, and let Katie know I was there. Once at my desk, I spread out my notes on the killings. Somewhere in these jottings was the key to these murders. Somewhere.

I rearranged the columns of the murders into different orders: age, sex, location. I looked at the victims' names, their histories, even the clothes they were wearing. Nothing came to me. I was about to put my papers away when Katie poked her head around the corner. "Dr. Dailey, were you expecting a Dr. Davis this morning?"

I pushed my chair back from the desk and looked up at her. "Bald-headed, beak nose, wire rims?"

"Yeah. That's him."

"Bring him back."

A few moments later Allan Davis rambled into the office. I greeted him, but he didn't say much. For the first time since I had known him, there was a look of contrition in his face. He seemed not to know what to do as he stood in front of my desk, so I motioned him to the chair. He sat down silently for a moment, took off his glasses and polished them with his tie, then began speaking. "Why is it every time I get involved with you, I begin to feel stupid?"

I glanced over at him, surprised to hear a self-effacing comment like that from a man who always held himself above the fray. "You're certainly not stupid, Al. In fact, you're one of the best forensic pathologists around."

"Then if I was so good, how did I miss that piece of glove in the jar?"

I could see where he was going. A mistake to Davis was like committing a crime. "Because sometimes you have to know you're looking for something before you can find it," I said.

"Well, I thought I would come down and talk with you. I know you've been looking at the Ishaki murder. A lot of people have been talking about the case."

"What do you think?"

"That's what I wanted to talk with you about. Everyone seems to think that someone else did the murder, that it wasn't the Issacson killer. I think it *is* the same person."

A chill went down my spine. "Why?"

He went on to explain that after dealing with so many deaths over the years, he could get a sense about how killers worked. He had done the autopsy on Stacey Issacson, and he had the feeling that it was done by the same person. "I thought pathologists didn't deal in feelings," I said. "Is there anything in particular?"

He shook his head. "Nothing I can point to specifically. That's why I haven't gone to the police. They would probably just laugh at me. But there is a certain neatness and precision about the deaths that seems similar."

"In what way?" I asked.

"Just the method by which it was done."

I wondered what he meant by neatness and precision. Was it the incision, the blood loss, preparation? "For instance?"

Davis seemed more animated than I had ever seen him. I got the impression that he genuinely liked the idea of being a sleuth. "The murderer planned bleeding the Issacson girl to death with extraordinary care. Instead of cutting a vessel, he used a needle. The wound was so neat, I almost missed it. It's like they do down at the Red Cross to take blood."

"What's that got to do with Hamoud Ishaki?"

"He was killed the same way, with the same attention to detail. Each strip of skin that was removed was in even rows, almost as if a straight-edge was used."

"It's hard to prove anything with that," I sighed. Davis's observations were interesting but vague.

"I understand, but I thought you should know. The police don't always see what isn't in the book."

"So why tell me?"

"Because you see things, Ben. Your view is different. You're . . . intuitive."

That was the closest Allan Davis would ever come to a compliment, and I thanked him for it. But how was anyone's intuition going to solve this case?

AFTER DAVIS LEFT, I had a few more patients to see. Around noon, I left to meet Jordan. She wanted to look at invitations. I agreed, though it seemed incongruous to me to be looking for wedding supplies while people were being tortured to death.

On the way over Sennett called me on the phone. He asked me to bring the note from my windshield and the slug from my briefcase. As far as the drive-by from last night, he thought they might have a make on the van and were chasing it down. When he was finished, I told him about my meeting with Davis. I could tell from the expression in his voice that he didn't care what Davis had to say right now. In fact, his only response was to tell me that Davis could speculate all he wanted, but he didn't have to make the collar. Then suddenly he changed the conversation. "You're right about one thing. It's all in the DNA. We have to get a sample from Stacey Issacson's body."

I was surprised that he had bought into the relationship of the murder. "What about the DA?" I asked.

"I've spoken to him, but he's reluctant to get a court order. All we have is speculation. And even if we get it, there's the matter of convincing the dead girl's family."

"You'd think they'd want to know," I said, suddenly thinking of Jordan and the baby.

"What do you say to a family whose daughter was killed fifteen years ago?" Sennett asked with a sound of irritation in his voice. "That family thought the case was closed. That's the toughest part, reopening old wounds." I could hear his gum snapping on the telephone.

"Are you okay, George?" I asked carefully.

"Honestly, I'm so angry right now my skin is crawling. If I could get my hands on that motherfucker, Masri, I don't know what I'd do. Somehow, he's behind this. I *know* he killed Yaldo. He *has* to be involved with these murders."

I didn't like Masri either, but I respected due process, and I knew Sennett did too. "George, can you be objective? I mean, you're a cop and this is a grue-some set of crimes. You're on the case to look for the killler, so you can't let this get to you like that. Something is going to break."

"I know, I know," Sennett huffed. I could hear the anger dissipate from his voice like steam from a kettle. "I'm just under a lot of pressure. It's hard, but I'll do what's right. You know that."

"I do."

"I'm going to make some calls and see what I can do," he said, back to his usual business-like tone of voice. "Where are you going to be?"

"Looking for invitations."

"Huh?"

"It's a wedding thing."

"Oh, that. Call me later." There was a pause before he hung up. "By the way, I'm going to have the boys watching your house again, so don't be surprised if a car shows up."

I felt better when he said that, but they couldn't go everywhere we did. I worried about every street corner I crossed and every person I met. It left me very unsettled.

Unsettled enough that, when I met Jordan, we changed cars and circled the block twice before going into the store. I assumed Jordan understood because she didn't say anything. Or maybe it was her fixation on getting the wedding invitations.

When I got married the first time, things were different. My ex's parents didn't have much and neither did I, so we didn't have a big wedding—my mom and dad, her relatives and mine, and a few friends. I was a resident at the time, and my first wife and I lived in a one-bedroom apartment. I thought I was the king of the road, making fifteen a year and working eighty hours a week.

Then I went into practice and started making money, and my ex suddenly learned how to spend it quickly—fancy purses, expensive jewelry, and above all dozens of pairs of shoes. I really didn't care. I thought we were a couple. What I hadn't understood was the magnetic pull that money and possessions could have. Forget my profession, my hard work, the struggle to succeed; I had re-ally become a means to an end. And when I was disgraced from the hospital, I found out just where that end was.

I vowed I would learn my lesson the next time. I never paid much attention to shopping, acquiring things, money. All I needed was a piano and my boat. That is, until I met Jordan. I found that I needed her more than anything I had ever wanted. And I learned something else: she didn't take money for granted. For her, shopping was an art form to be perfected with practice. Unlike my ex, Jordan expected value for what she spent.

And that is exactly what she got. We traipsed through six stores in an hour and a half before she found the one she wanted. It made me nuts, because each store we walked into was another set of people and another potentially dangerous situation. Going out in public was becoming a problem.

We, and I use the word in the broadest sense, settled on 12-bond paper with a linen texture. Jordan gave the order to the saleslady. The woman looked at the names to be printed. "Miss Jordan Elizabeth Dalkind and Dr. Benjamin A. Dailey." She looked up over her half-glasses. "Oh, you're not the famous Dr. Dailey, are you?"

Suddenly, I had risen in status. "Just a doctor, probably not the one you're thinking of. It's a common name."

I turned around and slowly walked to the door. It was clear outside, so I decided to sit on a bench in front of the store and enjoy the sunshine. I had just sat down when my pager beeped. I checked the number and called Sennett back.

"What did you find, Lieutenant?"

"The DA okayed the examination, but we have to talk with the dead girl's father first," he said.

"Okay. Then you'll be able to open the casket?"

"It's not that easy." Sennett paused on the other end. I could only imagine his discomfort. "Harry Issacson has not had the best relationship with the police department. In fact, he claims the police bungled the investigation of his daughter's death."

"Is he right?" I asked hesitantly.

"I doubt it, but murder cases are tough, especially when the dead child is your daughter."

I asked him if I could help. I think Sennett was waiting for the offer.

"I believe if you go over with me, it might ease my job. You know, doctor-to-doctor. He might be more predisposed to talk with his peers."

"I'm on wedding duty. Can we talk later?"

George and I hung up, planning to meet the next day. I looked over at Jordan. She was now outside, leaning against the car, rubbing her stomach and watching two women pushing strollers down the tree-lined street.

On the way back, Jordan called Gus and settled on the food. She seemed more content with the arrangements. That made two of us.

She dropped me off at my car, and I made it back to the office in time for the afternoon patients. My recent experience had changed my outlook on everything, including my practice. I know it was stupid, but I was suspicious, even of my patients.

I WAS READY TO GO HOME at seven when I got a call from the emergency room at St. Vincent's regarding a Frances Gallagher. They said she was in acute distress from a fishbone she had swallowed. She had asked for me.

When I called in, the ER physician assured me there were no airway complaints. By the time I reached the hospital it was eight o'clock. I walked through the automatic doors and back into Area A, where they put the critically ill patients. St. Vincent's had a class three emergency room that could take care of almost anything, including helicopter transfers.

I entered the area where Mrs. Gallagher was located, a ward comprised of thirty curtained cubicles around a central nurse's station. Two emergency room physicians supervised fifteen nurses and two residents, and every bed was filled. It was organized chaos, a tribute to the staff's skill and determination not to let adversity overwhelm them.

I looked for Mrs. Gallagher's name, then I walked over to her cubicle and pulled back the curtain. She was sitting upright in bed with a small plastic basin under her chin into which she was spitting. A tall, distinguished-looking man in his early sixties with a sun-tanned face, smoothly parted black hair, and a gray pinstripe suit with a three-point white handkerchief in his front pocket was standing by the bed.

"I'm Dr. Dailey," I said, introducing myself, offering my hand.

"Chip Gallagher." We shook hands. "Thank you for coming down to see my wife." Albert "Chip" Gallagher was CEO of Gallagher Industries, a major automobile supplier. I recognized his picture from articles in the newspaper and *Time* magazine.

I looked back at Frances. Her color was pale, and her face had a panicked look to it. There was very little resemblance to the haughty woman who owned the world two weeks ago. Sickness has a way of making everyone the same. I checked her oxygen saturation. It was good, and her pulse was normal. "Mrs. Gallagher, how are you feeling?"

"I feel terrible. We went out to a fundraising dinner tonight for Senator Murtaugh. They served whitefish, and there must have been a bone in it. I immediately had a catching sensation in my throat. Everything I tried, even eating bread, wouldn't clear it." I noticed as she spoke that her voice had worsened since I had last seen her.

"Can you point to a spot in your neck where it sticks?"

"Yes, it's just to the side of my Adam's apple." She pointed to the area with her forefinger.

"Did they take X-rays?"

"They're over here," a voice answered from behind me. It was Craig Talbot, the ER physician. I had known Craig for a long time. He was a competent, no-nonsense kind of doctor who had worked at St. Vincent's ER for twenty years.

I walked with him to the view box and studied the X-rays for a moment. I couldn't see anything abnormal, but I knew that wasn't unusual for fishbones. "I can't see anything on this film, Craig."

"Neither could the radiologist. Say, who is this woman anyway? I've been getting calls from everyone regarding Mrs. Gallagher; the Chief of Staff, the hospital president, even a call from a United States senator. They all want me to know how important this lady is."

"R-H-I-P."

"Huh?"

"Rank hath its privileges. Her husband is about as big as it gets in American industry," I said, suppressing a sigh.

"That explains it. What are you going to do?"

"I'm going to examine her larynx with a mirror first," I replied. "In the meantime, I'll need some lidocaine spray and Magill forceps."

While he went to get the instruments, I walked over to Mrs. Gallagher's bed. In view of my previous experience with her, I decided to tell it like it was. No sugarcoating. "The X-rays are negative, but I still think you have a foreign body in your throat, probably at the base of your tongue. I want to examine your throat first."

"Like you did in the office?"

I nodded. "Just like in the office."

"I'll do whatever you want as long as you get this thing out of my throat."

I pulled out my headlight and a small mirror from my bag. Once I had the light plugged in, I heated the mirror in hot water, took a small gauze square, and gently grasped her tongue and pulled on it. I shone the light on the mirror and, after some searching, found a fishbone protruding from the tongue.

"I see the bone in your throat, Mrs. Gallagher. I'm going to try and take it out here at the bedside."

"Will it hurt?"

"We'll freeze it with some topical spray."

Craig and his nurse had brought the airway cart over. I sprayed her throat with the anesthetic and waited for a minute. Then I placed another gauze square on Mrs. Gallagher's tongue and asked the nurse to hold onto it. When I was sure that she was holding it properly, I picked up the heated mirror along with the Magill forceps. The forceps were angled with a circular tip that could grab onto the fishbone.

With the mirror in place I could see the bone again. The image on the mirror was reversed, so everything had to be done backwards. Over the years it had taken me a lot of practice and a few missed attempts on patients before I had mastered the technique of working indirectly with the mirror. Fortunately, this case was easy, and Mrs. Gallagher was a very cooperative patient. I reached in and, on the first pass, grabbed the bone with the forceps. I pulled on it and an inch-long shiny sliver came out. I held the prize in front of my small audience.

"How do you feel now, Mrs. Gallagher?"

She swallowed several times.

"It feels perfect." A smile of relief filled her face. Then she said, "Thank you." I think those are the two words most physicians seek most from their patients.

"You're welcome," I replied, "but there is something else."

"What's that?"

"The lesion that I noticed on your voice box two weeks ago has grown in size. I would suggest that you discuss this further with your physician in New York."

"What does that mean, doctor?" Chip Gallagher asked. He had been quietly standing to the side of the stretcher during his wife's ordeal.

"To me, it means that it should be biopsied without delay." I figured I might as well be blunt, because they might be looking for the next flight to New York.

"How do you do that?"

"With a procedure through the mouth," I replied matter-of-factly.

"When would you do it?"

"Within the next two weeks." Then I added, "If you're intent on second opinions, that is your decision, but if I'm your doctor, you'll have to trust me." Was this guy ready to render judgment on my course of action, or merely curious? I regretted thinking out loud, a very bad habit of mine with patients in crisis.

As soon as I said it, Chip Gallagher spoke again. "I'm tired of Frances' games. This is serious stuff, not a supermarket where you can pick and choose your treatment."

"Your wife is in no acute danger right now, but if the lesion keeps growing at this rate, it could be serious."

"Call it like you see it, Doctor, just fix up my wife."

"I'll try. My office will make arrangements for the biopsy in a couple of days." With that I turned around and started to leave. I was tired and anxious to get home.

I passed by the nursing desk on the way to the door. Talbot was looking at some films on the viewer. "What does the lesion on her voice box look like?" he asked.

"I would suspect some type of malignancy," I said. "That's what I told Mrs. Gallagher when I first saw her in the office, but she just stormed out."

Talbot rustled some papers from the chart in his hand. "Someone once said that it is easier to be wise for others than for ourselves."

I nodded. "It's true. For all of her airs, I think she was honestly scared.

Sometimes you wonder how you'd be under the same circumstances."

"I guess you never know until it happens. I just hope it doesn't happen too soon," Talbot said with a laugh. "By the way, I almost forgot to tell you. When she first came in, we asked for the anesthesiologist on in-house call to come down and check her out. With her hoarseness, we thought she might have an airway problem. The guy that showed up was someone I hadn't worked with before. His name was Fair-something or other."

"Carl Fairchild?"

"Yeah, that's the name. After he listened to Mrs. Gallagher's story, he examined her and confirmed that the airway was not the problem."

"Did he recommend anything?" I asked.

"No, but he did say something that I thought was a little unusual. When he was done, he suggested they see a friend of his at the Massachusetts Eye and Ear Infirmary in Boston to check out her voice."

"Did the family tell him I had seen her?"

"Yeah, he said he was just trying to be helpful."

I thought to myself, maybe he saw what Mrs. Gallagher was like and was just trying to do me a favor by passing her off to someone else.

CHAPTER 19

I MET SENNETT AT HIS OFFICE at about two o'clock the next day. We were supposed to meet Harold Issacson at his house later in the afternoon. When I got there, the first thing he did was to ask me if I had brought the note from my windshield and the slug from my briefcase. I pulled both of them out of my pocket and gave them to him. He studied the note for a moment and then called in his sergeant, Paul Knudsen, and told him he wanted a make on the slug. Knudsen was in his late twenties with red hair cut close and a ramrod straight posture. I'd had dealings with him before, when Jordan had almost died. He had impressed me as someone who was ready to do great things, a high energy type, but due to some sort of karmic flaw, was never going to rise much above his current status as sergeant schlepper. We left Sennett's office, took the elevator to the police garage, got into Sennett's car, and left to see Dr. Harry Issacson.

I liked driving in the unmarked car. There was something about the crackle of the radio, the magnetic cruiser light sitting on the seat, the smell of gun oil, and the shotgun tucked out of view but within quick reach. It gave off a feeling of power and mystery, like one of those old Dick Tracy comics I loved as a kid. Those were the days when the police cars were black and white, just like the moral issues of that time. Or so I thought, as I remembered them.

We arrived at Harry Issacson's house a little after three. The weather was warm, but there was a stiff breeze from the southwest that made the air bearable. It was early July and the forecasters were already talking about a long hot summer if we didn't get some rain soon. About the time I reached the front step, I was thinking about taking my sailboat to Harsten's Island.

Issacson lived in a one-story house in Royal Oak, a middle-class neighborhood that was home to some of the best jazz bars in the area. The once-modest residences were viewed as valuable now that fancy restaurants and clubs had made the area popular.

His home was a small affair down a tree-lined street of other look-a-like bungalows. The builder must have given his architect strict instructions to make the houses the same on the inside but not make them appear that way. This was achieved by flipping the bay windows from one side to the other on the front of the house. This odd design feature gave an irregular pattern to an otherwise uniform street.

A couple of clay pots with white petunias sat on either side of the front porch of Harry Issacson's home. They needed water. I looked at the front door. Issacson was waiting for us.

I had a preconception of what a free clinic, abortion doctor would look like—unkempt hair, a beard, Birkenstocks and a pipe in his mouth. Harry Issacson didn't fit the stereotype. He was short, about five-seven, thin, with curly, short-cut gray hair and a wrinkle-free, ruddy complexion that gave him the appearance of a man in his mid-forties. He didn't seem anxious to see us.

Sennett introduced himself first, then me. When Issacson found out I was a doctor, he seemed a little relieved. We moved from the porch into the living room, which Jordan would have politely called "eclectic." In my mind that was a euphemism for disorder. There were two multi-colored oriental rugs at obtuse angles on a dull, dark oak floor. A television dominated the corner near the fireplace, resting on a cheap metal rolling stand. The window air conditioner hummed, but it was still stuffy inside.

Issacson motioned us to a green, overstuffed corduroy couch with a beige afghan. On the barn-wood coffee table in front of it rested the week's news-papers in various degrees of disarray. Issacson sat across from us in a worn, high-back, red leather chair. It was obvious he spent a lot of time in that room.

"Thank you for having us over, Dr. Issacson," Sennett began. "We're sorry to have to intrude on you, but we feel that you might have some information that could help us solve a crime."

"What could I possibly tell you that you don't already know?" he said in a defeated tone of voice. "The police found the murderer of my daughter. There's nothing else to tell."

"That's why we're here. There have been two recent murders of young men in the Detroit area. Perhaps you've heard about them."

"I've read about it." Issacson's face was drawn and his expression was flat. There's no getting beyond the murder of one's child, I suppose.

"In and of themselves, they wouldn't mean anything in this case," Sennett continued. "But the pathologist who performed the autopsy on your daughter and the two recent victims felt there is a similarity in their deaths."

Issacson raised his bushy eyebrows. "What about that punk they found in the river?" The way he spat out "punk" hardly concealed his contempt.

"Police aren't always right," Sennett said calmly. "They deal with the facts at hand."

"They can also be lazy," Issacson said icily.

I looked over at Sennett. He didn't flinch at the words. "Just like physicians, Dr. Issacson," I interjected. "Everyone makes mistakes. Have you ever made a wrong diagnosis?"

"I made enough mistakes in my life to fill a book." He glanced over at a picture on the end table of a young child. "That's Stacey. Stacey was one of the few things I didn't make a mistake about." I looked at the young, blonde-headed girl smiling at the camera. I hadn't been a father yet, but now that Jordan was pregnant, my eyes lingered on the photo. I noticed no pictures of his wife.

"I hope you don't mind me asking, is your wife alive?" Sennett asked. Issacson shook his head.

"How long after her death did your wife die?" I asked.

"A few years." His eyes shifted to the floor and his voice was cold and unemotional.

"I'm sorry to bother you. I know that every time someone interviews you it opens up another sore. I'm just wondering if anything else has come to you regarding your daughter's death?" Sennett asked.

Issacson paused before speaking. His eyes turned narrow as he looked at both of us. I could see him ball his fists with what seemed to be a controlled fury that belied his gentle appearance. "You saw who killed her. A fucking pro-life militant. What do you think? I was in charge of a clinic for indigent pregnant women who didn't want their babies. Why wouldn't a pro-lifer want to hurt me?"

"That's a good question, but maybe we've all jumped to conclusions," Sennett said calmly. "The crime lab discovered that there was a match between the DNA of the dead Arab boy, Ishaki, and the kidnapped young man, Zielinski, you've read about in the newspaper."

"So?"

"That means that both boys were fathered by the same man. If there was a similarity in the killings of your daughter and these two, then perhaps there was a similarity in their DNA."

It didn't take long for Issacson to figure out what Sennett was getting at. "Lieutenant, I'm sure you are trying very hard to do your job, but I am not stupid. Are you implying that I was not my daughter's father?"

"I'm not implying anything. Just trying to follow a lead." Sennett plowed on, as steady as a bloodhound on a scent. "If you had anything of Stacey's, like a lock of hair, that we could run a sample on, it would help us."

"I have none. The only DNA left of my daughter is in her grave, and you can forget about it. I will never give permission to disturb her peace." Issacson stood up and walked over to a corner of the living room. There was a large cardboard box filled with mail.

"You see that, Lieutenant? That's all mail I've received over the years regarding Stacey's murder. At first I used to open it and read the letters. It made me sick. Everyone had an idea. Finally, I just collected them and kept them in the box. I want nothing more to do with it."

"It would help . . . ."

Issacson stood by the box, one hand on his hip and the other pointed directly at Sennett. His face was red and perspiration covered his forehead. "I don't care about helping, dammit! My life is over. My career is over. My little girl is dead. I have no need to help you or anyone else. The murdering bastard took everything away from me. I only want to live my life out and pass on. For me, everything is over."

Sennett's shoulders sagged almost imperceptibly. He knew what would come next: lawyers, judges, endless delays. Just then his cell phone rang. I watched him as he listened intently. Then he clicked off. "We'd better go, Ben." Sennett rose from the couch and walked past Issacson to the door.

As I looked over at Issacson, our gazes met. I felt mine were novice eyes, a wannabe father in the presence of an ageless idol consecrated to paternal suffering. I stared for a moment at the floor and turned to leave without a word.

"What happened?" I asked Sennett as we got into the car.

"They found Masri's car in a wooded area in Rouge Park. There were some blood stains on the front seat. It matched the blood found on Brett Zielinski."

"Wonderful."

"There was something else. The bullet that was taken out of your briefcase was identical to the one that killed Bill Yaldo."

"Masri?"

He nodded.

"That's great. I try to help his family, and he tries to kill me. Go figure."

Sennett looked distracted. "Forget it for right now. We need to take care of some unfinished business." Sennett picked up his phone and in five minutes we were on our way to an address the dispatcher had given, 1501 Maple Avenue, in East Dearborn. It was the home of my friendly waiter.

FRANK MOLADI'S EAST DEARBORN NEIGHBORHOOD looked like any other middle-class neighborhood in America. It was not what I expected of a largest enclave of Arab immigrants. On our drive, I repeated to Sennett all the details of what had happened that night at The Oasis. He didn't seem surprised. He said, "Blackmail is business as usual in the police world." It didn't make me feel any better.

We drove down the tree-shaded side street looking for Frank Moladi's house. It was halfway down the block. Sennett did a drive-by first. The only thing we saw was an open garage door and a barbecue on the driveway.

Sennett parked in front of a neighbor's house, where three men were playing cards on the front porch. We got out and walked toward Moladi's home. I wasn't nervous until I saw Sennett check his piece. I think it was just a reflex, but I stepped a pace behind. I might have been scared, but the chance to see the man who had caused me such personal embarrassment was irresistible.

Sennett walked up the steps and knocked on the door. After a few seconds, Moladi opened it. I could hear a crying child in the background. My hiding place behind the lieutenant wasn't sufficient. When Moladi saw me, he tried to shut the door, but Sennett was too quick. His foot was inside, and his hand was on Moladi's sleeveless undershirt before I could blink. I never realized just how fast the big man was. He spun Moladi around and pushed his head against the wall. He was cuffed before anyone had a chance to make introductions.

We walked into the house. It wasn't a pretty sight. Two small children in diapers, huddled behind a woman in her early twenties. She looked terrified.

"I'm Lieutenant George Sennett, Detroit Homicide. I want to ask you a few questions. Do I have to keep you cuffed like this and scare your family, or do we have a nice quiet talk on the front porch?"

"You can't do this!" Moladi screamed. "This is America!"

"Yes, it is. It is not my goal to deny your rights. I would like to see your green card."

Moladi's eyes danced furtively from side to side, a caged animal looking for a way to escape. "Alright, I'll talk. But first take off the cuffs. You humiliate me in front of my wife."

"I will, but understand we are investigating a serious crime. It is possible that you might know something about the crime. We are not trying to deny you your rights." Sennett's voice was as even as a carpenter's level. He removed the cuffs and walked Moladi out to the front porch, where they both sat down on white plastic chairs. I sort of hovered over the lieutenant, waiting for my cue to be useful.

"How long have you been in this country?" Sennett demanded.

"About six months. Why? What do you want from me?"

"I'll ask the questions. First thing. Tell me about my friend's visit to The Oasis."

I studied Moladi carefully this time. His face was chalk-white and his thick red lips were pursed, as if any word he spoke would come with an expectant pain. As he listened to Sennett, he squeezed his hands until the veins stood out like blue rawhide. "There is nothing to tell."

"Think hard, Frankie, and while you're thinking and remember you have a green card. I want to know about the videotape."

I expected more resistance, but he was surprisingly talkative. "It was

Ahmad's idea. He told me to do it when I visited him at the jail. It is an old trick. We did it many times back home."

"Old habits die hard, right? Well, you live in America now. This is your home. This is the place where you scream about legal rights."

Moladi stared furtively at the peeling white paint on the porch deck.

"Go on," Sennett prodded.

"The idea was to get him drunk, put some opium in his drink to make him sleep, and then put him in bed with Fatima. Take a few photos. You know, scare him off."

"We use the term *blackmail* in America. That gets you ten years of ankle-grabbing at Jackson State Penitentiary." Just to make sure Moladi understood, Sennett pushed a forefinger of one hand back and forth through the circled thumb and forefinger of the other.

Moladi must have understood. Maybe the thought of anal intrusion sparked some memory. In any case, he was quick to back off. "Believe me," he pleaded, looking up at me. "Dr. Dailey did no wrong. He kept mumbling something about his wife."

"Thank you. Now I expect to get the original tape," Sennett rumbled.

Moladi nodded. Then he shouted something in Arabic to his wife in the house. After a couple of minutes, she came padding obsequiously out to the porch, handed a videotape to the lieutenant, turned around without looking at her husband, and went back into the house.

Sennett smirked just enough so his white teeth gave a snarl that Moladi couldn't mistake for kindness. "That's a good start, Frank. Just so we have an understanding, I'm going to keep this in my possession. If this surfaces again, I'm going to go to the DA with a complaint of blackmail and extortion against you. Now how about the incident the other night on Woodward?"

He looked genuinely surprised. "I know nothing." I wanted to throttle his fucking neck.

Sennett must have sensed it, because he put a hand on my arm as if to back me off. "Look, asshole, everyone says they know nothing, so let's quit the crap." Sennett recounted the chase and mentioned the spent bullet. As he listened, Moladi fidgeted with his belt buckle.

"This I swear to you.– I admit the business at the club. This other thing, I had nothing to do with it."

We listened as he claimed he had twenty witnesses, all of whom would say he was at The Oasis that night.

Sennett must have been satisfied at his alibi, because he asked him about Masri. "Your buddy, Masri, he was the enforcer in Lebanon, wasn't he?"

"No, I never saw him torture anyone, I swear," Moladi pleaded. "He merely prescribed the justice."

I was shocked at the confession. "You mean giving the order wasn't as bad as actually committing the crime?" I said angrily.

Moladi seemed unfazed at the reference. "There were atrocities on both sides. When some crime was committed against one of our people, he would order retaliation."

When Sennett asked him to describe the methods used, Moladi spoke of Masri as a genius in dissecting the body, claiming that he could find his way to any part of the body he wanted.

"What about mutilations?" Sennett asked

"Ahmad had a reputation in Lebanon. I had heard stories of the torture cell he ran. The descriptions of the victims were very bad. But human life is less important than being right. He had to send a message to his enemies."

"Do you know where Masri is?" Sennett asked

"I have not heard from him in several days. I don't know where he is."

"Any hints?" I asked.

Moladi maintained that he didn't know where Masri was, but when Sennett asked him if he had noticed anything strange about his boss, the waiter claimed he was worried about him after Hamoud Ishaki was killed. He claimed that Masri had been studying books and legal documents and acting very erratic. He said it was unlike him.

Sennett looked at Moladi for a few moments. His eyes stared at the man as if he were looking right through him. "What did Masri have against Bill Yaldo?"

"Nothing, nothing." Moladi's eyes shifted around the porch.

"I said, what did Masri have against Bill Yaldo?" As he spoke, Sennett locked one hand on his throat, lifted him out of the chair, and pressed his neck against the porch rail. With the other, he squeezed the man's balls. Moladi screamed in pain as his family watched from behind the screen door. For most men there was no greater shame than this kind of loss of face, and Sennett knew it. "Now tell me what the deal is."

Moladi was trying to catch his breath as tears ran down his cheeks. "I came here several months ago," he gasped, his voice raspy from the pressure on his throat. "When I got here, Ahmad invited me over to his home. He asked me questions about his wife. I told him that my uncle had said that her death had been a set-up. That Bill Yaldo had tried to save himself."

"What did Masri say?"

"He said nothing. But I knew the look. I had seen it many times in Lebanon. It was the look of death."

Sennett looked at Moladi contemptuously for a few moments, as if he was deciding his fate. "I'll tell you what, Frankie-boy. Don't leave town, because I know where you live."

With that, he let go of Moladi's throat and gave his balls another squeeze that dropped him to the floor. Sennett walked toward the porch steps, and I followed him back to the street. I was sure the message that he left was indelible in Moladi's mind. When we reached the car, Sennett got inside and turned the ignition. I followed him on the other side, and we both sat there for a moment, waiting for the air conditioning to cool down the cab. While we did, he explained that he had all the motive he needed to send Masri away for life.

Then he smiled at me without saying anything. "What else?" I asked, finally getting tired of waiting.

"I always knew you could never cheat on Jordan," Sennett said still holding onto his crooked grin. "It just took an asshole like that to prove it."

"Just make sure you get rid of that tape."

Sennett laughed and held up the cassette. "I don't know, Dailey. Maybe I should have something on you."

"Hmm, everyone else does. Why should you be different?"

"At the very least, I could save it for your old age, so Jordan could remember the man you once were."

"Drugged, impotent, and babbling her name to a sleazy whore. Great idea. I'll keep a few video caps pasted in our family Torah . . ."

CHAPTER 20

I OPERATED ON MRS. GALLAGHER two days later. I was able to take a biopsy and get a frozen section. The pathologist thought it was a verrucous carcinoma, a rare malignancy that is locally invasive but doesn't metastasize. I removed the lesion without taking out her voice box. The final sections came back with clear margins.

I was surprised when I made rounds on her the next day. The frightened woman from the other day was gone, and she seemed back in charge of herself. "I think this is going to work out, Mrs. Gallagher," I said confidently.

"I know. I'm committed to fighting this cancer thing. I'm supposed to start speech therapy next week. They tell me the most important thing is to maintain my nutrition. They call it positive nitrogen balance. I've already talked with a nutritionist from New York that a friend of mine told me about. He wrote a best-selling book on cancer and nutrition. He's going to fly in and meet with me. I've also arranged for my personal trainer to start on a new set of exercises." Her voice was surprisingly strong.

"That's great. A positive approach to disease definitely helps."

She looked up at me and smiled. "I wanted to thank you, Dr. Dailey." She searched for the right words, her voice getting higher and lower as she spoke. "I knew there was something wrong. I was worried, and I knew you were right. But I just didn't want to believe it, so I lashed out at you. I'm sorry." She extended her hand to me.

I held her hand for a moment and smiled. "I appreciate that, but don't be sorry. Just get better."

I walked out of her room and went back to my office. I suppose I should have been feeling better, but the shroud of killings and the recent note on my car left me with a feeling of dread. When I reached the clinic, I went back to my office and sat at my desk, distractedly sifting through some papers. Katie came back into the office, and I think she understood the look of consternation that must have cloaked my face.

"More problems, huh?"

"Yeah, more problems."

"There's a doctor on the phone for you. He wouldn't give me his name. Do you want me to put him through?"

"Sure."

When I picked up the phone, a soft tenor voice answered. "Dr. Dailey, this is Harold Issacson."

The gentleness of his approach startled me. "What can I do for you, sir?"

"I was wondering if we could meet. I wanted to talk with you about Stacey."

"Sure, I have a few patients to see. It will only take me a couple of hours. Let's meet around one. Your place?"

The two hours actually took longer, because of late patients and a couple of difficult voice problems. When a rock-and-roll singer with long hair and tattoos came in the office, I listened patiently as he complained about losing his upper register. Compared to being shot at, it honestly seemed inconsequential. Fortunately, it was a simple problem of the reflux of stomach acid onto his voice box, causing stiffness of the vocal cords. I gave him some medicine and a diet. He seemed relieved that there was an understandable cause to his problem, though doubtful that he could discipline himself to follow my instructions.

I arrived at Harold Issacson's house about half an hour late and found him waiting for me on the front porch. I apologized for being tardy, but he didn't seem upset. In fact, he looked anxious to see me. It took me a moment to discern why, then I noticed his eyes: They seemed alive, wide and bright.

He showed me into the house, but this time he took me into the kitchen. Unlike the living room, which reeked of memories and despair, the kitchen seemed friendly. A cozy spot, where Issacson probably read *The New York Times* and drank his coffee. It was a modest affair, clean, not particularly fancy; the kind of kitchen a lonely widower would find comforting.

He heated a cup of water in the microwave, put in a tea bag, and brought it over. I added a couple of teaspoons of sugar and let it steep for a moment. "I asked you to come back because of something the lieutenant said at our meeting yesterday. After he told me about finding the dead boy—I think Zielinski was his name—I realized that perhaps he was right. Perhaps I have kept this thing inside for too long."

"Why not call the lieutenant?"

"I meant what I said about the police. I have a basic distrust of them."

"Because of your daughter?"

He nodded. "They had knowledge of the threats against me and my family and never followed up on any of them." He stopped for a moment and reflected. "But I don't distrust you."

"Why not?"

"I checked you up on the internet. I read about your ordeal, how you resurrected your life after that malpractice case, and how you found a killer. It's quite a story."

"Things happen. It's past history."

"Maybe, but I don't believe in luck. That's why I wanted to speak with you. I need to explain something about myself."

He proceeded to tell me about his career, graduating from the University of Pennsylvania Medical School and going into obstetrics. He could have joined a fancy New York practice, but money wasn't his thing. That's why he accepted a staff position in Ann Arbor at the University of Michigan. His interest was preventive care of pregnant women. Eventually he took on the cause of unwanted pregnancies. When he had opened the abortion clinic in Ypsilanti, he felt that he had finally arrived at his mission in life.

I noticed he was no longer wearing a wedding ring, so I took the chance of asking him about his wife.

"There isn't much to tell. She worked as a nurse in the clinic. She seemed committed to the same goal I had. I thought we had so much in common. Sometimes you can't tell a book by its cover."

I thought about my ex-wife and nodded.

"Actually, at first things were all right between us. She got pregnant after I had opened the clinic. That's where my life starts to fall apart. When Stacey was born, I was surprised, because my wife had been sick, and we hadn't had relations for some time. But you know, I never suspected anything. Infidelity was something that happened to other people, not us. Besides, maybe the date of conception was wrong."

"And then she was born."

"I still remember the moment. I'm in the delivery room. The head starts to crown and all of a sudden, this gorgeous baby comes out. The doctor holds her up for my wife and me to see. It was strange because the baby looked nothing like either of us."

I found myself looking into my beverage. "You never know when a child is born what it's going to look like later," I offered. "It takes a while."

"That's what I thought. But as Stacey got older, I couldn't deny the child wasn't mine. She looked like a *shiksa*, for Christ's sake. No one in either of our families looked like her."

I looked around the kitchen. It was pleasant enough, but there were none of the mementos of a family, stickers on the refrigerator, a shopping list next to the phone, or even a rack full of spices. It made the cozy room seem some-how empty.

"Did you ever say anything to your wife?" I asked.

"What was I going to say? Who is the baby's father? It was evident to her, to me, to anyone who saw her. People used to make the jokes, it must have been the milkman. You know. It was as if we had adopted Stacey."

"But you still loved her."

Issacson's face suddenly lit up and a smile momentarily crossed his lips. It was a remembrance smile for someone who was no longer there. "Loved her? That's not the word. Stacey was the one thing in my life that kept me sane. I could only come to grips with my wife's infidelity by shoving all those thoughts out of my mind and focusing my love on that girl."

"What did your wife say? You must have had some conversations."

"She would never admit to an affair. When I confronted her with the fact that the child didn't look like either of us, and that she was sick at the time of conception, she wouldn't respond. She knew I was right."

I didn't want to ask my next question, reflecting on what would have happened if this had been Jordan and me, but I found myself blurting it out: "How could you stay together?"

Issacson pressed his pale, thin lips together. "We never slept together again. She asked for a divorce, but I would never give it to her. I wanted Stacey to have a home, and I wanted to be in that home. My wife agreed that we should do what was best for the child."

"Did Stacey ever suspect anything?"

"Not that she ever said." He explained that he tried to never argue with her mother. As far as his needs were concerned, the payment of joy he received from his daughter was worth far more to him than the pleasure of female company.

"Did you continue the clinic?"

He nodded. "Someone could have said that Stacey was the poster child for the pro-life movement, a child born who, in other circumstances, might have been aborted. I looked at it the other way. A child born to parents who loved her is a lot different than a child born without a father and without hope. It just reaffirmed my conviction that what I was doing was right."

"Until she was killed."

His gaze dropped to his tea, as if, finally broken and without hope, he was left with only the tea leaves to call forth his future. "Until she was killed. A note was left at her body. I remember it as if it were yesterday. It was clearly an anti-abortion statement. My conviction that I was doing the right thing with the clinic had ultimately taken from me the only thing that meant anything."

"And her mother?"

"I came home one evening after Stacey died and found another note, this one in our bedroom. She said she was sorry that my one joy in life was gone and that we both lived with such deep sorrow. She understood my anger and my devotion, but now that Stacey was gone there was no reason for her to stay. She said she never wanted to hurt me. It just happened. That was it. She left, and I never heard from her again. As far as I was concerned, she was dead."

I looked at Issacson's face. It was a mask with the blank look of a hurt so deep it could never be repaired. "Do you have a copy of the note left on your daughter's body?"

"I don't need a copy. I remember it as if it were tattooed on my forearm. It said, "God shall smite thee, thou whited wall.""

The way he pronounced the quotation it sounded practiced, as if he had repeated it so many times it was part of his daily prayer. "Who said that?"

"It's from the Bible, Romans."

"Any idea what it meant?"

"I'm sure it was an anti-abortion statement from that lunatic that killed her. No matter. They won. I shut down the clinic, resigned my clinical position at the university, and took a job with an insurance company reviewing claims. I'll run out the string, until my life ends."

He paused, waiting for a response from me. It came slowly, a bit too naive. I asked him why he was telling me this. He told me that he had reflected on what the lieutenant had said and concluded that if Stacey's body could in some way help the investigation, he would not stand in the way. Then he got up from the table and motioned me into the living room. I followed behind him.

Issacson pointed over to the corner. "You see that box?" It was the box full of mail regarding his daughter that he had shown to Sennett and me before.

"Most of these letters were sympathy stuff. I almost couldn't bear to read them. There was, however, one note from a woman in Chicago. It was barely legible. I thought it was a crank letter, so I never did anything about it. She told me about her teenage daughter who had been found dead, mutilated somehow. She said it was God's retribution or something like that. I was disgusted, so I threw it back in the box and never looked at it again. But I always remembered it. Now the lieutenant has opened a subject I can never forget. If there is some connection, I would hate to have it go unnoticed."

He reached into the box and pulled out a worn and yellowed envelope.

The return address revealed that the letter came from a Connie Lennell in Chicago. I looked at the envelope from both sides but saw nothing unusual. "You know I'll have to turn this over to the police."

"I know, but I want to have you involved. You're a doctor. You see things differently. I can see it in your eyes."

I softly snorted. There it was again, that doctor-detective thing. Both of us knew all too well that our crowd was like any other, human beings weighted down with the foibles of man and often consumed by failure.

I pocketed the letter, thanked him for letting me into his life, and walked outside into the fresh air. It had been three weeks since any rain. The lawns were turning brown, but the air still smelled sweet. I listened to the church bell down the street chiming out the hour.

Standing outside of his house, I pulled the letter from my pocket and stared at it again. I thought about how similar detective work and being a doctor really were, little pieces of information leading to a diagnosis. I wondered if it was going to happen here.

IT WAS FOUR-THIRTY WHEN JORDAN AND I got to her obstetrician's office for her check-up. Things were moving so fast, I was having trouble keeping track of everything. I sat down next to her in the waiting room and held her hand. She looked at me, radiating with a look that was probably duplicated by every expectant mother for millions of years: hope, joy, contentment, and a keen sense that she was protecting something very special, a one of a kind child that no one else had or ever would have.

We waited about thirty minutes until we were called back. The nurse took us into a room and had Jordan lie down on the examining table. She was used to the drill. She lifted up her blouse, and the nurse put a small microphone apparatus on the skin of her abdomen.

I heard the sound of my child's heartbeat. It seemed to be going like a machine gun, but the nurse said it was only 140 beats per minute.

"What's the significance?"

"It could indicate the sex of the child," she said. "But in this case, it's indeterminate."

For an instant I was insatiably curious, but Jordan and I had made a pact. The sex of our baby was going to be a delivery day surprise. Still, I was a voice specialist, not an obstetrician, so no one could blame me for asking about the heart rate. The nurse proceeded to tell me that a fast heart rate usually meant a girl and a slow rate meant a boy. In our child's case it was too close to call.

The nurse then handed me a picture of the ultrasound, and I looked at the fetus. My child, our child.

"Jordan, it looks just like me."

"You wish."

"If I had a dime for every father that said that, I'd be a millionaire," the nurse said with a laugh.

Her obstetrician, Tom Bromley, walked in as we were examining the photo. "Looks just like the mother," he said.

"See?" Jordan laughed.

Bromley placed his hands on Jordan's abdomen and gently pushed and prodded from both sides. "The baby is in perfect position." Then he put on the fetal stethoscope. "And the heart sounds perfect too."

As I heard the sound coming through the speaker, I thought about our home and how much we looked forward to having the baby. Harry Issacson came to mind. As much as you'd like to say you had control, there were some things that just happened.

I could understand his love for Stacey. Paternity wasn't the issue, love was. It was a feeling beyond description.

They drew some blood from Jordan and told her that she was due back every week until delivery. The frequent check-ups made the impending event seem more real. I had fought to keep these two alive—now it was going to happen. As we walked out of the building, I stopped and looked up and down the street. Jordan must have understood, because she squeezed my hand tightly.

Jordan and I walked back to the car. I had a few things to pick up at the office, so we drove the five miles from Bromley's office to the hospital while having an animated discussion about our impending progeny. We parked in the deck and walked to the elevator.

One thing I learned about being around a pregnant woman is that people always seemed to treat them a little nicer. It was that way by the elevator. There was a crowd at the entrance, but they let Jordan and me on first and parted politely when we exited.

We turned down the hall to my office, and my secretary looked up quickly as we walked in. "Lieutenant Sennett is waiting for you."

I wondered what he was doing here.

When we walked in, the lieutenant was inspecting a model of the larynx that was sitting on my desk. He looked up as we came in and smiled. "A person's voice comes out of this thing, right?"

"Not really. The larynx is the sound generator in your body, but speech and voice come from all of the structures in your throat, tongue, and lips," I explained. "The sound comes in waves called formants. It is then modified as it comes out by the other structures in the throat. That's what makes the human voice so unique."

"I thought it was all so simple."

"Nothing in nature is simple. It took millions of years to perfect it. It's still undergoing change."

"Change is a funny word. The more things change, the more they stay the same."

"What do you mean?"

"I heard a rumor that the judicial review board is going after Judge Pilkington for letting Masri out on bail." Sennett kept on studying the model on my desk. After a few moments he disclosed that Masri was still on the loose. "But," he said, "we did have one surprise. Harry Issacson told the DA to open his daughter's vault today and exhume the body. We did it today."

"I heard about it," I replied.

Both Jordan and Sennett looked surprised when I told them about my meeting with Issacson. I explained that I didn't realize that it would happen so quickly.

"Ordinarily it wouldn't, but I have something of a personal stake in this deal," Sennett said. I nodded in agreement.

"That's great, so you've got a DNA sample," Jordan said.

"Not exactly," Sennett relied in a dejected tone of voice.

"What does that mean?"

"We opened the vault, but all that was there was an urn full of sand. Someone had already been there and left a note in the casket. Now, without the DNA from her body, we can't compare anything. We're at a dead end."

"Shit. What sickness could make someone do this?" I growled.

"The same sickness that would make a killer take the life of an innocent child." Jordan turned to Sennett with a pained expression on her face. "How can you face Harry Issacson and tell him?"

Sennett turned the model of the larynx in his hands and looked at it for a few moments. I wondered if he was wishing the piece of plastic could speak for him.

"I won't," he said slowly. "At least not now. That poor man has suffered enough. Knowing that someone robbed his daughter's grave would tip him over the brink."

"What did the note say?" Jordan asked.

Sennett, who up until this time seemed under control, squeezed the plastic in his hand until I thought he would break it. "*God and the devil,*" he hissed. "Worse, the press has caught on to this now. They're calling him the FOD killer."

"Huh? What does that mean," I asked.

Sennett shrugged. "Friend of the Devil. And that's exactly what this person is. I think he has us beat."

"Maybe not," I said. "When I met with Harry Issacson this afternoon, he gave me this letter. I think you should look at it." I pulled the note from the woman in Chicago out of my coat and handed it over to Sennett. He scanned it carefully.

"Why didn't Issacson give this to us before?" he muttered.

"I think the police have to change their modus operandi."

Sennett wrote down a few words down on the yellow pad on my desk, then picked up the phone. When he hung up, he dialed another number and had a whispered discussion with some anonymous entity. When he was finished, he turned back to me. "How'd you like to make a trip to Chicago?"

"I thought you'd never ask."

Jordan, however, flashed me a dark, concerned frown. I knew she was worried about my safety. I was concerned too, but for a different reason. Sennett must have felt my anxiety, because he assured me that, as a precaution, his men would keep a close eye on Jordan. The lieutenant was a man of his word.

CHAPTER 21

I SHOULD HAVE KNOWN WE WEREN'T FLYING first class, but taking an early morning ride in Sennett's police issue vehicle wasn't my idea of a pleasant trip to the Windy City. I couldn't blame him for driving. With airport security, you had to get to the terminal two hours ahead of time. Then there was the one-hour flight to Chicago. That is, unless there was a holding pattern at O'Hare. Then a one-hour ride through traffic. Four hours by plane all told. It was four and a half hours by car.

Actually, the drive out I-94 wasn't that bad. Every fifty miles there was another town—Ann Arbor, Jackson, Battle Creek, Kalamazoo, Benton Harbor, Gary. We talked about a lot of things on the way, but mostly golf. I think Sennett dissected every club, every shot, every player on record and quoted freely from books by Hogan, Nicklaus, and Woods. George Sennett was a golf nut. After that he stared at the road ahead and didn't say anything for an hour. I wanted to draw him out by babbling about nothing, but I really didn't have the strength for it.

We stopped in Battle Creek for lunch. In addition to being home to Kellogg's cereal, the town prided itself on being the birthplace of George Armstrong Custer. Sennett found a Tim Horton's at the edge of town, where we ordered two large coffees and a couple of muffins, and then sat down at a small table near the counter. When you traveled with George Sennett, he didn't pad the expense account.

"Where did you learn so much about golf?" I asked. "I always thought of you as a contact sports kind of a guy."

He explained that he had been playing on the public courses for years. He said they called him the King of Palmer Park, the city course near his home. After listening to him talk about golf for two hours, I could understand why.

When he finished his explanation, he took a bite of his muffin, chewed on it for a while, and then looked up at me. "You're probably wondering how I got the department to let you go with me."

I nodded. "I thought they just liked me."

"I told the captain I needed your help,"

"Why? Your trigger finger sprained?"

"There's something about you, Doc."

"What's that?"

"You have a nose for this business, and the chief agrees."

Slightly intimidated by his praise, I felt I had to continue asking George about the case. "What did the Chicago police tell you about the murdered girl in Chicago?"

He went on to describe the murder. Janice Lennell was an eighteen-year-old sophomore at Northwestern. Apparently, she was a straight A student, involved in social causes and student government. She turned up missing one night, and the next day the police found her mutilated body near the stockyards in Chicago, naked and laid across the train tracks. A train had run her over while she was still alive. The police had no suspects in the murder. Initially, they suspected her boyfriend, but he had an air-tight alibi. At the same time a ConEd employee named Scott Terwiliger disappeared. They thought there was a connection, but no one ever found him or his truck.

"Alive?" I asked in disbelief. Sennett nodded. I shivered. "What do you expect I'm going to see in a fifteen-year-old murder?"

"Something I can't. I need to find something, Ben. This might be a big break." He stirred his coffee thoughtfully. "There was something else. The coroner made a note on the autopsy. It was hidden in the report and really didn't mean much until now."

"What's that?"

"He said that there was also a laceration on her left breast. Her nipple and the areola were found in her hand. Did I say that right?"

"Like my anatomy professor."

"Otherwise, the impact from the train's wheels made an almost perfect surgical excision of the limbs," he said clinically.

"Just like Allan Davis said." Sennett looked at me quizzically but didn't ask anything else.

We finished eating, returned silently to the car, and resumed our drive into Indiana and past the dirty steel towns of Hammond and Gary. With the haze from the steel mills filling the air, my mood had darkened considerably. The expressway skirted the rundown houses and partially silent factories that gave a glimpse of the poverty that fomented the unemployment/welfare cycle. Along with it came the gangs and crime that had given the area its reputation.

As we followed the highway along the south shore of Lake Michigan, the traffic became denser. I-94 turned into the Dan Ryan. Tenements housing some of the poorest and most violent neighborhoods in America ringed the highway, and through the middle ran the elevated trains. Chicago had a rep for being the Second City, but like New York, the problems were the same.

It wasn't long before we curved onto Lake Shore Drive, past McCormick Place, Soldier Field, and the Gold Coast. While we drove, Sennett told me what he had found out about Connie Lennell. She was in her early fifties and lived alone in a rented apartment. During the day she worked at Target and at night waited tables at a small diner near the Loop. As he spoke, I looked to the left and saw the Willlis Tower rising like a needle in the sky. Sennett had no trouble negotiating his way through the downtown.

"Like a native Chicagoan," I noted.

"I had a cousin who lived near Wrigley Field," he said. "We used to visit in the summer. I loved watching the Cubs play. Wrigley's the best park in America, that and Fenway. It's where baseball was meant to be played." By this time we had passed the downtown and were turning up Belmont.

"Where are we headed?"

"Lakeview. Mrs. Lennell lives in an apartment on Surf Street. I called a friend of mine at Chicago PD, who arranged for Mrs. Lennell to be there."

With the break for lunch it had taken us about five hours. Right on schedule, we reached a garden apartment complex, where an unmarked car was waiting for us. Out stepped a large man, maybe two hundred and fifty pounds, six-foot-four. He had a freckled, ruddy complexion and a boxer's nose. His name was Lieutenant Kelly Finnegan, and he was part of Sennett's old boy network. They had worked together on a drug killing in Detroit. From the way they shook hands and talked, they must have gotten along well.

We walked to the apartment together. There were eight units in the complex, and Connie Lennell lived on the second floor. It was an unassuming building in a middle class neighborhood. Small, tidy, brick houses and garden-style apartments were clustered along the tree-shadowed streets. The inhabitants were students, young professionals on the way up, and people like Connie Lennell, too old to be upwardly mobile and too young to call the undertaker; all people trapped by economics.

The apartments stood obliquely behind a wrought iron fence. Four story buildings with tight stairwells and no elevators. We walked up a flight of stairs and knocked on the door. Apartment 2C, C. Lennell was written on a little cardholder beneath the doorknocker. I assumed they used the paper nameplate for a reason. It didn't look like people lived in these units for a long time.

The door opened and a smallish woman, thin with large, round glasses, appeared around the corner. She was dressed in a red smock with her name pinned to the front. Below the name it said "Welcome to Target". Connie Lennell must have been five-foot-four if she stood on her tiptoes. She had mousy brown hair and a pale face that seemed to defy makeup. Her eyes looked watery and tired behind her glasses.

Finnegan showed her his badge and then introduced us as a police officer and a doctor from Detroit who had come to speak with her. She opened the door wide and let us in.

At first glance the apartment seemed warm and pleasant. A little kitchen and dining area sat to the right of a small living room. When I looked into the living room, I saw a large crucifix on the wall, surrounded by twenty or thirty photographs depicting a younger Connie Lennell and a pretty young girl, ranging in age from a baby to a teenager. I suspected that that was her daughter, and this was a shrine to her. Ten or twelve neatly labeled cardboard boxes were stacked in the corner nearest to me. I looked down at the boxes, which were filled with hair ribbons, photographs, clothes, and even some empty drug vials. I gazed around the room and peered behind the couch, where dozens of yellowed newspapers were piled in rows under the windowsill. Suddenly, the room didn't seem so neat and pleasant.

Mrs. Lennell must have caught my stare. "Those are my memories. I saved anything that concerned Jannie."

"Sorry, I didn't mean to stare" I apologized.

"It's all right. I haven't had anyone up here in a long time," she said softly. "I guess I can understand. Would you like to sit down?"

"Thank you."

Finnegan stood in the corner and Sennett and I sat in a couple of small armchairs with embroidered seats. I felt like we might have been the first people to use them. When she asked us why we had come to see her, we explained about our meeting with Dr. Harold Issacson and the letter she had written to him. She remembered the letter.

"I used to go to the library once a week," she said in a small voice, "and search for newspapers through the computer to see if there were any murders like my daughter's. Everything I read about, I put down in a book. I tried to keep a record of young people who were murdered."

"Was that because you felt there was a connection?" Sennett asked.

I noticed that Connie's face became more animated, she seemed more alive. "Maybe someone could find the person that killed Jannie."

"There are probably a lot of victims in that book by this time," Sennett remarked.

She sat a little more upright in her chair and looked directly at Finnegan when she spoke. "Unfortunately, yes. But the police couldn't or wouldn't help me. I think they thought I was a nut case. Researching these other murders was all I could do. It was my only hope. I kept writing to people and asking them if they had any clues that might help."

She described her efforts, cutting out newspaper articles, calling the police. According to Connie, the more she called, the more the police shut her out. I glanced over at Finnegan as she spoke. He was shifting from one foot to the other, looking down at the threadbare carpet.

"Lieutenant," Finnegan said defensively, "we have records of Mrs. Lennell's calls at headquarters. We looked into the murders, which she called us on. There were some similarities, but they were all solved."

"How do you know for sure?" I asked.

"We have a clearing house for murders like this," Finnegan explained. "Everything that went on with Janice Lennell and Stacey Issacson and anyone else is fed into a computer, and we've come up with no known connection."

Sennett nodded his head and turned back to Connie. "Did you contact these other people?" Sennett continued.

"I tried. I got newspapers after the murder. I still remember the names: Danielle Ianoulli, Virginia Ulanoff, Peter Davidson, and Helene Gustafson. After the Ianoulli murder, the parents both committed suicide. I can understand it. Relatives of the Gustafson family wrote me back. They expressed their condolences. Both parents were killed in a car accident. I could never find the other families."

"Did the police suspect any foul play in the deaths of the Gustafsons?"

"No. They were hit by a truck on the interstate. It was an accident."

"So, when you found Dr. Issacson, you thought you had a source of information."

"Yeah, but he never wrote me back."

"So that was it."

"What was I going to do? I called his home a couple of times, but he wanted nothing to do with me. After that, I quit. I'm not the police. I began to believe that nothing would happen. I finally gave up."

I reached across the small glass coffee table and picked up a picture of Connie Lennell and her daughter, taken at an amusement park. Both of them were smiling. I didn't see that kind of look in Connie Lennell's face today.

Connie took the picture from me, held it tightly in her hands, and stared at it as if it were holy. "We used to go down to Navy Pier on Lake Michigan a lot. I remember this picture. It was one of the best days of our lives. Jannie had just gotten accepted to Northwestern."

"Who took it? Her father?" I asked.

Another cloud.

Connie looked downcast, her face etched with the kind of resignation that comes from being sent to the principal once too often for discipline. "No, a passerby did. Her father and I divorced shortly after she was born. I haven't seen him since." I remarked to myself that she and Harold Issacson had something else in common.

"Mrs. Lennell," Sennett continued, "the captain here must have told you that the reason Dr. Dailey and I have come is because there might be a lead in the case of a dead boy in Detroit. We're wondering if there could be some similarity to your daughter's death."

When Connie asked how they could determine a connection from this long ago, Sennett said the answer might lie in her daughter's DNA. He seemed reluctant to proceed, almost as if he wanted to make sure she understood. Eventually he told her they wanted to exhume her daughter's body.

Connie sat stone-faced at the request. As we waited for her to reply, the room became eerily silent, except for the buzz of the window air conditioner. After a few moments she began to speak. This time her voice was firm and deliberate. "When Janice died, I was angry. I wrote people. I did things. I don't care anymore. Janice is dead."

"But someone else might die," Sennett said.

"It won't bring Janice back."

"We could get a court order."

"I'm an old woman now. You can do whatever you want. It won't matter. I don't want my daughter's body exhumed on the basis of some guess. I've suffered enough, haven't I?"

That was hard to argue, for sure.

Finnegan turned to Sennett. "Lieutenant, we ought to leave Mrs. Lennell for a while. Let's give her a chance to think this over."

Mrs. Lennell seemed relieved. She looked at her watch.

"I've got to be at work. Please, I must go."

Sennett and Finnegan walked toward the door, but I stayed behind. "Mrs. Lennell, I wonder if I might have a private word with you?" I asked.

"Please, I must go."

"It will only take a second. Can I see what you have on the murders?"

She shrugged her shoulders indifferently, then handed over a large scrapbook filled with newspaper articles, each neatly inscribed in ledger form. Dates and names. Types of murders. Age, sex, location . . . even references to newspaper articles. The murders for the most part happened several years apart. There didn't seem to be any rhyme or reason to the collection. It was a scrapbook of random killings.

"You mentioned there were several murders in particular that you notified the police about," I asked gently. "What were the names again?"

"Danielle Ianoulli, Helene Gustafson, Virginia Ulanoff, and Peter Davidson." Then she calmly began reciting the details as if she was reading from a history book. "Danielle was found with her belly button in her blue jeans. Helene had her stomach opened and her intestines laying on the floor. Virginia had her eyeball opened. Peter had his chest opened and his ribs taken out. I have all the information."

I found it difficult to believe that this woman could be so detached, as she showed me newspaper articles on the murders. "Do you think I could take these with me?" I asked.

"Sure. I have everything written down." She showed me a loose-leaf book with names and dates. I took the articles and put them in my hip pocket. "Now I must . . ."

"He wanted you to have an abortion, didn't he?" I persisted.

She stopped and looked at me. The large glasses gave me an amplified glimpse of the sorrow behind them. She nodded slowly and mournfully. "How did you know?"

"A guess." Maybe it was, but marital conflict wasn't. Hamoud Ishaki's parents split, Harold Issacson's wife left, and I suspected that the Zielinskis had an ugly secret that ran deep in their marriage.

"He didn't believe it was his. We had trouble conceiving, because he had a low sperm count. It was before test tube babies and all these drugs you hear about. I knew he was self-conscious, and all the doctor could do was have us keep a record of temperature, that kind of thing, so we would know when I was ovulating."

"Did you know when conception took place?"

"We had so much trouble, I was never sure." I could tell she was being evasive. Finally, she gave me the open look of trust that patients frequently give doctors before they admit their darkest truths. "Don had another problem."

"What kind of problem?"

"You know, the harder it was to conceive, the harder it was for him to get an erection. We talked about it with a specialist. The doctor called it performance anxiety. Don began to think it was all his fault. It made him feel depressed and inadequate. You would have thought that having his daughter would have made him ecstatic."

"Except that he didn't believe it was his child," I said, sympathetically.

She nodded with surprise. "How did you know?"

"Just a hunch," I said, trying not to sound smart.

"He studied the charts and everything and concluded that I had cheated on him. He told me he wanted an abortion, but after I had waited that long, I was not about to kill my child. I am a good Catholic. I would never have done that."

I decided that it was time to get to the truth. "Did you cheat on him?"

She stared at me for a moment as if searching for something in my words, then she began to cry, not a sobbing cry, but the gentle flow of tears of someone who had almost emptied her emotional bank. "Never, ever. I wouldn't do such a thing. It's one of the commandments. I think we just misjudged the time of conception."

Connie pulled out a small white hanky from her pocket and dabbed at her eyes. "So he waited until the child was born to see if it was his," I said sympathetically.

She nodded again. "She was a beautiful baby. When Don saw the child, he was furious. He said it didn't look like him or me. He said it wasn't his. It was awful. Yelling and screaming at me in the delivery room."

"Is that when he left you?" I asked.

"He never said a word. He left the next day."

"And left you penniless."

"He hired an attorney. He said the child wasn't his."

"Was she?"

Again a silent look.

"I never loved anyone except Don. I never slept with anyone but him. It was his daughter. He just said she didn't look like him."

"And you idolized Janice."

"I had nothing else. No money, no husband, no future. Jannie was everything."

"What about your family?"

"They loved Don. When they found out that he thought Jannie wasn't his, they abandoned me. Every one of them. They were good Catholics. In their eyes I never confessed my sins."

Connie Lennell picked up a scrapbook from one of her cartons and started looking at the pictures.

"Can I see that?"

In response she handed me the scrapbook, and I started leafing through the pages. "That's Jannie on her first day in kindergarten," Connie pointed out. "She was so cute. Always anxious to be involved."

I turned to the next page. "And this?"

"That's Jannie in the school play. She loved being the fish."

I flipped through the pages—Jannie on a pony, Jannie opening a Christmas gift, Jannie being a real person who no longer existed. Then, something at the front caught my eye.

"What is this?" I asked, staring at clear plastic Ziploc bag with some whitish objects in it.

"Those are Jannie's baby teeth. I don't know why I saved them, but I did."

I gazed stupidly at the small ovoid pebbles for a moment. "Mrs. Lennell, you have the potential answer right in front of you."

"What?"

"The teeth. We can use them for the DNA match."

She stared at the keepsake, a jewel never to be lost. "I can't. I can't give them up. It's my memory. I don't care what happens anymore."

"Yes you do," I insisted. "You care about the people who could have been saved, who may yet be saved. I'm sure you do."

She looked around the room, her gaze roving from photo to photo. It was as if she were glancing at old friends.

"There's a chance that you, too, could be saved, Connie."

"What do you mean?"

I walked over to the window for a moment and looked through the city-grimed panes at Finnegan and Sennett standing by the car. Finnegan had a cigarette in his hand and was puffing casually. I remembered Connie's words— the police couldn't or wouldn't. "I mean that you have been carrying the guilt of something you didn't do for over twenty years," I said, caught up in the heat of discovery. "It's time you did something for yourself. You did nothing wrong. Prove it. This is your chance. If the DNA matches with the other victims, we will establish a connection to all these murders. A killer is on the loose, maybe the same one that killed your daughter."

"But if the DNA matches the other murdered children, won't it mean that this person was the father? That would mean I cheated on Don. I swear by Our Lord Jesus Christ, that never happened."

"I believe you, Connie. Something has happened to you and several other people. How it has happened, I don't know, but it has ruined lives and killed children. This killer has killed at least three times, maybe more. Who knows how many?"

"Finding the killer won't bring Jannie back," she said gazing absently into the distance.

"Remember how you felt when you sent that letter to Dr. Issacson?"

"I sent that letter because I knew he ran an abortion clinic. That's what it said in the paper. I wanted him to know how wrong it was."

I was desperate. In that small plastic bag was the answer. In the heart of Connie Lennell was a grief so walled off and a religious fervor so permanent that almost no amount of persuasion could penetrate them. "Whatever the reason," I said, "you also wanted to find your daughter's killer. At one time you had a passion. You lost it in fighting the bureaucracy, and in your own misery. People can only take so much, and then they give up. It's human nature. Now you have a second chance."

She looked at me, and this time her eyes were focused intently.

"I talked with Dr. Issacson," I told her. "He understands, Connie, he understands. He doesn't want to kill babies. He wanted to help unfortunate girls. He told me he understood how you felt."

"I'll bet he did . . ." she retorted bitterly. Then her face opened as if releasing the evils of the world from a tight-packed box. "Really?"

I nodded. She looked for a moment. Tears welled in her eyes again and this time flowed in rivulets down her cheeks. "I have nothing," she said through her tears. "My husband is gone. I have had the scarlet A on my chest all my life." She took the small bag that contained the teeth and held it close to her chest, as if she were holding her child. Then she handed it to me. "Jannie was my one connection to society. If these teeth will help, then use them. Please."

I took the small plastic bag and folded the top. Then I hugged her. She flinched slightly at the unaccustomed warmth, then hugged me back with all her strength.

When I walked back out to the car, I didn't feel triumphant. I only felt sadness and confusion. Marital loyalty, the possibility of infidelity, the chance of abortion. It was unsettling.

Sennett was still standing next to the car with Finnegan. "What did you find out, Ben?"

"Well, I have baby teeth from the dead girl."

Sennett raised his eyebrows. "That should be enough to run a DNA test," he said, a touch of excitement in his voice.

"Mrs. Lennell also told me about the other murders that she thinks were similar."

Sennett seemed pleased with my discovery. "See, I told the chief that you had something special. Have you got the names?" he asked.

"Sure." I handed the newspaper articles over to him. He took out his cell phone, called Homicide in Detroit, and gave them the names and dates. "I want everything on my desk tomorrow," he demanded.

BY NOW IT WAS LATE AFTERNOON and we still couldn't decide whether to have the DNA tests on Janice Lennell's teeth run in Chicago or Detroit. It wasn't much of a decision. The prospect of driving another five hours made up our minds for us. We decided to take the specimen back to Detroit the next day and booked a room at a Holiday Inn near the loop. I thought it was a little fancy, but Sennett assured me it was on the department.

When I got to the room, I called Jordan. She said everything was fine and to tell Sennett she appreciated the police watching the house. I did too, I figured I'd sleep easier. I was wrong. After listening to Sennett snore all night, I spent breakfast trying to convince him he should get a sleep study. He wasn't buying what I was selling. From the distracted look on his face I knew his mind was elsewhere.

I tried making some small talk on the way back from Chicago, but for the most part, Sennett seemed deep in thought. Around Kalamazoo, however, he started talking, his voice was low and solemn. "Doc, did you ever lose anyone you thought you could save?"

I looked at him for a moment, not sure of what he was getting at. "Yeah, it's inevitable that some patients will die."

"No, I mean where it was your *fault*."

Sennett stared ahead at the road, staying in the right lane and easing the accelerator a touch. I knew he wasn't looking for doctor-speak.

"When I was a first-year resident," I told him, settling back into the car seat, "the chief resident sent me in to do a bronchoscopy on an indigent patient from the clinic. That's a procedure where you examine the inside of someone's lung. The patient had a cancer treated a few years prior and had been coughing up some blood."

"What happened?"

"I remember the situation as if it were yesterday. We were in the old county hospital. It was the middle of the summer, hot with no air conditioning. Only screens and fans to circulate the air. It must have been ninety degrees outside, and under the operating gown it was sweltering. It sounds terrible, but the county hospitals were a good place to learn.

"I had been a resident for about two months. In the operating room, it was just me and the second-year resident. I had performed a couple of the procedures before. At that stage of my education you could never do enough of them."

"Was there an attending physician there?" Sennett asked.

"Back in those days the residents ran the service. There was always someone you could call if you needed them."

"So what happened?"

I described the procedure in detail, how I put the long metal bronchoscope into the patient's lung and saw what I thought was a lesion.

"What happened?"

"I inserted an up-biting cup forceps into the bronchoscope and reached in to take a bite. As soon as I pulled the forceps out with the tissue, blood started erupting from the bottom of the scope."

It was difficult for me, even now, to discuss the episode. Nurses and other doctors running into the room, blood everywhere, and me sitting there with a feeling of abject helplessness as the patient bled to death. After listening to the story, Sennett stared ahead at the road. It took a few moments for him to speak. "That poor guy. What did you say to the family?"

"There was no one there. He was by himself. I didn't know who to talk with."

"You must have been devastated."

"Honestly, I felt like I was viewing this happening to someone else. I didn't know what to think. I went through a period of self-recrimination, wondering whether I had the right stuff to do this kind of work."

"What did you do?"

"I decided that I was not going to quit. Instead, I went to the library and started reading about what I had done wrong. They had a conference the next Saturday, and I had to present the case. I was pretty nervous. The chief was there and all the other residents, but I didn't try to hide anything and didn't try to blame anyone else. I told it like it was. It was pretty amazing the support I got from the other residents and the staff. They really helped."

"Did you do another one of those procedures?"

"The next week. It went without a hitch. But I have never forgotten the episode. Every time I go into the operating room, I think about that case and what happened. Things like that have a way of humbling you." Sennett watched the road intently, his face grim. "George, I know you too well. You didn't ask me that question just to find out if I had made any mistakes in my life."

There were no challenges on the road, especially in the right lane. Yet Sennett barely breathed. "It's all these murders. I wanted to ask you how you deal with things when they go really bad. I feel that this murderer is inside my head."

"Sometimes the truth can be hard to pin down," I replied. "Just look at Connie Lennell and her newspapers and boxes of memorabilia scattered around her apartment. Her search for the truth seems to have no end."

"Maybe it has. We'll have to see if Mrs. Lennell has given us anything substantial within the contents of that plastic bag."

"What about the other two deaths in the newspaper articles?" I asked.

"I don't know. I just don't know." The confusion in his voice insinuated itself in me like a cold, damp fog.

I looked at Sennett's face. His jaw was set, his eyes narrow and steely. Then he reached over, picked up his cell phone, and dialed Florence Clevenger. "Hey, Flo," he said, his voice surprisingly cool. "I'm dropping something off."

CHAPTER 22

I WAS IRRITABLE DURING THE ENTIRE RIDE home. It was the kind of unsettling crankiness that lasts all day and demeans my afternoon patients' complaints. By the time I picked up Jordan at her office, I thought I was starting to come out of my funk. On the way home I related my visit with Connie Lennell. It was almost as an afterthought inside the foyer when Jordan told me Carl Fairchild had invited us to his house for dinner tonight.

I was tempted to call with our regrets, but I felt obligated. He was a colleague and, behind his intellectual arrogance, a pretty interesting person. If he were extending the hand of friendship, I would take it. Then Jordan reminded me of their conversation at the art institute, as they discussed the nuances of Van Gogh's painting. The words *charming* and *interesting* didn't help my cause. So we went.

Fairchild lived on the northwest side of Detroit in an area called Palmer Woods. In the fifties it was Detroit's premier residential neighborhood, boasting large brick and stone Tudor houses, manicured lawns, and long, black Sedan DeVilles in every driveway. But time had deteriorated the city, and the rich professionals and businessmen who once inhabited Palmer Woods had long since bolted for the comfort and safety of the suburbs. Now, not every house had a Cadillac out front, but there was enough stateliness left so that the area retained much of its *panache*.

I had been invited to parties in Palmer Woods several times before. The people there still doggedly clung to the heritage of large houses and conspicuous consumption. They generally dressed stylishly, the men sporting silk ties of raucous design to contrast with the staid dark business suits they wore to work, the women careful not to let their hair or tailored suits look too Martha

Stewart. Even an economic downturn couldn't pluck the graceful old oaks and maples from their roots or mar the columns and gables that graced the houses.

Fairchild lived in one of the larger homes at the north end of Palmer Woods, at the end of a cul de sac that bordered a cemetery. As we drove up, my first thought was that, for a single person, it seemed a bit much. Four car garage, six bedrooms, seemingly endless gardens. Then I remembered Larry Schneider telling me that Fairchild had bought the house for a song from someone who had lost his shirt in the market downturn of 2000. I pulled into the brick-paved driveway, where three Beemers and a Land Cruiser were already defending the garage from the likes of my old Jeep. Fairchild greeted us at the front door. He was resplendent in a dark blue silk blazer, light peach linen shirt, white slacks, and sockless Cole Haans. He seemed happy to see us, but who could really know with him. He reached out and took Jordan's hand. "So nice to have you over," he said, smiling broadly.

"It's nice to be here," I replied.

He shook my hand. "Ben, have you got an anesthesiologist for Jordan? It looks like it's getting close." He seemed so different from the person I had seen at the hospital. Gone was the aloof, aristocratic east coast snob. He radiated a pleasant aura of suave urbanity that one could almost call delightful.

"The doctor says another month or so," Jordan answered.

"You know, doctors are like weathercasters predicting the next big storm," he said. "It's always a guess."

We laughed. I handed Fairchild a bottle Rutherford Hill merlot, my favorite wine.

"Thank you. Come on in. The guests are all on the patio." He led us through the wood-paneled entrance foyer, his shoes clicking on the polished slate floor. He stopped under the ornate chandelier.

"Your house is beautiful, Carl," Jordan commented.

"Would you like to see it?"

"Sure."

He turned to his left and showed us down another paneled hallway into the living room, a large space with stark white walls, black marble floors, and delicately modern furniture. "I've tried to incorporate different styles in each of my rooms. This is the modern room."

I looked around at the upholstered plexiglass chairs, freeform cocktail table, and couches that looked good in *Interior Design*, but were most likely impossible to sit on. Jordan looked at some of the wall art and began discussing the various painters. While she did, I strolled down the hallway and looked at the other rooms, an art deco library, a French provincial-styled sitting room, and past a room with intricately carved wooden doors. They were closed.

Before I could wonder what was behind the door, Fairchild was by my side. "Is that your study?" I asked.

"It is. I call it my sanctuary. I've been remodeling it, changing the ceilings and the lighting. I'm not ready to show it off yet. But I think the artwork in the room will be spectacular. It's going to have a Mission look to it."

I was about to say something else, when he grabbed me gently by the arm and said dinner was being served. He took us through the sitting room and past a state of the art kitchen, complete with two gas stoves, granite islands, and two cooks busily preparing a variety of dishes. To the right of the kitchen I saw the dining room with ornately carved beams and a large crystal chandelier glittering over an immaculately set table.

"What's for dinner? It smells terrific," I gushed. I was well on the way to nauseating myself with my charm.

"Broiled Alaskan char in a light beurre blanc sauce, Mediterranean couscous, and a side of mushrooms Florentine." He gestured broadly, as proudly as if he had actually dipped a ladle or turned a knob himself.

"My favorite." As I spoke, I thought about the Tums residing in my medicine chest.

A bell rang just as he spoke, and Fairchild walked us into the great room that overlooked his backyard. It was a large comfortable space with a wooden-beamed ceiling and overstuffed leather chairs. A huge floor-to-ceiling window overlooked the patio and the sparkling pool. Red and blue lights played off the pool's bottom. Other guests were out on the patio, holding drinks in their hands. Carl stepped outside and called them in.

Once back inside, he walked us all into the dining room, making introductions; a circuit court judge and a lawyer I had read about in the newspaper, the director of the symphony orchestra, a newspaper editor, the mayor and his wife, and last, but certainly not least, Julie McFarland. Not a bad collection of guests for a simple, low-brow repast.

Fairchild had Jordan sit to his left and Julie to the right at the polished mahogany dinner table as we drank red wine and talked. I was sandwiched between the orchestra and the law. The conversation was lively, and the food and wine were excellent. Fairchild took great pride in the wine, a 1986 barolo that he had picked up on a trip to Italy. I had to admit it was good.

Most of the discussion at the table was about the revival of the city. None of the schemes seemed plausible, but I didn't want to ruin anyone's dinner, so I kept quiet. Every now and then I would glance over at Jordan. Fairchild seemed engrossed in his conversation with her, but I wasn't so sure about Jordan. As for myself, I looked at the people assembled and the spread that Fairchild had arranged and wondered why I was here. Was it because of Jordan and her interest in art, or was Fairchild merely being friendly? It made me feel uneasy.

A little after ten, when the flourless chocolate cake had been served and the Columbian Supremo coffee had been poured, I could feel Jordan's gaze on my face. It was our signal that she was tiring. The guests were starting to get up from the table, and I took it as a cue to move over to Jordan's side. "You look tired." She nodded.

I turned to Carl and told him that I thought it was time to take Jordan home. He tried to persuade us to stay, indicating that Felix was going to play some Chopin etudes, but I declined. Fairchild seemed to understand and suggested that we do it again. Jordan said it would be nice, thanked him, and shook his hand. He held it for a second longer than I liked.

"Remember, Ben," he said jokingly, "if you need an anesthesiologist for the delivery, call me any time."

"Thanks, Carl. I'll remember that," I replied, hoping he wouldn't be on call the night that Jordan delivered.

When we got back in the car, Jordan slumped in her seat.

"Whew, I'm glad that's over."

"Why? You looked like you were having a good time."

"What, watching his girlfriend climb all over him?"

"Julie has two assets," I replied.

"I know, they're on her chest."

"No, that's not what I meant. She knows men like sex, and she likes to offer it."

"Oh."

"Don't worry. I don't like easy women with big breasts."

Jordan looked down at her protruding abdomen and chest. "What does that mean?"

"I mean that you're beautiful and it's not just your looks."

I drove away from the big house, still feeling uneasy. Fairchild was enigmatic. I could never read him, and, inevitably, he made me feel uncomfortable when I was around him. But then I felt the same way about Larry Schneider. Maybe it was something about the two of them.

I DIDN'T SLEEP WELL THAT NIGHT, suffering from the after effects of a rich dinner, the stress of the case, Jordan's impending delivery, and jitters about the wedding.

I had vowed not to let Ahmad Masri and the deaths of those young people get in the way of this special time, but I was getting in more deeply with each new revelation. Nor did my near-death experience ease my mind.

I got up early the next morning, checked my mail on the computer for half an hour, and went to the kitchen. I was surprised when Jordan came into the room. She poured herself a cup of decaf and maneuvered into a chair. Even though the morning sun was streaming into the room, she hugged her cup, as if her body needed warming. "I didn't sleep well last night, Ben."

"Are you all right?"

She shook her head. "It's not the pregnancy. Something's bothering me about this whole business, but I can't bring it to the surface. Do you still think that Masri was involved?"

"The DNA findings aren't consistent," I said. "They found DNA from the dead boys in Masri's home and in his car, but there was no paternity between him and the victims. It doesn't make sense. We know he's not the father, but I suppose he could be involved somehow. From what I've seen, he had ample motive to kill Bill Yaldo."

"What about the other murders in Chicago and Cleveland? They had nothing to do with Masri."

"It's true, Yaldo's murder was unlike the others," I said. "Maybe there were two killers, or maybe Masri and the killer were somehow a tandem."

Jordan was about to say something else when the phone rang. It was Sennett. He apologized for calling so early.

"What's the verdict?" I asked.

"Ben, the DNA from Connie Lennell's daughter was an exact match to the Ishaki and Zielinski boys." Sennett's voice was slow, measured, and police-hard, as the words echoed from the phone.

I sat there like a not-very-bright rock, trying to fathom the meaning of the news. Even though I had tossed around the possibility, the turn of events made my skin crawl. "How . . . how can this be?"

"Somewhere, somehow, the killer has met up with these women," Sennett droned.

We discussed the various possibilities, and came to the conclusion that Connie Lennell had nothing else to offer. She said she did not have an extramarital affair. Either she was lying or in denial or something else happened. At any rate, it was probably a dead-end to go back to her.

"That leaves Mrs. Zielinski," I said.

I waited for Sennett to respond, wondering what kind of deranged mind was out there concocting horrible and bizarre ways to kill innocent people. It gave me a sick feeling, the kind that wouldn't go away until the murderer was caught. I was brought out of my thoughts by Sennett's voice.

"Right. We have to talk with the Zielinskis again, but it's going to be a tough interview. I wondered if Jordan would come along. She seemed to have some rapport with the family. They might be more willing to talk with her."

"Pregnancy has a way of getting sympathy," I agreed, nodding with a weak smile at my startled bride-to-be.

"Ben, we have a serial killer that defies logic," Sennett murmured in his deepest bass profundo. "We need everything we can get."

We spoke for a few more minutes, mostly about the cases Connie Lennell had given me. They turned out, as Sennett said, to be pretty worn out. Worn out was a pretty good word for the way I felt. Where would the killer strike next, when would I receive another note, and was I a target? It made no sense, yet it seemed certain that someone was going to die soon.

CHAPTER 23

Jordan and I met Sennett at the Zielinski home on a humid, hot day, over-cast with scudding clouds that dripped with the prospect of rain. There was a scent of thunderstorms in the distance, a good sign for a community that hadn't seen a significant downpour in almost a month. I thought about how fitting the weather was for such an unpleasant encounter.

Sennett stepped out of his car with a few papers in his hand. "Here are some notes on those other murders you asked me about," he said, handing me some Xerox copies. "I can't make anything out of them, except that they were solved. Maybe you can find something."

I took the papers and put them in my pocket as we walked up the front sidewalk. John Zielinski came to the door and let us in. He was wearing a worn Central Michigan University t-shirt, faded blue jeans, and an angry expression. I probably would have been upset too, if I had been in his shoes.

He ushered us into the living room. As I looked around, I noticed that it was a lot different than the last time I had been there. Scattered around the room were a couple of open pizza boxes, some paper plates, and three or four opened cans of soda on the coffee table and even the floor.

Mrs. Zielinski was sitting on the couch, her hair pulled back in a ponytail. She wore no makeup and her red, swollen eyes stared off into the distance, as if she were waiting for someone to come home.

John Zielinski sat down on the couch a sizeable distance away from his wife. Jordan went to the large easy chair, and Sennett and I stood. It was us against them.

Jordan started talking. "We have a lead regarding your son's death. It's a complicated story, but we need your help. Some of the things I might ask you today may not seem very pertinent and may even anger you. I want you to know that we are not trying to antagonize you."

"What kind of information? It's too late for our son. As far as I can see, the police did nothing," Zielinski said defiantly.

"I know this is difficult. Everyone tried. But we may be up against a killer far more malicious than we ever thought." Jordan spoke with a soothing, controlled voice.

"What do you mean?" Zielinski demanded.

"I want to ask you a question. I know that it is going to be difficult to answer, because it's a personal question about your marriage," Jordan said.

I studied John Zielinski. His hands were clasped in front of him, the blood squeezed out of his fingers. His faced was bathed in consternation, his brow scrunched into a furrow and a glance that focused inward, almost cross-eyed. "What do you mean?" he snapped again.

"I need to know from your wife if she ever had a relationship outside of your marriage before Brett was born," Jordan said softly but firmly.

John Zielinski sprang from his seat and rushed over to where Jordan was sitting. Sennett moved at the same time, like a cat springing at its prey. Before I could react, he was standing between Zielinski and Jordan. I was surprised how fast a big man like Sennett could move.

"How dare you ask my wife that question? I don't give a fuck about your sanctimonious questions. My son is dead. It does no good. Get out, now!"

Jordan stayed calm. After all, even though she was pregnant, she was still a Fed. "Mr. Zielinski, we found out about a girl who was murdered in Chicago twelve years ago. She had the same DNA as your son and Hamoud Ishaki."

Zielinski stopped, almost as if he knew the answer to the question he was about to ask. "So . . . so what does that mean?" he stammered.

"It means that each of these victims had the same father," Jordan answered quietly.

Zielinski's broad shoulders and neck dropped into a hypnotic slump. His hands guarded his head gingerly, as if he had nowhere to put it down. Mrs. Zielinski calmly sat and watched her husband. After a few moments, John stood up, looked around dully, and then finally focused on his wife. "I knew Brett wasn't my child," he growled. "Mary Anne knew too."

"Why were you so sure, Mr. Zielinski?" Jordan asked swiftly.

"She was sick during the time Brett would have been conceived. I don't remember the details, but I know we didn't have relations during that time."

"Is that true, Mrs. Zielinski?" Jordan asked, smoothly interrogating the witness.

Mary Anne Zielinski looked vacantly at her husband. The defeat in this war had occurred long ago, and she was numb from captivity. When she wouldn't answer, Jordan took another tactic.

"Mrs. Zielinski, I'm carrying a child as well." Still no answer. Jordan continued. "Had you ever thought about an abortion?"

Suddenly, she picked her head up. Light flashed from her eyes. Jordan had skill as a cross-examiner. She knew how to find just the right word to awake the witness.

"Never!" Mary Anne cried. "The Lord created children to live, not die."

"What about Brett's genetic parent? Did you ever have communication with him about your pregnancy?"

"I don't know. I don't remember."

John Zielinski stood up. "How can you not remember? Mary Anne, you are our only chance to find Brett's killer. The DNA indicates that Brett's father was the killer."

She had a paper napkin in her hands, which she twisted back and forth in her fingers. All the while she remained silent.

"This is the same answer I've been given for seventeen years." John Zielinski sighed as he got up and paced the room. "I tried to understand. It got to the point where we stopped talking about it. I gave up ever knowing the truth."

"Had you ever sought professional help?" Jordan continued.

John went on to describe a series of psychiatric sessions, which ended without any progress. He said the last diagnosis from the doctor was that she was in denial. When Jordan asked him if he had ever met Ahmad Masri, the acid returned to his voice as he accused the police of letting a guilty man go free.

Sennett responded quickly. "Mr. Zielinski, the police had nothing to do with letting Mr. Masri out of jail. That was the judge's decision. But as a police officer, I am working day and night to bring him and anyone else who perpetrated this crime to justice."

"Too little, too late."

I could see that Sennett was trying his best to ignore the sarcasm. But what could he say? Zielinski was right. He was about to respond when Jordan spoke up. "I think we should leave, Lieutenant," Jordan said.

I knew the bulldog in Sennett wanted to stay, but slowly he got up. We made our way to the front door. Mary Anne Zielinski stayed in her seat on the couch, while John Zielinski stood in the middle of the living room. We let ourselves out.

We walked outside and stood by Sennett's car as he fumbled for his keys in his pants pocket. A group of young kids was playing down the street on a plastic water slide. The shrieks and laughter in their voices were a stark contrast to the grim Zielinski household.

Sennett looked at the children and then turned to Jordan. "Do you think you quit too early on them? I thought maybe you were making some headway."

"You saw it, George, there was nowhere to go. She wasn't going to tell us anything else, and that's that."

He nodded in resignation as we got back in the car and headed downtown. "What a shame. We're so close. If we could only get these women to talk," Sennett interjected, as he started the car and drove away from the Zielinski's house.

"Maybe they've told us all they know and we're not listening," I interjected.

"What do you mean?" Sennett asked.

"I mean, maybe she's telling the truth and didn't have an extramarital affair," I said matter-of-factly.

Sennett looked at me incredulously, like I was joking. "Great. Now that's a real good explanation. The only other time that was supposed to have happened, it changed the world forever." Sennett fixed his eyes on the road. He turned off I-75 at Mack and headed past the cultural center without saying anything else. Judging from his silence, I decided not to press the issue. Not at the moment, anyway.

Sennett dropped us off at police headquarters, where we had left our cars. Jordan and I asked him if he wanted lunch, but he declined brusquely. It wasn't like him.

I got back in the car with Jordan, who looked pale and tired.

"Are you okay?" I asked.

"Just the heat, and I'm hungry. The baby has been kicking a lot."

"We'll stop at Gus's. I wanted to see him anyway."

She paused for a moment and stared out the window. "Ben, I've been thinking. I really believe these women didn't know who the father was."

"It's hard to fathom, but I get the same impression."

"If they didn't know, then maybe they should have had an abortion. What do you think?" she asked.

"Jordan," I said, looking across at her, "when I can get pregnant, I'll deserve a vote on that question."

Jordan looked at me with raised eyebrows. Then she said, "I can tell you one thing. I understand how they felt. No matter what, I would never get an abortion. I want this baby more than anything I have ever wanted."

"I'm glad, honey," I said to her, reaching over and taking her hand.

We got out of the car and were greeted by the hot and muggy wind from the southwest, blowing like a blast furnace in our face. The promised rain still hadn't arrived, and the newspapers were making dire predictions of drought, water rationing, and burnt-up lawns. After a while you began to believe what they said.

We walked into Gus's place and sat at a corner table, looking out across the street. When Gus saw us, he hurried over.

"Hey, what's the matter? You guys look like you have the weight of the world on your shoulders."

"We do."

We ordered and sat back in the booth. Neither of us said anything until Gus came back with our food. He set the tray down in front of us. I looked up at him for a moment. There was a reason why I had come down here. Gus was my sounding board, a voice of simple reason that I had come to depend on. "Tell me, Gus. You've got a woman. She gets pregnant and then can't remember the man who did it."

"I see that all the time. They're a few hookers that work this area. Once in a while, one of them gets knocked up. They can't remember the father."

"It's not like that, Gus. These women aren't prostitutes."

Gus crossed himself. "Mother of Jesus. I knew a young girl back in the old country. She got pregnant. Nice family. Nobody could figure it out, until the girl comes clean and tells her father that her uncle did it." He told us they found the uncle tied behind a boat in the ocean. The crabs had gotten to him by the time he washed ashore.

Jordan, who was halfway through her sandwich, smiled up at him. "Too bad revenge doesn't work like that in America. We have a legal system that sometimes gets in the way."

"Yeah, well the legal system doesn't always work," Gus muttered. "Take the doc, here. He's got class, he's the kind of doctor everyone would want to go to."

"I'll drink to that," I said. "What's your point?"

"Well, you talk about having someone else's baby. They had this thing in *People* magazine about this doctor who lived in North Carolina, Cecil Jones or something like that. He was a female doctor. You know, he helped women have babies. You heard of them? They're called fertilizing specialists or something like that."

"It's fertility specialist, Gus, but what's the difference?"

He snapped his fingers like he suddenly remembered something. "Yeah, you know me, Doc, my English isn't always the best."

"And my Greek isn't so good either, so we're a pair of matched bookends. Now what was your point?"

"According to the article, they use other people for the sperm to fertilize the woman's egg. Seems kind of funny, but I thought maybe I'd be a donor. Easy money and someone would like to have my Greek bloodline. Kind of spreading the wealth." Gus winked. "And the work's kind of fun, too."

"Okay, Gus. I'll put your phone number on the obstetrics bulletin board. What happened with Cecil Jones?"

"Seems as though he thought a lot about himself, too."

"How so?"

"Every woman he fertilized was with his own sperm. He has dozens of Cecil Joneses walking around."

"Being a doctor allows you to exercise amazing power, Gus," I said.

"Yeah, but in the wrong hands it could be dangerous."

"*Primum non nocere.*"

"Huh?"

"*First do no harm.*"

"You doctors all use those Latin terms. They must give you lessons on how to speak so nobody will understand you. It makes you look smart."

"Actually, I got that one from the lawyers, during my lawsuit," I said.

Jordan put the unfinished part of her sandwich on her tray and shifted out of the seat. Gus looked perplexed, as if he had said something wrong. "What'sa matter, Jordan? Aren't you feeling good?" Gus asked.

"No, I'm tired, I just need to rest. Maybe we should go, Ben."

I didn't know what was bothering her, but I told Gus to wrap up the food, and we'd take it home. He seemed a little concerned about Jordan, but I told him not to worry and left a twenty on the table.

We walked out of the diner into the sweltering heat of late afternoon. When we got to the car, I opened the doors to let the heat out. As I did, I looked across the street again at the people working the slots. Nothing had changed, only the faces.

We got into the car and waited for the air conditioning to kick in. It was almost too hot to talk. After a minute of staring at the thermostat and feeling the cold air coming out of the vent, Jordan turned to me. "Three women with the same DNA and no known contact with the father," she said. "What about some kind of artificial insemination?"

I blinked a couple of times, as if a light had suddenly shone through the windshield. "I knew I could depend on Gus," I said.

CHAPTER 24

I BROUGHT JORDAN BACK TO THE TOWNHOUSE, but even with food, she continued to look fatigued. The heat didn't help. Ninety-degree weather with eighty percent humidity was as bad as a snowstorm in January. All you wanted to do was to stay inside. Then I thought about winter, the frigid temperatures, ankles deep in salt slush, and heavy clothes. It's a Midwesterner's dilemma.

Jordan changed into her pajamas and decided to spend the rest of the day on the couch. Once I got her settled with the remote and a glass of lemonade, I went to the study and looked through some papers I had on my desk. Among them were Connie Lennell's and Mary Anne Zielinski's phone numbers. It took a phone call to Sergeant Knudsen and an hour of impatient waiting to discover that the two women had different obstetricians. So much for Jordan's insemination theory.

Still, I thought, it was worth a call. Riley Jackson was Lennell's obstetrician. He had retired a few years ago, but I found his old office phone number through the AMA. According to the person I spoke with at Metropolitan Obstetrics, he had moved five years ago to a place in northern Michigan. It took another call to the American Academy of Obstetrics and Gynecology to find him. He lived near Elk Rapids, Michigan.

Retirement doesn't mean uselessness. Unfortunately, physicians who don't practice are like engines without cars. As soon as their practices stop, they are left out on the scrap heap by their public. I call them "used-to-be-doctors." But retirement isn't death, and retired physicians still remembered who they were and what they could do. That could be one of the reasons they loved to talk medicine with anyone who would listen. When I called, I found that Riley Jackson was no exception.

"Dr. Jackson, my name is Ben Dailey. I'm a physician in Detroit."

"What can I do for you, Dr. Dailey?" The voice was strong.

"There's an old patient of yours named Connie Lennell that I wanted to talk with you about."

There was a pause at the other end of the line. "I remember her well."

"Why?"

"Say, I'm not sure I should be talking with you. I may be old, but I still respect the Hippocratic Oath."

"Understood. What can I do to reassure you? This is very important."

"Where did you go to medical school?"

"Michigan, class of '72."

"My alma mater. Who was the professor of anatomy?" Jackson was no dummy.

"Russell Woodburne."

"Physiology?"

"Halvor Christianson."

"Okay, you pass. What's your specialty?"

"I do mostly voice work."

"Ah, an otorhinolaryngologist. If I hadn't been so interested in bringing new life into the world, I probably would have gone into that," he said with a sigh.

He spent the next five minutes telling me about his practice, his retirement, and his exercise program that would have sent me to the hospital.

"You sound like you are in pretty good shape."

"Yeah, I still jog and do calisthenics. I was on the gymnastics team in college. Used to be a cheerleader. Would you believe, I can still do a handstand at 78?"

"Amazing! I'm lucky if I can get out of bed in the morning." Then I told him he sounded too young to have stopped practicing. That opened the floodgates.

"I should never have quit practicing. I loved it."

"How come you did?"

"My associates. My partner and I were getting older, so we took in a couple of young kids. It all revolved around money. They thought they were so smart. An old fart like me was just in the way."

"There's nothing like experience."

"Yeah, they might have known molecular cell biology, but I could sit down with a woman and diagnose her problem in five minutes of talking." He spent another five minutes telling me about the practice of obstetrics, including the fact that you divide physicians by studying their physiques. He said most obstetricians were endomorphs.

After listening patiently, I figured I'd take the initiative. "Did Connie Lennell have a problem?"

"In what way?"

"This might be hard for you to understand, but I've been involved in a murder case."

"Wait a minute, are you some kind of criminal trying to get off the hook?"

I laughed. "No, I've been asked by the police to help them investigate a series of murders."

"A surgeon who's a detective . . . that's a new one to me."

"I know it sounds strange, but it's the truth." I was going to tell him I had a badge, but I didn't think he would believe me anyway.

"I'll tell you what. Before I answer any more questions, give me the name of the police official you've been dealing with. I'll call him and then call you back. You sound honest, but I've got to be sure."

Riley Jackson was no old fool. I gave him Sennett's name and cell phone. It took about ten minutes, but the phone rang. It was Jackson.

"Lieutenant Sennett says you're for real. I asked him how come a doctor was working on a murder case. He said that you've been helpful on a number of cases that he's dealt with over the years and asked if I would help you in any way I could. Yes, it does sound strange . . . a doctor investigating a murder."

"Sometimes I can't understand it myself," I responded truthfully enough. "I'm not sure if this is going to go anywhere, but I'd like to ask a few questions. You said you remembered Mrs. Lennell well."

"I do. It was one of the saddest cases I had ever had during my practice."

"Why?"

"Connie was a devout Catholic. For her to have an affair like that was a sin from which she could never recover."

"Did she tell you she had extramarital relations?"

"Not exactly. I assumed it." There was a lack of confidence in his voice. Then he continued. "Whatever it was, it ruined her marriage."

"But not her life. She still had the child."

"That girl was her whole life. Then Janice was murdered. I honestly don't know how that woman has survived."

I paused a moment for dramatic effect. "What if I told you that her murder was linked to several others? And that each of the other children had the same father."

"In Chicago?"

"No, the others were in Detroit."

"Any luck in discovering the father?"

"That's the problem. Each of the mothers has denied an affair. At least I can't get any information from them."

Couldn't or wouldn't get any information from them. The thought suddenly crossed my mind that if these two women weren't lying to protect something or someone, then they must have been unconscious when they were inseminated. I dismissed the thought as impossible

"Well, I'm not sure how I can help you solve this mystery . . ."

"The question arises as to whether these women were artificially inseminated."

"Not by me, doctor." There was an indignant tone in his voice.

"No implication to you," I explained hastily. "These women had different doctors. I'm just trying to find out something from their medical history that might give me a clue."

"Connie had a normal delivery, as far as I remember. Other than some back problems, she was a pretty healthy person."

"Did she have an internist?"

"No, like a lot of women, she relied on me for all her medical care."

Another dead end. "I suppose if someone was going to artificially inseminate a woman, she'd know about it."

"You have that right, doctor. She would have had to be drunk or taking drugs to have that happen," he laughed, "and that wasn't Connie Lennell."

Something about the way he said drunk or taking drugs struck me as peculiar, but I didn't have time to think about it. Riley started on a long discourse about Elk Rapids, and as soon as he mentioned how good the sailing was, I lost the train of thought. The sleeper area in Northern Michigan is what he called it, great beaches and not a lot of people. He even invited me to come up and see him. I think the idea of a doctor investigating murders had intrigued him. It made me feel a little strange, but I told him I'd look him up if I was in the area and thanked him.

It was around three in the afternoon when I went back to check on Jordan and found her asleep on the couch. I left a note for her on the table, closed the door quietly, and got into my car. Before I left, I checked for the blue sedan at the corner. When I saw it, I raised my hand and nodded.

IT TOOK A FEW MINUTES of driving to meet Sennett at a shopping center a couple of miles from our house. I left my car and we drove north in his sedan toward Maple Lake in the northern suburbs of Detroit. In other places, Maple Lake would be called Maple Pond, but in this exclusive area, anything bigger than a wading pool was deemed to be a lake. It was good for the real estate business.

The developers divided the land so that each homeowner got his 100 feet on the water. Then they let the builders have at it. Architectural control in these subs was an oxymoron. One ten thousand square foot house after another. Looking at the backside of these houses by the lake, I'm sure it appeared like a hodgepodge canyon of brick, steel, and glass.

Jack Weldon's house was no exception. It seemed like the architect couldn't quite decide whether the house should be modern or traditional. There were round windows and a circular turret of limestone in the front entrance. These were flanked by small and large square windows over the study and living room. Red brick pavers led up to the entrance that was protected by two large cement lions, each poised to snarl a warning to the would-be passerby.

The door was a heavy, dark oak. I was expecting someone from the Addams family to open it. Instead, a short, rotund man in shorts and a sleeveless t-shirt opened the door and introduced himself as Jack Weldon.

Weldon definitely fit Riley Jackson's description of the endomorph gynecologist. But as physicians go, that's where it stopped. He was bald, with deep bushy eyebrows. Gold chains hung from his neck, and a sapphire ring distinguished his pinky from that of the average working slob. When I looked at him, I thought of illegal abortions, payoffs under the table, or cheating on insurance.

But Jack Weldon seemed harmless as he ushered us into the marble-floored living room. Large round windows overlooked his white metal deck. Beyond that, I could see personal watercraft zooming back and forth on the narrow strip of water. For a peaceful afternoon, the noise was irritating.

Sennett and I sat down on uncomfortable, straight-backed, latticed chairs while Weldon sat on a chrome-edged couch with brightly colored, patterned cushions that almost made me dizzy. "You look pretty young to be retired," I offered. He proceeded to tell us that he got tired of practicing, so he got a friend to write him a letter saying he could no longer practice because of a disc in his neck. He claimed that his accountant—Manny was his name, got him to pay in pre-tax dollars so the income was tax free. He even offered to give me his name.

Sennett, who had remained quiet, shifted in his seat. The wood legs squealed against the floor. When he got Weldon's attention, he spoke in his best Joe Friday voice. "Dr. Weldon, we came over here today to talk to you about a woman who was your patient before you retired."

"Call me Jack. Who was the patient?" he asked.

"Mary Anne Zielinski." As soon as Sennett said her name, I could see Weldon's expression change.

"Now there is a sorry situation. Probably the sorriest case I ever had in my practice."

"What do you mean?" I asked.

Weldon crossed his stumpy, hairless legs, leaned back on the couch, and crossed his arms across his chest. His expression was that of a preacher who had heard thousands of confessions and never believed one of them. "I mean, they were Bible-toting, God-fearing, religious people. The last couple I would ever have figured to have been involved in some kind of hanky-panky affair. Hell, man, before this whole business, Mary Anne Zielinski would come into the office reading *The Word*."

"How do you know she was having an affair?"

He looked around suspiciously for a moment, as if someone might hear him. The room was silent except for the sound of the ceiling fan and the dull drum roll of the watercraft on the lake.

"Okay. I can't talk about her medical condition, but I could describe a fictitious patient. You understand?"

"Sure."

He told us how "this patient" had come to his office and confided that her husband wasn't the father of the baby she was carrying. When Weldon asked her who the father was, she said she couldn't remember having an extramarital affair. He said he almost laughed, but couldn't. Instead he told her he didn't have time for this kind of thing and maybe she should see a psychiatrist. I listened closely, wondering what I would have said in a similar situation. It didn't take me long to realize I could never be that dismissive.

When he finished, Sennett spoke again. "Do you know if she ever sought help?"

"As far as I know, she never did and she never mentioned the problem again," Weldon said with disdain.

I leaned forward on the couch. "Dr. Weldon, we believe she might not have had an affair."

"What do you mean?" he asked.

"Artificial insemination."

"From who, me?" he said smiling glibly, as if the initial suggestion was ludicrous. Then he stopped for a moment. "I guess it's possible, except not with Mary Anne Zielinski." He stopped again and thought for a moment, his eyes crinkling as if he just thought of something funny. "You know what I always told my patients. Spare the rod and spoil the child." As soon as he said it, he started laughing uncontrollably until tears came to his eyes.

Sennett didn't smile. Instead he waited until Weldon had wiped his eyes and calmed down, and then said that no one suspected him of anything. After he said it, I detected a sigh of relief from Weldon. As I watched him, I made a mental note to call Tom Bromley and check his schedule. I wanted to be sure he was in the delivery room for Jordan.

I turned back to Sennett. His face was impassive, but his eyes glared at Jack Weldon with a contempt that he didn't bother to conceal. "Dr. Weldon, we would appreciate receiving any records your office might still have," Sennett said softly and slowly, but with conviction. When Weldon said he'd need authorization, the lieutenant gave him Knudsen's name and told him the sergeant would take care of everything.

Sennett then rose abruptly, thanked Weldon for his time, and walked back to the sliding door. He seemed in a hurry to get out of there. I followed him out and walked back to his car in silence. When we got back in, Sennett started up the car and juiced the AC. I couldn't tell which was making him hotter, the weather or this case.

"Godammit, Ben, how do they let guys like that become doctors?"

"The same way they let policemen on the street who beat up innocent people. It's hard to define someone's character until they get into the fray."

"I suppose. But, shit, this guy's supposed to be taking care of human beings with care and compassion."

"What do you call the guy that finishes last in his med school class?"

Sennett looked at me with a blank stare. "I don't know."

"Doctor. Face it, Lieutenant, you've been reading too many novels. In real life, medicine is a business. Some doctors are in it for the income. That doesn't make them evil."

"No, just disappointing."

Sennett arranged for the records release by placing a few calls on his cell phone and then drove me back to the shopping mall to drop me off at my car. As I drove home, I thought about everything that had happened. It made me increasingly depressed. Depressed for the dead children, depressed for the parents, and especially depressed for my profession. Sennett's words had bit deeply into the flesh of my professional self-respect.

Jordan was up when I arrived home.

"Where did you go?"

"I spent the afternoon with George trying to determine whether medical education in America was living up to its standards."

"Huh?"

"We visited Mary Anne Zielinski's obstetrician."

"Anything come of it?"

"Just dead ends."

"George called a few minutes ago. He said he was faxing you some information from a Dr. Weldon."

"That's Mary Anne Zielinski's doctor. George is probably sending me the low-down on his last tax return."

I walked over to the machine. It wasn't a tax return. It was Mary Anne Zielinski's office records. At least he wasn't as neglectful as I thought he'd be, or maybe it was Sennett's tone of voice that convinced him to cooperate.

I put the record on the desk and started scanning it. Then I pulled out the information I had on the other victims' mothers, Jallila Ishaki and Connie Lennell. I separated everything I had into complaints, physical findings, and treatment.

That's when I saw it and suddenly everything made sense. I picked up the phone and dialed Sennett. He seemed irritated.

"I've got too many leads and nothing is panning out, Doc," Sennett said with frustration,

"Okay, then help me, Lieutenant. Maybe we were just using the wrong word."

"What's that?"

"Pain clinic. Each of the mothers had back problems. They all went to a rehabilitation clinic and possibly had some type of injection procedure for back pain. I don't have the other records, but I have Mary Anne Zielinski's. On October 15th, 1989, Jack Weldon noted that Mrs. Zielinski had a reaction to sedation during her treatment at Northside Pain Clinic by a Dr. Alfred Grodin. She had a bad back."

"So?" Sennett asked.

"It's the sedation. Riley Jackson, Connie Lennell's obstetrician, told me that she would have had to have been drunk or taking drugs to be inseminated. He said it as a joke."

"What's your point?" Sennett replied.

"Don't you get it?" I said excitedly. "They all had back problems. The treatment may have been an epidural injection. It would have been easy for someone to tell the patient they were going to get some sedation. Once the sedation was in, the killer could have inseminated her without her knowledge."

"Aren't you getting carried away with this, Ben?"

"It's worth a try. Whatever else we've tried isn't working."

Sennett growled in agreement. "You're right about that. I feel like the walls are closing in, and there's nothing I can do." There was a moment of silence. "What the hell," he said with resignation in his voice. "There's nothing to lose."

Chapter 25

WE FOUND THE NORTHSIDE PAIN CLINIC in western Oakland County, one of the biggest growth areas in the country. It has been said that Detroit is a series of small towns connected by bus lines. If it is, Farmington Hills was one of the main spokes. Urban sprawl, congested streets, and a myriad of tony shops and restaurants.

Orchard Lake Road was the main drag, carrying forty thousand cars a day. It sometimes defied logic to see traffic jams in someone's suburban utopia. Groden's office was in a one-story, stick and brick building, which had been built before Farmington Hills had been discovered.

We parked in the lot and walked up to the pink-bricked building. Flowers lined the walk. The sign on the clinic read "Alfred T. Groden, M.D., Rehabilitation and Physical Medicine." Below it was a list of the services provided: physical therapy, massage, strength and conditioning, medical consultation. It was a cornucopia of body repair.

The waiting room was full of people on crutches. There were two gumball dispensers near the front counter and three racks of magazines along the sidewall with issues ranging from *Car and Driver* to *Maxim*. Obviously, Dr. Groden was a man of many interests. We walked up to the sliding window. A man stood in front of me. He didn't seem like the rest, wearing a business suit and carrying a large briefcase.

"Do you know how much longer it's going to be?" He tried to talk softly so no one could hear, but standing right behind him, it was hard to miss the bite in his voice.

"I'm sorry, sir. The doctor is running behind."

"Doesn't he realize the importance of the Jenkins case? This matter could be worth a lot of money to our firm and, of course, the client." It was clear what the order of importance was.

"I'm sure Dr. Groden understands."

"Well, you go back and tell him I'm paying a lot of money to him for his time and his testimony and that I expect better service if he wants us to use him again."

"I'll be sure to tell him, as soon as I go back. Until then, you'll just have to wait."

The man in the suit turned and unwillingly retreated to the waiting room chair, sat down, and tucked his large briefcase between his legs. What could he do? He apparently needed Groden's paid testimony. This was obviously what medical consultation meant on the marquis—ambulance chasers. I had heard that it made up a large part of rehab medicine; giving testimony for a large fee in court cases involving auto accidents. It was worth big money to the doctors and the lawyers. It also made me sick.

Then it was our turn. As we approached the small sliding window, the receptionist looked up at us. Her nametag said Violet, which pretty much summed up her appearance. Violet-black hair, violet eye shadow, lots of foundation, and dark violet lipstick. In spite of the effect, she still looked middle-aged. Her annoyed demeanor didn't help.

Sennett stepped forward. Jaw jutted, muscles clenched. I hadn't seen him this agitated in a long time. "We'd like to speak with Dr. Groden."

"Do you have an appointment?"

"This is all the appointment we need." Sennett pulled out his badge. Her eyes grew larger, protruding out of their purple sockets. She scurried back to find her boss.

A medium-sized man in a white coat and an open-collared shirt came to the front desk. I looked at his face, a prognathic jaw with a large nose protruding in front of pin-point eyes that danced nervously from side-to-side. He had thick eyebrows and a full head of curly, dyed-brown hair that looked permed. "What can I do for you, gentlemen?" His voice trembled slightly, and I noticed a slight crook to the corner of his mouth.

"We'd like to see the records of Mary Anne Zielinski." The lieutenant spat the words out with a cobra's venom.

"Do you have a court order to see them?"

"How about I tell you that I'll put your name on TV, and you stick your court order up your ass?"

"Okay, okay. No need to make a scene," he said, looking around nervously at his waiting room. "Violet, give the gentlemen the records on Mrs. Zielinski and then a private place to sit."

Sennett glared at Groden. "Don't go too far away, doctor."

Groden didn't reply. He just scurried away, his eyes searching for the sanctuary of the deposition room.

Violet found Mary Anne Zielinski's chart and led us back to the lunchroom. It wasn't much, just a single Formica table, a toaster oven, a beat-up, small, yellow refrigerator, and a coffee pot smelling of burnt coffee.

The chart was thin, only a few pages.

"You look it over, Doc. Maybe we can find something."

I read the referral letter from the orthopedic surgeon that Mary Anne had seen. She had an L4-L5 radiculopathy, a pinched nerve, and he had advised her to see Groden for rehabilitation.

Then I read Groden's letter back. *Thanks for the referral. I've evaluated May Anne, and there appears to be nerve entrapment from a disc. She was given Demerol for pain but had a reaction. Because of this, I've suggested a cortisone injection into the nerve root at the Wallenbrook Clinic.*

Then a follow-up from the Wallenbrook Clinic. *Injection performed without incident. Please call me if there is any further information I can supply.* Signed, Dr. David Wilhelm.

There was another note in Groden's chart, indicating that Mrs. Zielinski was markedly improved. Other than that, nothing.

"Lieutenant, Mrs. Zielinski had an injection, but it wasn't here."

"What about Groden?"

"He's probably a scumbag, but not for the reasons you think. If there was a problem, it was where she had the injection."

Sennett sighed. "I just want to say goodbye to the good doctor."

We got up from the lunchroom and walked back to the front desk. Violet was at her post. "I need to speak with Dr. Groden," Sennett fairly barked.

"He's in a deposition." This time she didn't seem so sure. Her Mardi Gras face seemed even less human.

"Which room?"

"Third on the right, but it's . . ."

It was too late. Sennett barged through the door. Inside were two suits arguing over allowing a testimony about someone's income. It was always about money.

Sennett walked up to Groden, towering over the smaller man. He reached down and pulled him from his chair, bringing him up close to his nose. I was surprised at Sennett's violent approach. After all, this guy was a doctor.

"Hey," Groden protested, "what's going on? You've got no right to push me around."

Sennett dropped him back in his chair. "You see these two silk-suited fancy-dans with their yellow legal pads, Doctor?" Sennett said calmly pointing at the two lawyers sitting at the table. "My guess is that one of them is paying you big money for your testimony. How about I ask the IRS and the state bar to audit your return and see how much you were paid for your testimony and how much you declared? I bet we could find something interesting if we wanted to."

Groden looked around the room for an escape. When he saw none, his shoulders sagged in defeat. "Okay, what do you want?" he said in a soft voice.

"Who do you usually deal with at the Wallenbrook Clinic?"

"It's part of the university. I . . . I never know who the patient sees." Groden's eyes were twitching nervously and sweat glistened like small grease spots on his forehead.

"There was a report signed by a David Wilhelm. Who is he?"

"He's the director of the clinic. He signs everything that goes out."

"Listen to me, doctor, and listen well. If I find something wrong was done and you're involved, I'll be back for your balls."

Sennett appeared to have gotten what he wanted, so he turned and walked out. As I followed him, I wondered why Sennett bullied Groden. Then I looked at the lineup of ten other silk-suited men with slicked-back hair and large briefcases stacked up outside his door. I suspected that a visit from Detroit's finest was exactly what Groden didn't want, and Sennett knew it.

THE WALLENBROOK CLINIC was a large, well-respected university rehabilitation facility, named after Charles Wallenbrook III. The story was that he gifted the center in gratitude for the curative treatment his son received following a bout with polio. It was the kind of gift universities thrived on.

David Wilhelm was the director. I had heard of him; he had a national reputation in the treatment of muscular dystrophy. On the surface, Alfred Groden and David Wilhelm represented the two ends of the spectrum, greed versus academic good.

Sennett pulled up to the front of the modern limestone and glass building and parked in the no parking zone. When the attendant came up, he flashed his badge. The attendant backed away from the car, his hands in the air.

Next to the sliding glass doors was a plaque: *Our mission is to provide the highest quality care by the highest quality doctors.* We walked through the entrance and into the lobby, a marboleum. Marble everywhere, green marble floors, a red marble fountain, white marble countertops at the reception desk. Charles Wallenbrook III must have been in the marble business.

The receptionist pointed the way to David Wilhelm's office. We had called ahead, and his nurse was waiting for us with Mary Anne Zielinski's chart. She gave it to us, and then led us to a small consultation room.

The chart wasn't much, a letter from Wilhelm and an operative report of the injection dated June 28, 1988. I looked carefully at the document. It was stamp-signed by Wilhelm. Below his name it read: *Signed in Dr. Wilhelm's absence to assure quick response.* Under his name was the name of James Fogarty, M.D. His signature was signed in blue ink. When two names appeared on a report, it usually meant Fogarty was a resident or fellow.

We went back to the nurse and asked to see Dr. Wilhelm. She showed us to his office, which, in keeping with the building, was a spacious suite with three leather chairs and a large, expensive desk of varnished maple sitting in the middle of the room. There was nothing on it except an intricately carved pen set. I looked at the walls. There were no pictures, only diplomas. I secretly admired people who could keep their desk that clean.

David Wilhelm walked in. He was an unassuming, slightly built man, with ruddy cheeks and tousled, sandy brown hair that fell over his forehead. Thin eyebrows hung precariously over his steel blue eyes. He was wearing a white coat, but I noticed his Ferragamo loafers. Obviously, David Wilhelm didn't come cheap. He also didn't look like a killer.

We introduced ourselves. His handshake was a little weak, his fingers resting limply in mine. He never made eye contact, causing me to feel a little nervous, wondering what really caught his attention. Wilhelm went around to his desk and sat down in the green leather desk chair, one of those chairs with thirty-seven different adjustments. "My secretary told me you had called. I hope they gave you everything you wanted."

"We looked over everything, Dr. Wilhelm. It seems in order," Sennett replied.

"Could you tell me what you're looking for?"

"We're following up on a series of murders," Sennett said. "We have reason to suspect that the mothers of the victims were at one time assaulted, and that these attacks may have taken place when they were sedated. The only common factor we found from reviewing their medical records was that they all had back problems."

"And what brings you here?"

"One of the victims, Mary Anne Zielinski, was treated in your clinic. Her son, Brett, was murdered."

"How does his death affect our institution?" He stretched his fingers out in front of him. They were delicate, long fingers with neatly manicured nails. They didn't look like the kind of hands that would skin someone alive and cut off their manhood.

"She had a cortisone injection into the peripheral nerves in her back," I replied.

"I see. So you think I had something to do with it?" he asked with a look of consternation.

"That's a possibility, but not likely. We believe it may have been someone in your department." Sennett spoke deliberately in a voice that showed no emotion.

"What was the date on the procedure?"

"June 28, 1990."

"Well, that's a long time ago. But we keep meticulous records. I have to for the foundation that runs the clinic. Let's get my secretary in here and see where I was that day."

He called his secretary. She apparently went to her computer, because five minutes later a printout of his calendar was placed on his desk. "Let's see. On June 28th I was in Vienna, lecturing at the International Congress of Muscular Dystrophy."

Sennett looked at the calendar. "What about Dr. Fogarty? Where is he now?" he asked.

Wilhelm told us that Fogarty was still at the clinic. As he spoke, I looked again at Wilhelm's soft hands again and wondered how often he prepped a patient's back, picked up a syringe, and injected medication; probably not in years.

"How old is Dr. Fogarty?" Sennett asked.

"Probably in his mid-forties. Back in 1990 he was doing a fellowship in spine rehabilitation. Now he is chief of our functional rehabilitation program."

"Can you explain why both your names are on this letter?" Sennett asked.

"We get fellows from a number of different departments. We let them rotate through the clinic. They're the ones that do the injections. Dr. Fogarty was training at that time. I sign all the letters that go out. It's a departmental regulation."

"Even though you were not there?" Sennett asked.

"I know it sounds strange, but that's the way we've been doing it for years." He voice was calm, and he looked straight ahead. I couldn't detect a tone of deceit in his voice.

"It's a federal law to have a staff person in attendance when a resident performs any procedure, isn't it?" I interjected.

"No," Wilhelm replied, "these are fellows that come through the department to complete training in a specialized area. Most have finished a residency and are often board certified. They're as good as any person on the fulltime staff. We give them a lot of latitude so they can get a taste of running their own practice."

"So, we have a procedure done by someone, but we're not sure who, and the bills are being sent out under your name." Sennett's eyes narrowed.

For the first time, Wilhelm's calm demeanor changed. His back stiffened and his lips pursed, as if he had just smelled something offensive. "Are you suggesting an impropriety?" he asked haughtily.

"No, I'm suggesting that it is illegal to bill an insurance company for services without the person who is doing the procedure in attendance." Sennett stepped forward and took a confrontational stance.

"That would be a problem you would have to take up with the medical school administration," Wilhelm said coolly, though his right hand was now trembling slightly.

"No, I think it's going to be more of problem for you, Dr. Wilhelm," Sennett replied.

Wilhelm sighed. He and other colleagues had gone down this road before, I thought. "Look, it's difficult for lay people to understand. Part of our job is to train young physicians. This is a teaching institution."

"That's not the issue," Sennett said. "It's my understanding that it is a Federal requirement that physicians in training be supervised."

At that point Wilhelm went into what sounded like a canned speech on the need to train physicians and maintain a budget. I suspected he had given this speech many times to hospital administrators, lawyers, and insurance companies. He finished by saying he understood why the police were looking but doubted they would find anything.

"We're not sure right now, either, Dr. Wilhelm," I interjected. "We're just following up on one of the few leads that have been brought to our attention. Do you think we could speak with Dr. Fogarty?"

Wilhelm smiled. He welcomed a colleague who perhaps understood the structural integrity and related issues of running a teaching hospital. "Sure. He's right down the hall. I'll tell him you're coming down."

"That's not necessary," Sennett ordered in a demanding tone of voice. "Just tell us the room. We'd like to go in unannounced."

Wilhelm's face darkened. "Is shock and awe standard police procedure? If you investigate us, you'll find we don't treat our patients this way. You don't think Dr. Fogarty had anything to do with this, do you?"

"Not necessarily. We'd just like to go over a couple of things with him," I pointed out, playing good cop again.

Wilhelm gestured down the hallway to an open area with a series of small cubicles, separated by fabric-covered wallboard with glass at the top. "Last one on the left, gentlemen," he said. Fluorescent lighting illuminated the space. Obviously, the marble stopped here. We searched for Fogarty's office and found his name attached to the outside of one of the cubicles with a small, replaceable black sign indicating his name.

"Where did you pull that Federal law business about having a resident in the room from?" I asked, as we stopped a short distance from the office.

He gave me a slow, sad smile, his version of accepting a compliment. "A few months ago, I read some article in the newspaper about a lawsuit in New York," he replied. "The hospital was using residents to perform unsupervised treatment. It cost them millions."

"And all along I thought you were reading *Hustler*," I said, repressing a chuckle.

GENE RONTAL

"Just keeping up with the literature."

Nearing the area where Fogarty's office was located, Sennett was suddenly all business. We barged into the office unannounced. As we did, the man behind the desk was understandably surprised, standing up with a questioning look on his face. Fogarty looked like he was in his early fifties, a beanpole, six-foot-three, wearing suspenders and a slightly rumpled white, polyester shirt. His tie was a little too wide and his collar a little too frayed. He had a sallow complexion with a rather long nose that curved downward at the tip. There was a little hayseed in him until you looked at his intelligent, inquisitive eyes. "Can I help you?" His voice was deep and self-assured.

"I'm Lieutenant Sennett of the Detroit Police Department, and this is Dr. Benjamin Dailey. We'd like to ask you a couple of brief questions about this chart." Sennett flashed his badge and then tossed Mary Anne Zielinski's chart on Fogarty's desk. The doctor picked it up, looked at it, and put it back down.

"I'm sorry, but I don't remember this patient."

"You signed the chart."

Fogarty picked the chart up again and studied it. He seemed suddenly perplexed. "That's not my signature. Besides, it was eighteen years ago."

I studied Fogarty for a moment. I didn't know what a serial killer looked like, but his Norman Bates appearance didn't exactly sooth my disquiet.

"How do explain that your name is there?" Sennett asked.

Fogarty shrugged. "That's a mystery. We get so many different people coming through, it's sometimes hard to keep track. Perhaps the secretary mis-typed the dictation."

"When a chart is dictated, where do they leave them?" I asked.

"There's a box for each of us at the front desk," Fogarty explained. "They're left there for signing. Once we've signed them, we put them back on the secretary's desk for filing purposes."

Sennett tapped the chart with a beefy forefinger. "Do you have a recollection of where you were on the date of the injection?"

The doctor looked down at the chart, his brows knit in puzzlement. "I was a fellow at the time. Other than that, I have no idea. Maybe there is something on my computer." Fogarty went to his desktop, pressed a few keys, and pulled up his CV. He showed Sennett the results. Fortunately for him, his records showed that, during the time in question, he was attending a meeting on electromyography at the University of Washington in Seattle.

After he showed us the papers, Sennett opened his notepad and laid it on his desk. "I wonder if you would sign your name for me?" Sennett asked.

"What's this all about, anyway?"

"We're investigating a series of murders."

"Murders? If you think I had anything to do with it, maybe I should call my lawyer." Fogarty looked directly at the lieutenant. It was a piercing, candid look. There was a genuine fear in his voice, but not deceit.

"Right now we're just investigating, Dr. Fogarty," I intervened, trying to sound soothing. "Do you mind signing your name?"

"I suppose not," he said, relaxing a little and sighing in resignation. "You could get any one of the charts and compare it anyway."

Fogarty signed his name three times and then handed the paper back to Sennett. The lieutenant canned the paper and went to the door. As we left, he gave Fogarty the "don't leave town" line.

We walked back to the secretary's desk and had her make a copy of the chart and the letter. She had to fuss with the broken Xerox machine. Finally, the paper ejected, and we were on our way. As I stepped out of the pretentious glass and brick building, a feeling of anger and frustration swept over me. The name Wallenbrook Clinic didn't always mean anything when it came to taking care of patients. The patients thought they were getting David Wilhelm, but instead they were getting some resident or even an imposter, and that imposter could be a vicious killer. It made me sick.

Once in the car, Sennett turned on the ignition and waited for a moment.

"What was that last comment all about?" I asked. "The 'don't leave town' thing."

"Yeah, well, that's Police 101. Scare the shit out of the suspect, and maybe he'll do something stupid."

"You don't suspect that guy, do you?"

"Nah, he's got an alibi, and even a third grader could see the signatures aren't the same."

"So what's the deal?" I asked.

Sennett explained that the deal was with a clinic where procedures were done on patients and nobody knew who was doing them. He thought there was something strange about Wilhelm, as if he was hiding something. He even mentioned how peculiar it was that there were no photographs in the office. I thought about it for a moment. Maybe he was right.

He had just finished speaking when there was a ring on his cell phone. He picked it up quickly and listened intently, his jaw rigid, his eyes glaring out at no one. When he was finished, he angrily snapped the cover back on his phone.

"We've got another child missing, a seventeen-year-old girl, Rhonda Islington. She lives in Rochester Hills. Mother is divorced and never remarried. She works for Chrysler as an account executive. Good kid. Never in any trouble."

It was the same M.O. with no leads and no Ahmad Masri. The department's response was immediate, offering a $50,000 reward for a lead to the killer's capture. Sennett said that all they usually got from this reward tactic was a bunch of crank calls. I thought he was done giving me bad news, but he wasn't. He said the department got a note taped to the front door entrance. It read:

*The line between life and death is so fine. Who would think that
death could give me such pleasure? Aren't you glad for me?*
                                                Friend of the Devil

"He's taunting all of us," I said with an anger that stretched the limits of
my composure. "He knows we are on the case, and he wants us to suffer like
his victims."

Sennett nodded. "The wolf is on the prowl, Ben," he said in a steely voice,
"and I'm leading the hunt." I stared at his masklike face and furious eyes, and it
made me nervous. I'd seen him like this once before, and it had almost killed me.

Chapter 26

Before Sennett left to interview the Islington family, he asked me to go down to his office and look at Connie Lennell's newspaper articles and the handwritten ledger she had given me. When I asked him if Knudsen had them, I didn't even think he heard what I was asking. By now his captain was frantic. The television and print media were screaming for a perpetrator, and the national news was having a field day. They called it a terrible tragedy for the families and another blight on Detroit.

I felt bad for Sennett. He had to deal with his own feelings of helplessness while trying to prevent another crime. I could sympathize with him. Once, when I was first in practice, I found a small lump under my arm. I got the X-ray report while I was seeing patients in the office; my doctors thought it might be malignant. There I was, trying to tell Mrs. Jones that she was going to survive her cancer and wondering if I might survive my own. Fortunately, my lump was just inflammation and Mrs. Jones is still alive, twenty years later. Not everything works out that well, however. Even if Sennett and I could solve this case, all those kids would still be dead.

Instead of going alone, I called to pick up Jordan at the entrance to the Federal Building. Maybe it was my brain playing tricks with me, but as I watched her come down the steps, she seemed more pregnant than she had that morning. To a novice parent like me, she looked like she could have the kid any minute, and the thought unnerved me.

She was rubbing her stomach as she sat down in the seat next to me.

"Are you all right?" I asked nervously.

"Fine. Why?"

"You suddenly look so pregnant."

"Dailey, you always know how to say the right thing."

"No, seriously. Do you feel all right?"

She claimed that she had the same kind of pain she had been having for the past few weeks, and it made her anxious.

"There's nothing wrong with being scared," I reminded her. "That's what you have a doctor for. Call him if you don't feel well."

"Forget it," she said with a laugh. "Women have been having children for millions of years. Most of the time without doctors. Besides, I've got you. Now, what do we have to do?"

I sighed and put the car in gear. It took us a few minutes to drive to head-quarters and make it up to Sennett's office. By the time we arrived, Knudsen had the papers from the murders along with the medical records of Mary Anne Zielinski on the lieutenant's desk.

We both sat down in front of his desk and started arranging the files Knudsen had put out for us. I looked over at Jordan. She looked back with arched eyebrows, as if signaling, *what else were you going to do today?* I picked up one of the files.

"Where do we start?"

"Let's make a list of the killings," I suggested. "Where they occurred, age of the victim, what was peculiar about the autopsy, that kind of thing."

It took us an hour to get an overview of the deaths from Connie Lennell's list. The graphic details, especially inscribed in coldly professional "coroner-ese," weren't easy to read.

Danielle Ianoulli was found on a barge in the Mississippi River north of St. Louis about two years before Connie Lennell's daughter was killed. She had been cut open and a piece of tissue was found stuffed jeans pocket. The M.E. had identified it as her umbilicus. A note was found next to the body. It read: "Life is a dead end street." The quote was from H. L. Mencken. The killer had been identified as Albert Townsend, a known pedophile, who had worked as a nurse at a local hospital. The police shot him to death when he ran to avoid capture. Danielle Ianoulli's purse was found in his apartment, along with some photographs of her mutilated body. Case closed.

Helene Gustafson died a year after Janice Lennell. She was found tied to a chair on the shoreline of the Cuyahoga River outside Cleveland. Her abdomen had been slashed. The coroner had found an object wrapped around her right ear that was identified as her small intestine, the ileum. A note left attached to her big toe read, "For certain is death for the born." It was a quote from an ancient Hindu bible, the *Bhagavad Gita*, from 250 B.C. A known schizophrenic recently released from the state penitentiary after serving time for manslaughter was found dead on Euclid and 105th Street in Cleveland. On him was a knife with Gustafson's blood on it.

The other murders were similar, just the cities were changed. Virginia Ulanoff was found near a small pond outside Peoria, Illinois. Her neck had been slashed and her eye gouged out. A drifter was picked up two days later, hitch-hiking on an interstate exit. On his person he had her wallet and credit cards. He was convicted and sent to prison in Joliet. Two years later Peter Davidson was found dead on a running path near Lake Madison. He was a student at the University of Wisconsin and had been out drinking with his friends. They said he got a phone call and went outside. That was the last time they saw him alive. He was found with is chest cut open and his rib sticking out of his jeans. There had been several other attacks on the campus at the same time, and the police had a suspect. They finally cornered him in a farmhouse on the outskirts of the campus. Before they could arrest him, he shot himself.

It was hard to deny the similarities in the cases, but all of the murders had been solved. On the surface it appeared Janice Lennell had been a random act of violence. From the newspapers she read, Connie Lennell must have known that too.

We went back and looked at the recent murders, this time arranging the peculiarities of the crimes. When we were done, it became clear that the only people we hadn't interviewed were the nurses on the case. Knudsen called the Wallenbrook Clinic and arranged for phone interviews. After working with them, none of the nurses could place the date of treatment or nature of any of the nerve injections. It seems as if the good Dr. Wilhelm ran a regular assembly line of young doctors treating patients. So many, in fact, that from day to day no one could remember one from the other. As for Fogarty, they all knew him. They considered him to be a little eccentric, but a nice guy just the same.

Phyllis Issacson's chart was next. Sennett had left a note on the top of the file indicating that he had called Harry Issacson and found out where his wife had been treated. Among her records were reports from a clinic in Cleveland. The same story. A pinched nerve in the lumbosacral region requiring a steroid injection. She went to a clinic outside of Cleveland that specialized in back problems. Roughly nine months later, Stacey was born. After a few calls and a discussion with the police department, Knudsen found that the clinic and its records had been destroyed in a fire. According to hospital and AMA records, the doctor who ran the clinic, Edgar Fraiberg, was living in a nursing home in Florida, which turned out to be an Alzheimer's facility.

We were able to find Fraiberg's wife, but she wasn't much help. After listening to her story about her husband's dementia, I couldn't blame her for not wanting to talk. Her only lead was Mildred Cohen, who had been Dr. Fraiberg's administrative assistant. We found her on whitepages.com. She lived in Solon, just outside of Cleveland. Jordan called her, introducing both of us on the speakerphone.

"Excuse me for a moment," Mrs. Cohen said politely. "I have my grandchildren over." In the background I could hear her gentle commands. Her voice was high-pitched and chirpy, but there was no mistaking the ring of authority. I could imagine seeing her, a bustling woman, baking cookies and doting over her grandchildren. "Sorry, a four and six-year-old can sometimes spell trouble. Do you have grandchildren?" she asked sweetly.

I could see the look of consternation come over Jordan. "No," she said. "Not quite yet. But call me back in a couple of weeks and I'll let you know how having my first child went."

"Ah, how wonderful! Well, just you wait. You'll see. Your child will bring you great joy, and then, down the road, grandchildren. Mine are the loves of my life. I don't know what I would do without them. Now, what can I do for the police?"

"Mrs. Cohen, we're investigating a series of crimes. It is possible that one of the victims was treated in Dr. Fraiberg's clinic," Jordan said.

"What kind of crimes?"

"There have been several murders in the Detroit area." We waited for the effect.

At first there was no sound on the other end of the line. Then, "That's horrible. How can I possibly help you?"

"Dr. Fraiberg was an expert in the treatment of pinched nerves, wasn't he?" Jordan asked.

She went on to explain that Dr. Fraiberg had an extensive practice that drew from the entire state of Ohio. She called him a miracle worker. She also said he ran a tight ship.

"On average, how many injections would he do in a day?" I asked.

"Probably fifteen or twenty."

I told her I thought that was a lot of patients. "It sure was," she said. "But he was able to handle it, until he developed Alzheimer's."

"He was still practicing after that?"

"No one knew what it was then. He just couldn't seem to concentrate at times."

"How did he keep up his practice?" Jordan asked.

"He hired moonlighters, residents who were trying to earn some extra money. But I can't recall names. See, I took care of Dr. Fraiberg's practice. I knew where every scrap of paper was, every dime, and every patient. But when the fire burned the clinic, the records went with it. My introductions to the many faces that came and went were very brief and casual."

"Was Dr. Fraiberg there with every patient?" I asked

She hesitated. "When he began to falter," she began, "we lost a bit of control. This went on for about a year. Finally, I told Dr. Fraiberg that I couldn't keep working that way. He seemed unfazed, so I spoke with his wife. It was then that she told me that she suspected he had a problem. Shortly thereafter he retired."

"You wouldn't happen to remember a Phyllis Issacson, would you?" Jordan asked.

"The name doesn't ring a bell."

When I finished, Jordan took over the questioning. She tried every avenue, but after five minutes, it was clear that Mrs. Cohen didn't have anything else to offer. Jordan thanked her and gave her phone number in case anything else came up.

"Police work can be irritating," I lamented. "You think you've got something, and then it slips away."

"We still have Connie Lennell," she said, hopefully. "I think that's one lead we're going to have to talk with. From what you've told me, she's given up on the police, but I think she'll talk to you."

I thought about what she said for a moment. "You mean like a patient going to a naturopath or shaman after the specialists tell you there's no hope."

Jordan nodded. "I suppose so."

I called in Knudsen, and he contacted the manager at the Target store where Connie Lennell worked. In a couple of minutes, she came to the phone. I explained to her what we were doing but purposely left out the DNA results. I didn't think a telephone call was appropriate. When I mentioned a possible connection between Jannie's killer and the treatment she received for her back, she seemed surprised and a little put off. I wondered if she was angry with herself for not thinking about this angle.

"You don't remember the name of the doctor who treated you, do you?" I asked.

"It was Cozzo. That was the name on his coat. Like Bozo. You know how some names you can't forget."

"Sure. Anything you can recall about him?" I continued.

"Yes." She paused for a moment. "I've never told anyone this before, including my husband."

"What was it?"

"There was something about the way he looked." There was the tone of bitterness in her voice that comes with a bad memory. "He scowled at me, and his eyes seemed to look through me, as if I didn't exist."

"How can you remember that from so long ago?" I asked.

"You don't forget someone like that. I'll never forget the way he made me undress, for instance."

I shuddered to think that she might have been in the room with the killer and never knew the evil that was about to happen to her. "What do you mean?"

"He had me take off my bra and panties. Then he made me stand in front of him as he examined me."

"Was there a nurse in the room?"

"No."

"Did you think this was a sexual advance?"

She stated flatly that she didn't think it was. She called it more of a clinical thing, like he was buying a cow. When I asked her if she ever reported it, she said she didn't because she thought people would think she was nuts.

"Connie, was it before or after Janice was born?"

"It was before Janice was born. I know it, because I threw my back out on my birthday. Don and I had gone out to dinner and then went dancing. That night he gave me a necklace. I still have it, and I wear it now and then to remind me of the good times we had." There was a pause. "You don't think that the doctor did something to me, do you?" I was an expert on voices, and I could feel this one over the phone. It was a voice that was startled and suddenly tinged with guilt, as if Connie suddenly realized how badly she had been abused without even being aware of it.

"Right now, I don't know what to think," I admitted. "We just have to track down this lead."

"Please, if there is anything you can tell me . . ." She could say no more.

"We will, Connie," I assured her. "We will."

It turned out that there were ten institutes for rehabilitation medicine in Chicago, each with a different twist; The Institute for Pain Management, The Pain Institute, etc. *Institute* was a marketing gimmick that led consumers to believe that, if they were going to an "institute," they were going to a place of higher quality, a place where oversight was tight and talent was abundant.

It didn't always work that way.

Back in 1985, there were only two "institutes," both affiliated with medical schools in downtown Chicago. On the second try, we hit pay dirt. Connie Lennell was treated at The Lakeshore Rehabilitation Institute.

It took a couple of minutes of wrangling with a hospicrat and a call from Lieutenant Finnegan, but eventually the microfiche records of Connie Lennell's treatment came rolling off the fax machine.

Again, it was a clinic where the attending physician was countersigned by a resident or fellow. Connie was right, the name was Arnold Cozzo, M.D. Another name, probably another dead end. Another call to the AMA.

I looked over the actual injection sheet. There was a patient history and physical examination, all hand-written. At the bottom there was a signature and some other scribbling that was hard to make out on the microfiche. Everything seemed to be in order.

"Have we found Dr. Cozzo?" I asked Jordan. Jordan handed me a fax she'd gotten from the AMA.

"He's practicing in Toledo in a group of specialists," she said. "Bingo."

"Do we know where?"

"Toledo Institute of Rehabilitation Medicine, but he lives in Monroe, Michigan, just north of the Ohio-Michigan border."

Knudsen poked his head in the door and said Sennett was on the line. I picked up the phone. It didn't take long to recognize the tone of somber resignation in his voice. I tried to brighten him up. "We may have a lead." I explained what we had found, including my conversation with Connie Lennell.

"And the guy lives in Monroe?" Sennett asked.

"On the outskirts."

"What do you say I come and pick you up, and we go down to speak with the good doctor?"

"Tonight?"

"You got anything better to do?" he asked. I looked over at Jordan. She looked tired.

I thought for a moment. "Let me take Jordan home. Meet me at my house around four." I knew something was bugging him. "Anything on the Islington girl?"

"So far nothing. We can't find any trace," he said.

I looked over at Jordan again and told him I'd see him in a couple of hours. On the way home, I tried to convince Jordan not to go with us, mostly playing on the health of our unborn child. I told her that no chase would be worth endangering her or the baby. As I argued, I thought about myself and wondered whether it was worth putting myself in harms way. I couldn't answer my own question, so I let Jordan get away without answering as well.

It was no use. She felt we were on the verge of breaking a series of bizarre murders. I knew by the time we arrived at the house that she was going with us, no matter what. It was the prosecutor, not the mother in her, making that decision.

We stopped inside for a few minutes, and I waited while Jordan went to the kitchen to check the answering machine. I heard her calling from the kitchen. "Ben, I think you better come in here."

I walked in and saw her point to a red hair clip and a pair of Mickey Mouse earrings lying on the countertop. This time there was no note. I called Sennett and told him what we had found and heard him mutter, "Shit."

Then he told me that was what the Islington girl was wearing when she disappeared.

CHAPTER 27

SENNETT WAS LATE GETTING TO THE HOUSE. He had to arrange for his people from the lab to collect the hair clip and earrings and dust for prints. He said his boys would continue to watch the house. It didn't give me a lot of reassurance, since someone had entered the house and put the things on the counter while his men were outside. I didn't feel like asking him about it. I knew he was already upset.

I wasn't wrong. He was wearing the worried frown that could only come with a string unsolved of murders. The fact that Jordan was coming along didn't make it go away. I knew he had the same fear for Jordan that I had. But he knew her like I did. When she made up her mind, there was no stopping her. So neither of us argued.

We got in the car and made our way to I-696 and then on to I-275, past the new office buildings that ringed the suburban expressways. As we traveled, I went over my conversation with Connie Lennell once again. As I spoke from the backseat, I stared at his face in the rearview mirror. His jaw muscles had tightened, and his lips were pursed. In spite of the fact that we knew almost nothing about him, I almost pitied Arnold Cozzo.

About the time we crossed I-94, Sennett called the Monroe Rehabilitation Clinic. A nurse answered. Dr. Arnold Cozzo did work there, but he was on vacation this week, she said. From the look on Sennett's face, I knew next week wasn't going to make it. He pulled his SIG Sauer from the glove compartment and laid it on the seat next to him.

"Jesus, Lieutenant, is that safe, leaving it on the seat like that?"

"Relax, it's in a holster with the safety latch on."

"Yeah, but it could fall and go off, couldn't it?"

Sennett glanced at me in the rearview mirror with mock surprise pasted on his face. "Why, Doctor, you're beginning to think too much like a civilian. I'm not the kind to drop my guns or let them go off by mistake." He turned away, settling back in his seat.

"Ben, you worry too much. Sennett is a pro," Jordan said.

Duly chastened, I changed the subject. "Anything new on the latest victim?" I asked.

"Not much to tell," Sennett said. "Same story. Single child, parents estranged, mother went to a pain clinic for her back. It was so many years ago, she can't remember for sure."

"Estranged parents. Given what we're on the lookout for, I'm not surprised. Did you speak with her doctor?" Jordan asked.

"I did," Sennett replied grimly. "They can't find her chart. Can you fucking believe it? This doctor can't find her chart! We're trying to gather her medical history, but it could take weeks. We don't have that kind of time. I can't stand the thought of losing another kid. I just can't."

"The idea doesn't thrill any of us. Any notes?" Jordan rubbed her stomach and looked at her lap.

"Nothing. Just a missing child."

"It would appear that this killer doesn't kill his victims immediately. Maybe if this guy Cozzo is involved, we can nail him before he does any more harm."

"One thing bothers me about the connection with Connie Lennell and Harry Issacson," Jordan said. "Those incidents happened some years ago. If the killer is the same, why is he suddenly back in action? Something has stirred him to kill again."

"Killers have their own plan. Most of the time it only makes sense to them," Sennett replied.

As he spoke, Sennett slowed down and pulled the car to a stop on the shoulder. He took his flashing light from the floor and put it on top of his car. He waited for traffic to clear, then eased carefully back into traffic.

Once in motion he put the light on and accelerated. Cars moved to the side as we sped quickly past Metro Airport. At eighty miles an hour it didn't take us long to pass the southern suburbs of Southgate and Flat Rock, auto towns with ball fields, shopping malls, and thousands of people whose lives depended on the flow of cars out of the Motor City. About an hour into the trip, the clouds started darkening to the west, signaling that the drought might end that night.

It took another hour to negotiate the flat shoreline basin that led to the entrance of Lake Erie and Arnold Cozzo's home in Monroe. We turned into the town and spent fifteen more minutes finding the Riverview Heights subdivision where Cozzo lived. By the time we arrived, it was close to seven o'clock. The sun was still out, but the approaching storm clouds obscured the landscape.

Arnold Cozzo's address was a townhouse outside the city in a cluster housing subdivision called Riverview Heights, overlooking the Detroit River. They
should have named it Copper Corners. The architect must have had a love affair with the element; a copper sign at the entrance, copper cupolas over the
front doors, copper gutters, and copper mailboxes.

We circled several cul de sacs until we found 122 Waterland. Sennett picked
up the gun from the seat and clipped it onto his belt. We parked the car in the
driveway and got out to survey the house, a moderate-sized detached townhome perched on a hill. From its vantage point, you could see the freighters
plying their trade past Fighting Island, down the mouth of the Detroit River,
and then south into Lake Erie. From there it was a straight shot across the lake
and into the St. Lawrence Seaway.

It wasn't as hot out as when we had left Detroit, thanks to a fresh breeze that
accompanied the darkening sky and huge thunderheads moving in from the
southwest. The temperature dropped quickly, the wind picked up, and the skies
became darker. The drill of approaching thunder was like the distant artillery
of an advancing army. I looked toward the west again. The sun was now an
indistinct fireball ready to be put out by the approaching rain. In this climate,
tornado warnings were commonplace.

Jordan stayed behind both Sennett and me as we walked up to the front
door and knocked. No answer. Sennett rang the bell. The only sound was the
groan of the oncoming storm. He peered into the window and must have seen
something, because he motioned me to the back door.

"What is it?" I demanded.

"I can't see much, but it looks like there is someone in the living room."
Rain was beginning to pelt us from all sides. We went swiftly and quietly to
the garage and ducked under an overhang between the house and the garage
as the torrents of rain blew past. Fortunately, the wind was blowing from the
southwest, so the rear of the garage took the brunt of the storm. While the
fierce squall blew over, we peered in the window and saw a light blue Mercedes
parked inside. Sennett tried the garage door. It was locked.

It took about ten minutes for the first wave of rain to pass over. As the storm
started to abate, we dashed for the back door of the house, and Sennett knocked
again. No answer. He tried the door. The latch clicked and swung open.

As soon as we entered, a sour and pungent odor hit us. It was a familiar
smell, I just couldn't place it. We turned the corner and walked into the living
room. Sennett had his gun out.

"Whoa," I whispered to him. "You first."

The room was finished in wood paneling and thick wool carpeting with
an elegant mixture of art deco and modern furniture. In the middle of the
room, in front of the marble hearth, there was a very large leather chair

with its back to us. In the low-profile, modernly furnished room, it looked strangely out of place.

We walked around the chair and found the source of the stench. There sat a slender man in his forties in a blue blazer, arms in his lap, and his head resting against the back of the chair. I was about to say something when I noticed the single hole in his forehead and a dark line of congealed blood across his left eye. I looked at his hands. He was holding a steel blue revolver, his finger still on the trigger. I stepped closer to the body and saw a large exit hole through the side of his head and some brain tissue splattered on the copper hood over the fireplace. Arnold Cozzo wouldn't be doing any more doctoring in this world.

The first thing I did was to glance over at Jordan. She seemed pallid and a little clammy. "Are you all right?" I asked.

"I'm okay. Probably something I ate."

Sennett took out his handkerchief and put it over his mouth. I wasn't so lucky to have one, so I went over to the windows and opened a couple of them to let the swirling storm blow itself into the room.

By this time Jordan had opened the front door and moved outside to the covered porch. There was a bench there, and she sat down. When Sennett and I had reached her side, her color had returned. I sat down next to her and waited. After a few seconds, Sennett pulled out his cell phone and dialed a number. I watched, numbly fascinated, as he calmly called the local police, identified himself, and described the situation.

When I was sure Jordan was all right, I left her and went back inside with Sennett to search the house. Whatever caused Arnold Cozzo to commit suicide, he must have been in a hurry. He hadn't left a note. Sennett patted his coat. "His wallet is still in his pocket," Sennett said in a flat voice.

We searched the house from top to bottom, trying not to disturb anything as we looked for Jessica Islington, the missing child. There was nothing: no pictures, no documents, no letters, no other person. It was as if Arnold Cozzo never existed.

By the time the Monroe police arrived, we had finished a preliminary search of the house. The police walked in with guns drawn. Then Sennett showed them his badge. That didn't seem to make them any friendlier, but Sennett acted as if he was used to it. As soon as he mentioned that he was the chief investigator on the recent series of murders in Detroit, and that Jordan was a federal prosecutor, their demeanor changed. I identified myself as a physician and showed my badge. They didn't seem to be impressed.

The arriving officers started peppering Sennett, Jordan, and me with questions, and Sennett calmly explained what he had seen, to the last detail. Jordan added her findings. By the time they got to me there wasn't much left to say.

After they were done with the initial interview, we waited on the porch for the next squall. While we were talking, the forensic boys arrived in a van.

Three men in civilian clothes piled out, each with a suitcase in his hand. They appeared professional enough as they put on masks and gloves and went through the living room collecting fingerprints and taking photos. It didn't take long for the body bag to come in and the corpse to be removed. I thought about Allan Davis. He'd probably be salivating at the chance to figure out what had happened.

As the Monroe forensics team combed through the house, the three of us sat on some deck chairs we found in a gazebo off the back deck. Jordan sat next to Sennett while he wrote down notes, adding her thoughts. For my part, I just stared at the water, wishing I were somewhere else. When forensics had gathered their last scrap of evidence, we went back inside, just in time for rein-vigorated thunder and rain. I watched from inside the house as the ambulance cut through the stream coming down the front drive. The red lights flashed on the top of the van, illuminating the water along the curb like the flow of blood.

Sennett and Jordan went upstairs, so I turned back to the living room and looked around. The body might have been gone, but the smell of Arnold Cozzo seemed to have permeated every corner of the house. I had become extremely sensitive to it, so I went back to the front door and opened it wide. I didn't suspect anyone was going to care if rain stained the wood floor in the entrance hall.

I stayed at the entranceway as the downpour continued pelting the front driveway. When I started to get wet, I went back inside. Looking at the living room chair, I could still visualize Cozzo's twisted face and blown out cranium. I gazed around the room, trying to get a hint as to why Arnold Cozzo took his own life. On either side of the bay window were a couple of Lucite Pace chairs from the seventies. There was a highly polished wooden table between them, with straight legs capped with brass at the bottom. Neither the table nor the chairs looked like they had been used much.

Over the mantel was a modern art print, with heavy, carved bookcases on either side. The shelves were filled with thick, scholarly books. I looked at some of them: Durant's *The History of Civilization*, Churchill's *The Second World War*, Foote's *The Civil War*, and various art books, mainly collections from the Prado, The New York Museum of Fine Art and the Louvre. There were a couple of missing spaces on the shelves.

I walked up to the wrought iron and glass coffee table next to the chair and looked at some art books on the table, scattered haphazardly. I felt that some-how staring at them was an intrusion into the private life of Arnold Cozzo. Yesterday he was alive, and now he was on the way to the morgue. I picked up one of the art books and started looking through it. There were a few turned corners. I looked at the reproductions on those pages and read the inscriptions. Picasso's *Guernica*, Degas' *The Green Room*, and Michelangelo's sculpture of

David. Cozzo had eclectic taste. Under different circumstances, Jordan might even have enjoyed a conversation with him over a bottle of rich Medoc.

I put the book down and looked around the room again. The worn brown chair, creased from years of use, intrigued me. It looked so incongruous next to all of the modern furniture that filled the room. I ran my hands over the leather, wondering again what tormented compulsion forced Cozzo to pull the trigger. I pulled back the cushion of the chair, not sure of what I was looking for, but certain that every man's easy chair had something under it. Hardly a buried treasure, the discarded paper clip that I found, open at one end and lying on the cloth backing on the seat, seemed out of place in the fastidious home. I pushed the cushion back and looked at the lined and creased leather arms.

It took a lot of will power, but I forced myself to sit where Arnold Cozzo had been seated. From this vantage point, the creases in the leather arms seemed less random, more coherent. I looked more closely. It appeared that words had been scratched into the leather. I thought I read the letters GOOG, OLGA, 1541. Then I looked again, wondering if the horror I had seen was playing tricks on me. Trying to clear my mind, I shook my head. I looked up at Jordan and Sennett as they returned to the room. They both gave me that *what-in-the-hell-are-you-doing-sitting-in-that-chair* look and proceeded to the front door.

I shrugged my shoulders and got up. Before I left, I wrote down the letters on a piece of paper and hustled out to the car. The whole thing was getting to me.

It was nearly midnight when we left Cozzo's house and turned onto the expressway. Jordan said she had to be in court early the next morning. The next thing I knew she was asleep.

I thought about what had transpired. We had a dead man. Whether he was associated with the murders was another question, mostly a matter of DNA and circumstantial evidence. The police took their samples and hustled them down to headquarters.

Sennett tried to put a lid on the murder until he had concrete evidence, but there are always leaks. No one ever seemed to know where they emanated from. The following morning the newspapers and television stations were a non-stop rattle of misinformation. Somehow a blue Mercedes had been identified as part of the killer's MO. Every time there was a sighting, there was a hysterical news flash.

I WAS IN THE LIEUTENANT'S OFFICE that afternoon when Flo called with Cozzo's DNA results. From the look in Sennett's eyes, I knew this wasn't what we were looking for.

"They didn't match any of the victims," he muttered with a tone of irritation. "Shit, Ben, we're back to square one."

"So, Cozzo's not the father. That doesn't mean he isn't involved."

"Well, we've got the homicide guys down in Monroe talking to everyone. So far nothing's come up."

"What about the hair clip and the earrings from our place? Were they from the Islington girl?" I asked.

Sennett told me they showed them to the mother, and she identified them as belonging to her daughter. He said it was a pretty emotional scene. Then I asked him about DNA samples from Cozzo. "Did Cozzo have any friends or acquaintances?" I asked.

"From the people we interviewed we found out he was a loner. A good doctor by all reports. Never married, no love interests."

"Was he gay?"

"Not that we know of," Sennett said. "We checked the people at his office and the hospital where he practiced. We showed his picture in a couple of gay bars around Monroe and even in Toledo. No one knew anything. The people at work never mentioned the possibility, either, but you never know. Some guys never come out of closet, and the closet rarely opens willingly for questioning cops."

"What about college, medical school, his residency?"

Sennett pulled a few sheets of paper from a stack on his desk. "Arnold Cozzo was born in South Bend in the early sixties. Went to high school there and then attended the University of Indiana. He went to the Indiana University Medical School. Graduated near the top of his class."

"What year?"

"Around 1980."

"I know Raleigh Farmer, he's the chief of head and neck surgery down there," I said, excited by the prospect of following up the lead. "He's a lifetime Hoosier, and he's about Cozzo's age. Let me give him a call. Maybe he knows him or his friends." Sennett was eager for me to call him.

As I went to pick up the phone, I thought about Raleigh. I had met him several times at the national meetings. He had a specialty in head and neck cancer surgery. I had referred a couple of patients to him, and they were exceedingly pleased. When I called, he came to the phone immediately.

"Ben, how are you doing?"

"Fine, trying to stay out of trouble, but somehow trouble finds me," I admitted.

"Problems, huh? Big or little?"

"I'm afraid this is a big one." I explained that I had become involved in an investigation but left out the details.

"Didn't this happen to you once before?" he asked.

"Like I said, I have a penchant for trouble."

"What can I help you with?"

"I'm wondering if you know a doctor named Arnold Cozzo," I inquired.

"Arnie? Of course I know him. We were classmates at IU. He's the most benign person I know. What kind of trouble could he be in?"

I explained the series of murders and Cozzo's suicide. When he responded, I sensed that he was surprised. "Did Cozzo have something to do with it?" he asked expectantly.

I looked at Arnold Cozzo's history lying on the paper in front of me. It certainly didn't have the word "killer" stamped all over it. But then, neither did Gary Ridgeway or the BTK killer.

"We're not sure," I replied. "What do you know about him other than medical school?"

"I lost track of him after medical school, besides the usual alumni update stuff. I think he went to Chicago to do rehab medicine. At the ten-year reunion we were going over old classmates, and someone said he was practicing in Ohio. Tell me square, Ben. I've read about the murders in *The New York Times*. Was Cozzo involved?"

"His name appeared in a case where the woman involved had a nerve block. Her daughter was murdered several years ago. The police thought they had the murder solved, but there are some recent happenings that have made the authorities suspicious."

"You're not telling me everything here, Ben."

I looked over at Sennett sitting across from me. He had his forefinger across his lips. "You're right. I can't divulge the entire story, but it's possible that Cozzo or possibly a friend of his might have been involved. The police have asked me to follow up and see if I can find out any information on him. I wonder if you remember any of Cozzo's friends, men or women. That might be a good starting point."

"I don't think there will be any women," he said carefully. "No one could ever prove he was gay, but we all suspected it. He never talked about girls, and he always hung out with some guy who was a couple of years older."

"Do you remember who the guy was?"

"I don't know. He used to come down from Chicago. I think he was a doctor, at least Arnie always called him Doc. That was it. I saw them together once and awhile."

"Did Cozzo ever get into trouble?"

"Arnie? You got to be kidding. We always kidded that even his underwear was pressed."

I didn't know what else to ask. This looked like it was coming to another dead end. "I guess there's not much more to say."

I was about to thank him for his help and hang up, when suddenly he said,

"There was one other thing. It was always rumored that Cozzo was an orphan. He was on scholarship and was always scrimping for money. You know, the free drug company eats, getting an extra tray in the hospital from the food service. The word was Cozzo would do anything for money, at least as long as it didn't compromise his squeaky-clean rep. Know what I mean?"

"Yeah, I think I do. Do you think he would kill for money?"

"I couldn't begin to believe that. He was so benign. Why don't you ask his friend, Doc, or maybe his foster parents?"

Raleigh was right. Orphans had families, and they should be traceable. I wrote the words, "Cozzo—foster parents," on a slip of paper and passed it over to Sennett. Raleigh and I chatted for a few more minutes about some mutual friends and then thanked him for the information and hung up. I sat there wondering where this was leading us and if it would help find the missing girl.

It didn't take Sennett long to track down Arnold Cozzo's foster parents. We found their names on a mortgage application he had with a local bank in Monroe. Fortunately for us, they lived in Brighton, Michigan, just outside Detroit.

BRIGHTON IS ONE OF THOSE CAN'T-MISSES in the real estate developers' handbook. At the junction of two major highways, about sixty miles from the center of Detroit, it represents the farthest outpost of the megalopolis, mostly white-collar workers and white homeowners.

We found the Cozzos at home in a small subdivision on the western side of town. Their home, like most of its neighbors, was a white farm colonial with dark green shutters, a neatly cut lawn, crisply edged beds with red and white begonias, and a fresh coat of paint. When we arrived at four o'clock, it was still hot, but the skies were clear and less humid with a strong breeze from the northwest that had followed the thunderstorms.

Marie Cozzo met us at the front door. She was in her late sixties, overweight, with sagging, fleshy arms, and gray hair neatly drawn back in a bun. She had a long turkey neck that wobbled when she spoke, and deep-set wrinkles around her mouth and eyes that seemed to get deeper when she found out Sennett was a police officer.

When we asked if her husband was at home, she escorted us to the backyard. Paul Cozzo was sitting on a deckchair, drinking a longneck. He was a burly man with plaid shorts over beefy legs that stuck out like tree trunks and fleecy gray hair poking over his white sleeveless tee shirt and covering his arms. The color reminded me of an aging Persian lamb coat. Looking at his ample roll, I guessed that he must have weighed two-seventy-five. His riding lawnmower was standing guard near his chair.

"She's a hot one today, ain't she, gents?" he asked as we walked up.

"Yeah, but you have to expect that in July. You're Mr. Cozzo?" Sennett asked.

"Sure am. Why don't you take a seat?" He motioned us to sit down on a couple of lawn chairs. "What can I do for you?"

"I'm Lieutenant George Sennett from the Detroit Police Department, and this is Dr. Benjamin Dailey, who is helping me on a case."

"The police, huh?" Cozzo hung on the word *police* as if it were a word in a prayer in church. "Did I miss paying a traffic ticket?" He roared at his own joke, then looked over at Marie, who smiled politely with forty-years-of-marriage resignation.

"No, this is in regard to your foster son, Arnold," Sennett began.

A cloud came across Cozzo's face at the mention of his name. "What's he done, robbed a Seven-Eleven?"

"Mr. Cozzo, something has happened to your son," Sennett continued. He looked over at Marie. She had a frightened and puzzled look. "We found him in his townhome outside of Monroe. He had been shot in the head."

I expected tears, anguish, and some remorse. That's not what we got. Cozzo's wife stood silent and emotionless next to her husband. "How'd it happen?" Cozzo asked clinically.

"It looks like a suicide."

I carefully studied the two of them, wife standing next to her husband. They looked like the suburban version of American Gothic, stoic and unsmiling. "Can't say as I'm surprised. He was an emotional kid. Maybe it was over a break-up with one of his boyfriends."

"So you think Arnold was gay?"

"We suspected, but never proved it. But what would you expect?" he asked derisively. "The kid hated sports, walked like a girl. Always reading books and doing these stupid puzzle books."

"Do you remember anything about any of his friends?" Sennett asked.

"Not really. Look, if you want a story about Arnold, you won't get much from Marie and me. He hasn't spoken to us in over twenty years."

"Really?" I interjected, both surprised and disappointed.

"Yeah, I guess it's what most folks would refer to as *gratitude*."

"How so?" Sennett asked.

"Well, we were his foster parents and then finally adopted poor Arnold when he was about twelve. We were living in Indiana at the time. We had tried to have children of our own, but it never happened. We saw him in an orphanage down there. He was a pitiful sight. We kind of felt sorry for him, like an unwanted puppy at the pound, you know."

I thought of an orphanage and a scrawny kid in cotton pants, a shirt and tie, and his face scrubbed with the prayer in his eyes that someone would take him. There were the Cozzos, young and hopeful, taking home the child they never could have on their own. Now all that was left was death and bitterness.

"Yeah, I guess so," Sennett said.

"Seems as though no one else would have him. I have to admit he was a peculiar-looking kid, but we looked past that. We provided him a good, God-fearing home. Even tried to help him with his schoolwork, but he was much smarter than my wife and me."

He went on to tell us that Arnold never was much for social life, but when it came to science and math, he was a whiz. He said he was so smart he got a full ride to Indiana. Then, just after his twenty-first birthday, when Mr. Cozzo was transferred to Brighton, Arnold left home. They never heard from him again.

"You must have some mail, tax returns, something," I said.

Cozzo shook his head. That's when Marie piped up, "C'mon Paul, tell them about Mrs. Frick down the street. She said she was in Toledo and saw a Dr. Cozzo. She knew we had a son who was a doctor, so she asked him if he was related. He told her he had some relatives in this area, but hadn't seen them in a long while."

"Well, that's not like saying we knew anything, Marie," Cozzo grumbled.

"What orphanage did he come from?" Sennett asked, his pen hovering over his notebook.

"Actually, he had been in several homes before we got him," Marie responded. She said she thought that's why he was such a loner.

"Any one person in particular that he talked with on a regular basis?" I asked.

"He used to get calls from a kid that he lived with in the orphanage. That's about all."

"Any idea about the other homes he was in?"

"When we got him, he was pretty messed up. He had been abused. We didn't ask all the details, but it wasn't too pretty. It took a year before he would start talking. Even then, he seldom laughed. Always so serious."

"Did you ever try to find him after he left home?" Sennett asked.

"To be honest with you, Lieutenant, I regretted ever having fostered him. I was so ticked off, I didn't want any part of him. I mean, think about how ungrateful that kid was. All that my wife and I did for him and he just ups and leaves without a word."

"What about friends?" Sennett asked again.

"Like Paul said, just the friend at a foster home that he used to communicate with," Marie replied quietly.

"What was his name?"

"I don't know. They used to write letters back and forth," Mrs. Cozzo answered.

"Did you ever see any of the letters?" Sennett inquired.

"Yeah, Arnold left some of them on his desk. Mostly they were over this game they played through the mail."

"Game?" I asked.

"Yeah, it was kind of like that game hangman, except it was different," Marie said. "There were pictures of a heart or a stomach, things like that."

Momentarily, Sennett and I caught each other's eye.

"Did you ever ask Arnold what they were about?" Sennett continued.

"I had told him that I had accidentally picked up one of the letters and read it. It was filled with all kinds of weird drawings. I asked him what all that stuff was about."

"Was he mad about you reading his mail?" I asked.

"No, just the opposite," Marie continued. "He was excited to tell me. He said he and his friend were playing 'organ hangman.'"

"What was that?" Sennett questioned.

"They tried to spell a word, except the clues were always organs of the human body. One of them would think of a word. Except, instead of guessing a letter, they would guess a part of the human body that started with the letter. If they guessed the right organ, they would write down the first letter. When one of them didn't get the right letter, they removed that part of the body. He had a textbook, and they would keep on looking for body parts. If they removed enough vital parts, the patient died, and the game was over."

"Sounds . . . interesting," Sennett commented, then shook his head, staring down at the notepad.

I looked around the yard while they were talking—neatly clipped bushes, deep green, manicured lawn, and beds of flowers without a weed in sight. I thought to myself that these were their children.

"Apparently it was, because Arnold would spend hours doing the game. It was amazing how quick he became at saving the patient. But when one of them failed and the patient died, Arnold became very depressed."

"Did you ever find out who the other player was?" I asked.

They both said they tried to find out, but Arnold just said the letters were from a friend at the orphanage. To the parents the game seemed innocent enough, so they never pursued it further.

"Did they ever stop playing the game?" Sennett asked.

Marie hesitated as if she were having a hard time remembering. "After a while the letters stopped coming. I asked Arnold about it, and he said he was getting tired of playing. He said he wanted to find some way to make it more interesting. Then he said someday he would make the game mean something. I never knew what that meant."

"Did he ever contact his friend again?" Sennett continued.

"I was never sure. A few months after I thought the letters had stopped, I know I saw him reading something. It looked like another letter, but I was never sure. When I asked him, he became very defensive, like I was intruding."

"Did he ever tell you of his plans for the future?"

"Nothing, except he and his friend wanted to be doctors," Paul Cozzo interjected.

"Have you ever heard from them?" Sennett asked.

"Funny you should ask that," Paul replied with a smirk on his face. "Every Christmas I get a card addressed to me from a different part of the country. It's usually a funny card, like a bunch of doctors throwing pieces out of a body like it was an automobile and then asking for replacements. That kind of a thing. It was never signed. I always thought it was from him. Typical slap in the face, you know."

"Is there anything else you can tell us?" Sennett asked.

"That's about it. Twenty years and no information. Pretty lousy if you ask me," Paul replied in a voice heavy with resignation.

"Yeah, it's pretty lousy all right," Marie added sadly.

"What about Mrs. Frick? Is she still around?"

"She's gone to visit her daughter in California," Marie replied. "She won't be back for six weeks."

Sennett looked at me, as if he expected me to ask another question. When I didn't, he got up, and I followed. We thanked the Cozzos. There was no sadness in their goodbyes, only the tone of relief.

When we got to the car, the lieutenant stopped at the side of his sedan. "The killer is playing a game and Cozzo was part of it."

"Except Cozzo committed suicide," I said. "What's the point? Now the game is over," I concluded.

"Maybe it's not over. We still haven't found his friend, and we still haven't found the Islington girl," Sennett said. "His friend may still be playing, and he wants to finish it before someone finds out. It probably explains why he is killing now."

I mulled Sennett's concept over. The killer was a psychopath, and he was smart. Was this series of killings somehow related to a game of hangman, and did the peculiarities of the deaths bear some kind of meaning?

"Lieutenant, most answers to problems are simple. Occam's razor. As time goes on, they become complex. If the game is still on, then the killer is trying to spell something. Maybe it's in the names of the victims or the organs that have been removed, just like their game. It's like a code. If we break it, we find the killer."

"Code?" Sennett stroked his chin. "I was always lousy at code games."

On the way back, Sennett called in. No leads on the Islington abduction. Sennett looked frustrated and frantic.

"Your theory is a long shot at best, Ben."

"Have you got anything better?"

"No. This whole affair has been driven by longshots. We're going to follow it up. In the meantime, I'm going to try and find out what orphanages Cozzo lived in. There might be a lead somewhere."

As I drove back with Sennett, I was silent. My mind was churning. The killer was performing premeditated murders, all for the sake of a game. Who was next and what goal was he trying to achieve were the questions we needed answered. Theoretically, answers were right in front of us. Unfortunately, if we didn't hurry up and find them, another innocent kid was going to die.

CHAPTER 28

I ASKED SENNETT TO STOP BY MY HOUSE on the way back. I knew Jordan was there. We needed someone to analyze the facts, and, when it came to logic, Jordan was the best I had ever seen.

When we arrived, her car was gone. I walked into the house and looked around. On the small table in the foyer was a note, something about going to the mall and trying on shoes. I took Sennett into the kitchen and brought a pad of paper with me. I was about to start writing when the front door opened. It was Jordan. She carried in a few packages.

"Looks like pregnancy hasn't diminished your buying urge," I chided her.

"I've got to plan for the wedding. Pretty soon I'll be too big to get anything."

"We could always get married after," I said.

Jordan wrinkled her nose and shook her head. "Uh, uh. I don't want my child to have an unmarried mother when he or she is born."

Sennett winked at me, but that was it. I think he was too upset with the events that were swirling around him to be jovial about much of anything, so he got right to business. "Ben tells me you are the most logical person he knows."

I held up my hand. "No, Lieutenant, what I said was that she got a perfect score on the LSAT, which, in large part, is comprised of logic games. That means that someone else agrees with me."

I think Jordan might have been a little embarrassed by the compliment, because she quickly put her packages down on the counter and asked Sennett what he needed without any further discussion about her credentials. He immediately recited our visit to Arnold Cozzo's foster parents, and the friendship Arnold had with a person known only as Doc. Then he told her about their game of hangman, and our hunch that the killer was murdering his victims to develop some kind of perverted code.

After listening to Sennett, Jordan and took out a pad of legal paper from the small desk next to the kitchen table. She said the first thing we needed to do was make a list of the victims and see if we could detect some kind of pattern. With that she began writing down the names of the dead children—Ianoulli, Lennell, Gustafson, Issacson, Ulanoff, Davidson, Ishaki, and Zielinski.

Sennett's cell phone rang just as she was about to start rearranging the names. He opened it up, spoke for a moment, and then listened. I watched as his face tightened and his huge fists clenched so tightly that his nails blanched. When he was done, he clicked the phone off and shoved it back in his pocket. "They found Jessica Islington," he rumbled. "She was in an empty lot near the Ford Rouge Plant. Her lower lip was cut off and strung around her neck like a necklace."

I felt sick and depressed.

"Was there anything else?" Jordan asked quietly.

"There was a videotape left at the site in a plastic garbage bag," Sennett said.

"I'm afraid to ask what it contained," I said.

"You should be. According to forensics, it was gruesome. It was set in a dark room with a single light shining on a table. The Islington girl was naked and strapped to the table. The video was shot from behind and shows the dark form of the killer. He asks if she is ready to meet her fate. The girl is awake and starts screaming, pleading for mercy. The killer pays no attention. Instead, he speaks in a voice that is garbled for the video. He tells her it is time to atone for her sins and that he is God's messenger. She screams again as he takes out an instrument of some kind. Then there's nothing except the whirring sound of something that sounds like a saw. There is another scream and then silence, except for the sound of the machine. After about five minutes the killer takes out something cylindrical on a string and holds it up to the camera. He makes the sign of the cross and then holds up two fingers in the peace sign. Then he utters the words, 'Justice has been done.' After that the tape goes blank."

I watched Sennett sitting there, silent, without words to express his frustration, anger, and helplessness.

"How long had she been dead?" Jordan asked.

"Within twenty-four hours," Sennett replied somberly.

"That means the killer is still on the loose," she concluded.

"There was something else," Sennett added.

I couldn't imagine any worse news, but there was. The Monroe forensics team had reported that Arnold Cozzo hadn't committed suicide. They concluded that the angle of the bullet was in such a direction that it could not have been self-inflicted.

I got up and walked around the kitchen, finally standing in front of the refrigerator and staring at the bag holding Jordan's shoes. It was green with a pretty floral pattern, a marketing design for summer. I thought about the Islington girl. For her there was no summer, no going to the beach, no hanging out with her friends. No new shoes ever. A flower dead before it could bloom.

Sennett stood up from the table and opened his coat. In a swift motion he pulled out his gun, checked the chamber, and put it back in his holster. He looked over at Jordan and then at the yellow legal pad with the names written down. "We've been following these leads and getting nowhere. I've gotta go back to basics and do this the police way. I need something more concrete than this puzzle exercise. This killer is on the move. Something has prompted him to finish whatever he set out to accomplish fifteen years ago. I appreciate what both of you are doing, but I can't wait around to find out that we're on the wrong trail. If you find anything from those papers, let me know."

I was about to say something, but before I could, Sennett got up from the table and left without another word. After he was gone, I sat back down with Jordan. She was twisting a pencil nervously in her hand, looking down on the papers scattered on the table.

"Maybe Sennett is right and we are wasting our time," Jordan said, pulling the sheets of paper together in a neat pile and fastening them together with a paper clip. It reminded me of something I had almost forgotten.

I reached into my pocket and pulled out a piece of paper that I had written on at Cozzo's home. "Jordan, I never told this to Sennett, but, when I was at Cozzo's home, after they had removed his body, I found a paper clip under the cushion of the beat-up leather chair."

"So? Lots of people have stuff stuck in their chairs."

"Not Arnold Cozzo. He looked too fastidious for that."

"Okay, so he left a paper clip there on purpose," she said. "What does that mean?"

"The chair was cracked and creased, but I thought I could make out some letters."

I showed Jordan the paper with the letters on it. It read: GOOG, OLGA, 1541. She studied it intently, looking at it on both sides, turning it upside down.

"Why didn't you tell Sennett about this?" she asked.

"You can see what he's like. He would have laughed it off. He's a pro, and I'm just a doctor. What do you make of it?" I asked.

"I'm not sure, but the only "goog" I know is Google, the internet search engine," she said. "Maybe Cozzo was trying to tell us something before he died. I'll check the internet."

We went into the library and turned on the computer. I wasn't particularly facile around computers, but I had Jordan on hand, and it wasn't long before she had the screen papered with Google pages.

I felt a little stupid as she worked the search engine by typing in Olga. There were several Olgas on the screen, including OLGA, the Online Guitar Archive, the OLGA and the HFA threat site, and Olga's Gallery, the online art museum.

We looked at the guitar site. It was a submission site. If you had a song and wanted it on the service, you submitted it. After studying it for a while, we gave up. Even Jordan found it too complicated. OLGA and the HFA Threat was even more bizarre, featuring a court order to cease and desist the website. That left us with Olga's Gallery. Jordan opened it up.

"It says here that this is one of the largest online collections of art works."

"This makes more sense. When we went into Cozzo's townhouse, there were art books all over the place," I explained. "Mostly those coffee table art books."

"Did you go through them?"

"I remember thumbing through a book on the table. There were a few pages that were creased at the corner."

"Do you remember what they were?"

"You're stretching it, Jordan. I'm not an art person, and I only remember two of the photographs." I paused to think. "One was a picture of a bull by Picasso. I remember it from college."

"*Guernica*," she said excitedly. I snapped my fingers.

I went to the bookshelves, pulled out an old art book of Jordan's, Jansen's *A History of Art*, and started turning the pages aimlessly.

"What are you looking for?" Jordan asked

"There was a green picture of a ballet dancer on one of the pages. She wore a tutu and toe shoes. Her feet were resting on an instrument of some kind. It was kind of a dark painting. It wasn't modern, but it wasn't like one of those realistic portraits either."

"Degas painted ballet dancers in the 19th century. He had a famous painting called *The Green Room*."

Jordan took the book from me and found the section on Degas. She found a picture that looked very similar. "That's it. How did you know that?" I asked.

"The same way you know what artery is behind the tonsil. Remember, I had an art history minor in college."

"I recall the last photo I saw in the book was the David sculpture by Michelangelo."

"What about the 1541? Is that a page number?"

"Who knows? Maybe it's a date."

"Well, if it's 1541, that leaves out Picasso and Degas. Let's look up Michelangelo." Jordan thumbed through her battered copy of Jansen's to the section on the famous Italian artist. There was a timeline for the year 1541 at the beginning of the chapter. "1541 was definitely in the time of Michelangelo. Let's see what he was doing during that period."

She found the section on the famous Italian artist. Her eyes seemed transfixed as she read about the artist and turned the pages slowly. When she came to the Sistine Chapel, I could see her stop.

"What is it?"

"It says here that Michelangelo completed the last fresco at the Sistine Chapel in 1541. It's called the Judgment Day."

"So we have a Judgment Day. A judgment for what? It doesn't make sense."

"In the Last Judgment, God renders his decision as to who goes to heaven and who goes to hell. Twenty years passed between the time he painted the eighth and the ninth, or last, fresco. It was much different than the other paintings, darker and more solemn, his vision of Judgment Day. God is in the middle as both the consecrated and the ruined plead for mercy."

"Are you saying that in the murderer's last judgment, it is he who is playing God?"

"Remember, Ben, we're dealing with a psychopath," Jordan said with a frown. "Reality and fantasy can be hard to distinguish. To the killer this may all be a part of a game, like his game of hangman."

"Yeah, except this was much more complicated," I said. "They used body parts to spell words."

"And you believe that the killer is playing a spelling game with these murdered children?" Jordan asked in disbelief.

I nodded. "Remember what Flo said. All serial killers are playing some type of game. It wouldn't be beyond reason to assume that the names of the victims and the organs may have some significance based on the order in which they were killed or how their names were spelled."

Jordan picked up her papers, spread them out on the table again, looked at the names from the list, and then stopped for a moment. "There have been nine murders and nine body parts. That's a lot of permutations," she said, as if talking to herself and then began again. "There has to be some order to this. Let's write them down in chronological order of their murders." She proceeded to list them in vertically.

Ianoulli
Lennell
Gustafson
Issacson
Ulanoff
Davidson
Ishaki

Zielinski

Islington

When it came to the organs she started and then stopped again. "You're going to have to help me out here."

I went to the library, pulled out my copy of *Stedman's Medical Dictionary*, and brought it back to the kitchen. "Okay, let's write down the organ removed next to the victim's name," I said. "Ianoulli was the first." I sat down next to her and pulled out the reports that Sennett had given me. Then I picked up the yellow legal pad and carefully wrote down the names in a second vertical column next to the victim's name.

Umbilicus

Nipple

Ileum

Vein

Eye

Rib

Skin

Arm

Lip

We both stared at the list. "In time sequence, Danielle Ianoulli was the first victim in St. Louis," I said. "She had her umbilicus removed. Janice Lennell had her nipple cut off and placed in her hand. Helene Gustafson had her ileum removed. Stacey Issacson had her internal jugular vein opened. Virginia Ulanoff had her eye taken out. Peter Davidson had his rib removed. Hamoud Ishaki had the skin of his body taken off. Brett Zielinski had his arm amputated. Rhonda Islington had her lower lip removed."

"In the game hangman, I always remembered that it was the first letter of the name that was the letter you used," she said.

Using that logic, she wrote down a list of all the first letters from each name and body part, put them in random order, and then studied them. After a few minutes, she put her pencil down, exasperated. "Doing it this way doesn't make any sense. There must be some order to the letters."

"Why don't you place them in the order of the murders?"

She wrote down the letters again, this time in order of occurrence:

I-L-G-I-U-D-I-Z-I

She followed these with the first letters of the organs:

U-N-I-V-E-R-S-A-L

Jordan studied the list carefully. "I know you're going to think this is crazy, but there is one phrase . . ." She paused.

"What is it?"

"It's Italian: *il* means the. Now let's look up *giudizi*. I have an Oxford English/

Italian dictionary that I bought for a trip to Italy a few years ago. Let me look." She went back to the library and returned with a worn paperback. I watched as she flipped through the pages. Finally, she came to a page and spread the book open. "The only thing that is close is the word *Giudizo.*"

"What's that?"

"It's Italian for judgment or the judgment."

"Like the page Cozzo had open in his book. What was that called?" I asked.

"The Last Judgement."

"Perhaps Cozzo was trying to tell us something before he died. What is Italian for Judgment Day?" I asked.

She looked again in her Italian/English dictionary. "The idiom for the Last Judgment is *il giudizio universale.* Let's write the victim's names down on one side and then line up the other letters of the organs continuously. She wrote them down carefully:

I-L-G-I-U-D-I-Z-I-U-N-I-V-E-R-S-A-L

She then glared at the line for what seemed like an eternity. Finally, she spoke: "There are two letters missing, O and E. If he is playing hangman, then those are the two letters left to play."

"How do we know which letter is a victim and which is an organ?"

"I would bet on O for the person and E for the organ. That's the way they have lined it up. In game theory there has to be consistency. That would be the order of insertion. The killer is too compulsive to change the rules. He would consider it unfair."

Unfair? Unfair applied to sporting events and tests and punishment from your parents. Jordan was right, only a psychopath would consider switching the order of letters in a deadly contest unfair. "What do you think the chances are that we're right?"

Jordan shrugged. "This is all a game. Who knows what the truth is? What organ could he be dealing with?"

I looked back at the dictionary and wrote down a few words. I realized it was fruitless. "Just like the notes on our door and the videotape, the killer is taunting us," I said angrily.

"He's a psychopath and probably deeply involved in medicine, nursing, biology, something like that," Jordan responded clinically.

"Wait," I said, "maybe that's part of his game. Maybe he wants us to *think* he is a doctor. Have you considered that? I've got to see Sennett."

I snatched up the list and raced out of the house.

I FOUND SENNETT BACK AT HIS OFFICE. He was grumpier than he had been at the house. He had no leads, only frustration, and he seemed unwilling to listen to any ideas outside of the police book. It took about ten minutes of explanation before Sennett would begin to consider my crazy idea. I emphasized the idea, point by point, tapping on the notepad I had opened on his desk. "George, it's the only thing we can even begin to hang our hat on."

"How in the hell are we going to find that O person?"

"There was one victim in Chicago, one in St. Louis, one in Peoria, one in Madison, and one in Cleveland. The rest were killed in the Detroit area. The common thread that runs through these murders is the rehab clinics."

Sennett went back to the coffee pot and poured himself another slug of sludge. He asked me if I wanted some, but I was already too wired. I think it would have given me a heart attack.

"We have no leads in St. Louis," I continued, "and a presumed perpetrator found dead with items from the murdered victims. We checked out the clinic in Cleveland and nothing turned up. We've checked out Chicago and found Arnold Cozzo. We followed him to Monroe. Now he's dead. That means all we have are the clinics in Detroit."

"What are you getting at?"

"All of the recent victims were from Detroit, probably from the Wallenbrook Clinic," I said.

"The Wallenbrook Clinic is a huge place. There were thousands of patients treated there. How do we know which ones had our killer?"

Sennett was right. We had to narrow the scope down. I thought about the murders and the age of the victims.

"Some patient with the last name starting with O who had a nerve root injection about fifteen to twenty years ago." Sennett remained dubious. "Have you got a better lead?" I asked.

Sennett was hard-headed, but not stubborn enough to miss a potential source of information. It took a brief but explosive phone conversation with Wilhelm to get the medical records department of the Wallenbrook Clinic to crank up their computer. A half hour later we were sitting in Sennett's office when the computer list came off the fax machine. There were sixty-two names on the list. Seven of them started with the letter "O."

It was agony going through the list. Two of the patients were dead. Of the other five, their medical records indicated that four of them had grown children. One of them, Christine Overton, had a fifteen-year-old daughter, who lived at home with her mother.

Knudsen looked surprised as Sennett dropped the list on his desk and rushed out of the office with Christine Overton's address in his hand and me trailing at his heels like an obedient dog.

CHAPTER 29

I TOOK US ABOUT TWENTY MINUTES with his bubblegum light on to reach the northwestern suburb of Novi. We passed a couple of huge shopping malls on either side of the expressway and exited south on Novi Road. As we did, I looked at the parking lots filled with cars and shoppers with eager dollars in their hands. It was a far cry from the city.

Chittingham Downs, the Overton's subdivision, could have been in the Cotswold. The entranceway was made of wrought iron and limestone blocks. A divided boulevard at the entrance was surrounded by a lush garden of red, white and violet flowers, and carefully manicured hedges.

The Overton house was on Chilton Court. It seemed like any other normal house in a neighborhood of large four thousand square foot limestone and brick Tudor homes on half-acre lots. There was a Lincoln Navigator and an Escape in the driveway. One for Mom and one for the teenager. Normal fare in a community dominated by Ford Motor Company.

We walked up a red brick walkway to a front entrance with a brass coach light on either side of the door. It opened and a tall woman in her mid-forties wearing a sleeveless V-neck shirt and mid-length Polo shorts came out on the front stoop. She had sweptback, straight blond hair, blue eyes, a tanned face and arms. Her left hand was pale in comparison to the rest of her, probably testimony to some serious time on the golf course.

Sennett showed her his badge. "Mrs. Overton, I wonder if your daughter is at home?"

"Why, has Christy done something wrong?" In her voice was the fear of a parent's worst nightmare.

"No, not at all. However, we're investigating a string of crimes around the city and your name came up as a person who was treated several years ago at the Wallenbrook Clinic. That treatment might have some relationship to the investigation."

"What relationship does my daughter have to this?" The voice came from a tall, athletically built man in an Izod shirt who walked up to Mrs. Overton and put his arm around her. I could almost see him on the first tee, Titleist over-sized club in hand, twisting his lean body through the drive and ramming the ball two-fifty down the middle.

"Are you Mr. Overton?" Sennett asked.

"Yes. And this is my daughter Christy. Now what is the problem?"

Christy peered at us from behind her parents. She was a carbon copy. Same blond hair, same upturned nose, same blue eyes. Besides, she was wearing a golf shirt. It made you believe in genetics. There was no question of paternity here.

Sennett looked at the scene and dropped his eyes.

"Now that I've seen your daughter, I think we've made a mistake, Mrs. Overton. We won't bother you anymore."

"Aren't you going to tell us what you came for?"

"I think we had a case of misidentification."

"Oh," Mr. Overton said, as if that was all that could come to his mind.

"Thank you for your time."

We walked back to the car, depressed. If this weren't so serious, it would have almost been comical. Our best lead had melted away.

We drove back to headquarters and waited impatiently in front of the shiny brass elevator doors. An uncomfortable silence emanated from the people around us, some of them in uniform. It was as if they expected Sennett to give them an answer they knew he didn't have. I could see why he was agitated.

When we got back to his office, he opened the door, made for the desk chair, and slumped downward in dejection. "Shit, I thought you were on to something. Another dead end, another dead child."

"I'm sorry, Lieutenant," was all I could manage.

"Me too. Did you see all those people in the department staring at me as if I were the sole person responsible for this fiasco?"

"Yeah, I'm sorry." I knew I was in trouble when I started repeating myself.

Sennett's eyes were downcast as he picked his nails irritably with the open end of a paper clip. "It's almost as if the killer is outthinking us, and I'm to blame."

"You're not to blame," I insisted, moved by the utter misery of his voice. "We're dealing with a very clever psychopath."

"Well, he must be smarter than me, because right now I'm coming up with *gornisch*."

I looked at him quizzically. "Where did you come up with that expression?"

"C'mon, Doc. You eat at the delis I eat at and you learn a lot of words."

"I should have known that with you it would come down to some visceral response," I said, not really in the mood for witty repartee.

"Yeah, visceral. That's a good word. I need a visceral response, maybe even an epiphany."

"I still believe in the day of judgment," I said stubbornly. "I've looked at all the murders. I've looked at each case. There are too many coincidences. I think this psychotic has invented a very complex game."

"It seems like it," Sennett agreed. "Any suggestions?"

My pager went off as we were talking. The office. One of my patients needed pain medication. I told Sennett to wait for a moment as I dialed the patient's pharmacy near the hospital.

I waited endlessly for the pharmacist to come to the phone, then another impatient minute as he asked me a list of questions, including my DEA number. My narcotic identification was important. It was like a PIN number to pharmacists, allowing me access to their drug bank.

It was an irritating intrusion, but the call gave me an idea. I turned back to Sennett. "We need to find out if Mary Anne Zielinski ever had any prescriptions filled in the last twenty years."

When I explained that we might be able to trace her doctor's name through old prescriptions, he picked up the phone and called for Knudsen. It took Sennett about ten minutes to come back with a list from Mary Anne Zielinski's chart. Nothing popped out from the medications, so I asked him if the state kept a record of narcotic prescriptions. It took another call to the state capitol in Lansing to find out it did and another thirty minutes to receive a fax. Sennett brought the copy of Mary Anne Zielinski's pain medication into the office.

"It's a doctor I've never heard of," he said.

"Who is it?"

"Dr. Larry Schneider."

"I know him," I gasped.

This was becoming a nightmare. I had known Larry for twenty years, since he first came to St. Vincent's. He was a good doctor, and I left it at that. To even think he may have had something to do with these deaths was beyond comprehension. Then I remembered his performance at the M and M conference. Was it possible that Larry's anger went beyond a temper tantrum? Could he be the killer? Maybe. It gave me the shivers.

"We need to speak with him, Ben," Sennett said with some urgency.

"He's easy to find. His office is across from mine in the medical arts building next to St. Vincent's. He runs a pain clinic there in the afternoon." As soon as I said it, I knew what Sennett was thinking. Things were adding up quickly. I just found it hard to believe.

It took us twenty minutes to get to the St. Vincent's medical building.

Sennett left the car in the circle in front of the building and jumped out. The admonition from the guard at the front was no match for his badge. He brushed past him and took the stairs two at a time to the front door.

We found Larry's name on the directory and took the elevator to the third floor. Walking into the cramped waiting room, we found the front desk behind a bevy of wheelchairs and patients on crutches. There wasn't a happy face among them.

An elderly woman was at the counter, trying to fish her Medicare card from her purse. Sennett looked at her and then up at the receptionist. He didn't wait to sign in. Instead, he pushed through the door and was in the back office.

Larry was coming down the narrow hallway with a chart in his hand. He looked at me and smiled with surprise. As he was about to say something, Sennett thrust his badge in front of his face. Schneider looked from side to side, then down the hall. It was the look of someone who had been busted before.

Before I could say anything, Larry turned and led us back to his office. It was a corner room with a small antique desk, a thick wool carpet, and some ornamental Japanese prints on the wall. There was a small, polished mahogany table adjacent to the desk in front of a window that overlooked the parking lot and the hospital in the distance. On the sill were some framed photos. In a different environment it might have been a power office.

Larry walked calmly in and sat down at the table in one of the ornately carved modern Chinese wooden chairs with thick green seat cushions. He motioned us to join him. As I sat down, I looked at the photographs on the sill. I thought I recognized one of the men.

"What can I do for you, gentlemen?" There was a little belligerence in his tone. Sennett ignored the tone and replied in a measured voice. "As you may or may not know, Dr. Dailey and I have been investigating the murders of several young adults in the metropolitan Detroit area."

Schneider looked over at me with surprise. "What does that have to do with me?"

"Your DEA number was found on a prescription bottle in the possession of the mother of one of the victims, Mary Anne Zielinski."

"I don't remember the patient. Let me see if I have a file on her. What was her name again?"

We wrote down the name Mary Anne Zielinski, and he gave the note to his nurse. She scurried back to her files, and two minutes of silence later, she came back. There was nothing there. "I don't know what to tell you, gentleman," he said. Strangely, the usual belligerence was out of his voice. It was replaced by a tone of empathy I had not heard from him before.

Sennett wasn't about to give up that easily. "I know this might be difficult, but I'm wondering if you could establish your whereabouts in August 1988."

Schneider looked puzzled. "That's a long time ago. I usually throw out my log records from that far back." He paused for a moment. "Perhaps I have some type of record, maybe something on my CV."

He walked over to a cabinet next to his desk and pulled out a sheaf of papers. After a minute or two of looking them over, he pulled out a single sheet and handed it to Sennett. "I was out of the country at a meeting."

Sennett wasn't about to let a piece of paper make him give up that quickly. "Anyone that can verify your story?" Sennett asked after looking at the sheet.

"Yeah." Schneider hesitated a moment. "David Wilhelm."

I looked at the picture on the windowsill and now recognized Wilhelm's face. I pointed it out to Sennett, and he nodded. It was a complete package, and we both knew it. I felt bad for accusing Larry. Sennett didn't seem fazed.

"Why don't we get Dr. Wilhelm on the line and see if he will vouch for you."

Schneider hesitated for a moment, and then reached for a polished brass phone at the edge of his desk. He dialed a number he obviously knew by heart.

"David, this is Lawrence. I have a Lieutenant Sennett here from the Detroit Police Department." There was a pause at the other end. "He wants to know where I was in August 1988. Maybe you could tell him."

He handed the phone to Sennett, and I waited as they spoke. I could see Larry looking at me. There was a hurt expression in his eyes, like I had let him down, and I was beginning to think I had. Then Sennett hung up the phone and got up from the table.

"Thank you, doctor. We might be in touch with you. I'm going to leave you my card. If you think of something, call me at that number. It's important." He dropped the card on Schneider's desk.

I was going to say something to Larry, but he was already out the door. I knew I was guilty by association. We walked out of the office, a little bewildered, and stopped in front of the elevator. "Wilhelm made his alibi," I guessed. Sennett nodded. "The killer is playing games with us, Lieutenant."

"Games?" Sennett said. "It just makes sense. Schneider runs a pain clinic. His number is on the pills."

The thought that Larry Schneider could have murdered someone made me sick. "So you think he did it?" I asked.

"It's too pat," Sennett said. "Yeah, his alibi is good, and I don't think he fits the picture of the type of psychopath I've been carrying around in my head, but I don't know . . ."

"I thought you didn't believe in hunches."

"I don't." He stopped for a moment, as if he had forgotten something. "Don't get me wrong, I'm going to check him out, believe me. We'll run a DNA test on him."

"What's next?"

"Sometimes I think I'm playing games with myself," Sennett sighed. "I know you believe in this Judgment Day theory, but I have a murder to try and solve. It's too tough trying to track down these leads. I need to get solid facts."

"I think I'm right."

"Then you keep thinking that and leave the police work to me."

Sennett fumbled in his pocket, pulling out a pen and a notepad, announcing to all that would hear that he had forgotten his damn cell at the office. After a couple of more frustrated seconds of digging, he finally found some change and took it out.

"Do me a favor. Don't give up on my theory. There has to be a connection," I said.

Sennett didn't answer me. Instead, he stopped at a phone in the lobby and called his office to pick up his messages. He just stared at the elevator doors and said nothing as he listened. I was getting used to the intent look of his face. It meant trouble. "I've got to run," he said grimly. "Someone called in with a tip, saying they knew who killed the Islington girl."

"You think it's for real?"

"It's hard to say. We've investigated so many tips, and they've all come up empty. But I can't take a chance."

Sennett didn't say anything else. I could feel for him. The angel of death was lurking in every shadow, and so far we were powerless to stop it.

We went to the entrance door and waited for an old man in a walker with his wife to go through. I watched for a moment as they struggled down the hall, the wife with her arm under her husband's. I thought of Jordan and me. Would that be her holding me up? Or would I still be active at that age? At my age I wondered whether I'd be around long enough to enjoy my child. The thought unnerved me.

We didn't say much on the ride back. Sennett dropped me off at his office where I had left my car. He told me he would be in touch and drove off.

I walked back to my car, disconsolate. I didn't know where to turn. All I was convinced of was that there was going to be another murder. I stopped just short of the car when I saw the note attached to my windshield. I had no doubt who it was from. I picked it up and read slowly.

Life is a game and death is its aim.
You can wait for my joy or suffer in pain.
Your choice.

Friend of the Devil

What choice was there? I would never wait for anything.

CHAPTER 30

I WENT BACK UP TO HIS OFFICE. Knudsen was used to me being there, so I nodded as I went in. I wasn't sure about many things, but I knew if we could find a bottle with a DEA number, we might find the killer. I also knew I was on my own now. Sennett was under too much pressure, and my ideas were too obtuse for him. I sat at Sennett's desk, frustrated. Dammit, I thought I had it figured out, but the killer outguessed us. Larry Schneider was just a ruse. But Connie Lennell might not be.

I called her again. She was at her apartment. When I told her about what I had found, she seemed to come alive over the phone. "Connie, I know it was a long time ago, but I'm wondering if you had any papers or prescriptions from the doctor that treated your back?"

There was a silence at the other end. Then she spoke. "Yes," she said in a breathless voice. "Why do you ask?"

"What were they?"

"Just some old bottles for pain medication. After Jannie died, I cleaned the apartment and found them lying in the back of a linen closet. I was going to throw them away, but then I looked at the date. It was around the time she was conceived. I know it sounds crazy, but I saved anything that in any way could have been related to her. To me they were like a link to the past, a link to Jannie. I couldn't throw any of that away, no matter how insignificant. If I did, I felt I would be losing part of her."

I was almost breathless. The evidence was right in front of us while we were standing in her living room. If we had only known. "Can you get them for me?"

"Why?"

"Because whoever wrote those scripts had to use a narcotic number," I explained. "Maybe the killer got careless and left his number."

Again, there was a loud silence before she spoke. "You mean all these years his name was right under my nose?" I knew exactly how she felt.

"It's too early to say that, Connie. Get the vial and read the numbers to me."

I could hear her in the background and imagined what was going through her mind as she rummaged through her daughter's memorabilia. In a couple of minutes she came back to the phone. "Here it is. It's old and the writing is faded. It looks like A-E, although the E looks fuzzy. The numbers are either 4-4-9-6-4-2-2 or 4-4-8-5-4-2-2."

I wrote them down. "I'll call you back, Connie. Thanks a lot. Now I need to do some checking."

I called Jordan and asked her to chase the numbers down through her contact at the DEA, but she said it might take a while. I sat for a moment at Sennett's desk and stared at a line of photos of the victims. I assumed it was for motivation. Personally, I didn't need any.

I was putting some papers back in my briefcase when Knudsen walked in. He looked a little sheepish as he held some pages in his hand. I could see they were from the Wallenbrook Clinic.

"Dr. Dailey, I don't mean to be sticking my nose where it doesn't belong," he said, "but I was looking over this list. I know you're searching for a family with a last name beginning with O."

"Yeah, we found them. Nothing panned out."

"I think you missed one."

"What do we mean missed one? We scanned the whole list three times."

"It's not that. It's just in Nordic languages the O sound is often produced by A. Let me show you. There's a patient on the list with the name Grace Aakesson. In Swedish that would be pronounced Okeson."

"How can a guy named Knudsen be so sure?" I asked.

"My mother came from Lund on the southern coast of Sweden. I'm pretty fluent."

"A name like Knudsen, I should have known Scandinavian ancestors," I said.

"You never know when your ancestors might come in handy," he replied and handed me the woman's address and phone number. I thanked him and sat back down at Sennett's desk, staring at the number. Was this another false lead, or was the killer taunting us one more time? I decided that I would find out for myself. Sennett wasn't up for another wild goose chase.

I called the home number, but no one answered. It was impulsive, but I decided to go there myself. Before I left I called Jordan. There was no answer, so I wrote a note and asked Knudsen to call her later.

I got directions to Grace Aakesson's home from Knudsen and pocketed it. It didn't take me long to reach my car. I sat behind the wheel for a moment and looked at the address. It was in St. Clair Shores, a working-class suburb northeast of Detroit and one of the critical "swing" districts, the ones the politicians love to focus on—auto industry, blue collar, core values.

Grace Aakesson lived in an older subdivision off I-94. Built in the late '60s, it had at one time been the home of baby boomers. Now it was filled with owners ready to sell to the next generation.

It was late when I arrived. The heat from the day lingered, and the mosquitoes were everywhere. Dusk had fallen, and the afterglow of the sun cast a yellowish gray haze throughout the neighborhood. Searching for the address in the dwindling light was difficult, but I finally found the right house at the end of a cul de sac. It was a neat, white aluminum-sided ranch with a light on over the front door. The street was quiet, and a couple of bikes were out on the front lawn. From the hum of the air conditioning, I suspected most people were inside, hiding from the heat.

I got out of the car, walked up to the front door, and rang the doorbell. There was no answer. In the receding light I peeked through the window and saw only drawn shades, so I walked down the steps and followed a tall, thick hedge next to the driveway to the back of the house.

When I reached the back corner of the house, I turned and surveyed the yard. The sounds of deep summer clearly resonated among the backyards and open spaces; the bark of a dog a few houses down, songbirds intimidating caterpillars with their trills, a hose nearby spraying soap off a car before it got too dark.

The rear door was in front of me. I looked around and then reached for the handle. I heard a sound and turned just in time to see a truck come up the driveway. I was like a deer in the headlights.

It was a Ford F-150 King Cab. A huge man slid out of the front seat. He had a hanging mustache, a long mullet down his neck, and a series or tattoos on his arms. One of them spelled *Semper Fi*.

"What's your problem, buddy?" he asked.

"No problem," I said hesitantly. "My name is Dr. Benjamin Dailey. I've been working on a case with the Detroit Police Department. I needed to ask you a couple of questions."

"Yeah, a doctor, huh?" By this time he was in front of me. I could smell what was probably the afterglow of the six Budweisers he had sucked down at the local pub.

"That's correct." I was about to say something else, when he grabbed me by the arm and flung me against the truck, knocking the wind out of me.

"How about I kick the shit out of you and leave you for the police? Trespassing is an offense in this neighborhood."

"Wait," I gasped. "Let me take the wallet out of my back pocket and show you my badge. I'm telling the truth."

I don't know if it was the alcohol or the tone of my voice, but he let go for a moment as I reached in my pocket for my wallet. I extracted it and pulled out my shield. It was my only hope, before this giant kicked the crap out of me. I shoved it into his hand.

He looked at it for a moment, staring at the writing. "So you're a doctor, huh? What the hell you doing here?" His hand was raised threateningly.

"Do you have a daughter?"

"Yeah, what about it?"

"I'm worried about her, Mr. Aakesson."

His raised hand stopped in mid-air. "Why?"

"I've been investigating a series of murders with the police. I have reason to believe that your daughter might be in danger."

"Impossible."

"Why?"

"I dropped her off at the train station this morning. She went to Chicago to visit her mother."

"Did you see her get on the train?"

"Sure did."

A wave of relief followed by an intense feeling of stupidity came over me. "I'm sorry. I thought I was following a lead."

"Are you the police or just a doctor?"

Just a doctor? What did that mean? "Look, call Sergeant Knudsen at this number. Check me out." I gave him Sennett's office number.

"I will. Until I do, I'm going to just make sure you don't go anywhere." He found a rope in the back of his truck and wrapped my arms tightly. I had no choice. If I ran, he would have chased me down and killed me. When he was done, he tied me to the bumper. I sat down on the ground as the mosquitos bit at me. It was torture as I waited.

Ten minutes later he walked out of his house. "Your sergeant vouched for you. I'm going to release you. If you do anything fancy, I'm going to kill you. Do we have an understanding?"

I nodded weakly as he untied me. When the ropes were off, I started rubbing my wrists. "Listen, do me a favor and call your wife when your daughter gets to Chicago. Just make sure she's okay."

"Grace ain't my wife anymore. I kicked her sick ass out of the house after my daughter was born."

"Just call her," I pleaded.

"I'll think about it. Now get the hell out of here and don't come back."

I skulked back to my car, my pride wounded and my confidence shaken.

I turned the engine on and waited for the air-conditioning to kick in. That's when my cell phone rang. It was Jordan.

"Ben, where are you?"

"Just getting some bug spray. Why?"

"I checked on those DEA numbers," she said anxiously. "One is a doctor Eagleton in Missoula, Montana with that number. He's a retired GP who worked overseas for the Foreign Service."

"Another dead end," I said dejectedly.

"Not necessarily."

"What do you mean?"

"I was always taught in law school to look for similarities in cases," Jordan said. "You know, a V could look like a U and an F could look like an E. On a chance I asked if that number belonged to someone else with similar first letters. They came up with an AF 4486422. It's someone we both know."

"Who is that?"

"Carl Fairchild."

"Fairchild? Are you sure?"

"It's what the computer spat out, Ben."

It could make sense. Fairchild knew Schneider and they were always at each other's throats. Maybe he set him up. Fairchild was an anesthesiologist. He was used to giving spinals and could very easily masquerade as a fellow in a pain clinic. But killing innocent people . . . was he capable of that?

"I'll call you back. I need to speak with Sennett."

"Don't do anything rash, Ben. You don't know if this is a coincidence or not." There was a panic in her voice as if she knew what was going to happen.

"I'll be fine."

Then she uttered the three most favorite words of the patient going into the operating room and a husband talking to his wife: "I trust you."

"And I love you too," I said, not knowing what else to say and hoping she would remember it.

I called Sennett's office and Knudsen answered.

"Honestly, Dr. Dailey, I don't know where the lieutenant is. He said something about seeing a doctor at a rehab clinic somewhere."

"Any news?"

"Nothing, except I think you might be interested that I got a call from the Chicago police regarding a Mrs. Woods. She was expecting her daughter to arrive by train this morning. She's been frantic. No one knows where she is. She asked me to place a missing person report."

My blood froze. "What was the kid's name?

"Dawn Aakesson."

"Shit! If you get a hold of Sennett, tell him I've got a lead, but I don't want to string him on. Tell him I'm going to check out a Dr. Carl Fairchild, and I'll call him. Tell him I want to be sure this time." Knudsen tried to ask me something else, but I just hung up and took off.

It was already late when I called the hospital and asked for the operator. I waited impatiently while she got number of the chief of anesthesia, Fred Black, hoping he was still there. If anyone would know about Carl Fairchild, he would. Black answered on the first ring. He seemed a little surprised to hear from me.

"What's going on, Ben? Emergency vocal cord surgery?"

"Maybe worse. What do you know about Carl Fairchild?"

"In terms of what?"

"Where he came from, his past training, who are his friends?" I asked impatiently. "There's a chance he might be messed up in something real bad at the hospital."

"Like what?"

"I can't say right now. Off the record, what do you know?"

"He transferred from Samaritan," Black said, a little shaken. "I spoke with Bill Jeffords about him. A little bit of a prima donna. He trained at St. Joseph's University Hospital in Chicago. Medical school in Indiana and Yale undergrad. Always thought he was a little smarter than everyone else, like that day at the conference. Never married, but his sexual proclivities are unknown. Never sued, no criminal record, if that's what you mean."

"What about research?" I pressed.

"Interesting. He did research on cadavers, regarding alveolar-capillary block."

"Anything peculiar about it?"

"Come to think of it, I did have a complaint from one of the assistants in the dissection lab that Fairchild was performing dissections on other parts of the body, intestine, eyes, things like that."

"What happened?"

"I asked him about it. He said that he was trying to understand some of the problems that surgeons had with their own surgery. I basically brushed it off. Hell, it was a cadaver."

"Yeah, it was just a cadaver."

"Other than that, nothing else."

"I guess that's that. I appreciate the help."

Black stopped me before I could hang up. "There is one other thing that I almost forgot. About a month ago I got a call from a doctor with a foreign-sounding name. It was Ahmad something or other. It was hard to understand him. He had a thick accent."

"What did he want?"

"He asked many of the same questions you did."

"What did you tell him?"

"Honestly, I didn't know who he was. I didn't tell him much. Once in a while we get calls like that. You never know who you're talking to, so I generally refer them to the medical staff office."

"Did he ask you what he was looking for?"

"It was crazy stuff. Things about insemination of women in pain clinics while they were sedated."

I smiled inwardly. Masri seemed like a smart cookie. Always one step—no, a whole leap ahead—of the rest of us. "Did you ask him if he had any proof?"

"He mentioned Fairchild's name. When he did, I ended the call. There are so many people out there trying to say and do things, and this was out of my province."

"Did you tell Carl?"

"Yeah, I mentioned to him that I had this phone call. I even mentioned the guy's name. He laughed when he heard it, and I didn't think much more about it. Carl doesn't run a pain clinic and doesn't do anything except for what's monitored in the operating room. We have to be careful about accusing people without proof. You above all should know that."

"No doubt about that. Did you ever follow through with the medical staff people?"

"I called up there the next day. They never heard anything. I thought it was a crank call and forgot about it."

I thought about my own experience with the medical staff. I wasn't surprised. It was a don't ask, don't tell organization. "Yeah, well, it probably was. Do you remember anything else?"

"There is one other thing."

"What's that?"

"The QA committee is supposed to meet on that case that Fairchild brought up at the conference."

"Fred, do me a favor."

"What's that?"

"Tell them they need to worry more about who they let on the staff."

CHAPTER 31

I THANKED HIM AND HUNG UP THE PHONE, trying to figure out the best move. I didn't want to go down another blind alley with Sennett. Telling him that Ahmad Masri was checking out Fairchild would have been more than he could accept, especially with the way he was feeling.

These thoughts tumbled through my head as I guided my car down Seven Mile Road past the Seventh Precinct station. I half-wondered if I should stop. Who would believe me? A doctor doing detective work. Besides, I doubted whether there was much time.

That's when the little man in my head began torturing me again. The idea that Dawn Aakesson was going to die unless I did something quickly overrode my caution. I had to go after Fairchild. There was no comfort in the realization that what I was doing was crazy, but I was helpless to say no.

As I turned off of Seven Mile, I realized that it all made perfect sense. Fairchild, the ultimate effete snob with his fancy dinners, his art, and his "eclectic" decorating. A man who was so perfect he couldn't stand anyone suggesting he had a flaw. I would bet that, deep inside, he knew he was inadequate to the bone. An anesthesiologist would fit in perfectly. They frequently ran pain clinics. His friend, Cozzo, had given him access. After that it was easy. Work in a university setting where they needed help. Masquerade as a fellow or a resident. Steal someone's identity. Fill in other doctors' names.

Once inside, he was in the clear. Sedate the women, inseminate them and wait. He fathered the children, now he could take his time. The game might take a while, but it would be worth it.

The only other question was why. Why murder your own children? For a game? Even Fairchild wasn't that shallow. There had to be a deeper reason.

Murder, his only solace. And what was his relationship to Ahmad Masri, acquaintance or accomplice?

By the time I arrived at Strathcona, it was dark. An early evening thunderstorm had just passed through, leaving a dense haze in the warm, humid air that seemed impregnable to the widely spaced streetlights. The full moon helped, shining between the lofty maples that lined the streets. I looked around at the houses on his block, each an island set apart from the others.

I found his home next to the large cemetery that bordered Woodward Avenue. The house was dark except for a single light shining from the entrance hall window. In the muted light, the large house was more imposing than I had remembered.

I thought a moment and then reached in the glovebox for the Walther PPK that Jordan had insisted I carry. I had used it on the target range, but never close up. I'd never shot anyone. Could I do it now? If I fucked up and shot somebody wrongfully, I'd be in seriously deep shit. I pocketed it and stepped out of the car, feeling less and less confident about what I was doing.

With my conviction fading, I took out my cell phone and dialed Sennett's number. Nothing but a busy signal, the kind that comes out when there is no connection. I tried three more times, then threw the phone on the seat in disgust and walked away from the car.

I looked at the single light in the entrance hall. It seemed to dare me to enter. Fingering the revolver in my pocket, I walked up the driveway. I shouldered past the sinister looking, densely packed ivy that covered the walls. It seemed malevolent, reaching out at me with a sharp, pointed finger. I stared at it again. A torn piece of plastic was hanging on one of the bushes. Beneath it was a pocketbook. I picked it up and looked at the contents of the pink wallet inside. There was a driver's license with the picture of a beautiful girl with blonde hair. It read: Dawn Aakesson.

I threw the purse down and walked quietly along the garage door. My pistol was in my hand as I made my way to the front entrance. The thought of whether I would actually use it shot through my mind again. But I knew it was too late for second thoughts. If I waited, the girl would be dead. Or maybe she already was.

Standing to the side of the door, I looked through the window panel. No movement. I pushed on the heavy oak door. Surprisingly, it sprung open. Carefully, I walked onto the parquet floor, again looking from side to side. A plain wooden table stood in the entrance, bearing a simple copper lamp that cast a dull light over the dark, wood-paneled foyer.

I looked to the right, where a light was coming from around the corner of the hallway. I backed against the wall as I made the turn, holding my gun next to me. What I saw almost made me gasp. In place of the large Motherwell print was a full-length oil of the devil, with his red hat, fiery eyes, black cloak and evil fingers reaching for me. I wanted to leave but couldn't. My weighted feet moved themselves inexorably forward, as if drawn by a magnet to the room with the light.

The light was coming from the study that Fairchild had been renovating. The door was cracked open. I went to the opening and looked into the room. There was a single leather chair with a small table next to it. On the table was a small brass lamp with the bulb lit. It partially illuminated a large, domed-ceiling room with the shutters closed. I looked up at the ceiling and struggled to make out the scenes painted with some type of fresco-like designs. They looked like photographs.

I walked into the room further to study the ceiling more closely. My heart fell to my stomach as sweat poured off my face. When I looked up, I saw in the dim light a photographic montage. In the center was Fairchild's picture, beneficent and smiling. Surrounding him were the photographs of nine mutilated bodies, each representing a dead victim. There was one space still blank. It was Fairchild's almost completed *Il Giudizio Universale*.

I turned again and stepped forward, sensing that someone was in the chair. As I came around the front, I froze. There, sitting in the chair, was the nude body of Julie McFarland. Her legs were apart, exposing the fine hair between her legs. Her hands were in her lap in a strange sense of repose. I looked at her face, ghastly pale with bright lipstick and rouge on her cheeks. Her mouth was gaping at me, jaw frozen and eyes wide open. I looked again, hoping she would say something, but then I realized she was dead. Her tongue had been cut out.

Suddenly, the light in the room became brilliant.

"Poor, beautiful Julie. It's a shame isn't it?"

I spun around quickly and stared into the face of Carl Fairchild, dressed in black, a black walking stick in his hand, and a twisted smile on his face. My gun rose automatically, but I was too slow. That's the last I remembered of the room.

I woke up in a daze, my head throbbing. I tried to reach up to feel my temple. That's when I realized that my hands were tied down. I shook my head back and forth, trying to clear my eyes. As they opened, I looked down at my legs and saw that they were strapped to wooden legs. I looked down at my feet. I was in a sitting position on a chair. Where was I?

I looked at the chair again. It was a rounded chair with spindles on the back. I could feel them with my hands. I felt the rope around my hands. They were fastened tightly to the upright wood of the chair back. I struggled to move them. There was precious little give.

A light shone in my face, and I felt as if I were sitting in an electric chair, waiting for execution. I glanced around again. The place had the feel of an operating room, but it smelled damp and musty. The unmistakable odor of formaldehyde filled the air.

I looked up. There were wooden beams over my head, like those in a basement. I looked to my right side again at a variety of tables encircling the room. They were filled with instruments and test tubes. There were mirrors lining the entire room. A laboratory?

I craned my head to the left, and that's when reality finally set in. There, strapped on an operating table, was a man with a familiar gray beard. I stared at him in disbelief. It was Ahmad Masri. He was supine, his arms bound in heavy Velcro, his gaze dancing furtively around the room. He seemed to beckon me to look to the right again.

I heard a noise from across the room in that direction and looked toward the sound. There was another operating table. On it was a stand holding metal stirrups, the kind used in a gynecologist's office. A naked girl lay on the table, with her firm white legs bent open and her feet in the stirrups, her pubis shrouded by a tuft of blond hair. I looked up along her body.

I was overwhelmed by the horror of her bound arms, taped mouth, and eyes darting wildly across the room was horrific, just like the video of Jessica Islington. I wanted to say something, to try and comfort her, but it was useless. My mouth was taped too.

The glass door to the room opened and in walked Fairchild in surgical scrubs with a mask partially covering his face. "Ah, the great Dr. Benjamin Dailey, surgeon to the stars, champion of the downtrodden. Welcome to my private operatory." As he spoke, he reached over and yanked the tape off my lips.

"You sonofabitch, Fairchild. I should have known." My mouthed burned from the tape.

"Should have, but didn't. Almost figured it out, but didn't. Shoulda, coulda, woulda. You're a big old ex-jock. Aren't those the words of the loser?"

"You couldn't kill me with the van, so now you've got your chance."

"It's true. I thought I had you in that Arab caterer's van. No one would have ever guessed it was me. If it hadn't been for that missed shot and . . ."

"Where are we?" As I spoke, I looked at the metal operating table next to my chair, where a variety of medical instruments were displayed. Some of them I recognized.

"Oh, you don't know? My house. My surgical laboratory. My own private operating room, all supplied by the closing of Samaritan. Can you believe it? They even made me pay them a dollar to make it look like a real business deal, and then they delivered it." He laughed in a high-pitched gurgle that echoed across the mirrored, musty room.

"Why did you kill Julie?"

"Ah, poor thing. She became too nosy for her own good. She found my operatory. What was I to do? Forget about the slut—I have. An inconsequential in my list of inconsequentials. Not bad to look at, but for all her talk, she was really quite an ordinary fuck. By the way, her death was extraordinarily exciting." Saliva gathered at the corner of his mouth as he spoke.

"Do all your inconsequentials die?" Fairchild circled around me as I spoke, examining me closely.

"Death is a punishment to some, to others—a rare few, I might add—a thing of indifference, and to many a favor. Seneca said something like that, in case you didn't know." He continued to stare at my arms and hands.

"What's it to Masri?"

"Bad luck for Masri. It's such a shame he had to be here with us, but he was too smart for his own good." Fairchild looked contemptuously at the old man's darting eyes. "He didn't trust the police and started his own investigation. He was actually quite good. I was surprised at how close he was getting. Fortunately, it was only a small glitch that actually became a very fortunate turn of events. Masri was a very useful decoy. Everyone is looking for this poor regrettable cretin."

"Just like James Carrington, a surrogate for your evil."

"That, my friend, was the perfect match," he said, his eyes glittering with pride. "I killed him, planted some information, and that was that. The police are so interested in solving murders that they forget to *think*. It was child's play. It was the same in St. Louis. Peoria was just luck. That drifter stole Virginia's wallet and got caught. Now that was true justice. I planned Peter Davidson's death when I heard about the attacks on the campus in Madison. That was another stroke of luck."

"The amazing Dr. Fairchild. You impregnated all those patients, didn't you?" My hands struggled against the rope. Still no give.

"Of course, can't you see the family resemblance?" He glanced over at the girl on the table and then gestured toward her like an impresario showing a circus crowd his latest rare animal. "My daughter, Dawn Aakesson."

"The missing O."

"Tsk, tsk. Right again, Doctor. You were so clever to guess the pronunciation. My only disappointment with you has been that you were slower than I thought you'd be catching on to my game."

I ignored his admonition. "And each of those other dead children is yours also," I said, "impregnated in a rehab clinic. How did you do it?"

"The wonders of anesthesia. A little touch of narcotic put these women to sleep. I sent the nurse out for some impossible task, and then I impregnated them."

"But never had intercourse with them."

"Horrors, never. Sex is such a beautiful thing, not to be marred by the game. They were all artificially inseminated." Fairchild lectured me in the same way he had spoken at the conference—indifferent, superior, unfeeling.

"Then, you sick bastard, you watched as their families fell apart."

"Similar to the way my family did."

"Your family?"

"That's right. My own sick and demented family. My mother lived in Haight Ashbury during the sixties. She must have slept with a lot of men. My father was the lucky one who knocked her up."

"And then he split."

"And so did my wonderful mother. Leaving me in the orphanage."

"The good Mrs. Fairchild."

"No, actually her name was Lehmann. I chose my name to honor the best thing she ever did."

"Where is your mother now?"

He paused, letting his lips curl just enough to see his sharp canines. When he spoke, a drip of saliva fell from the corner of his mouth. "I killed my mother by severing her trachea and watching her die. As she expired, I held up a sign that said, 'I am your son.' I buried her in a landfill outside of L.A. A nice touch, don't you think? Putting her in a garbage dump where she belonged."

"For a psychopath like you, it's appropriate," I uttered, trying to buy more time. "Somewhere there's a shithole waiting for your sorry bones." Fairchild leaped at me, waving his scalpel. I stared him down. "Careful, Prince of Darkness. You'll fuck up the suspense of what you are going to do. By the way, what about your father?"

Fairchild stiffened and drew back a foot or so. "An unworthy fellow. Drummer, hophead, anti-war militant, and finally maintenance man at a high school outside of Massilon, Ohio. His name was Rocco Bagnasi. I was surprised when I finally found him. Fat, dirty, and unkempt. Hardly a man I would introduce as my father."

I needed to keep him blathering until one single idea came into my head about how to escape. "What did you do with him, beat him to death with drumsticks or drown him in a janitor's bucket?"

"I used a sledgehammer. I found him in his car drinking a beer after school. It didn't take much to get him. I offered him a toke. Once he was in my car, I bound and gagged him. I never said a word to him, but I showed him a sign. It read, 'And my father sold me while yet my tongue / Could scarcely cry 'weep! weep! weep! weep!' The miscreant just looked at it. No appreciation for Blake. Really quite a disappointment. That's why I tapped his head with my hammer, a simple blow that sent the natural seams of the skull into a rather violent eruption." There was no remorse in his voice, just a simple statement of fact. "Quite a mess, I must say."

"And you buried him in another garbage dump."

"No. Actually I burned his body on a raft on a little pond out in the country near Niles, Michigan. It was at night. No one around for miles. It was really quite magical and a fitting end for these two embarrassments. They left me. Can you believe that? They left Carl Fairchild to fall prey to foster parents, animals who abused me for years. How would you like to be fucked by a forty-year-old alcoholic truck driver?"

He seemed to stiffen momentarily at the thought, his charred mind playing ancient tapes once more, the psychopathology of his abused childhood caught in the syntax of his suffering. Really, I might have started to pity him, except that the bonds on my hands and ankles kept me very current regarding my own predicament.

"I'm surprised you didn't kill them also."

"I did. Every one of them. The police will never know. I made the deaths all seem like accidents."

I struggled again. This time there was a little more give in the back. I had to keep him talking. "Nietzsche at work? A fitting philosophic groundwork."

"These were people not fit for life. Nietzsche would have approved wholeheartedly."

"Nietzsche was a philosopher who hated murder. He was a conscientious objector in World War I, an ambulance driver. He never proposed euthanasia."

"No sense splitting hairs," he said, shrugging his shoulders. "Life is, after all, based on one sort of philosophy or another, isn't it? And everyone has to pay for his beliefs."

"Yeah, what's your sick philosophy?" I continued struggling, trying to find some means of escape.

"Perfection. That is my philosophy. Truth. Rebellion."

"Is that why you killed your own offspring?"

He looked at me quizzically, then smiled. "My, you are a good student, aren't you?"

"You killed them, because in your eyes, none of them could match up to your standard. Isn't that right?"

I could see his nostrils flare slightly and his eyes, as hard as marbles, squint and redden like the devil's own. "None of those children were . . . quite *right*."

"And you are God deciding their fate."

He shook his head solemnly. "No. I am God's superior. The Rebel Angel, the Truth that struts behind all the sniveling lies. My children were imperfect. Take Hamoud Ishaki. What a disgrace, selling drugs across the border. And Stacey Issacson, whose father performed abortions."

"That was her fault?"

He was quick with an answer: "I chose to make it her fault."

"What about this poor girl next to me?" I tried pushing back on the chair. There was a slight give.

Fairchild moved over to the girl, took a large dissecting knife off the table, and stroked it slowly over her pubis, then across her breasts. Then he took the handle and pushed it roughly inside her vagina. The girl shuddered and cried out.

"Poor Dawn. How did that feel compared to your boyfriend?" He looked at me like a pettish schoolmarm. "She slept with her boyfriend before they were married, you know. Now she must pay."

He turned away from me and began arranging his instruments. As he played with her, I tried looking at the mirrors. I quickly looked forward again as the poor girl's moaning stopped.

"It's because *you're* not perfect, isn't it?" I taunted him.

He paused, glancing sharply at me. "What do you mean?"

"You just suck in general. You're a lousy person, a lousy anesthesiologist, a lousy lover. You hate yourself, therefore, you hate everyone else who might seem better. You kid yourself that you're some sort of satanic deity just so can get up each morning and take a piss. Right, you worthless piece of shit?"

His eyes flamed, but he was shaken. He attempted a smile. "Actually, I am very good with the women." He walked over to me, fingering the scalpel. I fixed my gaze on the metal instrument that glinted in the fluorescent light. "You want this blade much, don't you, doctor?" he said, passing it just under my nose. "Well, it's very sharp, you know. You could cut your hands, and, as a surgeon, you never know when you may need them." Something about that statement seemed familiar. I had heard it before.

He pulled the knife back and stepped to my side. "Now where were we? Ah, yes. As for being a lousy person, as you put it, even my mother knew she was unworthy to raise me. I *am* the deity she could never worship."

"That's right, Lucifer, the beautiful bearer of light. Give me a break, asshole. All your artsy 'classical perfection' bullshit is just a cover for your worthlessness."

Right then I was praying to my own deity to help me bust out of the chair before I got the bastard really pissed off.

"And that woman who you impregnated, who had no ring on her finger, is merely a fool pretending to be an art critic. A fool fucking a greater fool."

"*Il giudizio universale.*"

He paused. The twirling scalpel froze, twinkling. "Intriguing that you should have guessed the game." He stepped closer again. I watched the blade hand. "Michelangelo understood perfection."

"In his art he created perfection, unlike real humans," I said with a touch of irony in my voice.

"So true, so true," Fairchild replied with an added tone of diffidence. "Someone asked him once, how he created the statue of David. He replied, 'I cut away everything that wasn't David.' Now I am doing the same. My fresco is like his, each dead supplicant pleading for mercy from God."

"And you are God." I looked at the mirrors around the room, searching for my own god, but instead, strangely, an image of Frances Gallagher, my high-society patient, swirled in my mind.

"I am. My judgment is final."

He stiffened. Then I saw on the table next to me the significance of Mrs. Gallagher, a Magill forceps.

"Ah, yes, the Imperfect God, Lucifer, He who Fucks Up . . ."

The blade rested sharply under my right eyeball. I backed off.

"Will you mock me?"

"No, not with that blade in my eye. I can be accommodating."

Evidently, it wasn't the right moment in the pattern for me to be carved. He stepped back again, breathing deeply.

"Arnold Cozzo," I said. "What was his imperfection?"

Fairchild needed to confess. Every gesture, every intonation evoked the drowning man gasping for air, deprived time and time again of the perfect witness to his perfect crimes, the one anchor of sanity upon which he could moor his delusions, pleading for approval. "Poor Arnold, he gave up on the game. You know I love puzzles, the perfect art form. I thought Arnold was my Bartholomew, holding his hidden skin. I tried to convince him, but he gave up on me after all those years. He let me into the clinics, I implanted my seed, but he never really knew what was going on, never appreciated my Grand Design."

"But he found out that you were actually murdering the victims, and he wanted to quit the game. Right?" I said, stealing another glance at the forceps. I kept talking, realizing that the delicate instrument held my freedom, but was useless unless Fairchild left the room.

"Playing a game by yourself is no fun. I had to let him see my genius, so I kept sending him clues. He finally caught on when I killed Hamoud."

"And then you killed him."

"I was going to prolong the game for a few more years, but then I asked myself, *why*? The canvas was nearly complete. Arnold's intransigence became an annoyance. I no longer needed him. I needed no one, ever, you see. So, when Arnold threatened me, I finished him quickly."

My mind was racing. I knew I couldn't keep Fairchild talking forever. I needed to get that instrument. "And you had to make it look like a suicide."

"Well, wouldn't you?" He spoke as if he thought I understood his madness. I was hopeful he would keep talking, and even more hopeful that he'd leave the room.

"They'll catch you, Fairchild."

"Not likely. In fact, the way I have it planned, they're going to find Masri's semen inside my little daughter."

"He'll never let you do that." I looked over at Masri, his eyes burning with defiance.

"He won't have to let me. There are ways to get his semen out of him without his consent. Obvious ways," he said, smiling at Masri's outrage. "The despicable Ahmad Masri raping and murdering this poor teenage girl. And then having his daughter tainted by the memory of a criminal father. The press will love it. It's perfection."

"Don't forget about me, O mighty one."

"Yes, you." Fairchild stroked his chin, and then looked down at the scalpel. "Persistent and perceptive. You have truly gone where angels fear to tread."

He stepped behind me and tested the bonds on my wrists, then bent over, examining the ropes on my ankles. "True, you are an oversight, a small smear on the fresco. But I'm nothing if not thorough. I am going to kill you and put your body next to his. The police lack imagination, as has been adequately demonstrated thus far. They will assume you tried to catch him, but he proved too clever and killed you first."

I thought about Jordan. I tried arching my back again, but nothing moved on the chair. "Pretty slick, Lucifer. You've thought of everything."

"Absolutely. I am going to bleed you to death. Imagine the slow darkness, the drifting away of consciousness as your blood drains. Maybe your last thoughts will linger on the child you'll never know." He gloated. "Or maybe just before all is dark, you'll wonder, ever so fleetingly, what I'm going to do to that whore you love afterwards."

My arms flexed involuntarily, pulling at the bonds.

"Afterwards, I am going to slit your throat. It will look like a typical Arab revenge killing."

"It's your house. They'll find you."

"Please. Don't pretend you're stupid. The bodies will be gone. You know I've become expert at cadaver disposal."

The ropes tightened on my arms as I continued to strain against them.

"And the 'E' in your sick game?"

"Ah, the 'E.'" Fairchild beamed with pride, Lucifer's pride. "It's so perfect. Estrous is the final clue. Therefore, I remove the ovary, the source of all life. The place where everything begins and the source of all the imperfection in life. A fitting end to my game."

He picked up a piece of cardboard and took the autopsy dissection knife. "Now, I must be getting on with this." He lifted the cardboard between his thumb and forefinger and cut the edge. He must have pressed too hard, because the blade snapped against the hard paper board.

"Dear, dear, I mustn't be so rough. It will just take me a moment to replace it. So don't go anywhere, I'll be right back." He came back over and re-taped my mouth. Then before he left, he turned on some music. It was "Death and Transfiguration" by Strauss.

A fitting finale for my last minutes on earth, I thought.

My heart sank as he walked out. I looked over at Masri, shaking his head defiantly. I looked at the Magill forceps on the table next to me. At this point the instrument was my only hope. Then I glanced over at the girl, whose eyes were becoming more panicked with every moment. The words, "You could cut yourself. You never know when you may need them," echoed in my mind. It was then that I realized where I heard the comment before. The police sergeant who had inspected my badge.

I pushed my feet against the floor and raised myself upward to the metal table. Looking in the mirror in front of me, I could see the Magill forceps reflecting off the mirror to the side. I remembered Mrs. Gallagher and the foreign body in her throat. I had to remove my badge from my rear pocket, just like taking out the fishbone.

My hands were aching as they grasped the rounded Magill forceps. I had no feeling in my fingers. The instrument started to slip, but I clasped my palms together and held it before it clattered to the tile. I brought the chair back to the floor and sat for a moment, exhausted at the effort.

It took a moment for the blood to start flowing into my hands. When the feeling returned, I stared intently at the mirror to my side as I inched the instrument downward toward my back pocket. I could see the tip of the leather wallet.

Sliding my butt forward, I opened the forceps, grasped the leather, and pulled. Nothing happened. I grasped it again. This time there was a slight give. I pulled once more and felt a sliding sensation as the wallet slid out of my pocket.

I held the instrument with one hand and inched it upward until the tip that held the leather case was in my other hand. Then I let go of the Magill forceps. It clattered noisily to the floor, the sound almost drowned out by the loud harmonies of the music in the room.

With both hands I opened the wallet up and slid out the metal shield. I could feel the sharp edge of the badge. I took it in my hand and started moving it up and down against the ropes. The sergeant was right, it was sharp. Slowly the fibers began to give, one after another. After what seemed an eternity, there was a tear and most of the pressure was gone. But I still wasn't free, there must have still been a few strands left. At that moment Fairchild walked back in.

He was still dressed in black, but now he wore a black hood over his head. He had painted his mouth and drawn lines down his face with red lipstick. His skin-tight black pants were broken only by a hard-on, mute testimony to his intentions.

"God has summoned you, Dawn," he said softly. As he spoke, he stroked himself with the handle of his knife, gently, just a touch, just a slight encouragement to tremor. "You will die for your imperfection, and I will live to continue meting out justice."

He moved over to the table where Dawn was lying and placed the knife on her abdomen. As he did, I could feel the rope give way on my right hand. He raised the knife and made a cut on her belly, just a superficial incision, a prelude, the first stitch in the pattern of his sick mind's tapestry, with many stitches to go. I saw the blood running down her side. She was moving her head, eyes shut, tears smearing her cheeks, desperate.

"That, my dear, is just the beginning. I am going to let you watch your friends die first. Besides, I want to prolong the pleasure of watching you expire." As he spoke, he turned the operating light back to me.

"Now, my dear Dr. Dailey. It is time for you to return to the God of Abraham."

He pulled out a large rubber tourniquet, pulled up my pant leg, and exposed the large saphenous vein near my ankle, where he wrapped the elastic band. As he cinched it down, I struggled to surreptitiously pull my hands through the loosened rope. Sweat poured off my face and chest as the blood vessel in my leg became engorged. Then he brought out a huge needle and deftly pushed it through the large blue vessel. No matter how hard I tried, I still couldn't free myself. I knew what he was going to do.

"I am so lucky to be an anesthesiologist and have all the tools I'll ever need." He removed the needle and methodically pushed the plastic sheath into my vein.

"Have you ever watched someone die from exsanguination?" he asked in mockery. I thought about my residency and the poor unfortunate man who had bled to death during a bronchoscopy. The thought flashed through my mind that perhaps this was God's way of punishing me for my mistake.

"It really is quite remarkable," he continued. "Seeing life ebb from someone, especially someone you loathe, is such a marvelous feeling. It happened to my daughter, Janice Lennell. It was ingenious, laying her across the railroad tracks. The police never figured out that I had cut her teat off before I put her there. It was a special moment, watching the train dismember her."

In the background I could hear the solemn music playing. Fairchild hummed along with the orchestra as he brought a large vacuum bottle under the tubing and attached it.

"It happened with Jesus, the so-called Christ, too, you know."

Fairchild was mad as a hatter, completely delusional. The streaked make-up on his cheeks gave him the horrible aspect of the damned from Dante's inferno.

He finished hooking the tubing to the bottle. Suddenly blood was coursing into the container. "Don't worry. Death for you will be agony. It will take ten minutes." He turned back to a table at the corner and became engrossed as he gathered some tools.

I continued fighting to break the bond that held my hands as I watched my blood flowing into the bottle. I could feel myself becoming lightheaded and my struggles more difficult.

With one last surge of energy I struck at the bonds with my shield and they snapped free from my hands. Slowly, I raised my numb arms and fingers to the side of the chair. It seemed like an eternity as I reached down and yanked out the needle. The bottle was half full. I looked over at Fairchild, whose back was turned to me, seemingly consumed in organizing his next murder.

I was quick, quick like in my college football days. My arms ached from their bondage, but I freed my legs and lurched upward. I was dizzy from the loss of blood, but I staggered to my feet and stumbled over to Masri, pulling at the Velcro that bound him. The enemy of my enemy had suddenly become my friend.

Fairchild saw me next to Masri and leaped backward, dropping his tools, as I sank to the floor. I looked at Fairchild as I began to collapse. A dense anger consumed his face. He turned around, quickly picked up the knife and rushed at me. Weakened and nearly defenseless, I rolled to the left, behind the table. I grabbed onto the edge and tried to lift myself up. He was on me now, his hot breath pressing against my face, his arm grabbing my throat. I was surprised at his strength.

"You are making things difficult for me," he growled. The razor-sharp blade hovered for the briefest moment near my throat.

Suddenly, two hands appeared from behind him. They grabbed his arm and yanked backward. I heard a snap as the radius cracked at the wrist. Fairchild let out a cry of agony as the knife clattered to the floor. Masri stood over him, small and wiry.

"For pigs like you, we have special treatment."

Fairchild looked up from the floor, a trapped animal. Masri stooped and reached for the knife. Fairchild, whimpering in pain, suddenly rolled to his right and grabbed it first with his left hand.

"Masri, look out!" I yelled.

Fairchild's mania endowed him with superhuman speed. He slashed at Masri's neck. Masri clutched his own throat, the blood erupting from the laceration as he went down. Fairchild jumped on top of him and raised his knife again for the *coup de grace*.

I reached out helplessly, as far as I could, but at that moment the door burst open. All I could see was the silhouette of a pregnant woman. I wanted to call out her name. Before I could, there was a flash and a scream as the knife clattered to the floor. Then a second flash and Fairchild collapsed on the brown tile floor.

As he fell, I struggled toward Masri's motionless body.

CHAPTER 32

I T WAS THE BEST WEDDING I had ever been to, and not just because it was my own. Granted, it was delayed several weeks until I recovered, but considering what had happened, it was a small price to pay.

My parents stood next to me under the *chuppah*. I was happy for them. At their age, I knew it was satisfying to see their son married and in love.

Then I looked at Jordan, showing off for her parents. Jordan looked beautiful and smugly radiant, not only because she was going to have a baby as an honest woman, but because she was in full control of her fate, with her job, her man, her life. Her parents beamed with pride at their daughter. Her old man kept nodding sagely at her, as if cueing to her that he hadn't had a single doubt about anything all along. Every once in a while, he'd flash me the high-five sign, in appreciation for my going through with the wedding. I'd smile back and raise my wineglass. Then I'd wonder what it would feel like for me when the day came and I'd be standing there with my own daughter, saluting the bastard who knocked her up, just beating the disgrace deadline by a hair. If it happened, I just hoped her husband loved her as much as I loved Jordan.

The rabbi made it short and sweet. When I broke the glass, there was a large roar from the hundred and fifty guests. Then the party started.

The flowers were beautiful, and Sid's music was fantastic. As for the food, Gus was in a league of his own: lamb chops, Greek salad, stuffed grape leaves, and a dozen other items I had never seen before. It was more wonderful than I could have ever imagined. I stopped him at the dessert table. Gus filled a bowl with rice pudding covered with minced pistachios and handed it to me. Sennett was next in line.

"I knew you were good, Gus, but this is unbelievable," I said.

"You know, Doc, this is the first time I ever catered a Jewish wedding."

"Well, you must be doing all right, because Jews appreciate food. So far, I haven't seen anybody sending their dinners back."

"You know, in the old country, if the food isn't good on the wedding night, it's a bad omen. That puts a lot of pressure on me."

"You came through, pal."

"Say, what's this I hear about Jordan saving your life?" Gus's enthusiasm made me think he had been dying to ask me all night.

"You got it right," I said.

"How does a six-month pregnant woman shoot this guy?" Gus asked.

Sennett came up next to me. "She didn't just shoot him," he said. "She shot him in the arm, and then hit him in the kneecap."

"Why didn't she just kill him?" Gus asked.

I laughed. "You know lawyers, they're always looking for a good case to try." Then I shrugged my shoulders. "It's just her way."

Gus looked at the swirling white silk of Jordan dancing with her father. "Damn," he said, "She's . . . *impressive*."

"If you listen to her tell it, it was routine," I said. I remembered the picture of Jordan in the SWAT outfit. Maybe it was routine.

"How did she find you?" Gus wanted to know.

"I left my cell phone on when I left the car. It has GPS. Jordan and Sennett tracked the location down."

"They said his basement was fitted out like a surgical suite," Gus said, amazed at the dancing woman's dauntless courage.

"More like a morgue," Sennett opined.

I studied the guests conversing, dancing, enjoying Gus's banquet. This moment of religious communion grounded in sheer joy, unimpeded by ritual or prayer, warmed me. I grew thoughtful. "What causes a man to be so evil?" I mused, mostly to myself.

Sennett looked around, seemingly absorbed with the sights, the sounds, the smells. "I'm damn sure Fairchild never enjoyed anything like this growing up," he asserted. "This teaches you how to be happy. How to love."

"I thought love comes naturally," Gus said.

"That's 'cause you Greeks are born with party hats on," Sennett responded, broadly smiling. Then he looked at me, catching, I suppose, a somewhat dour look on my face.

"You're the groom, bud," he said. "You should be the happiest of all. You're certainly the luckiest." He tilted his glass to my smiling Jordan, who waved at him from across the room.

"I guess being so close to so much perverse evil leaves a lasting impact." I absentmindedly adjusted my tie.

"Well, we won't have to worry about him anymore," Gus said. "He'll be gone until he's dead. The key is thrown away for that sick sonofabitch."

"Yeah, but even in prison I'll bet he still figures he's better than everyone else," I commented. "I can just see him waltzing around with that superior attitude."

"I think the inmates will take care of that, Ben," Sennett advised.

"In his case, there is no hell bad enough for him," Gus said with a scowl.

"Hell's his kingdom, Gus," I pointed out. "He's always lived there, and always will. We just sort of moved him indoors."

Gus surveyed the room to make sure his servers were hopping and that nobody wanted for food. Then he asked Sennett, "Now what about Masri?"

"More sad stories, Gus. Masri went to Yaldo's house to talk with him and forgive him. When he got there, Yaldo was dead. The death of his only grandson and his daughter and his implication in the death of Masri's wife were too much for him. He was tortured with guilt. Suicide was Yaldo's only out, sin or no sin. He left a note apologizing to Masri for what happened to his wife. Masri picked up the note and the gun and took it with him. He didn't want his old friend shamed by suicide."

"So that explains why the bullet matched the one that killed Bill Yaldo," I said.

Sennett nodded. "When Fairchild abducted Masri, he found the gun. That's when he decided to kill you with it. It would have been a perfect crime."

"Another good plan gone awry," I said ruefully.

Just then there was a trumpet fanfare and a drum roll. Sid motioned Jordan and me up to the dance floor and started playing "Hava Nagila."

As we stood in front of the band, listening to the clapping around us, she reached over and whispered in my ear:

"Ben, when we were standing on the *bema*, you gave me a long stare. What were you thinking?"

"I was thinking that if we had a daughter, I was going to make sure she was married first."

We started in line, snaking around the dance floor. The music crescendo'd, as small circles developed in the crowd of dancers. She was about to say something, when a couple propelled us toward the circling dance. The woman was beautiful with dark hair, deep red lips, and an exquisite smile. She was holding on tightly to a slender man in his late sixties with a gray beard and fierce dark eyes. But this time the eyes held no anger, only love, as Ahmad Masri looked at his daughter, Karin.

I looked at Masri's neck closely. The red scar on his neck was now almost completely covered by his beard. I was told that, before I had dropped into semi-consciousness, I had grabbed a towel from the floor and put enough pressure on his wound to stop the flow until the ambulance arrived. The surgical team did the rest.

Masri and Karin waited until the dance was over and then slowly approached Jordan and I with his right hand across his chest. "You do us a great honor, Dr. Dailey, both for saving my life and the life of our family, and by inviting us to your wedding."

"The honor is ours, sir. I understand your love for your family. We come from different places, but we all live in the same world. If Karin was my daughter, I too would have tried to protect her. After all that we have gone through, I would like to consider you as my friend." He smiled as he nodded his head.

Karin looked at Jordan. "Are you sure you should be doing this? Dancing, I mean."

"I'm not sure, but I know this is the last time I'm getting married, so I better dance while I can."

Suddenly, Jordan stopped short and started laughing uncontrollably.

"What could be that funny?" I asked.

"I think my water broke."

I stood there motionless, wondering what to do next.

I needed a doctor.

G ENE RONTAL, M.D. has always had an interest in telling stories. From his experience as a head and neck surgeon, Dr. Rontal learned both the personal and professional stories behind the world of medicine. Those stories, combined with a passion for mystery writing, turned into five medical murder mystery novels starring Rontal's main protagonist Dr. Ben Dailey. Dailey, a surgeon who finds himself reluctantly playing detective, winds up in action adventures that that explore the fascinating practice of medicine, while entertaining the reader with spellbinding plots. Dr. Rontal resides in Chicago, Illinois.

www.ingramcontent.com/pod-product-compliance
Lightning Source LLC
Chambersburg PA
CBHW011516100726
47899CB00010BD/3383